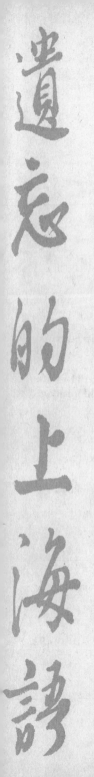

W9-CZJ-527

The LOST *and* FORGOTTEN LANGUAGES *of* SHANGHAI

◼ ─────────────────────

Ruiyan Xu

ST. MARTIN'S GRIFFIN
NEW YORK

THE LOST AND FORGOTTEN LANGUAGES OF SHANGHAI. Copyright © 2010 by Ruiyan Xu. All rights reserved. Printed in the United States of America. For information, address St. Martin's Press, 175 Fifth Avenue, New York, N.Y. 10010.

www.stmartins.com

Designed by Kelly S. Too

The Library of Congress has cataloged the hardcover edition as follows:

Xu, Ruiyan.
    The lost and forgotten languages of Shanghai / Ruiyan Xu.—1st ed.
        p. cm.
    ISBN 978-0-312-58654-6
    1. Brain damage—Patients—Fiction. 2. Neurologists—Fiction.
3. Americans—China—Shanghai—Fiction. 4. Triangles (Interpersonal relations)—Fiction. 5. Shanghai (China)—Fiction. I. Title.
PS3624.U3L67 2010
813'.6—dc22

2010029210

ISBN 978-0-312-61415-7 (trade paperback)

First St. Martin's Griffin Edition: October 2011

10 9 8 7 6 5 4 3 2 1

"A thoughtful disquisition upon the power of language, Ruiyan Xu's remarkable first novel is also a compassionate and perspicacious examination of the nature of human relationships."
—Ross Gilfillan, *Daily Mail* (UK)

"[A] lyrical contemplation of language and how it shapes our identity, as well as a subtle commentary on the slippery sense of belonging in the new China . . . Ruiyan's writing style is often delightfully evocative and she summons up beautiful tableaux with her carefully crafted prose."
—Siobhan Murphy, *Metro* (UK)

"A moving debut full of insight into how language shapes us."
—Marissa Cox, *Stylist* (UK)

"Ruiyan Xu's intriguing plot and unaffected writing provide a fresh take on a tale of linguistic and cultural difference . . . the fundamental links between language and identity are minutely explored."
—Catherine Taylor, *The Guardian* (UK)

"[An] edifying exploration of the limits of language . . . Xu's emotional fluency is what makes this novel work: The love in this book is unfettered, and from this she draws out complex and intriguing questions about language, culture, and understanding."
—Mary Fitzgerald, *The Observer* (UK)

"A sensitive and moving exploration of what happens to a marriage when love is lost in translation . . . [a] tale of loss, love, and loyalty."
—*Marie Claire* (UK)

Praise for *The Lost and Forgotten Languages of Shanghai*

"There's a kind of useful symmetry at the outset of Xu's appealing first novel. . . . Novelist Ruiyan Xu writes in English, so she doesn't enunciate the four tonal variations of Chinese. The tone of her story about love in modern Shanghai seems just right."　　—NPR

"Xu lovingly re-creates 1999 Shanghai and skillfully shows the culture clashes among the city's native, immigrant, and expatriate populations, swinging gracefully between these worlds."　　—*Publishers Weekly*

"Precise and elegant."　　　　　　　　　　—*Kirkus Reviews*

"What a gem of a debut. This is the most literary kind, rarely found in fictions about new China. There is such deep silence in her prose, hinting at the depth of human suffering, anguish, and hope. A gifted novelist, she gives us the insight into a Shanghai that is at once strange, and familiar, old and new, creating a literary landscape for its dwellers that is vast and beguiling, which is precisely the spirit of this metropolis, and of this fine fiction."　　—Da Chen, author of the *New York Times* bestselling memoir *Colors of the Mountain* and *Brothers*

"One part medical mystery, one part love story, *The Lost and Forgotten Languages of Shanghai* is an engrossing novel that will enchant you from beginning to end."　　—David Ebershoff, *New York Times* bestselling author of *The 19th Wife* and *The Danish Girl*

"From the explosion of its first pages to the searing emotion of its last, *The Lost and Forgotten Languages of Shanghai* is a novel that burns with the heat of clashing cultures and love transformed. Ruiyan Xu is a wonderful writer with a perfect ear for both the words and the silences that define us."　　—Peter Manseau, author of *Songs for the Butcher's Daughter*

"In her captivating debut novel, Ruiyan Xu paints an absorbing portrait of modern Shanghai. When a terrible explosion leaves husband and father Li Jing without the language in which to communicate, the Li family must rediscover who they are and how to live. *The Lost and Forgotten Languages of Shanghai* is a richly nuanced and compelling story of loss and grief, betrayal and redemption by a gifted new voice."

—Gail Tsukiyama, award-winning author of *The Samurai's Garden* and *The Street of a Thousand Blossoms*

"This is an intelligent and thoughtful exploration of the terrifying isolation that can come from loss of language. The novel skillfully examines the complex relationship between language and identity, seeing beyond the words themselves to the way in which they mold our thoughts and shape our personalities. With sensitivity and perception, Ruiyan Xu penetrates right to the heart of the dilemma of translation, the etiquette that is embedded within each language, the nuances of tone. This is a novel that makes us think beyond our boundaries, that opens up a fresh understanding of our relationship with language."

—Clare Morrall, author of The Man Booker Prize finalist *Astonishing Splashes of Colour*

"Her writing is delicate, evocative, and eloquent. . . . An eminently readable part allegory of China's views on national identity and be-longing, foisted Americanization, and external temptation."

—Alex Bartleman, *Sunday Express* (UK)

"A beautifully executed, moving debut about the articulation of love."

—Kate Saunders, *The Sunday Times* (UK)

For my parents,
Xu Jingdong
and
Chen Yuanchun

The LOST *and*

FORGOTTEN

LANGUAGES *of*

SHANGHAI

■ ——————————

Later, she would remember the crack in the building: a line splitting the cement, a body of veins crawling everywhere. It happened in slow motion. On a balcony two blocks away she watched the crumple of the Swan Hotel. Aortas feeding into arteries, capillaries branching off, slender, disappearing into the façade of the building. Carrying blood away from the heart.

The hollow, sickening boom of it sucking all air out of her lungs.

For a second Shanghai looks exactly the same, some haphazard perfection brimming out of the skyline. There is silence for a still moment, until the city rushes back to the clatter of horns, bulldozers, airplanes blazing across the eardrum. A gust of wind sweeps by, carrying a trace of gas, of combustion. There is a halo of dust around the hotel, and she watches it swarm upward and outward like a pack of locusts, expanding darkly into the sky.

She sees the sway of the building, pieces loosening, cement crumpling off the sides, glass shattering and buckling. The entire structure begins to melt away, the bottom giving out, the floors sinking down. She watches the middle of the building sag, walls crushed between sky and street, windowpanes that shone bright being obliterated, a solid shape in slow disintegration. The noise keeps pouring in, heavy and thudding, ceaselessly, pounding everything else out of her body, filling up her insides. She has to close her eyes but she can't stop listening. The sound of stone against stone the only thing in her ear. It would not stop.

Later, standing on the same balcony, she would look down at the debris on the site and see a wound that refuses to heal.

I

THE SWAN HOTEL

He leaves work early, walks down thin strips of sidewalk, and meanders over the bridge, his hands tightfisted at his sides. It is one of those spring afternoons when the skin begins to pucker in the sun, when the heat of summer hints at the back of the neck, and instead of driving home he forces himself onto slow-moving buses, lets himself be carried along by crowds and their murmurs, gives himself the luxury of time to notice the city around him as he walks under the shadows of high-rises. He looks up: the city is new and strange and the skyline startles him, the way it changes constantly, month by month. His memories are slightly skewed, an older print, already out-of-date; the last time he looked up there was the same city but different—emptier—stretches of sky.

The lobby of the Swan Hotel stretches cool and marbled, and he walks in nodding at the bellhop, the receptionist, the maintenance worker moving a trolley of old bathroom fixtures out the door. The afternoon light saturates the carpet beneath his feet, exposing motes of dust, bleaching navy into a muddy blue. Up the stairs, the glass doors of the restaurant are half shut and streaked with a light layer of grease. Two waitresses shelling lima beans over tea and gossip jump up when he pushes through the door, chirping, "Welcome, Mr. Li!" in his wake.

His father is already sitting in the corner, poring over sketches with his glasses pressed up tight against his face. At the sound of Li Jing's greeting he looks up and cocks his eyebrows, stretching his thin, angular face even longer.

"So it was you on the phone after all, not an imposter. Tell me"— Professor Li makes a show of looking at his watch—"to what do I owe this unexpected pleasure? How long has it been since you left work voluntarily at five o'clock in the afternoon?"

Li Jing shrugs but does not meet his father's eyes. "Why not? I felt like a drink."

Side by side, a subtle resemblance between father and son reveals itself in the same broadness of the shoulders, in the same bulging black eyes. But Professor Li is tall and skinny with a long, horselike face and a pouf of white hair; his son is all compression, thick-bodied, with a broad nose and a locked jaw.

A waiter comes to stand behind their shoulders, angling a long stalk of bamboo with the tip sliced open to pour threads of tea into their cups. The two men tap the table with their index and middle fingers in thanks at the same time and lean back against their chairs, the younger man sighing, closing his eyes.

"Is everything well? You've been awfully quiet the last few days."

Li Jing takes off his suit jacket and flings it over the back of his chair; his pale blue shirt hugs his body, dark pools of sweat gathering under the armpits.

"It's just work," he says. "I got impatient last week and jumped on something without confirming the tip. Ended up taking a pretty big loss—it's been a rough week. Anyway, things are volatile in the domestic market right now. I really should have stayed with the American stocks. Their market's booming, but still steady."

"But American stocks are expensive, and isn't Wall Street on a bull's run? It's going to have to come down at some point."

Li Jing looks up from the menu in surprise.

"I keep up," the professor shoots back at him, smug. "I drop by the English department on campus and read the *Herald Tribune* when I get a chance, and sometimes when I've finished everything else, I glance through the financial pages."

"It'll be fine. I can handle it." Li Jing wipes his forehead with his shirtsleeve and gestures with his chin, eager to change the subject. "What's that? Did you get roped into judging another architectural competition?"

"A memorial this time. They're going to build it in Hangzhou, by the lake. I wish they'd leave that area alone—it's already overdeveloped. But if they insist on erecting something, I have to make sure that it won't be completely hideous."

"And you say I work too much? You're the one who's supposed to be retired."

"You do work too much." Professor Li gives Li Jing a slow, assessing look. "You should spend more time with Pang Pang and Meiling. Work isn't everything, you know?"

"Dad . . ."

"Before you know it, Pang Pang will be all grown up." The professor closes his eyes, sighing loudly before shaking his head.

The restaurant manager sets a covered blue-and-white bowl on the table with a flourish. The inside of the bowl hisses, sounding an occasional wet plop against the porcelain. A waitress brings a tin box of long, skinny matches and takes the cover off the bowl. The tiny curls of shrimp inside stir, their gray, translucent bodies thrashing in the liquid; some of them jump out of the alcohol and dive back in, their torsos shuddering, their antennae swishing in desperation.

The match tip strikes against the box and a small red flame erupts, contracting and expanding in the manager's hand. He dips his wrist, and the entire bowl of shrimp is now engulfed in crests of fire, orange and red and tinged with blue. The shrimp dance more desperately now, their shells burnt and crackling, their bodies tossed up through the fingers of the flame and tossed back down into the liquid. The smell of burning alcohol perfumes the air, sickly sweet; the shrimp sizzle and gasp, buzzing in the ear. The manager slides the cover back onto the bowl. The hiss of the fire snaps off into silence. Professor Li and Li Jing pick up their chopsticks, lean forward, but both draw back in surprise when a phone rings under the table.

"Do you mind if I take this? It's business." Li Jing flips open his cell phone and slides out of his chair without waiting for a response, already walking away.

"Should we wait for Mr. Li?" The restaurant manager bows at the waist.

"Business, business all the time," Professor Li mutters under his breath. "I don't understand it. He's on that phone nonstop, nights and weekends. He's working himself too hard."

"I'm sorry, Professor."

"Never mind, never mind."

"The shrimp?"

"Let's not wait. I'll get started now."

Inside the bowl the shrimp glow a lurid pink. Professor Li dips his chopsticks into the dish and draws slow circles in the liquid.

"Are you expecting Ms. Zhou and Pang Pang to join you this evening?"

"Not today." Professor Li scans the room for a sign of Li Jing before wiping his hands and turning back to the sketches. "But that reminds me, we were supposed to pick up some dinner for them. No hurry, we'll take it when we go: winter melon with ham, a big container of seaweed soup, that spicy boiled beef, and some bok choy with mushrooms."

"It'll be waiting when you're ready to leave."

"And where are our other appetizers? Fried oysters? Scallion pancakes?"

The manager grimaces. "Many apologies, Professor. The gas stoves are being a bit temperamental, but we'll have it fixed in no time. I'll head back to the kitchen to check on your food now."

The floor rumbles slightly. The manager takes a step and his long legs register a tremor on the ground. The professor finds a shrimp and breaks its neck with his teeth, sucking flesh out of the body, spitting its neon shell onto the table.

THE WALLS SHAKING.

The walls shaking again, wildly. Pieces of gold plaster from the ceiling explode and scatter, falling down onto tabletops, gold dust drifting onto plates of food. The lights flash once. Then darkness.

There are screams and gasps. Metallic clatters from the kitchen. People crawling under tables and rushing to press up against the walls. The walls shaking again.

A high-pitched "Keep calm!" rattling out of the manager's throat.

Then the air ripping apart the ground in uproar and a burst of sound unfurling so loud that there is no pitch, there is no shape, there is only sheer volume, only the black mouth of noise opening, gulping everything into its dark, cavernous belly. The noise swallows the building whole. There is no escaping it.

THE GROUND SHIFTING like a prehistoric animal. Fire in the kitchen stretching out its wings, flapping, frantic. Fissures mutate in the walls, mapping out an eventual collapse. Glass and metal utensils and shattered plates fly up from the tables. Smoke everywhere. The sound of the initial explosion ricochets off the walls, grows smaller, fades away into silence. A stray car horn howls a lonely blast, and then the noise of the city rushes in from the broken windows like sandpaper across the eardrum.

Everything feels so still for a moment that the people in the restaurant are afraid to move a centimeter, then they let out their breaths, and whimpers and moans fill the dark room. They shuffle their feet and call out to each other. "Are you hurt?" "What happened?" They begin to grab the edges of tables, trying to stand up. A child cries out and his mother mumbles soothing sounds, her voice lilting. "It's all right," she says. But then another huge swath of noise crushes down, the floor sags, and they can feel something heavy pounding from above, rocking the foundation of the building, tearing apart the plaster.

LI JING OPENS his eyes and the whole world is extinguished. There is noise everywhere, inside his skull, vibrating in his bones, everything shaking, the walls hysterical against his back. It smells like sulfur. He closes his eyes again—it's sweet and heady, that smell, and the noise making everything oblivious and he wants to fall back to the ground and go under but he has to open his eyes, he has to keep his eyes open.

His eyelids feeling heavy, drawing closed. The floor beckoning with gravity, with rest. There is the noise, the smell, the darkness, and then pounding again, thudding rocks, jerking him awake. Everything hurts, but pain keeps him lucid, gives him a sharp edge to hold on to. His fingers find the wall and he pulls himself up to stand only to rise into a cloud of smoke, plaster raining into his hair. He lowers himself down to all fours, his hands roaming across rubble and broken glass. All he wants is just to find a way out.

A pale, muddy light comes in through the windows, but all it does is make visible the calligraphic tendrils of smoke in the air. When he squints he can see the outlines of bodies, denser than smoke and bent over, moving toward a door on the other side. He stays down but crawls with more speed, bumping into chairs and broken plates and hot, gelatinous soups and the edges of knives. Things keep raining down, hitting his head with dull thwacks, and he grabs a tablecloth, flinging porcelain and metal into the air, and drapes the pink polyester over his head to prevent debris from falling into his eyes. He looks up and there is a thin quiver of light thrown up against the walls, illuminating fissures that look like the geographical maps he studied in school. No neatly drawn political boundaries, just the twists and curves of rivers, mountain ranges.

The rivers begin to run over; the mountain ranges shift their thudding feet.

He crawls forward, glass slicing across his knees, dodging around chairs and table legs, trying to keep the door on the other side of the room in his sight line. Everything looks dreamy, with soft, painterly edges. The gilded ceiling, faintly visible through the smoke with its dull glow, is splitting apart, pieces shedding away, floating into the darkness like flakes of golden snow. He lets his eyes follow the drift of plaster, watches a flake of gold hover in the air for a second and then land on a strip of hair so pale it flares bright, having caught some of the light in the room.

Knees stumbling across glass, knees on fire, but he has to crawl faster, he has to get there now. He hauls himself over to his father's body and cries out, but there is no response, not even a flicker across the face. He shakes the torso in front of him, feeling his own fingers sink into soft, silent flesh, shouting, "Come on. Come on." The building pulses hot and alive around them. The torso lies as still as driftwood.

Li Jing begins to drag his father toward the door, lifting him by the shoulders, pulling him across debris. Broken plates tear at his father's clothes, splitting fabric, slashing past the surface of skin. He swings his father up into his arms and props him up, puts his own shoulder under a slackened armpit, lets the dead weight gather and fall into him, this gaping, empty face by his ear. If only he could tell whether there is a heartbeat or the sound of a breath being taken, but it is too loud, too dark, and he has to get going, he has to get them out of here. The light is dim, but he can hear shouts and sirens outside the door, the rumble of the building a constant underneath everything. He takes a short, fluttered breath and crouches down, flings his father over his shoulder in a fireman's hold, and stands up straight into the smoke. His spine cringes at the extra weight, his eyelids are heavy and thick, the noise of the world comes stabbing into his ears like dull razors, but he holds on, his father's body bent over his shoulder, and lurches toward the exit.

———————

THE SIRENS ARE louder now: there are several different ones looping into strange patterns as he staggers out the door and into the second-floor lobby of the hotel. People with face masks holding stretchers rush toward him. He goes down on his knees and allows someone to take his father out of his arms. There are voices and smells and images in the blink of his eyes but it is as though his senses have been scrambled, the taste of smoky darkness imprinting itself on his tongue. Every noise bleeds together for a narcotic buzz, the hot air presses down on his skin like an iron, and there is a thumping inside his head, heavy beats hypnotizing him to sleep.

A bead of light shines across his eyelids, penetrating through skin. He opens his eyes, squints, and turns away in fear. "Baba . . ." He can barely open his jaws. His mouth is filled with ashes.

"He's on one of the stretchers heading out of here. He'll be taken to the hospital right now." The flashlight wavers and drops away; the medic's voice tumbles out. "You just passed out on me there. You all right now?"

"Sorry . . ."

"We have to get you out of here. Now, try to stand. I've got you."

It is slow and dark going down the stairs but then he sees the brightness of day outside the glass doors, the sun casting a dazzling square into the hotel. His shoulders stretch out, his mind hollows, and a memory flickers to the surface, thin, unanchored: he sees himself as a boy, lying in a pool of orange light on a brown velvet coach, waiting for his father to come home. They lived in America then. It was the year after his mother died. Every day after school he'd get off the bus at the top of the hill and walk down the slope, a latchkey kid coming home to rooms still filled with his mother's things. Hours would pass, and he would eat leftovers from the restaurant for dinner, peer into living rooms across the courtyard to see televisions all lit up. Late at night every set of footsteps in the hall held possibilities, and he'd struggle to stay awake, but he always fell asleep on that couch with the light still on, still listening, still waiting for his dad to come home.

THE SIDEWALKS RUMBLE and then they are still. Asphalt shivers under tires but then cars lurch forward, oblivious. The boom had been unmistakable, loud at first, a shock against the eardrums. But then it subsided, and from far away, it is easy to imagine that nothing had happened. Only if you listen carefully, close your eyes and stand still for a second, you can feel it, that dangerous bass line, so low-pitched that it hovers just beneath the threshold of hearing, the almost-silence of a building going down.

Shanghai, 1999, the middle of spring. The city is covered in haze, the light gritty, the air corrupted. Noise from cornices and subways and construction crews and flea markets thrusts upward, collecting in the atmosphere. The weather is still mild, but the sun glares down with a detached menace, sharpening its claws, waiting for July.

On the façade of the hotel the metallic swans glare through the smoke, their bodies adrift, desperate to hold on. The two sculptures hung huge and heavy on top of the main entrance, the curves of their pale necks meeting up to form a heart, their red beaks garish against the concrete backdrop. Glass and cement shatter. The swans dip their necks. A fissure splits the building, dividing it in two. The swans hang on, precarious, their bodies beginning to sink. One of them loosens its hold on the other, breaking the heart between their necks, swinging its body downward with reckless velocity and swinging back the other way, its upside-down head like the pendulum of a clock, swerving through a wide arc just above the doorway. Now it is attached to its twin only by the white bulge of their bellies, and as it dangles and moves, gravity seduces it away from coherence. The swan pulls itself farther and farther away from the building, from the other swan. Metal stretches and groans. A swan lets go of its twin.

Six tons of steel crash into the marbled entranceway, bounce once, and come back down again. The ground jolts in shock, the building leaps up and comes down again, disconcerted, crushing its already wobbly foundation. The walls shake epileptically, crumbling even faster, even more. The momentum of the building's ruin gathers and accelerates, blowing out beams as everything crumples toward the ground.

INSIDE THE LOBBY, the men trying to get out are down again, knocked into walls and pressed into the carpet. The medic rolls over on his stomach and covers his head. Li Jing lifts his neck and looks up.

Later, he would remember the last thing he said before his body was pierced. It was the last bit of Chinese he would utter for a long, long time.

"*Tiānna.*" The two syllables gasped out of his mouth. *Good heavens.*

A blur of glass whistling across air and bolting into his forehead.

CHAPTER 2

When she closes her eyes she sees it again: cracks widening in the façade of the building, thick dust swirling in a skyscraping column, how the entire structure shifted and faltered, the crush of it, its slow-motion collapse. She had stood on the balcony two blocks away with one hand stretched, grasping empty air, the dust from the explosion whipping by, stinging her face. "Mom?" She remembers Pang Pang's voice above the murmur of the television, but she couldn't open her mouth to answer, couldn't let go of the sight of the building going down, couldn't shake off the pit of certainty in her belly, filling her body with fear.

"Mrs. Li?"

A voice and then a light touch on her shoulder. Zhou Meiling rubs her face and stares up at the doctor. He smells like cigarette smoke, and she shrinks away for a second before standing up and leaning in.

"Is he . . . ?"

"He's alive."

She sinks back into her seat, boneless. The lights above her seem to dim and flicker. Memories of scenes from other hospitals billow out like sails and she has to close her eyes. *He's alive.* She tries to take a breath but her heart is still so tight that it feels like there's no air in her lungs. They are all the same, hospitals, the same grimy benches and walls, the people in threadbare pajamas with unfocused expressions, all of them inhaling the same smell of herbs and disinfectants, slowly losing their minds.

The doctor speaks again. "He's not out of danger yet."

She blinks, letting the words sink in.

"He's in surgery now. He'll be in surgery for at least another four hours. There was damage to his brain during the explosion. If all goes well, we'll know more once he wakes up."

Meiling is familiar, too, with surgery. With the thin gowns rubbing against the skin, with the anesthesia swirling, muddying up everything inside.

"I'll wait," she says. "I want to be there when he wakes up."

"It's going to be a long time."

"It doesn't matter. I want him to be able to see me as soon as he opens his eyes."

He had waited for her through the back surgery she had undergone for her herniated disk at twenty-three. He had waited, despite the fact that if the surgery went badly, she could have been paralyzed, or unable to carry a child to term. She tried to play the martyr, told him he should find someone else, someone whole and healthy. All along she had wanted to endure the pain of her back in silence, by herself, but he would not leave her side. She remembers waking up from surgery and seeing his face above her. His features were foggy and her eyes wanted to slip shut again, but then he grabbed her hand and she could feel the warm sweat that had pooled on his palm.

"Mrs. Li?" The doctor again.

She has always disliked being called "Mrs. Li," but now the sound of his last name is a comfort, the clean, stretched-out syllable wrapping around her body, keeping her warm.

"I'll come back when the surgery is finished. Try to get some rest until then."

Meiling nods, knowing that she will not sleep tonight. She leans back against the chair and holds her breath, thinking about his face above hers when she woke up, thinking about how it is now her turn to wait for him.

PROFESSOR LI OPENS his eyes and looks around, clears his throat, tries to speak. His voice is a thin, wobbly line that he cannot recognize.

"Jing Jing?" He calls out for his son, and the two syllables barely move through the air, tiny sound waves that collapse before they reach beyond the door of the sickroom. The effort has exhausted him. He lets his limbs go slack, shivers, gathers air into his lungs. His body feels as though it's been wrung out, the muscles withered away, the skin ready to tear.

He closes his eyes. Images scramble out of his grasp before they can gather into shapes: the spring air rushing into the hotel lobby, the taste of shrimp and bourbon in his mouth, something beating wildly in his chest, this booming that would not stop. Then nothing, as if all sound and sight and smell have been wiped clear. Now this mush of a bed beneath his body, exhaustion clouding over, making everything blurry. He has lost his glasses but even when he closes his eyes the world is still unfocused, without a rim to hold on to.

Nurses come and go. He gapes up at them with his jaw open, aware of the spit trailing out of his mouth, too exhausted to wipe it away. Someone puts a cold palm across his forehead, making him shudder. Someone else pulls down the hem of his gown, patting him on the thigh.

Awake is around the curve, maybe, but he can feel himself getting pulled back to a dull sleep, the world flickering, darkening.

"Dad!" A woman bursts into the room and then slows down, her heels tapping on the linoleum floor. Her face is fuzzy, but it is unmistakably Meiling; he can smell the barest hint of her perfume. He takes a deep inhale, letting his bones sink further into the mattress.

"I'm so glad you're all right." She brushes his arm and bends forward as if she is going to hold him. He feels his body reaching up for her touch, the skinny arms of this skinny girl that his son is married to, wanting comfort from her, wanting to be held. It has been so long—he doesn't even remember how long—since anyone has taken him in their arms and held the world at bay. Her face comes into focus now, the high forehead, the big, calm eyes that have always unnerved him, the pale hollow beneath her cheekbones, and he tries to hold her gaze, but she is looking away, she is looking anywhere but at him.

Without touching him she pulls her body back and turns her head away.

"Li Jing?" He can barely move his tongue. He closes his mouth, pain oozing out of his joints, into his neck, his heavy brain.

"He's coming out of surgery now."

"Surgery?"

"After the first explosion there were aftershocks. Glass from a blown-out window flew across the room . . . He got caught by some of it."

Her voice clips by, rushing through the words. He lifts his hand off the bed and she catches his fingers in her own, quieting his tremors.

"He's going to be fine."

He stares hard, tries to find answers in every line of her face. "But—"

"He's going to be fine."

THERE IS NOTHING to do but wait. She calls to check in with the nanny, calls his office and hers, calls her parents in Sichuan just to hear their voices, calls a doctor friend for advice, hanging up before the cries of sympathy erupt in full force. Whenever she sees a nurse she engages them in bribes and complex negotiations, wrangling promises of special attention and a nicer room in exchange for envelopes of cash. The nurses come back again and again, but they have nothing new to report. "Professor Li is stable. Mr. Li is still in surgery," they tell her, and when they look at her with well-practiced expressions of calm sympathy, it makes her want to throw up. She digs her fingernails into her palms instead.

The night is spent in the waiting room with everyone else. She looks around the room, sees bodies slumped over in half sleep, half dread, and wonders if they are the family members of favorite bellhops or waitresses, wonders who else is lying on operating tables or in morgues.

When she is finally led to his recovery room it is the late morning of the next day. There is more waiting, only now he is in the same room and they are breathing the same air. It makes her want to hold her breath so that the air he breathes is cleaner, so that there's more of it, so oxygen is pulled in through his nose and curls into his body, seeps into his brain, regenerating cells as he sleeps. She stares at the pale bandages binding his head, the thin black lines of his closed eyes and his faded, watercolored eyebrows. There is dirt under his fingernails, and bruises and cuts on the parts of his neck and his bare arms that she can see. A stunted forest of hair creeps across his jaws, poking through skin, and dark red cuts streak his face like drops of rain ticking across a pane of glass. He looks like a stranger to her, but she wants to touch him. She wants to put her palms on the smooth skin stretching across the sides of his stomach, press her cheek to his face and feel the sting from his stubble, run her hand over his scalp, letting his thick, wiry hair slip between her fingers. Sleep holds him tight in its grip and Meiling hovers by his side, staring at him, mesmerized, missing him. The warmth of his body anchors her in place. She sits still, waiting for him to wake up.

WHEN SHE OPENS her eyes she sees him looking back at her and for a moment she is puzzled, not quite remembering why she is here. But his face is stunned defenseless and bandages are taped to his head and wires wind out of his body and into a machine in the corner and— knowledge, and with it, this jumbled mess of feelings, comes flooding back in.

Her fingers reach out toward the bed, not quite touching him, but then she sets her hand next to his face and crouches down, bites her bottom lip to tamp down her smile of relief. She lays her face down on the mattress, inhales the vinegary scent of the sheets, and looks him in the eyes, taking him in. "Li Jing," she whispers.

He says nothing. He coughs a little and grimaces hard. She nuzzles her head softly into his side before standing up to get him a glass of water, feeling light-headed and light on her feet.

There is a fan stapled to the ceiling and its blades cut slices out of the air and cast moving shadows on the bed. She wants to laugh, hug her body to the length of his, stand him up and kiss him everywhere, but she touches her fingers to her lips and then touches a bare spot on his skull instead.

"Thank heavens." Her voice is like a thin flame, jumpy, flaring bright. "I was so scared. When I saw the building I couldn't breathe. I couldn't find you. I didn't know how to find you. I wanted to run in there myself and I didn't think they could get you out and they wouldn't tell me anything . . . No one would tell me anything." She cuts herself off and lifts her face up to his. "But you're fine. Thank heavens. They got you out in time. You're going to be fine."

The adrenaline that had filled her leaks out of her body, and now exhaustion takes hold, sapping tension from her limbs, leaving her collapsed.

"Okay. I . . . okay." He squeezes her hand.

The sounds curve out of his mouth in little round packets. She shakes her head to clear her brain.

"Say that again." She laughs softly, squinting her eyes.

"I . . . okay. No . . . Don't worry." His tongue lumbers in his mouth. The words strain forth, rolling into the room.

She looks at him with furrowed brows.

"I don't understand." Something pulls at her, a sense of fear now slightly elongated, slightly distorted from its shape, before. She takes a small, quivering breath. "Say it again."

"It's . . . okay." He speaks in English, slowly, careful to pronounce every syllable. She stares at him with a blank face, and he says it again, opening and closing his mouth with deliberation. The body on the bed

is his, that same face, but she leans away, panic bubbling inside her, looking at his mouth, shaking her head.

"*Don't . . . worry.*" He keeps talking, enunciating more and more clearly, every syllable so hard that he looks like he might choke.

"*It's . . . okay. Don't . . . worry.*"

Her eyes shutter up and down. She pulls her hands away from his body. His face shifts and shudders, and she knows it is because he has caught the horrified expression on her face, but she can't look away, she can't make herself stop. She keeps staring at him with her mouth open, this sense of desperation bleeding out with every breath, wanting different words, another language, wanting to understand.

CHAPTER 3

The first few days after the explosion Meiling watched him wake up as if he were gasping before going underwater again. It was not quite sleep, his states of unconsciousness; he lay huddled under pale blankets, his eyes closed, his body tossing as if trying to throw off shackles. From the neck up thick strips of white bandages wound around his forehead like a misshapen bandanna, with raw bits of scalp poking out, purple bruises on his cheeks, swallowing up his eyes. She stood by his side for hours while he slept, stared at the thin, stretched skin of his eyelids, the blistered tips of his ears, the way his nostrils flared out with every breath. Sometimes his eyes flickered in dreams, and she bent down until her ear hovered above his mouth, listening to his breath, waiting for a sound or a murmur.

"The thing is—" Dr. Feng is the head of neurology and wears her competence like a sash across her short, narrow-hipped body. She opens her palms across the desk and looks at Meiling with her mouth pressed into a thin line. "It's still quite early. There's a lot we don't know. But there is a significant possibility of severe language impairment."

"But he's talking."

"In another language."

"Doesn't that count for something?"

"Yes and no."

"Yes and no?" Meiling looks up at the ceiling. "What do you mean, 'yes and no'? Is he going to be able to talk again or not?"

Dr. Feng flips open a folder and shuffles through the report, holds a translucent page up to the window.

"According to the scan, parts of the frontal lobe, which includes areas of the brain responsible for language production, were damaged during the explosion."

"What does that mean? He can still speak English, so . . ."

"That means things are complicated. The presence of another language doesn't necessarily indicate that he'll be able to recover his Chinese." Dr. Feng looks at Meiling and softens her eyes. "Did he speak a great deal of English?"

"No. But it was his first language."

"And he was fluent, before the accident?"

Meiling turns away, trying to remember. When she takes a breath she registers the false note of her perfume, how it clashes against the astringent smell of the hospital. The perfume had clung to her scarf from days ago, a different life now winding about her throat again. Back then he spoke English rarely, but she'd hear him tossing it off on the phone, sometimes, and other times, when he was frustrated with his father, a sentence or two of English would come flying out, as if Chinese weren't enough to contain his anger.

"He might have been, but I'm not sure."

"And how old was he when he switched over?"

"Ten." Meiling says the number with certainty. "Professor Li moved back when Li Jing was ten. It's been over twenty years."

Dr. Feng is silent for several seconds as if doing complex calculations in her head. "Our initial diagnosis is aphasia—"

"Aphasia?"

"A condition characterized by the disruption of speech. His MRI findings correspond to a particular type of this condition called Broca's aphasia, which means that he can understand what you're saying, he can probably even read some Chinese, but he can't produce it: he can't write it down, and he can't talk back to you."

"But he can talk back. At least in English he can . . ." Meiling stares at the doctor, pathetic with hope.

"And that's definitely encouraging."

"So what do we do now?"

"Well—" Dr. Feng tries to reassure. "We'll be taking a number of approaches toward Li Jing's rehabilitation. The human brain has an extraordinary amount of plasticity, which means that it's amorphous and self-protective and very flexible. It's definitely possible that Li Jing will recover some, if not all, of his speech abilities in Chinese. The frontal lobes are very large, and in this case, only his left frontal lobe was damaged. The brain has the possibility of shifting particular functions elsewhere, and I've seen patients with very large tumors who have continued to operate very well in their daily lives. But I don't want to give you false hope either; the trauma to Mr. Li's brain was severe."

"And it's called aphasia?"

"Specifically, the diagnosis is Broca's aphasia in a bilingual patient, which is a very rare condition. All the neurologists on staff have had significant experience with aphasia. It's not an uncommon condition in stroke victims. But the severity of the damage, coupled with the temporary loss of one language and preservation of the other, leads me to think that Mr. Li would be well served by someone who specializes in bilingual aphasia."

"Is there anyone here who does that?"

"Unfortunately not. There are very few true bilingual speakers in China, so the field is not well developed here. I've contacted the other hospitals in the area and I'll let you know if someone turns up. But I have to admit, it's a long shot."

"We can—" Meiling bites back her words but then rushes to keep talking. "We can pay for their expertise. Money is of no concern. We can do whatever it takes."

"It's not quite that simple, Ms. Zhou. It's more a matter of finding the right person. There are a very limited number of people who have the kind of expertise we're looking for."

"And what will we do in the meanwhile?" Meiling reaches across the desk and picks up the film, studies the colors patterned across its impenetrable transparency.

"In the meanwhile we will work with Li Jing on language and occupational therapy. A significant portion of linguistic recovery in aphasic patients occurs in the first twelve weeks, so we'll stimulate his brain and attempt to rehabilitate him as much and as quickly as possible. There are a number of approaches that we'll take, courses of treatments that have been shown to be effective immediately after the neurological trauma. What's important is that he works with us as much as possible right now. Speed is of the essence."

LI JING HAS begun to dread the late afternoon. It is the sixth day of his stay in the hospital and he no longer gags at the smell of talcum powder and ammonia. The cuts across his ankles and up his calves have begun to scab and heal; the soreness and atrophy of his muscles have settled in; and his left shoulder, which had been wrenched out of its socket, is now throbbing back in place, muscle and sinew and bone seizing up again. The pale-colored universe of the hospital has become everything, has become real, and at four o'clock every day, as the shadows stretch long on the floor of the speech therapist's office, he can see Meiling begin to swell with hope as she sits by the door, staring at him with this molten love in her thin face, smiling her small, encouraging smile, as if through sheer determination she could will him into saying the right words.

"Let's try counting again today." Dr. Liu makes a fist with his hand and then unrolls his fingers one by one. *"Yī, èr, sān, sì, wǔ."*

"Yee—" What comes out of his mouth is slurred and muddy, the pitches off, the tones nonexistent. He looks away and exhales through his mouth, shaking his head.

"Keep going. *Yī, èr, sān, sì, wǔ.*"

"Yee . . . Lrgh . . . Theen . . ." He hears each syllable in his head as if it were a marble, smooth and perfect, but without traction, without a crevice to hold on to.

"Great. Now let's focus on one sound and its four tones. Let's try this: *yī, yí, yǐ, yì.*" Dr. Liu smiles, showing off his crooked teeth. He enunciates each syllable slowly, matching the motion of his index finger to each inflection: the first one a flat line, the second one rising, the third dipping, and the last falling. "Now you: *yī, yí, yǐ, yì.*"

"Yee, yee, yee . . ." Li Jing tries to approximate the shape of the doctor's mouth, exaggerating his lips, separating his top and bottom teeth. The sounds come out as a series of long, flat drawls without contour, each one a sloppy version of the same thing.

"Good." Dr. Liu pauses for a second, looks down, jots something in his notebook, and nods with practiced indifference. "We're doing very well."

Li Jing shakes his head. He can't speak, but he can still hear, can still understand, and his own failures echo clearly within his skull: his pathetic utterances bear little resemblance to speech. It's all wrong, he knows it's all wrong, but he can't quite grasp the right sounds. He only knows that the words are in there, embedded deep in his brain, but for some reason, he can't extract the right ones. It is as if all the little individual packets of sound are now mushed together, no longer discrete, no longer making sense.

She is sitting by the door of the room, and without lifting his head he can see the two tips of her shoes pointing toward each other, not quite touching. Her shoes are a midnight blue, the toes round, the heels as thin as pencils. He has never quite figured out how she walks in her high heels, but he knows it doesn't matter whether she is in heels or barefoot. She is always the one his eyes are drawn to; she will always be the most graceful girl in the room for him.

The first time he saw her they had been freshmen in college. He was laughing in the middle of a crowd when he noticed a skinny girl walking away from the group. The girl was wearing a yellow backpack and a short navy skirt. He couldn't see her face, but something about her—the way she glided down the sidewalk—made him stop laughing. He couldn't look away. After that, he began looking for the yellow backpack whenever he walked around campus. When he saw it in the library two weeks later he sat down across from her and leaned in, forcing her to look up. "Hello," he said, thinking that her face already looked so familiar. "I've been looking for you everywhere."

He looks at her now, helpless, wanting to say, "Don't be scared, everything is going to be fine"; wanting to say, "I will always take care of you." But his mind is like a swamp, all the right syllables buried deep in mud, and he knows he can't explain things to her in a way that she will understand. He just wants her to understand.

A word tickles at his throat and he opens his lips. *"Love."* He says it out loud and lifts his face to look at her. She looks back and smiles, opening her eyes wide. *"Love,"* he says it again, and this time he listens to the sound of his own voice, waiting for it to slide into its groove, waiting for meaning, wanting it to make sense. He touches his fingers to his throat, repeats the word again, and shakes his head in horror, feeling his pulse flare beneath the skin.

She keeps looking at him, keeps smiling, but her eyes blink, just once, and he can tell by the way that her face has gone absolutely still that she cannot understand him, and that she is devastated. He has always loved her face, not just because it is hers, and not just because it is beautiful. There is an expressive quality to her face despite her calmness, so much that lurks just beneath the surface; her face is never quite still: if you know to look for it—and he knows better than anyone else—there is always something that gives her away. He has studied the faint flush of the skin by her temples, evaluated her responses by how many millimeters apart her lips sat, pinpointed the thin, dark eyebrows and their exact arc on the occasions of her every mood, watched her smile with a quirk of her mouth because of some joke he'd made. And now he is looking at her face again, noticing a tiny speck of dead skin dangling from her lip, the way her eyelids swell pink and dull, erasing the crease above her eyes. Her face looks like it has collapsed, and he can tell she is trying to keep her muscles absolutely still, as if she is too exhausted and too afraid to register a new emotion. He has to look away. He cannot bear to see what he has done to her.

HE DOES NOT keep track of the days. At night he wakes up gasping, his throat clogged, his body seizing in panic. There are images inside his head: he sees plaster falling like snow, plaster falling apart at the seams, and plaster the size of clouds, crashing down from the ceiling. Noises too: he remembers a boom that rang warm and thick and electric, and then sirens, and later, the hiss of scalpels.

In his hospital room with the lights off and the shades pulled down he is caged in a dark, airless cell of silence and terror, without the use of language as a release valve. Memories come, fears, inchoate desperation, and they gather at the base of his brain, piling on, accumulating in weight, wanting to burst out of his skull. He waits it out. He tries to take long, even breaths and drain the thoughts out of his mind the way he would empty a bathtub. When the nurses come in the morning to change the sheets they find frayed holes where he has bitten the fabric, desperate attempts to keep from screaming in terror in the middle of the night.

He stays awake for longer periods of time. His treatment fills up the days. From morning until late afternoon he is poked and prodded, he undergoes physical and linguistic rehabilitation, tests and measurements, until finally, he is forced to fall asleep again. All his therapy sessions boil down to a colorless sludge, but it is preferable to being alone in the dark, watching black, formless thoughts course around in his head. When he sees his father they exchange resigned, desperate snippets of English, but he does not want to say too much; every phrase in the other language feels like a betrayal. When Pang Pang is in the room he clenches his fists to stop himself from grabbing the boy and hugging him so tight that they can never be parted. He looks away in shame when Pang Pang asks him a question, turning that smooth, round face up to him.

Under the care of doctors his body responds to treatment. He begins to exercise his muscles; his legs fall under his command again; he learns to find his open mouth with a toothbrush without having to look in the mirror. But things are different during speech therapy; he cannot manage to write down a single Chinese character, he cannot seem to repeat a simple word of Chinese with accuracy. Every afternoon at four hope seeps out of him as he tries not to look at his wife, as he squints his eyes and opens his mouth, as sounds wobble out of his throat, flare into the room with a single moment of possibility before the acoustics die down and disappointment sets in.

"New approach today. You're doing great, but let's try something else. I want to make sure we're doing as much as we can." Dr. Liu runs a hand through his comb-over, patting his hair down on one end, and smiles the same unflagging smile he's been wearing for a week and a half. "Let's try proper names. We'll start with your name: *Lǐ Jǐng*. Can you repeat after me? *Lǐ Jǐng*."

"Le . . . Nnnnnnnng." He struggles and swallows, leans back in his chair like a trapped animal. The sounds he produces are as imprecise and toneless as everything else he's tried. He shakes his head and swallows hard, biting the inside of his mouth.

"Let's try to get the consonant sound on *Jǐng*. Can you try that? Try saying the word *Jǐng*. We're looking for the third tone—there is a dip in the sound of the syllable."

Meiling is standing by the door, wearing a soft green shirt and sharp gray slacks. He has begun to take a mental snapshot of her each day, and at night, he tries to see her again, pores over the details of her outfit, remembers the way she wore her hair, holding on to the image of her as he is wrenched into sleep. She looks back at him now, softly mouthing, *"Lǐ Jǐng."* He can see the pink tip of her tongue between her teeth for the first syllable, and then it disappears as her teeth come down like a gate on the second.

"LeJnnng."

"Good job. But let's try again," Dr. Liu says.

"Le . . . Jnnng."

"Good. You got the *J* on *Jǐng.* That's very good. Now let's try another name—this one should be pretty familiar too. Let's try *Zhōu Mèi Líng.* Do you think you could try to say that? Slowly now. *Zhōu. Mèi. Líng.*"

"Choo—Chu . . . Meeh . . . Lunn," he manages. The words flat and heavy. Syllables dropping like stones.

How strange to be thirty-two years old and trying to learn the tones of words again. When he was a child he shifted from English to Chinese so easily, finding the tones without effort, exchanging one set of words and syntax for another, changing universes in the process. Back then he never thought about the particularities of Chinese, its single-syllabled words, its dependence on the shift in tones to produce meaning. Now he can hear the differences, but finds it impossible to enunciate the four variations. It's like hearing a piece of music and then looking at the black and white keys of a piano, not knowing how each note corresponds to the identical-looking keys before you.

"Mèi Líng." She stands up and walks toward him, pressing her palm to her chest.

"Mèi Líng." Dr. Liu repeats her name. The first syllable falling, the second one rising.

A pitch falling, a pitch rising. The discrete tones of every word in Chinese suddenly impassable. She crouches down in front of him and peers up into his face, repeating her name over and over as if wanting to carve it into his brain. Her fingers touch his temple, slide down his

cheek, and brush across his lips. She nods, waiting for him to repeat
after her, waiting for him to say her name.

Just two syllables: *Mèi Líng*. He can understand them, can hear the
tones of each one, and knows that they are a bridge into the arms of his
wife, but his brain can't deflect the sounds, can't turn them around and
rush them to his mouth. A breakdown in delivery and only the empty
echoing air. A synaptic collapse between the frontal lobe and the operculum. He closes his eyes and absorbs the impact of her voice into his
body; there is nothing to do but withstand the blows without screaming. He opens his mouth, wants to try again, but he knows he is going
to fail, knows he can't say what she wants him to say. The sound of her
name is still there, in the room, still reverberating, still hewing into his
head with its serrated edges. He keeps tracing the syllables again and
again in his mind, opening and closing his mouth, wanting to say those
two words, wanting to say her name.

"Meh . . . Lun." The roar of blood so loud in his ear that he can't
hear his own voice for a second. But he knows he has failed, knows it
by the bitter taste at the back of his throat.

Her face in defeat still looks like the face he knows so well, but it is
bloodless now, completely wrung out. For a moment it is as if everything has come to a stop, as if neither of them would be able to go on
from this moment, and he leans back, away from her, reveling in the
stillness, wanting an end to this violence. But he keeps looking at her
face, and he sees a tear slide down the dull pane of her cheek. It is as
if she were seizing his heart in her desperate, clawing hands. He lets
out a breath but none of the pressure inside his chest is expelled.

She touches his face again. Her fingers stumble across his nose, press
into his mouth, stab at the hollow beneath his cheekbone. She touches
him as if he were a stranger, as if the pressure of her palm on his jaw
could mold him into someone else, and he pushes his face into her hand,
nuzzling hard into her palm before pulling away, shrinking back into
himself.

For what right does he have to touch her? He can't even say her name. He tries to think of it again: *Zhōu Mèi Líng*. The words dart around his skull, evasive, refusing to be charted. With the absence of those syllables he sees her stand up and turn her back on him in order to cry. Without being able to say her name he watches helplessly as she slumps her shoulders in exhaustion, giving up. Her presence drains out of the room, and when she takes an unsteady step away from him, he knows she has been out of his grasp all along.

He stops trying to speak. Every day after that he stares down at his lap and refuses to make a sound. The speech therapist comes in the afternoon and is met with silence. Professor Li pleads and Pang Pang stares puzzled and they are both met with silence. Meiling comes every day and sits in the chair by his bed, holds his hand. His silence, which he erects to keep her alive, grows between their bodies, erasing everything.

II

ROSALYN

The patient asleep on his side, the metal bars of the hospital bed framing his body. A row of black stitches carves across the left side of his skull, visible underneath patches of newly grown hair. He is murmuring indecipherable syllables, pushing out compressed air through his teeth. His eyes flicker beneath the lids, and she wonders what he's dreaming of, what words float through his unconscious, which language threads through his nights, what he will say to her when he wakes up.

A car ride to the Oklahoma City airport. Flight to San Francisco. Flight to Tokyo. Flight to Shanghai. A man with a placard outside the arrival gate with DOCTOR ROSALYN NEAL in big, blocky letters. It was Alan, her hospital-appointed interpreter, and he kept pushing his glasses up the bridge of his nose, answering her questions in a fluent, accented English that she found charming. She insisted on heading to the hospital first, and when they arrived she unbuckled her seat belt. Across the front of her white sweater was a fat streak of dust: this was to be her first souvenir of Shanghai.

She blinks and focuses her eyes on the clipboard she has been given: his original chart with its intimate, handwritten Chinese characters; a translation into English, typed; an MRI scan dotted with color, bright on black; a reckless, hand-drawn illustration of the brain with X's and O's in the language of physiology, of localization.

Left frontal lobe. Operculum. An unlikely open head injury. Immediate surgery for the extraction of foreign matter and the containment of original trauma. Wound concentrated at fields 44 and 34 with extensive neurological damage extending into premotor and motor regions, underlying white matter, basal ganglia, insula.

His virtuoso wound.

She shivers with a discreet sense of thrill. Even in her prodigious reading of case studies, she has rarely seen this type of originating trauma. Aphasia usually resulted from strokes; clots cutting off oxygen, withholding blood from the brain, snuffing out neurons in casual cruelty. Occasionally, a patient's aphasia was the result of a cerebral hemorrhage; in those cases, it was as if a cluster bomb had been dropped into the skull, destroying everything—speech, movement, recognition—in its path. But the collapse of a building, a sheet of glass slicing across the air, a body placing itself so specifically across the wrong path at the exact wrong moment—the precision of the damage was excessive, almost unthinkable in the way it zeroed in on the areas responsible for lexical retrieval, fluency, syntactical processing.

She stares at his bare feet, the scarred slopes of skin poking out of the covers, and finds herself astounded by the sequence of events that has brought her here, to this room, this city, the sleeping man by her side.

"Dr. Neal." Alan stands by the door, not quite stepping into the room. "Shall we head to your residence now?"

"Yes—" It is the familiar-sounding words *Dr. Neal* that snap her back into herself. She clutches the clipboard to her chest and backs away from the bed, still staring at her patient. *My patient*, she mouths the words, testing out their shape as if she had never formed them before. "Yes, let's go."

FOUR A.M. AND the bamboo sheets cool beneath her. Rosalyn sprawls across the width of the bed, wide awake, but she doesn't know where the light switch is, and so she lies there, draws the blanket up to her shoulders, waits. In time the darkness loses its density, she can begin to see the shapes of cabinets, chairs, mutely packed bookshelves. This strange new city. An eleven-hour time difference. May morning halfway across the world.

As part of her research fellowship, the hospital offered her a stay in an absent doctor's home. The apartment is small and dark, on the ground floor of an institutional-looking building situated at the back of what Alan called a *longtang*—a dense, dithering alleyway—that was lined with stoops and bicycles. When she arrived she took a walk around the neighborhood, and she found the area littered with these little alleys, each of them like a twisted secret, giving off the smell of burnt coal and powdered soap, full of voices and their echoes. It took her an hour and a half to find her way back to the right alley, the right apartment. By the time she walked through the door her enthusiasm for exploration had deflated, and she spent the rest of the afternoon opening cabinets and drawers, fighting off sleep.

She gets up to open a window and tries to inhale the early morning, wondering about the woman who lives here, the classical music station on the radio, the ginseng roots wrapped in newspaper nestling in the refrigerator, the two men's dress shirts hanging in the bureau next to wispy skirts and blouses. The woman's solitary life is left intact here, in the apartment, and she, Rosalyn, steps in as if trying on a pair of shoes.

She is here because she wanted to run away, she thinks; she hadn't thought much about what she was running to. The foreign city and the exotic patient had been only abstractions, before, but now they are real and waiting, with their own thorny demands. Rosalyn walks back to bed and sits down, grabs her knees and pulls them to her chest. Despite the heat, she is shivering, uncontrollably so. What has she gotten herself into?

The e-mail that had circulated on the aphasia research Listserv two weeks ago had been cryptic. She had read it twice, trying to decipher the message.

Seeking neurologist with specialization in bilingual aphasia. Paid eight-week research fellowship in Shanghai, China (Shanghai Huashan Hospital) starting ASAP. Patient with Broca's aphasia and secondary damage, near-complete loss of primary language (Chinese), some expression in first, non-fluent language (English). Opportunity to focus on a single case in a world-class facility. Experimental rehabilitative methods welcome. Research and on-site data-gathering highly encouraged. Generous compensation and housing included. Please contact immediately for more information.

She had been drinking, that much was true. It had seemed like a good idea at the time to send an e-mail back expressing her interest with a copy of her CV attached. She had limited expertise in rehabilitation work, and she noted in her e-mail that she spoke no Chinese at all. There was little chance of her being selected for the fellowship, she thought, but she seized the opportunity for a temporary leave like a lifeline. When she fell asleep that night she forgot to turn the lights off, and she woke up the next day to an overcast sky out the window and warm, orange light flooding out of the ceiling. By the time she dragged herself to the kitchen, clouds were gathering in black herds outside the glass-paneled doors, rain starting to fall across the backyard. When she checked her e-mail she found a response from Shanghai with a point of contact, a detailed summary of the case, paragraphs of travel information, and a request to start immediately.

The case was strange and tempting: traumatic head injury causes a man to lose language he'd been using for the last twentysome years, an older, more primitive tongue from his childhood gurgling out of his throat. The invitation was formal and authoritative: it made her acceptance of the fellowship sound like a foregone conclusion.

She asked for a sabbatical from the university believing she wouldn't be granted one. Dr. Reddy called her into his office and tilted his head to the side, talked to her in the same hushed voice he used with patients: "It is the end of the semester, after all, and if you're ready to combine your research with direct therapy, then this is a great opportunity. And Rosalyn, I know things have been difficult for you recently. Maybe a change of scenery would be good. Maybe this case is exactly what you need right now." She called Alice and asked her for advice, thinking that they could have a good laugh together. "Rosalyn." Her sister took a long breath and the shrieks of the kids playing in the background filtered through, making her miss them. "It doesn't sound like such a bad idea. You told me last week that you were at the end of your tether. Why not get away for a while, focus on your work instead?" When she flew to the Chinese consulate in Houston for her visa two days later, the in-flight magazine featured Shanghai as its cover story, and she thumbed over the pages, staring hard at the panoramic photos laced with bright lights. There wasn't nearly enough time to be scared, no time for second-guessing, and despite the fact that she has never liked traveling she packed her suitcases in a hurry, a sense of relief outweighing whatever trepidation she might have felt.

Her sabbatical lasts for the entire summer. She does not know anyone in this country, nor does she speak the language. She is away from home, finally, away from that big, empty house where she wandered from room to room in the dark. The morning of the day she left, she finally pulled out the divorce papers that had been sitting in her desk drawer for three weeks. She could barely look at them, but she signed her name again and again on the dotted lines. On the way to the airport she shoved the envelope into the mailbox. When her plane took off, she finally felt as though she was leaving it all behind.

She shakes her head at the strangeness of all this: a gas pipe explosion, a piece of glass, a man trying to get out, one language lost but another rising to the surface. There is a shift in the degree of darkness out the window. It is evening. It is morning. Her patient is waiting for her. She is in Shanghai, time upside-down.

AT DAWN. LIGHT breaking into the alley from above, light stretching through the half-open gates. She wanders out of the apartment and the streetlamps are still on, the yellow lights glowing in pink sunrise. Over her head there are balconies with metal frames and stalks of bamboo stretched out—clothes hung on them, tiny red T-shirts and flowering dresses and gray button-downs, thin, diaphanous stockings swinging in the breeze. The clothes are everywhere, on every balcony, drifting, drifting, these gardens in the air. She brushes hair out of her eyes and takes in the frames of houses hugging each other for support, curls of paint peeling away from the walls, perfect arches in the roofs; the crumbling façades shimmering in the morning light.

The sky is tinted the barest blue, and there are uncluttered silhouettes of buildings rising in the distance, power lines and telephone poles, treetops and rooftops. She watches people starting to rise, wanders past shutters being opened, gates being unlatched, metal doors rising up and exposing storefronts and restaurants. There are old, empty buses lined up one after the other across the street, and she stares at their long, dull bodies, the black accordion folds in their midsections crumpled, the advertisements on their sides covered by layers of dust.

She follows a greasy, savory scent to a little stand on the sidewalk and waits in line behind people with Tupperware and stainless-steel tins. Some of them turn around to look at her, and as if it had been waiting for an audience her stomach grumbles twice, making everyone laugh. Rosalyn smiles back and tries to take a peek around the line. The tiny proprietress of the stand takes the lid off the biggest cast iron pan Rosalyn has ever seen. The smell of meat and green onions and charcoal rushes out. In the pan, crowded against each other, are small, perfect bundles of flour, the bottoms charred brown, the tops puffy and pale, scattered with flecks of green. Rosalyn watches people in front of her walk away hoarding their containers, and when it is her turn she holds up six fingers to the tiny woman, who stares at her with a bemused smile, says something quick and friendly that she cannot understand. Rosalyn takes a twenty-yuan bill out of her wallet and then holds up six fingers again. The woman laughs and takes the money, shoving a clatter of change back, muttering, her black eyes animated. The buns are doled out to a small wax bag, but when Rosalyn tries to reach for them the woman makes a shooing gesture to show that she isn't done. There is another bag of six, and another, and only when she fills out the sixth one—for a total of thirty-six buns—does the woman put them all in a pink plastic bag, which she holds out with an impish smile while Rosalyn giggles, happy to be in on the joke.

In a nearby square she sits down on a bench and watches the early morning traffic rush across the avenue. She brings one of the buns up to her lips, stares at it for a second, wondering what's inside the dough, and takes a bite. Her tongue gets slightly burnt, but she can still taste the succulence of meat, the smooth envelope of dough wrapped around it, the smoky, dense bottom flaking apart in her mouth. She swallows the bun and wipes her mouth, already grabbing the next one out of the bag, and allows herself a small smile between bites, feeling the triumph of having conquered breakfast on her first morning.

It must be around six in the evening in Oklahoma, and images of the empty house unspool like a film reel in her mind. She sees the tall, wooden bookshelf gaping and bare next to the sofa, the single towel strung across the bar in the bathroom, the crib that Ben never finished gathering dust in the basement, with only half of its slats nailed in, and she wonders what Ben is doing now, whether he is in his new apartment, whether he has found shelves for all the boxes of books that the movers took out the front door, if he looks forward to going home at the end of the day. She had dreaded it, dreaded the fact that she always drove up to a dark, hollow house after he left, dreaded the empty, rattled feeling that wouldn't go away no matter how many lights she turned on. The house had stopped feeling like home, and the places where his things used to be began to look wounded, marked by absence. She is glad to be out of there, she thinks, glad to be in dizzying new spaces and rooms, but it comes back to her despite this distance, that house and how much it needed him. She wonders if she will ever be able to fill up that house by herself.

On the street more people walk out of buildings and *longtangs*, and Rosalyn gets up to join the crowds going to work, the crowds heading to the market. She sees a little girl and her mother emerge from around a corner, holding hands, a bright pink backpack strapped onto the girl's tiny body. She stares at them, the girl's dark head bobbing as she turns her face up to her mother to tell her something, the sound of her voice, bright and impenetrable, cascading over the street. The scene makes Rosalyn's heart lurch and she comes to a standstill, looking around wildly, taking in the faces of strangers swarming forward. They gawk and point, walking around her as she stays rooted to the same spot. She has to close her eyes for a second to remember exactly where she is.

HE'S AWAKE. AND handsome, she thinks, despite his uneven hair, the pale green bruises circling his neck, the slightly grimy bandage on the side of his head. His is a squarish face, with two rosy knobs of flesh for cheeks, a jaw so defined that the lower half of his face looks like a spade, and large black eyes that follow her as she closes the door and enters the room.

"Good morning, Mr. Li. My name is Rosalyn Neal. I believe you've been told that I was coming. I'm here from Oklahoma City, where I'm a bilingual aphasia specialist at the University of Oklahoma."

When he doesn't respond she sits down in the chair by the window, crosses one leg over the other, piles her hands together in her lap with the palms up. Being here in this strange hospital makes her feel uncertain and inexperienced, as if all her authority and self-assurance have been siphoned off during the plane ride. The white coat she had been handed in the morning was too small for her, and so she left it unbuttoned, the thin fabric stretching so tight across her shoulders that she can barely raise her arms.

"I'm very eager to work with you on your language rehabilitation, and I'll also be doing some of my own research on your case. Now, I've spoken with all your doctors, and we've decided that I should spend two hours with you, five days a week. We had a very productive meeting this morning and worked out a schedule for you. I'll be coming here to your room every day at ten-thirty a.m. until you are well enough to visit my office."

The meeting in the morning had been long, disconcerting, a little bit torturous if she is honest with herself. She met with the entire team and tried to memorize names and specialties, took copious notes on her laptop, nodded over and over again, darting her eyes about the room. All the other doctors kept looking at her during every pause in the conversation, but it was impossible to read their expressions through the veil of another language, another set of habits and practices. She smiled quietly and nodded often, not sure if they were waiting for her input or if they thought her stupid. While everyone else had their say she watched and listened, not volunteering anything unless she was asked.

"I've been told that you speak and understand English, so I'm very glad that we're getting the chance to talk now. I'll be working with you on language rehabilitation in English in hopes of spurring your production in Chinese—both writing and speaking. I'll also be working with your neurologist on some neural-stimulation therapies, and mapping your brain function for research purposes. How does that sound to you?"

Li Jing leans back on his pillow, raises his eyebrows for a second, and then shrugs, looking away.

"Well, good." Rosalyn looks down at the floor, nodding out of habit. "I'm glad that we're getting together today. It's good to be here, and I'm looking forward to working with you for these next eight weeks. Do you have any questions for me?"

It is afternoon but the room is dark. The shades are down, and the ceiling fan keeps going around, humming its own listless song. She tries hard to keep looking at him, tries not to be nervous, but his silence sets her on edge, and she takes a deep breath, counting out the seconds. Finally, he turns around and looks at her again, and this time she sees an intimidating cast to his face, something slightly thuggish in his features. She looks at his chart again, at the typed passages of English black on the page, and tries to remind herself that she's the doctor here, she's the one who's in charge.

It has been a long time since she has worked directly with a patient on their rehabilitation. Her own work focuses on the research side of things, and when not teaching, she spends most of her time collecting data sets sent in from other neurologists to create computational models that mapped brain function in bilingual aphasics. Theoretically, she is well informed about all the developments in the field, including assessment methods, drug treatments, and therapeutic approaches. But in the States, language rehabilitation usually falls under the domain of a therapist rather than a neurologist, and she had been slightly astonished, during the morning meeting, at how much direct patient contact she was expected to have.

"Mr. Li, the hospital brought me here all the way from America to work with you. Obviously, this isn't the typical setup for aphasia therapy, but because of the special circumstances around your case, I think they thought that a specialist without a large caseload might be best suited to the situation. I'm here to focus on your recovery. Hopefully, we'll be able to make some significant progress."

His head is tilted backward on the pillow and he gazes at her from beneath hooded eyes, scanning her face with something that looks like contempt. He shakes his head and rolls his eyes, mocking her, but she lifts her chin and tries to hold his gaze.

"Really, Mr. Li. It's not going to be easy. It's going to take a lot of work. But I really do think—"

He rolls away to face the wall as if he is tired of listening to her now. She can feel a blush spreading hot across her cheeks and takes a deep breath.

"Working on your English could assist with your production in Chinese . . .

"My expertise is in the field of bilingual aphasia with an emphasis on computational modeling . . .

"If you just work with me I really do think . . ." She trails off and starts again. "I really do think we can make a lot of progress. What do you say?"

It is as if she weren't even there. He stays absolutely still on the bed, faces the wall on the other side of the room, breathing in and breathing out at even intervals, locking himself back into silence and solitude.

IN THE HOSPITAL cafeteria the task of ordering food by pointing and gesturing leaves Rosalyn worn out. The food on her metal tray is unrecognizable, the afternoon grows longer and longer, and her eyes are heavy-lidded. All she wants is sleep. But she is aware of her solitude, the color of her skin, the red hair she has put up in a bun in order to obscure its flamboyance. She is aware of everyone else looking at her, aware of their conversations, syllables raining down and skidding away from her, whole, inscrutable.

She knows he is hoarding mouthfuls of English, thinking the words precious, the open air dangerous. After sitting in his hospital room for half an hour, trying to wait out his silence, she wanted to shake him, loosen his tongue, pry sentences out of his mouth. Instead she left with a promise to come back in the morning, let her "Goodbye" drift into the stale, humid air of the sickroom, the sound of it expanding and then dissipating without response. Now there are words all around her, words fluttering in the air, words thickened with the sound of chopsticks rubbing against each other like insect wings, the sound of metallic spoons scraping against porcelain bowls.

"Dr. Neal. How are you getting on?" Without her notice Alan had maneuvered his tray onto the table and his body onto the seat across from hers. He nods at her as if she is his great obligation and mounds some cooked greens onto a small pile of rice, scooping the whole thing up with his chopsticks, bringing it to his mouth.

"Alan!" Rosalyn says the name with relish. "I'm so glad to see you."

"Yes." He peers down at his food again, composing another bite as if he were mixing paints.

It is not that Alan is unfriendly. He has already offered to accompany her to the drugstore and given her the phone numbers of teachers who instruct foreigners in rudimentary Chinese. But he does not let her engage him in conversation. He simply nods while she unleashes a desperate torrent of words whenever she sees him. She cannot tell if he approves or disapproves of her, if he even likes her, if it matters at all what she says.

She wants to talk to him about the case of Mr. Li, about bilingualism and translation, about the intricacies of Chinese and its single-syllabled efficiency, about the way the loss of language tears away so many unexpected facets of memories and experiences. Alan, who performs a strange alchemy from one tongue to another, seems as though he can make sense of all of it, but when she tries to ask him about his thoughts on the case, he responds dutifully, offering no insight. His impassive face shuts down any attempts at conversation. Still, she wonders, what language does he dream in?

She asks for a translation of the word *aphasia*.

He says: *Míng   Shī   Yǔ   Zhèng*
          Name Loss Language Disease

She remembers from her study of linguistics that the Chinese language is always divisible, each character, each sound its own self-revolving planet of meaning. Strung together, the language creates something new without losing the building blocks. You can break it down and still hold on to each unit, its pitch, its implication.

But to hear the word *aphasia*, with no breaks in sound, no method of subtraction or division, anyone would be at a loss.

Aphasia—a disturbance of the complex process of comprehending and formulating verbal messages that results from newly acquired disease of the central nervous system.

Without etymology, without history: an empty vehicle of vibrating waves.

A   -*phasia* (She translates from the Greek.)

No Speech

At the end of Rosalyn's first week she has already stumbled into an exotic routine. At six-thirty in the morning the sports and recreation field behind her apartment building starts blasting music over its loudspeakers. She wakes up to the Chinese national anthem, or a brass and horns cover of "Moon River," or Bach's Brandenburg Concerto no. 3, her limbs still sagging with sleep, her brain disconcerted by the music. After her shower there is always half an inch of water on the floor of the tiny bathroom. She wades through the puddles in her flip-flops and mops the floor again and again, leaving the bathroom with a thin film of sweat clinging to her body, a mild ache in her shoulders from bending over.

When she walks to the hospital at eight the sunlight is still thin but the crowds are already swarming over the streets. Some people steal looks at her from the sidewalk; others turn around and gawk without shame. She pastes a friendly smile on her face but avoids eye contact. In time she begins to recognize the two young women lounging listlessly at a hair salon down the street, the police officer on the corner whose whistle pierces the air every morning.

She buys breakfast each day from the same stand she found her first morning, gesturing and smiling at the owner, walking away with her arms full of buns and pancakes. There is a flower seller at the corner of Zhongxing Road and Hengfeng Road who watches her approach and says, "I love you" in English every day, each syllable hard, as if he does not know what the words mean. She nods at him and says, "Good morning" back, taking a small measure of comfort from these new routines.

Her office is, in actuality, a supply closet without windows in the psychiatric ward. There is no outlet in the tiny room and so an extension cord snakes its way in from the hallway, emitting a constant buzz. Every time Rosalyn plugs in her laptop she half expects an electric shock and withdraws her hand quickly, but the machine always hiccups and then starts, the screen blinking blue and bright, the modem connection gurgling to life. When her e-mail begins to load, each line unscrolling across the screen in slow increments, she leans back in her chair, looks up at the clothbound medical texts lining the walls, tries to pretend for a second that she doesn't need this thin, hissing connection, that she hasn't been desperately waiting for it all along, before turning back to sweep her eyes over her inbox, clicking madly for the news from home.

The mornings stretch on. She spends far too long reading the few e-mails from her friends. She waits for the news, box scores, the weather in Oklahoma City to download onto the screen. Outside her door she can see nurses careening through the hallway, doctors with their white coats bunched behind their bodies, moving past her office in syncopated steps. Everyone is always in a hurry, walking at the fast pace familiar to hospital corridors everywhere, making a mockery of her leisurely schedule, her one-and-only patient.

In the hallways, the bitter, brewing scent of Chinese medicine mixes with the smell of bleach. Beneath her feet the floors are always grungy, despite the custodians pushing their muddy mops back and forth. The elevators are packed every morning for the start of visiting hour, and when she squeezes onto them she is always conscious of being large and awkward, always muttering apologies no one will understand. They stare at her, the women with plastic bags hanging from their wrists, the old men pressing themselves against the walls, away from her. But she is getting used to being stared at, getting used to being in the way, and she can only look down and count off the floors before getting off and breathing out.

When she turns the handle to his door she is greeted by the same sight every day: Li Jing lying in bed with his back to her, the shades down, the lights off. She says the same chirpy "Hello" every morning, pulls the shades up, and sits down by the door. Alan had attended two sessions with her, stood at the wall, refused to meet her eyes. The silence was embarrassing, and she asked Alan to not come anymore, not wanting to waste his time.

So it is just the two of them, Rosalyn and her patient, trapped in the same room, breathing the same air. She tries to remind herself that this is a familiar scenario for aphasia patients, that withholding language is often a patient's only means of control, but it's different here, in Shanghai, more nerve-racking somehow. In a different country, in this strange hospital where sentences and charts, signs and labels, all unravel in a different language, she has no colleagues to confide in, no other cases to take up her time, no excuses for the lack of progress. She sits next to Li Jing and there is only the fan and the tick of the clock interrupting the silence, her own voice stuttering and grasping, sometimes pleading, mostly waiting. The hours go by slowly. Sometimes it seems as though he falls asleep. She tries different intervention approaches, brings notepads and music and picture books, but still, there is not a word from him, barely any reaction, and when their time is up she has to keep herself from wrenching the door open and running down the hall. Instead, she keeps her voice steady, says, "Thank you" and "See you tomorrow." She takes slow, determined steps out the door, vowing to try harder next time.

In the afternoons she goes to the consultation and debriefing with the other doctors. They meet in the smoking lounge: the head of neurology, the internist, the Chinese speech therapist, the occupational therapist, and the psychologist on the case. The speech of all the other doctors filters through Alan. Rosalyn smiles and nods as they offer platitudes like "Give it time" or "Just be patient." She cannot tell if they're being polite, trying to spare her feelings. She tries to look at them as they're talking, study their faces and look back at Alan to see if he is softening the blows through translation. But his eyes are inscrutable behind his glasses; his small, concave mouth keeps moving. He is always the man who hears everything and then empties himself of it, a shallow and temporary container of language.

"He'll come around," Alan says.

"We've all seen this before. He can't hold out forever," Alan says.

"Time," Alan says. "In due time the patient will realize that this stubbornness is getting him nowhere. In due time he'll start trying to talk again."

If there's one thing she does not have, it is time on her side.

The other doctors are all politeness, but none of them offer much in the way of help. She can't get a read on the situation, doesn't know how to conduct herself among these new colleagues, doesn't know how to assert her authority, demand more effort from Li Jing's psychologist, or ask for insight and help. After twenty minutes the meetings inevitably meander and dissolve, with doctors called away one by one to more pressing cases, new admits, other meetings, until Rosalyn is left alone with Alan. He fiddles with his watch, asks, "Is there anything else?" while picking up his briefcase. By now it is mid-afternoon and the jet lag has kicked in again. She says goodbye to Alan, spends another hour in front of her computer, and heads out into the city sleepy and delirious, the sounds of Shanghai thick in her ears. There are always errands to run, groceries to buy, places to explore, but it is so painfully bright outside, the air shimmering and viscous, weighing down on her, that all she wants is the cool dark of the apartment. All she wants is for the day to be over, to close her eyes and succumb to sleep.

HER EIGHTH MORNING? Or was it her tenth? It feels like she's been here for a month, walking the same path from her office to the elevator to the sickroom on the ninth floor so often that there should be indentations on the linoleum from the heels of her clogs. It is still early enough in the morning that she has hours until jet lag sets in, a time of day when she is still clearheaded, when everything still looks sharp, in focus. But she knows she is in for another two hours of frustration, and she has begun to resent her patient—her silent, dead-eyed patient, this sloping shape under the covers, face perpetually turned toward the wall—for this pointless occupation of her time.

"I'm back. I know you're surprised to see me again, but here I am. Ready for yet another round of our scintillating conversation." It's unlike her to be so sarcastic, but without anyone to talk to she has begun to resent the city, the way it seems determined to shut her out. She sweeps in through the door with a mocking smile pasted on her face. She has half a mind to curtsy.

The boy sitting next to the bed looks very much like his father, the same slightly flattened shape of the head, a baby-faced indecision between aristocrat and thug. He is bent over a small, handheld electronic device, his face fierce with concentration. At Rosalyn's entrance he gawks at her for a moment and then turns to look at his mother, who stands at the foot of the bed, a hand pressed flat against the windowpane. Between them Li Jing lies stiff, wearing an expression that Rosalyn has never seen on him before. He turns to look at her with panic in his eyes, as if wanting rescue, as if she could somehow make things easier. She stares at him in wonder before turning away.

"HelloHowAreYou!" At a nod from his mother the boy begins shouting in English. He hops off his chair and bows once in Rosalyn's direction.

It takes an enormous amount of effort just to drag a breath into her lungs. She stares at the boy, and all at once she feels a soreness in her heart, as if the muscle is worn out from overuse. How much like his father he looks. Ben had always said that he wanted a child with her red hair and his Roman nose. For years they imagined children with affinities for medicine and history, with her goofy sense of humor and his long legs. "They're not just going to be miniature versions of us, you know!" she remembers telling him, before they knew better. "They'll be perfect," Ben said, "they'll be ours!" He put a hand on her belly and laughed into her neck.

She turns back to the boy and flashes him her biggest smile. "I'm fine. How are you? Did you come to visit your father?"

The boy pauses, looking lost. "HelloHowAreYou," he says again, his voice more uncertain now.

The woman by the window walks over to stand in front of her and Rosalyn extends her hand. "You must be Mrs. Li. *Nihao.* It's so nice to meet you."

"Nǐhǎo." The woman seizes Rosalyn's hand with both of her own. Her face is feverish, with an expression so desperate that it has made her beautiful features slightly grotesque. *"Xièxie nǐ, Neal yīshēng. Wǒ zhēn de hěn gǎnxie."*

Rosalyn opens her hand to indicate that she doesn't understand, and the other woman nods, laying her palm against her chest. Pang Pang presses buttons on the tiny machine in his hand, and a robotic voice comes out of it with flat syllables of English: "Thank you, thank you very much." On the bed Li Jing flinches, turns his face toward the wall. Rosalyn looks at mother and son, and finds the other woman staring at the device in the boy's hands with suspicion, as if she is unsure of its faithfulness. The boy, though, seems pleased. He says something to his father, and then leaves the device on the bed, next to the curve of Li Jing's back. When he turns away, his small, inherited face is jumbled in anxiety and hope, and looking at him, Rosalyn can feel something sharpening into focus within her, this affection, for someone else's son, a determination to make things better for the sake of the boy.

"*Wǒmen zǒule,*" the other woman says, helping her son strap on his backpack.

"Goodbye!" Pang Pang says in English. "Goodbye!"

Rosalyn looks back at the bed. Li Jing is so still lying there, his body the same misshapen lump under the blanket she is greeted with every day. She paces the four steps to the opposite side of the room and starts back, shaking her head. He breathes out through his mouth, a gravelly, tortured sound. The heat of the room traps the smells of sweat and herbal medicine as if they are part of some fermentation process, stewing away.

"Your son is very cute. He looks so much like you." She sets herself down in the seat the boy has just vacated, next to Li Jing, and picks up the electronic dictionary, turning it over in her hand. "I'm sure he misses you very much, and he really wants to talk to you. Don't you think you should try to talk to him? If you hadn't wanted your dad to translate for you before, now you can do it through this."

She leans back in the chair but lets her neck hang loose. Peeking out from the curtain of her hair she sees him absolutely still on the bed, not even a tremor, not even a glance in her direction. Remembering the boy's face, with fear and hope rippling across the smooth skin, she holds the electronic dictionary up to the light and then puts it down, standing up again. The man's silence is a noose tightening around her own throat.

"Are you trying to make some kind of point by not talking? What good is that going to do?" She is pleading, and her voice sounds shrill to her ears. She can feel the thin veneer of her calm slipping away from her, but she's not quite sure she cares. "Do you know how lucky you are to have such a beautiful son? To have your family? You're being really unfair to them. They must be so scared for you."

It's been five weeks since the explosion. She had been told that after struggling through speech therapy during the first week Li Jing had completely shut down. Since then he has not said a word to anyone.

She looks over and wants to shake him hard, wants to shake the words loose from his throat. She has begun to have these dreams at night where she is talking to Ben again, trying to explain why she can't go through another round of shots and dashed hopes, but still trying to work it out. Only they are underwater and every time she opens her mouth to tell him something she swallows more water. She wakes up choking and hysterical, dreading the day, dreading another session with Li Jing, dreading the hours of silence that always press into her, mute and relentless. There are things she wants to say, thoughts beating against the inside of her skull, wanting to erupt. What she wants is a conversation, but there is no one to talk to here, and she has begun talking to herself on the street like a madwoman, just to hear the words out loud.

"Come on. Don't just lie there." There is something about seeing the family: the child's features so much like his dad's, the woman's grief etched on her face. Rosalyn gets up and opens the window. The air outside is just as heavy, just as muggy, and it hits her face like a hot breath. She slams the window shut again.

"There's no reason you can't be up and about walking around. There's no reason you can't try to talk to your son or go outside with him. I know your physical therapy is going well, so why are you staying in bed all the time? I know this is hard for you, but think about somebody else, think about your family. Think of how they must feel."

The bed creaks beneath his body, but she is beyond noticing, pacing back and forth, raking her fingers through her hair.

"You're not even trying. Try, for god's sake! I know you can talk to me in English. I know you can say something."

He tucks his knees into his chin, tries to bury his face in the pillow and sink into the mattress. She is barely looking at him, spitting out syllables with force, biting down on her fingernails, stripping thin layers of them away with her teeth.

"Don't you want to get better? Don't you even care how this affects everyone else? Or is it that you're just trying to prove some point, be the tough guy? Don't you want to talk to your son? Your son, who's a part of you, who clearly adores you, and wants you to be okay? Just say something." She jerks herself to a full stop at the foot of the bed, clutches the metal railing and snorts in disgust. "Say something. Say anything. But say *something*!"

He lifts his head and his face is murderous. He puts his hands up to his ears and presses hard against his skull as if he wants to crush it to powder. He screams—a long, thorny snarl erupting out of his body—and then he opens his mouth wider and the sound expands and fills the room, metallic and full-throated, savage in its vibrations. It makes her duck her head and cover her ears with her hands, back away into the wall. He is shaking wildly, his arms pounding into the mattress, his body rocking back and forth, making the bed swing and groan on its wheels.

"Stop it!" She is screaming too, but she can barely hear herself. He keeps shrieking, jagged edges of sound that whip across the room, and he crushes his fists into his skull again and again, the muffled *thwack* of bone hitting bone coming through in a regular rhythm. "Stop it!" Now her voice is so high-pitched that it registers a notch above his screams. "What are you doing? Just stop it!"

His eyes are shut tight and his face is twisted up in a grimace, the skin quivering, blooming into blotches of red. He closes his mouth abruptly, makes a dry gagging sound, and now she is the only one still screaming, her "Stop it!" ragged in the air, his gulping breath underneath the sound of her voice, counting time. He picks up the electronic dictionary and hurls it across the room. The crack of plastic meeting concrete is disappointingly quiet. "God," she breathes out, her shoulders shaking, and bends down to his body on the bed, pries his fists away from his skull. Her hands press his down to the mattress but he makes no motion to resist, just lies there defeated as she heaves and mutters, "What are you doing?" By now she is whispering and still her voice sounds too loud in her ear. "What are you doing? What are you trying to prove?"

She swallows and closes her eyes to keep from crying.

He focuses on her face for a second, and then he looks away and rolls over to the wall again. There is silence now, then a set of footsteps getting louder and then softer outside the door, the intercom cackling with electricity, some unintelligible sentence distorted and spit out. She looks back at the bed, but he has not moved a muscle, has not made a noise again. And so she walks out and closes the door behind her, making sure it is shut tight before slumping her shoulders in defeat.

SHE WANTS A nap. She wants to go home. She wants another patient. She wants to give up. Rosalyn throws off her jacket and slings it over her shoulder, prowling past the intersection, her hair loose behind her as brilliant as a flag on a pole.

A malicious May sun gathering in the pavement all day, and now, in late afternoon, the heat glowers on the sidewalks, wringing sweat out of skin. She feels as though she is wilting, the city and every step exhausting her, her patient completely impossible, every casual encounter demanding too much effort. This whole trip has made her so tired and she just wants to go to sleep, she wants to be in her parents' house with the radio on and the bathwater running, she wants to be under the blanket on the couch, Ben bringing her ginger ale and a grilled cheese, Ben reading by her side. Sweat drips down her neck, past the collar of her shirt, and the air is so thick and hot that she can barely breathe. There is something about being in this foreign city that makes her feel pathetic and helpless, but all she can do is trudge forward, hungry and exhausted, and try to find a place to sit down, some food, a few seconds to close her eyes.

She has wandered away from the familiar route between her apartment and the hospital, and now she doesn't know where she is, the convoluted streets closing in, the street signs in hieroglyphics. A McDonald's logo glares red and yellow in the distance, but she resists its familiar allure and heads down a side street, dragging air through her nostrils, following the crowds. Past a large pane of glass she can see a clean, bright restaurant bustling with people, veiled in steam from the kitchen. Families gather at huge, round tables covered in food; couples sit across from each other, their chopsticks flying, their faces animated. The door swings open at a touch and inside she is overwhelmed with the scent of food, webs of conversation, all this laughter, particular pitches of excitement and family that she can only recognize in abstraction, but which fill her with a wobbly and tremulous feeling so that she almost begins to cry. Before she can gather herself, a hostess walks up and smiles, says something that passes by too quickly, and holds up one finger. Rosalyn nods and finds herself following the woman to a table in a brightly lit corner. She slumps down in her seat and opens the menu. There are pages and pages of Chinese characters, no translations, no pictures, no chance of her understanding any of it. But of course—she shakes her head and squeezes her eyes closed and tries to silence a groan—what was she expecting? She looks around the room again, all the people, the cheer of the place, the voices arcing across tables. She knows that she can't be a part of any of this. Now there is nothing to do but rush out with an apology in English that no one will hear, head back to the street, keep walking, looking for something else. What that might be, she doesn't know.

She keeps walking along, each step exhausting her, surrounded by restaurants, bars, people munching on snacks and laughing with each other, teenage boys in packs cutting through the crowds. There's no place to stop, no place she can rest. There's only fear pounding away inside her, its steady rhythm beating beneath the pulse. She knows that it makes no sense, being afraid, but every face that peers at her with curiosity makes her want to shrink back into herself, every Chinese character on street signs and neon billboards feels so daunting. Finally her eyes land on a sign in English, green script on a white sign proclaiming DELICIOUS CHINESE FOOD HERE with a flourish. She stops at the sign, finds a misspelled plaque in English at the door directing her to the sixth-floor restaurant, and gets on an elevator, passing by men and women in suits getting out from a day at the office. When she gets off she finds an empty restaurant as big as a ballroom, with immaculately set tables, damask tablecloths, tall young women at the entrance in *qipaos* whose sole purpose seems to be greeting the nonexistent diners. The hostess utters a practiced "Good evening," thrusts a menu written in English into Rosalyn's grateful hands, and leads her to a table by a window. She sits down, exhaling, and closes her eyes.

She is so lonely, and though she has been in Shanghai for only a little while, she can feel her skin close up into itself, as if the impenetrability of this other language has erected a shield around her body, some glass cage that she can only press up against. She remembers telling Alice a few months ago, before Ben left, that she was so lonely in her house, despite him living there, despite the easy way they talked to each other, the way they've always talked before. They didn't speak in future tenses anymore. It made her painfully aware of a time when he would no longer be at her side. But it is different, a different kind of loneliness here, everything is different. She is in a city with fifteen million people, the sounds of them constantly pressing up against her skin, the sheer density of them making sure she is never really alone. The street below is a narrow pedestrian lane, and Rosalyn looks down at neon signs in every color blaring into dusk, the streetlights shining on a sea of black hair, the crowds following the curves and angles of the crooked street endlessly. In Shanghai she has found a whole new solitude.

CHAPTER 6

Rosalyn opens the door of his room cautiously this time, clutches her clipboard tight against her chest. "Good morning," she says, trying to keep her voice even-keeled, striding in with as much bravado as she can muster.

His wife is there again, along with an older man who sits in a wheelchair by the bed, his hair as white as his hospital pajamas.

Rosalyn starts to excuse herself. "Oh, I'll just come back later . . ." she says in English before shutting her mouth and backing out of the room.

"Stay, Dr. Neal." The old man's English is crisp and lightly accented. "Please come in. I was hoping to run into you."

"Hello!" Rosalyn takes a step forward and smiles. "You must be Professor Li. And *nihao*, Mrs. Li. It's nice to see you again."

"I'm not much of a professor in this wheelchair, but yes, that is me," the man says. "It's a pleasure to finally meet you, Dr. Neal. My daughter-in-law, whom I believe you've met, is named Zhou Meiling."

Zhou Meiling gives Rosalyn a small, closed-mouth smile before bending down to tug her husband's blanket across his bare feet.

"It's wonderful to meet you, Professor. And I must tell you, it's such a pleasure for me to speak English with someone these days." Rosalyn's smile broadens.

"It's a pleasure for me as well, Doctor. Do I detect a Southern accent in your voice?"

"I grew up in North Carolina."

"I spent a few years not too far from there, in Charlottesville, Virginia."

The old man wheels himself over to her. Shaking her hand he holds on to her for a second longer than necessary, his thumb stroking the back of her hand as if trying to recover a memory. "Quite beautiful out there, especially around this time of year. All that tender green, the dogwoods blooming."

"It's wonderful." Her accent deepens and her voice slows. "I love it out there. I live in Oklahoma now, and I like it. But I still miss North Carolina a lot."

Professor Li gives Rosalyn an inscrutable look, lifting his eyebrows. "Do you know that Li Jing grew up in Charlottesville?"

"Oh yes, it was in his file." Rosalyn turns from father to son. "It must have been quite a shock going from Charlottesville to Shanghai. Still, Virginia was probably a wonderful place to grow up."

Professor Li snorts lightly. Li Jing does not even turn his head.

"I doubt Li Jing would consider his childhood idyllic, Dr. Neal. But I don't really know. He claims not to remember most of it. As for me, well, the 1970s were an interesting time to live in the American South. I remember all of it very well."

Rosalyn nods, dropping the subject. "And how are you feeling today, Professor?"

For that she gets a dismissive wave of the hand, something in the professor's gesture reminding her of Li Jing.

"I'm fine. Please don't fuss over me. It's my son you're here to concern yourself with. Isn't that right, Li Jing?" The professor wheels himself over to the bed. "I understand that he's been extremely uncooperative, and I apologize on his behalf, Dr. Neal. Please know that we are very pleased you are here in Shanghai, and don't hesitate to let us know if you need anything at all."

"Thank you very much, Professor. I'm glad to be here, and I hope I can help. But . . ." Rosalyn trails off and glances over at the bed. "I just wondered if there's anything else that might account for Mr. Li's reluctance to speak."

"Believe it or not, Dr. Neal, Li Jing has always been a man of many words. Just ask Meiling. I believe that sometimes in the past she has wanted her husband to—what's that wonderful American colloquialism?—she has wanted him to put a sock in it."

Rosalyn glances over at Meiling, admiring the other woman's face, subtly and expertly made up, the way her black hair falls sleek and perfect onto her shoulders. Rosalyn tries to imagine what they look like together—her patient and his immaculate wife—but it is hard to imagine the bandaged and bruised man standing next to this woman, holding her manicured fingers in his hand, whispering endearments into her ear.

"But he is stubborn. He doesn't like not being able to do things well. He reminds me of his mother that way," Professor Li resumes, looking pointedly over at his son. "He'll come around, though. You'll see, Dr. Neal. This is very childish behavior, trying to prove some kind of point instead of just working hard to make things better."

"Actually, aphasia patients are often reticent to even try speaking when they first realize that they've lost their fluency. They feel like they'll make a fool of themselves as soon as they open their mouths. Aphasia can be a very isolating condition, and though Mr. Li's silence has lasted longer than we would have hoped, he has undergone a great deal of trauma, so his behavior is perfectly understandable and not at all uncommon."

She's not sure why she feels compelled to defend her patient, but something about Professor Li's imperiousness rubs her the wrong way, and it is not as if Li Jing can defend himself. She sneaks a glance at the bed, but his face is still turned away. Professor Li gives a small harrumph in dismissal, and barks out two sentences in Chinese before gesturing for Meiling to follow him out the door.

The professor pauses and looks Rosalyn up and down. "I have no doubt that you'll be very successful in your work with Li Jing, and I expect to hear updates and progress reports on a regular basis. After all, we brought you in specifically because of your expertise. Feel free to drop by my room anytime to discuss his case."

The door closes behind Professor Li and Meiling, and it is as if some of the tension in the room drains out. Rosalyn lets out a loud breath, and when Li Jing turns to her there is the slightest bit of amusement in his eyes before his face is blank again.

"Well, I feel like a student who's just been dismissed by her teacher. I liked your dad, and he obviously cares a great deal about you, but he's a bit intimidating. From the tone of his voice, it sounds like I better make you start talking, or else!"

When Li Jing doesn't react, she sits down in the chair next to his bed and touches his shoulder lightly.

"I'm very sorry about yesterday," she says. "My behavior was un-professional and unkind, and you have every right to be upset with me. A lot of that had nothing to do with this case, and I shouldn't have taken out my frustrations on you. I hope that I haven't damaged our relationship permanently, and I hope you can trust me enough to work with me for this next month and a half."

He doesn't say anything but nods very slightly, turns his head just a little toward where her hand is resting on his shoulder.

"What I told your father is true. It's perfectly understandable for you to not want to talk right now. The thing is—and you know this—the sooner you start trying, the sooner we can really assess where you are and work out a plan for your rehabilitation."

She stands up and paces to the window, clears her throat. "And your wife Meiling . . . Am I saying that right? She seems lovely. I'm sure you're eager to talk to her, and to your little boy. How old is he?

Around seven or eight? I have a nephew who's seven—it's such a great age. Anyway, people must say this all the time, but your son looks so much like you, in the shape of the face, in the eyes too. You're very lucky to have him, you know. I'm sure he misses talking to you very much."

Rosalyn's sentences pour out as if a faucet has been opened, and she keeps talking, she cannot stop herself. The room is tiny, but she paces back and forth with slow steps, stretching out her throat, letting her voice arc up and down. She wants to entice him into conversation, build a defense for language, show him its cursive pleasures, remind him of what he is missing.

"Do you know that this is only the second time I've ever left the U.S.? Can you believe it? I'm thirty, and the only other time I've been abroad was a semester in Dublin junior year. We never had the money growing up, and after college there was medical school and my residency and then my job. The past few years, especially, have been so busy and exhausting that I've barely gone anywhere. I guess I'm just a small-town girl at heart. I don't do very well out of my comfort zone, so this trip has been quite a challenge. But you must travel a lot, being a businessman. Do you like it? Traveling, that is?"

He lies facing the wall, his eyes closed, his breath even, his back falling, rising.

She keeps talking, wanting him to listen, wanting to hear the sound of her own voice speaking English ripple across the air. She tells him about growing up in North Carolina, what the light looked like slanting through the bare trees in winter, the way she would watch the sun set in the valley behind their house, letting her eyes unfocus, letting the light burn her retinas before looking away. During dinner the radio would always be on, tuned to the country music station, and her dad with his blackened baseball cap would sit dull and exhausted at the head of the table, motor oil under his fingernails, smelling of gasoline. "I went to Syracuse for college," she says. "I got a full scholarship there, but my parents were aghast. The farthest place they had gone before that was D.C. God, it was cold up there in New York. That first winter I lived on warm milk poured over cereal. My roommate thought it was disgusting. But then again, my roommate thought a lot of things about me were disgusting. She was from Boston, and to her, I must have seemed like such a country bumpkin. I couldn't wait to get away from Syracuse and go back South. Ended up going to medical school in Oklahoma, and I've been there ever since."

Her monologue grows longer and more haphazard. She leaps from one train of thought to the next without ever looking back, tells stories whose middles become the beginning of other stories. There are details where she bares herself, a kind of longing that hums beneath every word, places and names and feelings that illuminate tiny patches of her history, leaving context and time in the dark.

Here is this room, this man who refuses to open his mouth, a silence that threatens to choke them both. So she keeps talking, taking deep breaths, expelling words into air as if trying to fill up the room. In this space she wills English into being, watches it flower, coaxes it to grow so tall and profuse that it cannot be denied, not even by his silence. And so she goes on telling stories, asking questions without demanding answers, revealing her fears and vulnerabilities, delivering sound waves at a constant speed.

When he finally speaks, it takes her a minute to hear him.

"What did you say?" She lets her mouth hang open and gapes at him in shock. When he repeats the sentence in a rusty, stuttering English, she smiles with her back to the window, sunlight filtering through the red halo of her hair. He looks up at her and on his face is a mixture of defeat and exhaustion. He repeats himself again, the dribbles of English making her clasp her hands together, making her bright with joy.

ROSALYN RUNS INTO Alan on a block not far from the hospital. From across the street his face is animated as he chatters on his cell phone while eating an ice cream sandwich that drips down his fingers. "Alan!" she shouts with an extravagant wave, and ducks in and out of traffic to get to his side. By then, he has already hung up the phone. He wipes his hands on a handkerchief, having thrown the half-eaten sandwich away while she crossed the street.

"Dr. Neal." He is all business, as usual.

"Alan, I got him to talk!" Rosalyn throws her arms up in the air and then promptly hugs the interpreter, drawing stares from passersby.

"Congratulations." He pats her on the back like an awkward father. "Very good."

"Thanks!" She is breathless with excitement. "I know! It was so strange, you know, since I've been here I've been trying to get him to open up. Well, you saw how it was. It made me so frustrated. I didn't even tell you the half of it. He was all clammed up, and for the life of me, I couldn't get him to open his mouth at all. It was driving me crazy!"

Her voice is as loud and quick as a train slamming through night. Her hair has soaked up the humidity and now tumbles out of her scalp, frizzy, curls combing through the air. She laughs, oblivious to the little kids who point at her with unabashed curiosity. Alan inches closer, looking around in embarrassment before dropping his head.

"Good, good." The words are so soft he's almost whispering, but she keeps talking with that fever in her throat, not taking the hint to lower her voice.

"I don't know. I just started talking to myself, just rambling on and on, remembering things I haven't thought about for ages. He must have been bored to death. It's just that it's been so long since I've talked to anyone. I miss my friends back home, but it's impossible to get any-one in the States with the time difference, and here, well—it's not like I can just strike up a conversation with the other doctors, you know? So I was just going on and on, and then for some reason I started talk-ing about my parents. They'd always had completely different politics from each other, and I said that the last presidential candidate they had both voted for was Richard Nixon. Suddenly I hear this noise from the bed and I swear, I had almost forgotten he was there. I had to ask him to repeat what he said. 'President Nixon. Great man,' he says to me. Can you believe it? I wanted to keep him talking so I said, 'What about Watergate?' 'Americans,' he said, 'care about stupid things.' Can you believe he said that to me? It was slow going, but he finally wanted to talk. He talked about how Nixon established ties between the U.S. and China, and how that made it possible for him and his father to return to China. 'More important than break-in,' he said. God, I just kind of stood there and nodded. I didn't really know what to say back to him."

Alan has discreetly maneuvered their bodies away from the middle of the sidewalk and into the mouth of an alley during her monologue. Rosalyn feels a cool shade on her face and looks up to see the arms of an oak tree arching over her.

"He wasn't fluent, of course, and his speech in English was riddled with agrammatisms and paragrammatisms. But part of that could be because he hasn't spoken very much English over the last few decades. I don't know, tomorrow I'll do more testing to pin down his linguistic skills, and I'll have to consult his other doctors. But it's amazing, really! I can't believe it—he actually opened his mouth and talked to me!"

"Very good, Dr. Neal. Now, if you'll pardon me, I have to go catch the bus." Alan shakes her hand and begins to walk away. "Get home safely, and see you tomorrow."

"Alan!" Rosalyn leaves the shade and stumbles after the interpreter. "Alan, wait! Where do I . . . ? What do I do to celebrate?"

He turns around and there is a look of slight triumph on his face, as if he'd been expecting this question all along. "Of course, Dr. Neal. I will tell you where to go."

Alan steps into the street and shoots his arm out. A taxi zips to a stop in front of him, almost knocking over a bicyclist. Cold air rushes out of the car when Alan opens the door and gestures for Rosalyn to get in. "Portman," he says to the driver, and Rosalyn can't quite tell if he has spoken in Chinese or in English. "It's the bar on the second floor." He smiles for a brief moment before slamming the car door shut.

"Por-ta-man," the driver repeats, breaking the word up into three discrete syllables while the car lurches ahead into traffic. Rosalyn leans back against the seat, alone and giddy, letting herself be carried away.

THE PORTMAN RITZ-CARLTON on West Nanjing Road rises out of a cluster of lower buildings in a wash of blue lights, towering over everything. Rosalyn presses herself against the taxi window as they pull off the main road and into the compound, noting a change in the atmosphere. There is a Hard Rock Cafe on her left, glass-enclosed walkways suspended in the air, carpets of grass that glow green and lush in the evening light. When the car stops in the middle of a long, circular driveway and a bellhop opens her door, says, "Good evening" in a near-perfect American accent, she lets her shoulders loosen and her face relax and tips the taxi driver a decadent 50 percent before swinging out of the car and in through the revolving doors.

At the top of the escalator a young man in uniform motions her toward a set of black leather doors before she can even open her mouth. She walks into the bar, her shoes slapping against the hardwood floor, and pauses for a moment, tries to take it all in. It's getting dark now, and the wide, continuous windows are blurry, alight with reflections of martini glasses, the flicker of candle flames, sparkling jewelry on wrists and earlobes. There are people dotted against plots of dark leather and expanses of glass tabletops, a saxophone's quiet wail beneath the thrum of conversation, and she takes slow, gingerly steps toward the bar, smooths the fabric of her skirt and drags her fingers through her hair before sitting down.

A cell phone rings loud and brash near her ear. Someone picks it up and Rosalyn is startled to hear "Hey! How are you?" in a New York accent. She listens harder and finds threads of conversations in German, Chinese, English, Spanish, English again. Looking around the bar she notices people with pale skin and bright hair lounging across booths and laughing by the window. It is like stumbling into a secret club, and she flashes back to Alan's face right before the taxi pulled away, his uncharacteristic smugness. Does he think that this is where she belongs? That she would be more comfortable here, surrounded by other expats? Before she can figure out whether she is insulted or relieved, a blond man in a pale pink polo shirt sits down next to her and says, "Hi there," a little too close to her ear. He gestures the bartender over with a small wave and turns back to Rosalyn with a sheepish smile. "Can I buy you a drink?" She nods, slowly, looking at him and then looking down at the lacquered black of the bar.

His name is Danny. He has a mop of curly blond hair and a face that looks a little like Charlie Brown's. He tells her he is a cellist with the East Sea Regional Orchestra, has lived in Shanghai for seven years, can't imagine going back to America to stay, and calls himself an "old China hand" with a grin.

"But what about your family?" she finds herself crying out, the wine in her blood shifting her body toward him.

"My family's a mess," he leans in and whispers back. "In fact, I think I might have come here to get away from them. This is a great place to get away from yourself, you know? I think a lot of people I know came here to start over."

The first notes of "Summertime" float over the room. Rosalyn turns to the stage just in time to see the tall, blond singer wink at Danny. An overweight man in a three-piece suit slaps Danny's back on his way to the bathroom. A group of loud, boisterous Americans tries to wave Danny over. He nods at them but stays by Rosalyn's side.

"Do you know all these people?" she asks him, incredulous.

"More or less."

She empties her wine and gestures to the bartender for another glass. "Really? That's amazing."

"The expat community is not so big," he says. "And we run into each other all the time, whether it's here, on Maoming Road, or at some of the places on the Bund. Shanghai might seem overwhelming at first, but once you get the hang of it, it stops being so big and scary. You get to know everyone sooner or later."

"I've been here for almost two weeks, and I haven't met anyone."

"We'll have to fix that." Danny takes her hand in his with a shy, beatific smile. "You'll have to meet all my friends. Shanghai's fantastic, really, and full of great people. Stick with me. I promise that you'll have a great time here."

The alcohol seeps into her muscles, putting her at ease. The music swims into her limbs, the slow, drowsy notes making her sway on the bar stool. Danny's eyes are a clear, glassy blue, almost liquid in the dim light, and when she stares up at him for a beat too long he blushes and looks away before looking back at her. It fills her with a small dab of affection, his shyness, and so she rests her hand on his shoulder with the barest hint of pressure, lets the almost-forgotten gestures of flirtation trickle back into her body, reveling in his obvious approval.

"So, Ms.-Dr.-Rosalyn-Neal," Danny says, singsongy. "Tell me more about this whole medical case. I've never met anyone who's come to Shanghai for medical purposes before. It sounds so glamorous, crisscrossing the world with scalpel in hand to save lives."

"Hardly. And I'm not a surgeon. I'm a neurologist. But the case *is* totally fascinating." She leans toward Danny, her face now animated, transformed, drawing him in. "You speak English and Chinese, don't you? Can you imagine if suddenly you lost the ability to speak English? I've been working with aphasia for a long time now, and it's still hard to really know how the patients feel, what it's like to not have access to language on the inside. But it's strange, I've actually been thinking about it differently since I've been in Shanghai, because I don't speak Chinese. It's devastating, how much your loss of language cuts you off from. It reshapes your entire personality, it makes you different in this unimaginable way."

"Wow," Danny says. "It sounds fascinating."

"I'm sorry. Am I boring you?" Rosalyn lets out a laugh and tilts her head, looking at him sideways.

"Not at all." Danny puts his hand on her bare arm and looks into her soft, flushed cheeks. "Keep talking, please! Have another drink—I want to hear more about you."

For the rest of the night her ears are packed full of words, her head is spinning with them. After being so lonely in Shanghai it is a relief to talk to someone easily, and she glows bright and careless, laughing often, feeling as though some facet of herself has been returned to her. The familiarity of the language makes her so happy that she talks to Danny as if he were a close friend, teasing him and confiding in him at the same time. He listens hard to what she has to say. She lets herself fall into soliloquies and then rambles into a torrent of questions. At times she slows her sentences down, lets them fill with languor. Other times she speeds them up and races through, as if she's been running to the finish line all along. They laugh at each other's jokes, hear each other's stories for the first time, and it is lovely, she thinks, to get to know someone new, to really talk to them. It is the first time she has felt at ease since she's arrived in Shanghai.

This is what she has been missing all along, this conversation tilting back and forth between bodies, this symmetry of sounds. There are words unrolling from her mouth and his, interruptions and laughter, sentences eclipsed by other sentences, thoughts building off one another. Danny presses in close and whispers the punch line of a joke; she has lost the thread of the joke but throws her head back and roars in laughter. His voice and her own and the voices of all the people around them condense into this swath of pleasure, wrapping her up, enveloping her. Paragraphs accumulate with clarity and ease. This language like a lover.

III

HUANGMEI DAYS

Meiling had fallen asleep on the couch and she wakes up with her jacket shrouding her face, blocking out the light. She has not opened the windows in the apartment for days and a stale, musty smell drifts past her nose. She walks across the living room and opens the sliding glass doors, steps out onto the balcony. At the site of the Swan Hotel a pile of rubble stews in the sun, glaring back at her from its stump of disaster, an occasional flash of metal flaring bright.

What time is it? What day of the week? What day of the month? How much longer can this go on? At times, before waking up, her body clenches itself tight as if wanting to hold on to dreams, as if not wanting to wake up. Consciousness always comes as a disappointment—the real seeping in, memories of the way the building buckled, the shiny, knotted scar tissue on his skull, those lips that refuse to open.

She's not used to this silence, the way the apartment is so still without the constant chatter from Li Jing and Professor Li. Visitors come and go, the dining table gets buried under gifts and casseroles, but in the evenings, the quiet stretches its sinister wings. When Pang Pang's thin voice erupts, it seems to knock into walls, echo in the room. Pang Pang will ask, "When are they coming home?" Pang Pang will ask, "Will Dad ever be able to talk again?" And she can only let his questions go unanswered, can only hold him close and hide her face in his back, trying not to shake, murmuring, "Everything's going to be fine."

The solitude of being the one still left standing exhausting her; their absences expanding and contracting, marking the passage of time. It was not uncommon for her to fall asleep alone, before, but now she wakes up with a start in the middle of the night, the bed empty, the blankets on the floor. Without his body next to her, anxiety thrashes up, and she is afraid of slipping into sleep again, afraid of being alone in the dark.

His voice in her ear these past fourteen years. She can barely remember what life was like before he firmly planted himself by her side.

When she met him, Meiling had just left Sichuan to attend Fudan University in Shanghai. Young, unsure of herself, she stood at the periphery of their group of friends, preferred listening to talking, tried to absorb the world through her pores. She was a stranger to the city, ignorant of the local dialect, awkwardly navigating intricate customs, watching other girls out of the corner of her eye in dorm rooms and classrooms, registering their easy mannerisms, studying their casual sophistication. Her heart pounded with anxiety when she was surrounded. She felt ill at ease in Shanghai, its catty, elaborate habits confounding her. But she already had a hint of the power that her beauty had given her, and she kept the knowledge of it tightly wound inside, where it slowly grew into a self-assurance that coursed beneath the skin.

He was the gregarious one at the center of their social group. He was its sun. He was a quick study, athletic, with a certain glamour clinging to him from his childhood abroad. Other students talked about him often and without malice. He was one of those campus stars whom everyone knew on sight. Without trying, Meiling learned that his father was the famous architect Li Shenjian, his mother a Hong Kongese beauty who died in a car accident when Li Jing was a kid. He had spent the first ten years of his life in America before moving to China.

Despite his entitlement he was well liked by nearly everyone who met him. Around campus, there was much admiration for his quick wit, envy of his effortless good grades, and rumors of a terrible temper, which added an element of danger to him, giving his careless charm even more appeal.

She saw him in the middle of crowds, heard his booming voice crack jokes after class, but she didn't pay much attention, finding him indiscriminate in his tastes, far too casual with his affection. Until he set his sights on her, she was one of the few women at school not under his thrall.

How he seduced her was with words. He stole up to her side and asked her questions, tilted his chin. He excavated her mind for her theories of history, her opinions on literature, her preferences among various forms of poetry. Tell me about the body of water closest to you, he would ask her, the book you loved most as a child, the last time you laughed out loud. Unused to this kind of attention she trembled and withdrew for a few weeks before his sincerity sank in past her skin; when he continued his pursuit she unfolded herself like an artichoke opening up to the sun, her rich, succulent petals slowly easing away from the dark, spindly heart of her. He whispered in her ear and took her face in his hands. She held herself still and told him everything he wanted to know. Conversations accumulated between the two of them until one day, she discovered that his words had built an entirely private universe between their two bodies. By that point she no longer wanted to escape his grasp.

A little post outside her dorm: one meter by one meter, about seventy centimeters high, circumscribed by brick and topped by mud and grass. Intended for flowers, the pillar had long been neglected to a dismal, uneven patch of green. They sat on its borders for late-night conversations. They called it "our garden."

Once he pulled out a handful of grass by its roots and handed it to her, as solemnly as he would a bouquet. Another time he coaxed her into standing on top of the pillar with him, barefoot, swaying to some song he was humming. He murmured in her ear. The streetlight shone on them every night for a semester. When it rained the light was dazzling.

When she was in pain he would gather her tight against his body and hold her, absorbing her tremors. While she sat in lecture halls trying not to cry out, he would wait outside; after class was over he would slip her yellow backpack off her shoulder and carry it to her next class for her, waiting outside again. When she needed to go to the hospital he would pedal her there on his bicycle no matter what time of day it was, whether or not he had classes or exams. There were times when she tried to push him away, when she felt herself a burden. She tried to be cold and distant, she would insult and ignore. He would leave her in a huff, but then he'd return, rub her shoulders and kiss her face as if he could lift the pain out of her, as if he wanted to draw it out of the herniated disk in her back and take it on himself.

Later in their courtship he gave her a notebook, keeping its twin for himself. During the day, he instructed, they'd write down the things that happened, what their thoughts were, the times when they would think of each other. At dusk, they switched notebooks and read them side by side, silent, smiling. If infatuation became a matter of record, inscribed in ink, with words, then it would acquire a permanence that neither of them could deny. The pages filled with words. The notebooks became the archive of their love.

She can see their youth so clearly, but has he changed in the years since then? Who is this man lying silent in a hospital bed, his face slack with defeat, his tongue straining under the weight of another language? And who is she, what are they together, without his voice, which had always drawn her back toward him when she wavered in her devotion, when she might have drifted away? Meiling stares out at the gray of the city, the thick blanket of pollution hovering over everything, and when the ringing of the telephone saws through the apartment she grips the balcony railing tight in her hand as if to steady herself before walking back into the living room.

"Mrs. Li." It is Dr. Feng—the neurologist—on the other end of the phone, grave and kind. "There's been a development. Yesterday afternoon, Dr. Neal made a breakthrough with Li Jing. He's started talking again—in English. I wanted to call you and let you know before you came to visit so that you'd be prepared. We'll have the translator on hand so that you can talk to him."

Meiling walks out of the apartment building, into a humidity that makes the throat clog up, and hails a taxi to the hospital, keeping her knees pressed tightly together in the backseat, trying not to let the hope in her chest flare too bright. His voice again; the way it pitches high, almost like a teenager's voice; the easy swells and dips of every phrase off his tongue. She tries to remember the last thing he said to her in Chinese. It was just hours before the explosion. He had startled her when he called to say he was leaving work early. "Dad and I'll bring home dinner," he had said, and she was barely listening, already hanging up when she heard his voice again and put the phone back to her ear. He said: "I'll talk to you soon."

"I'M FINE," HE SAYS, lying there in his hospital bed.

In translation the words are bare, stripped of emotions.

"Don't worry about me. I don't need anything."

Meiling searches his voice for meaning, listens to his slow, painstaking enunciations, the syllables gathering upon each other, the sentences proceeding at an uncertain gait. Then silence as he refuses to meet her eyes. His gated face like a stranger's. She holds her breath to wait him out, wanting him to talk more. A few minutes later, he begins again, Alan converting the phrases in a transparent voice. *"Yes, I'll cooperate. I'll work on my English, and the Chinese."*

Her face flickers. She wants him to say something more . . . personal, but then she snuffs out her own desire. "I'm just glad," she says, all tenderness, without demands, "I'm glad you're talking again."

"I'm back." Rosalyn Neal strides through the door, flashing a sunny smile. Alan begins his translations again, this time with more speed.

"I just took the scans down to the lab and consulted with Mr. Li's other doctors. Everyone's very excited about the new developments. We're restructuring your schedule, Mr. Li. You'll be in speech therapy with me for two sessions of two hours every day now. I swear, you'll be sick of me by the time this is all over."

All morning long Meiling had followed Rosalyn Neal around as she whirled into offices and laboratories with an unshakable sense of purpose, a decidedly authoritative tone in her voice. Alan started his translations before she finished each sentence, smothering her voice, relaying her words so fast that Meiling could barely keep up.

"—We'll administer the Boston Diagnostic Aphasia Exam every week to gauge his improvements."

"—And I'm starting him on a low dosage of propranolol. Studies have shown that it may have short-term benefits for aphasia patients. There are side effects, but we'll monitor carefully."

"—I'll be working with Dr. Liu to measure brain activation during Chinese and English speech attempts with functional MRIs, with an eye on integrating his English speech therapy with his Chinese speech therapy down the line."

Meiling watches Rosalyn, the woman's pale skin, her red hair thick and tangled down the back of her white coat—and remembers how sure Rosalyn had been of herself, how almost happy, obliviously so, she was, the pleasure she seemed to take in her work. There is a kind of warmth to her, a softness in her body, an openness on her face. Meiling is not quite sure if Rosalyn—with her ungroomed eyebrows and her bare face, her sloppy outfits and her big feet—could be considered beautiful, but her smile is so easy and genuine that it is impossible not to be drawn in by her. It is as if by stepping into her sphere the world would become a simpler place.

In the halls of the hospital everyone stared, the other doctors unblinking each time she addressed them, the nurses narrowing their eyes. They looked at this woman and it was as if a character had walked out of the television, or off a billboard, waving her ferocious excitement at them. They listened to her voice, speaking with a particular rhythm, but in some key that they couldn't decode. The translator sounded like everything else they had ever heard, so they watched her mouth move instead.

The contours of her voice beautiful. English a beautiful language: milky, round-shouldered, some voluptuous dream.

"For now, we'd still like to keep him under observation." Rosalyn walks over to Meiling and nods, then looks at Li Jing, addressing him. "But in a week and a half, if nothing goes wrong, you'll be able to go home. I would recommend that you purchase another one of those electronic dictionaries. While it's fairly unsophisticated, it'll at least allow you to communicate on a basic level."

"*Thank you*," Li Jing says in English.

"Please let me know if you have any questions, and thank you again, all of you, for your patience. Mr. Li, I'll see you tomorrow morning."

Alan gives them a small wave and unfolds himself to walk out the door with Rosalyn.

"Wait!" Meiling calls out, and when they both turn around, she stammers, not looking them in the eyes. "Alan, can you . . . ?"

The translator had introduced himself as Shao Anli the first time she met him, peering over his glasses and twisting his mouth into an expression of sympathy. There was a sense of discretion to him that she liked right away. She had given him an envelope of money, the same kind of bribe she gave to everyone else, but he took it matter-of-factly, with no false protests, nodding in thanks and slipping it into his pocket without counting the bills. "Alan," she heard Rosalyn Neal call him again and again, the only thing she could understand out of paragraphs unwinding into the air, and so she calls him that too, abandoning the familiarity of his real name, clutching on to "Al-an" as if it were an anchor, two syllables within her grasp.

When Alan comes back to the room, alone, Meiling closes the door behind him, letting the crisp metal of the doorknob bite into her skin for an extra moment, fighting off nausea. Is this worse than silence, needing a translator to talk to her own husband? She pauses for a moment and then charges ahead. "Everything's being taken care of. Don't worry about anything, just focus on getting better."

She talks as if she's giving a report, updating Li Jing on the latest details of the diagnosis for Professor Li, making assurances about a speedy recovery. She talks about Pang Pang too—the end of his school year, his summer school schedule, the karate lessons and computer classes and English tutoring that he'll receive; how Nanny Chang has been a godsend, watching Pang Pang when she hasn't had the time. She does not talk about herself, does not tell him about being afraid to fall asleep most nights, does not tell him that taking care of a child and a home, making arrangements and bribes, and running back and forth to the hospital has her completely exhausted, too worn out to even wash her hair at the end of the day.

Through Alan he says, *"Fine."* He says, *"I see."* He does not say anything else about how he feels or if he misses her or whether he regrets having withheld himself during these weeks.

How strange to be talking with her husband through another person, her voice and his crisscrossing each other with only the translator to make sense of it all. She looks at Alan, the way he stands pressed up against the wall, as if making himself as unobtrusive as possible, and thinks about all the things left unsaid, the impossible-to-translate sentiments stuck in her throat.

"Tell Pang Pang not to worry about me," Li Jing says.

The English is a blur in her ear. Despite his slow, laborious enunciations the syllables bleed together, this soft, shapeless thing that she cannot grasp. She wants to listen, really listen, follow the curve of everything he says, parse out the sounds, find correspondence, equivocation, understanding, but Alan is waiting for her response, and she has no choice but to go on.

"Your office has been calling." She has saved this for last and says it, now, with a dropping feeling in her stomach.

A grunt emerges from the bed. He throws an arm up over his face.

"I don't know what to tell them."

"What . . ." He struggles and then the sound dies down. Alan waits for Li Jing to speak again. *"What do they want?"*

"They want to know when you're going to go back to work. They were quite insistent: they need to talk to you as soon as possible."

"What should I . . . what should I do? Should I call them?"

Even without understanding the words she can hear his uncertainty, can see, from the way his eyes are blinking and his short, rushing breaths, that fear has infected him, holding his entire body taut in its grasp. Meiling glances over at Alan but the translator doesn't look up. He simply turns Li Jing's shaking voice into a flat, impassive strip of Chinese. *"I don't know. What am I supposed to do? Maybe I should . . ."*

"Why don't I go to Pudong?" Meiling cuts in. There is something terrifying about seeing him like this, and she has to look away from his face, she has to fill the room with her voice, which she tries to hold steady, to erase the memory of his doubt. "I'll go, and find out what's happening. You don't need to call. You should rest, get better."

There is a quiet, grateful moan of assent from the bed, and Meiling squeezes her eyes shut at the strangeness of the sound—it was so small, so pathetic, unlike anything she had ever heard from Li Jing before. But then she shakes her head, unwilling to acknowledge his weakness. She takes a few more steps away from the bed so that she is facing the window, with her back to him. "I'm sure everything is fine with the company. I'll call, I'll take care of it. When you get better I'm sure you'll jump right back in. But for now, you don't need to worry about a thing."

CHAPTER 8

On the subway the world looks different, sleeker, the people crowded to-gether but impassive, pouring in and out at each stop. The early morning stupor inside her head is punctured by her ears popping as the train ac-celerates under the river. Meiling walks out at the first stop in Pudong with men and women in somber suits, with briefcases and stony faces. She looks up into the polluted, silty air, the endless skyscrapers, the wide, empty boulevards, seeing only buildings, cars, construction cranes gawk-ing in the sky. There are no children here, no old people, no one practic-ing Tai Chi on the sidewalks, no shouts from vendors hawking food or batteries. There are only ugly blasts from car horns in the ear, only people in suits speeding down the street. She hurries her steps, falls in with the crowds of office workers heading to their cubicles, and keeps her eyes on the cement beneath her feet, trying to stay calm.

When she walks into his office the young woman behind the re-ception desk calls out loudly, attracting everyone's attention. "Mrs. Li! How are you? How's Li Jing? Can I get you a cup of tea? Would you like to sit?"

The sound of chairs scraping across carpet fills the room now, and voices chiming in, telephone rings going unanswered. In a minute she is surrounded, with hands pawing at her shoulders, concerned faces gaping at her, questions swirling in the air. "Is he all right?" "Of course he's all right, but when's he coming back?" "Tell him he better get back here soon!" "We miss the boss man!"

A tall, broad-shouldered woman in her forties steps forward and clears her throat. "Back to work, everyone. Let's give Ms. Zhou some space. Can I get you anything, Ms. Zhou? Why don't you wait in Li Jing's office for me?"

"Thank you, Vice President Wu."

Meiling is glad for the other woman's steady, booming voice, the way she shepherds her past the cubicles and into his office. She listens to the clatter of the keyboards, the phones ringing, the voices so thick and constant that they weave together into a tapestry of noise outside the door, and sinks into his chair, spinning around to face the window, stare out at the forest of skyscrapers, and farther off, plots of lush, green fields, glowing through the gray light.

She takes a breath, smelling him, and presses her palm down on the desk as if she might still feel the heat of his body. The desk is clean and ordered, and she knows that someone must have come in to put everything away in the last few weeks. She opens the top desk drawer and finds a mess of business cards and folded-up paper, a half-eaten chocolate bar, an electric razor. When she lifts the razor out and runs her thumb over its craggy surface, tiny snippets of hair caught in its grooves loosen and fall, shaking onto the desk like confetti.

"Thank you for coming." Vice President Wu walks in and closes the door. "I hope we haven't been too persistent with our phone calls. We're all very concerned about Li Jing's health. And it's not like him, don't you think, to not check in with us for so long. Some of the staff tried to go see him at the hospital, but . . ."

"That's my fault." Meiling gives the older woman a sheepish smile. "I asked the hospital to restrict visitors. I didn't want him to wear himself out."

"What really happened? Nobody has been able to get a straight answer."

"He was having a drink with Professor Li at the Swan Hotel on the night of the explosion. And he was terribly hurt. They both were. But I'm just so grateful that they both got out alive. When I think of those other families—"

"We're all very grateful," Vice President Wu interrupts. "And the injuries they sustained? I'd heard that Li Jing was hit in the head. Was there . . . lasting damage?"

Sitting in his seat, Meiling lifts her chin as she looks across the desk at the vice president. The other woman's forehead is shiny, reflecting the overhead lights. *Lasting damage*—what did those words mean anyway? When she opens her mouth, it's as if she has known what she would say all along.

"Of course not—the injuries, while serious, were all physical. At first, Li Jing suffered from a bit of shock, especially because of his dad's condition. But now, it's really a matter of his body healing over time. I'm afraid he's already driving the doctors crazy, chatting all the time, demanding to be released. I definitely won't let him overexert himself, though. He's going to be fine, but he needs his rest."

Vice President Wu's small, wide-set eyes blink once, and then she exhales. "Oh, good," she says. "Someone was talking about possible brain damage the other day—"

"Oh no! Not at all." Something about the space of his office, its polish and sheen, seems to hold no room for the complexities of the truth. It would be impossible, she thinks to herself, to explain what has really happened, how he really is. After all, he has already started speaking English, and he might recover his Chinese at any moment, all the words rushing back in.

"Well, that's good news. We all wish him a quick and complete recovery."

"That will take awhile yet." Meiling forces her cheeks into a smile. "He was just joking yesterday that he looks like Frankenstein's monster with all his bandages. I told him I didn't care what he looked like, and he said he was hurt, since he assumed I only married him for his looks."

Vice President Wu chuckles and chats, asking after Professor Li and Pang Pang, biding time. The tension in the room lingers on, and the second hands of the four clocks on the wall move around the dial, ticking off the seconds in Shanghai, London, New York, Tokyo. Outside the office door someone's shout of "Damn!" darts out of the low, constant thrum of voices, making the vice president flinch in her seat. Meiling looks down at the worn patch of carpet beneath the chair. The room smells wrong, antiseptic and stale, and something about all this—the office, the people, the black computer screen glaring back at her— makes her shiver, sending a sense of unease up her spine.

"Xiao Zhou." Vice President Wu sits up taller and slips into using the diminutive. "I'm so glad you called, and finally came by. And so glad to hear that Li Jing is fine, and getting better. The truth is, things have been really tough here, and we need Li Jing to come back into the office as soon as he can. I need to talk to him about our strategy going forward immediately. Tomorrow, or maybe the day after that."

"I'm afraid that won't be possible."

"I'll just call him—we won't even need to meet. But I have to talk to him. And he should really make a few calls himself."

"I'm sorry, but I won't allow it."

"You won't allow it?" Vice President Wu's disbelief peers through before she hides it behind a bland look.

"He's recovering from a punctured lung, whiplash, a broken ankle, and other injuries. He needs to focus on getting better. This is no time to talk about work."

"Xiao Zhou, be reasonable. I don't think you understand what's at stake. I assure you Li Jing would want to take care of things here."

Meiling shakes her head and spins her chair to look out the window again. In the distance, at the edge of where the buildings stop and the rice paddies begin, there are construction cranes angling their booms, mounting new beams, erecting new skeletons.

"Just an hour, Xiao Zhou." The vice president's tone is now half pleading, half condescending. "That's all I'm asking. I don't want to bore you with the details, but the company is not doing very well. It's been a volatile time in the market, our clients have been clamoring for Li Jing, and we've made a few moves that have backfired. I really need to talk to him before something else happens."

"It can wait until he gets better."

"No. It really can't."

A year after they got married Li Jing announced that he was quitting his well-paid government job to start his own investment company. Professor Li gave his blessings and a small amount of capital, and Li Jing began building the company, which he named SinoVenture, with one other employee and eighty hours a week of his time.

During those early days she would hear him in the middle of the night, still asleep, mumbling numbers, murmuring orders to buy, orders to sell. All over their low-ceilinged one-room apartment she found little slips of paper that had been folded over and over again until they were tiny shards. Unfolding the pages she saw that they were covered with calculations and currency rates, names and phone numbers, arcane notes about state-owned enterprises, tips and dates and inexplicable symbols she barely recognized. His slanted handwriting had pressed into the paper so hard that it made indentations, little ridges and hollows on the backs of the pages that she fingered with pride.

It was 1992. The stock market in China had opened two years earlier, and the economy accelerated like a young stallion, furious, skittish, unsure of its own stamina. Li Jing had seen the possibilities and charged ahead with a mixture of youth and bravado. Three years later he leased office space in Pudong, Shanghai's developing business district, where a new building seemed to spring up every day. Since then, SinoVenture has grown into one of the most successful investment companies in the city. Outperforming the market by more than 5 percent six out of its seven years, it now handles upward of 250 million yuan.

"Xiao Zhou." Vice President Wu sighs again, and when Meiling turns around she catches the woman rolling her eyes. "I didn't want to burden you, but you must believe me when I say that the company is in trouble. Some of our largest investors have been skittish, talking about pulling out. The market's already on a downward swing; if these investors go, that could cause a chain reaction. The entire company could be jeopardized."

"You must be exaggerating. I thought the company was in good shape: it's only been a few weeks since the explosion."

"Everyone's nervous about the market, afraid the Shanghai and Shenzhen markets will crash the way the Tokyo stock market crashed in '97. Timing is so important right now. And Li Jing had contacts everywhere, especially in the government, so we used to always be a couple of steps in front of everyone else in terms of knowing when to buy and sell—we haven't had that advantage since he's been gone. He also used to handle the bulk of client relations with all the large investors—they love him, and now that they can't get ahold of him, and they've been hearing rumors of his ill health, everyone's getting nervous, wondering if it's time to bolt. If enough of them do that, the whole company could go under."

"How is that possible?"

"The market moves very quickly."

When they were young they were poor. But everyone was poor then, and it never occurred to her to mind. Young married couples usually lived with one set of parents, but they had wanted their own place, and so they rented a studio over Professor Li's protests, and she cooked all their dinners on a small hot plate, permanently staining the walls behind it with splatters of oil and soy sauce. She gets nostalgic for those days sometimes; they were so close, but that closeness seemed impossible to sustain later on. Back then, it was as if the rhythm of their days converged into a single beat, and she still remembers their two chipped white bowls nesting together on the bookshelf, how they'd share a single clementine section by sweet section after dinner.

Once he started SinoVenture they rarely ate dinner with each other anymore. He came home late most nights, and was often away during the weekends. They spent less and less time together. Their lives un-wound themselves from one another, and it felt as though they were on parallel tracks, hurtling forward simultaneously, but never quite con-verging. At moments, she felt almost indifferent about Li Jing, and longed for the intensity of being completely engaged with someone, the way they had been, before. But there was Pang Pang to take care of, and soon there was more money—it appeared in their joint bank ac-count with regularity, in increasing sums. His success meant a car, a new apartment, designer clothes, vacations to exotic locales. It also meant that she could continue working as an editor without minding her abysmal salary. Despite working only part-time after Pang Pang was born, she built up a solid reputation for herself, acquiring and editing obscure contemporary poets, rising up through the ranks. Friends and colleagues changed careers to work in television or advertising, but she was happy to stay exactly where she was.

Around the city, the open pursuit of money, which had been ma-ligned and unfeasible for so long, was now celebrated. Meiling found the frenzy of it distasteful, she hated it when people asked her for Li Jing's stock tips or made discreet inquiries about their wealth. Still, she had to acknowledge her privilege; it was, after all, his ability to charm investments out of clients and manipulate the rhythms of the market that afforded her the ease and luxury of her life. She had not thought much about the things that they had given up, in return, except in the moments when she remembered what their life had been like before.

"The company has been around for a long time. How could it just unravel like that? I'm sure it'll take some hits, but right now, Li Jing's health is more important."

Vice President Wu's face is etched in dogged determination. "Trust me, Xiao Zhou, I wish it weren't happening. But even before Li Jing's accident things were rocky. For the last three months the company has been on thin ice."

"He didn't say anything about it to me," Meiling says in a tone of betrayal.

"I'm sure he thought he could fix it, and maybe he still can."

"Fine. I'll talk to him." Meiling stands up and grabs the strap of her purse, clutches it tight in her hands as she walks to the door. When the other woman calls out again she almost keeps walking, not wanting to hear any more, but then she slows her steps and comes to a stop, standing with her back to the room.

"Thank you, Xiao Zhou. Should I call his room tomorrow?"

"No." She shakes her head and does not turn around, not wanting Vice President Wu to see her face. "Please don't call. I'll take care of it. I'll talk to him, and I'll call you, I promise I will."

CHAPTER 9

Rosalyn sees Danny at the end of the block, straddling his moped at the stoplight with all the other riders, helmetless, his golden hair plastered to his forehead. This makes her laugh, and so she abandons the awning of the hospital doors and steps out into the rain, waves hello. He is in the middle of all the commuters who ride their bicycles and mopeds steadily forward, wearing surgical masks to filter the dirty air. Danny's is the only face that is animated. His is the only face she sees.

It's her first date in years. The rain stipples the landscape, making everything blurry.

"Get on!" He is glowing from the kicked-up dust, the radioactive pollution.

She looks down at the delicate sandals she just bought this morning, feeling precarious on the tall, skinny heels. She smoothes her hands on her skirt, the light passing through the fabric to silhouette her legs.

"No!" she says, waving her hands in the air. "You're crazy. I can't ride that thing. The traffic here terrifies me!"

"You'll have to, Ms. Rosalyn. Tonight, it's my way or the highway," he drawls, water dripping down his forehead, his body hunched in a pose over the compact, rusty moped, throwing her a feigned look of toughness.

Everyone stares at them, the golden-haired Americans who seem to give off their own light in the rain. She bites her lip and starts to shake her head, but then looks up at the thick throng in the street, all the people driving past them, and shrugs, climbing onto the moped with a whoop, letting her legs straddle the black plastic of the seat.

In Oklahoma, in late afternoons under the blistering sun, she'd ridden in the beds of trucks with dry wind scrubbing her face, the roar of the engine blazing down stretches of road between tall fields of wheat, surfing through endless, golden waves. She had liked the speed, the strange seclusion of hurtling through space. The silence of wind.

But this! She screams in delight by Danny's ear when they edge another bike so closely that her dress almost catches on its tailpipe. This is like being in the middle of a wet, dripping beehive. The moped weaves slowly in and out of the vehicles packed on the street. Thatches of buildings rise in front of them, gleaming windows mottled by the haze of the city. Her breasts are pressed against his back, his damp shirt is beneath her fingers. She can feel sweat pooling at her armpits, the fabric of her skirt fluttering around her knees, the drowsy hum of the engine between her thighs. They are snared in traffic, vehicles hiccuping forward around them, riders in helmets and slickers honking at one another, crawling down the same boulevard. Ten lanes stretch out, sluggish with cars, mopeds, bicycles in slow motion. Rain and heat in the air.

The moped turns sharply into a side street and now there is a new tension beneath her, the unpaved surface of an alleyway. A sudden acceleration like breaking through glass. Raindrops a different slant on her body now.

"Hold on tight!" he yells out.

She opens her mouth and swallows threads of water, dirty air, the smell of fish and watermelon hitting her in the face. The wind and wet particles of dust slice through her hair. Faces pass by in a blur. Tattered apartment buildings slouch next to each other. Bleached grass soaks up the rain. People walk fast and furious, hunched under umbrellas, edging away from the center of the street to avoid the mud splattering everywhere as Danny and Rosalyn speed past them.

THE HUMIDITY IN the air presses against her skin; the wind brushes her skirt against her legs. Danny has taken her to the Bund, the stretch of old Shanghai where the extravagant façades of art deco buildings rise up on the west bank of the Huangpu River. The rain has stopped, but the humidity lingers on, and it gives everything in the distance a wavering quality, the scenery miragelike. Across the river in Pudong skyscrapers glint cold and bright. The Oriental Pearl Tower, shaped like a space shuttle, blinks pink while airplanes swoop down in slow motion. Rosalyn turns away from the futuristic skyline on the other side and looks at the colonial bank buildings on the Bund behind her instead, noticing their well-worn crevices, taking in their antiquated grandeur.

"So how's your patient? The one you were so excited about last time?" Danny puts a gentle hand on her elbow and guides her past the vendors selling food and disposable cameras in a mishmash of English and Chinese. "Is he chatting up a storm? Talking in Chinese yet?"

"I wish." She shakes her head. "He's talking a little in English, but I'm not sure I'm the best language therapist for him. It's not really what I do, and I haven't made that much progress. The other doctors are getting concerned—I'm afraid they think I'm a hack. Hands-on rehabilitation is much harder than I thought it would be. I have a lot to do in the next six weeks."

"Maybe you'll have to stay for longer than that," Danny says. "I was only supposed to be here for the summer after I graduated college. Seven years later, I'm still here."

They stroll down the street side by side, murmuring, stealing glances at each other. The Huangpu River smells vaguely of garbage. The water darkens as the sun begins to bleed out at the horizon, and Rosalyn can hear the barges pass by, their long, steady horns singing strange songs.

She breathes in: the air is still polluted, but the dusk has its own magic. They drift into the crowds on the bank of the river, everyone's steps slow and soft, the heat melting the hustle of Shanghai into night languor.

The promenade is as wide as a football field, thick with people strolling slow, stopping for photographs and ice cream. The sky is finally dark, and all around Rosalyn and Danny there are flashes of neon across billboards, hurricanes of light. On the other side of the river the shore is so bright there is a translucent band of light shimmering just above the horizon. She has still not gotten used to the size of the city, its fearless combustion, its fathomless sprawl. The night scenes all seem cinematic, constantly astounding her with their scope and clarity.

Rosalyn motions for them both to sit down on a bench facing the river, but she stays silent, keeping her eyes on the other side, staring at the advertisements and skyscrapers glowing out of the hum of night. Danny turns and looks at her face, searching it with an intensity that prickles the skin. There is a kind of privacy in the shadows now, now that night has fallen, and she leans into Danny's arm, feeling its heat on her skin.

She doesn't know what she's doing—in this strange city, with this strange man. It's as if she has been airlifted out of her life and dropped into an entirely new one. But the slant of her body against his feels effortless, dictated by the evening. She is surprised at how easy it is to fall into the sly looks and teasing rhetoric, the touches ghosting over each other's arms, the pattern of glances skittering away before they are fully registered. Danny's affection makes her feel safer somehow, makes it easier to forget her other life, her real life that she has to return to someday soon. Here, in Shanghai, she can leave all that behind for a while, and let herself get lost in the lights.

"so I HAVE a plan for dinner," Danny announces in a mock-English accent, looking pleased with himself. "For the first course, we'll travel to the north of China, where various species of dumplings are studied and perfected. But be careful not to eat too much there. That's just the opener." He begins to lay out a complex itinerary, coaxing laughter from Rosalyn as he shifts accents to match regions of the world. ". . . And then, we'll go to this Brazilian barbecue restaurant. They fly the beef in from South America every week, and the steaks there are out of this world."

She watches him ticking off restaurants like a talking guidebook, his enthusiasm both endearing and embarrassing. Is this what dating is supposed to be like, she wonders, full of plans and activities, an agenda for every half hour? He falls in step next to her as they walk away from the river, still talking about the best place to get gelato in the city. Rosalyn arches her neck to look up at the sky, but with the white light blazing all around them, there are no planets, no stars, just the sliver of a yellow moon.

". . . What do you think?" Danny asks, tugging her hand and guiding her across the intersection. It is strange not to have to make her own way here, in this world, even if it's just for a few hours, but she likes it, she thinks, she likes the feeling of being taken care of, the ease of being led by someone else.

"It sounds lovely," she says. "I'm putting myself in your hands."

Looking at the sea of taillights from the back of his moped, she closes her eyes and throws her head back. She doesn't know where they're going and she doesn't want to know. The evening air hums across her face.

They stop by the Underground Dumpling House, noisy with shouts and chopsticks clanging against plates. She watches him hail a passing waitress with an easy phrase of Chinese. They wash down the pile of pork and chive dumplings with lukewarm beers, making appreciative slurping sounds when the conversation begins to lag. The young couple at the next table smiles at them, shyly, in recognition, before turning back to each other, and Rosalyn grins to herself, liking the picture of herself with Danny.

In an open-air stall he introduces her to stinky tofu—white, silky masses crowding across the surface of a bowl of broth like rotting flower petals. When she grimaces in distaste at the smell he is almost pleased. "It's an acquired taste," he says, "takes an epicurean's palate to really appreciate this stuff, I've always thought." She rolls her eyes and he winks at her from across the table, emboldened by her giggles.

"But at the end of the night, does the epicurean get kissed?" she asks with a smirk, enjoying the bright blush on his cheeks.

They ride past winding streets with open-faced shops selling snacks, strings of tiny lights canopying above them like a lifted veil, the simmer from pots and pans rising, absorbed into the heavy night air. Piles of fruit shine in dull, metallic shades under the yellow lights on corner stands everywhere, watermelons gleaming green, mounds of strawberries a bloody blur. The city, as always, is dense with people, and there are families strolling down boulevards, old men playing cards on the sidewalk. She leans into Danny's back, puts her head between his shoulder blades, liking the solidity of his body, the way she can close her eyes as he drives them to wherever it is they are going, somewhere else in the night.

"LAST STOP: MAOMING Road." Danny shuts the engine off and leans back into her for a second before helping her off the moped.

"My stomach thanks you." She shifts off the seat and grabs Danny's arm with an exaggerated groan. "Not that it wasn't all incredibly delicious."

They had threaded their way past converging taxis to pull into a street that seems even more lit up than the rest of Shanghai. Slow, thorny music drifts past them while the scent of magnolias infests the dark air, and the shadows of women slouching against buildings in short skirts ripple across the sidewalks. Danny leads her past a garden into a large, stately manor that looks like someone's country estate. She gawks at the opulence of the bar before sinking into a plush couch in the back room, and she looks up into Danny's glazed eyes in the candlelight.

"What do you think?" His voice wavers ever so slightly.

"It's perfect," she whispers into Danny's ear, letting her eyes flutter with the barest suggestion of sleep.

A beautiful girl appears next to them in a tight *qipao*, the embroidery on the brocade dress discreetly outlining her breasts. Rosalyn stares at her, transfixed by the shimmer of her dress, while the girl takes their drink order in a breathy, halting English. On the walls illustrations of seductive, sleepy-eyed women with tins of powder or tubes of lipstick stare out next to candelabras and under half shadows.

"Danny!" A curly-haired man barrels across the room to pump Danny's hand up and down, a drunk, vigorous smile blurry across his face. "It's good to see you, man! We were just wondering where you've been hiding. Come on, come sit with us."

"Patrick, this is Rosalyn." Danny gestures at her with an open palm. "It's Dr. Rosalyn, actually, from Oklahoma City. Rosalyn is new to Shanghai, so I've been showing her around. Rosalyn, this is Patrick Helton. Patrick came from Texas a couple of years ago. Patrick, tell Rosalyn how fun Shanghai is! I don't think she's convinced yet, but I'm determined to make sure she has a good time here."

"Why Dr. Rosalyn, we're practically neighbors!" Patrick picks up Rosalyn's drink and laughs all the way to the other side of the bar. A crowd of people look up and wave hello, squeezing down to make room for her around a long wooden table. "El Paso to Oklahoma City's what, a ten-hour drive? And to think, we had to come halfway around the world to make our acquaintance. About damn time, I'd say. And let me tell you, you couldn't ask for a better guy than our Danny to show you around this crazy-ass city."

"Patrick." She is so happy to hear another Southerner that it makes her lengthen her drawl and bat her eyes. "Wonderful to meet you."

"Everyone, this is Rosalyn. She's new in town." Between kisses on the cheek and slaps on the back, Danny's eyes keep returning to Rosalyn, making sure she is settled.

Soon she has met Clarissa from New Jersey and Josh from Vancouver and Maia from Chicago and accumulated more names and faces than she can remember. A crowd of ten or fifteen people gathers around, mostly Americans, a couple of Canadians, an Australian accent in the corner. Drinks come in rounds and empty glasses litter the table, catching candlelight and scattering it everywhere. She looks back at Danny, perched halfway down on the other side of the table, and raises her eyebrows in disbelief and delight—where have all these people come from?

English sprays out from mouths in a shower of sparks, clattering on the wooden table, cartwheeling through the cigarette smoke, absorbed into the soft carpet beneath their feet. Rosalyn laughs at the sound of her own voice, sharp and eager; she laughs at Patrick's already-familiar drawl, the way it booms sweetly, shouting everyone down with its muscular charms; she laughs at the talk of movies and apartments and prices of flights to the U.S., the ease of it, all the different voices chiming in but still making sense, each word, each sentence imprinting itself into her mind. She closes her eyes and sips her drink, letting the sweet bubbles of tonic shiver on her tongue, letting her ears fill with English, happy to be listening in.

"Saturday?" She turns to her right and expectant faces shine up at her, smiling, waiting. "I don't know. I don't have any plans for Saturday. Actually, I don't have plans for much of anything here besides my research at the hospital."

The woman with the cat-eyed glasses—Clarissa from New Jersey—nods in sympathy. "Saturday you'll be coming with us to a party on the Bund. Let's get dinner beforehand. Which district do you live in? Maia and I can come and pick you up on our way. Let me get your number before I forget." Clarissa starts digging through her purse for her cell phone.

"What are you going to wear?" Maia—a long-haired blonde taking a year off from college—turns around to join the conversation.

"I don't know," Rosalyn says.

"It's a fashion party—"

"So we'll take her shopping," Clarissa interrupts, turning back to Rosalyn to plead. "You'll come, won't you? Let's make a day of it. Shopping and then dinner and then party. Shall we pick you up at two?"

Her newness is part of her allure, she knows, but she is still flush with attention, letting the slow, syrupy pleasure of being courted churn and puddle in her belly. She nods and laughs—"Saturday. Sounds great"—and compliments Clarissa on her scarf, lets herself be absorbed into a conversation about people she doesn't know wearing designers she has never heard of. The evening is hazed over with gossip and plans. Clarissa and Maia are sharp and charming. Rosalyn is infatuated with their ease, their quickness, and their flattery, and she giggles and flatters in return, making quick friends of everyone around the table. Her gregariousness, throttled for too long, has finally found an outlet, and as she looks around, she thinks for a moment about her friends at home, thinks about drinking with Carlos and Sue and everyone else at the bar on campus. During the last few months she began spending more time at the bar. There she tried to laugh it up, she tried to convince herself that she still had a future. But even thinking back to those nights fills her with an ache so quick and sudden that she has to sweep the memories aside, she has to take a gulp of her drink and let the alcohol flood her with warmth so that she can forget before joining the conversation again.

The hours sluice by, the drinks pile in, and the glow of conversation wraps tightly, warmly around her body. She gets up and takes a new seat, next to Danny this time, and lets her head fall on his shoulder. "I have to go," she whispers in his ear. It is three a.m., and when she staggers to stand up everyone else begins to protest. She feels drowsy but content, blows loud, wet kisses at her new friends, waving in slow motion. Danny starts to get up, reluctantly, but she shakes her head with an indulgent smile.

"Well, I'll walk you out," he slurs, puts his arm around her waist. "Get home safely, you hear? I'm going to call you tomorrow to check up on you."

Outside the bar identical burgundy taxis line the street, idling their engines, waiting for the next fare. Streetlights and headlights shoot through the maple trees so that the leaves shine a pale, bright green, rustling softly in the night.

"Good night, sweet Rosalyn," he says.

"Good night Ben."

The slip of her tongue wakes her up with a shudder, and she blinks, focuses on Danny's pale, hopeful face. But he doesn't notice, just keeps smiling, and bends forward, holding open the taxi door, brushing his lips against her cheek so softly that she can barely feel his kiss.

CHAPTER 10

Another Sunday afternoon in the hospital. Rain all day long. The air is thick and suffocating, the sky so dark that all the lights have been turned on. Outside the door, Professor Li can hear two men playing cards, muttering to each other with exaggerated venom. Earlier in the day, a man died in the next room. After the clamor of the attempted resuscitation quieted, the wheels of his death-cart squeaked down the hall. Everyone else stayed silent; they—the sick, the elderly, the infirm—waited.

Meiling and Pang Pang step through the door, and Professor Li stares at them hungrily, taking in everything. Pang Pang has a tight grip on his mother's hand and scans the room. Meiling's face looks worn out, as if her skin has been rubbed raw. What is left is a layer of skin so thin, so fragile that a light could shine through it.

"Meiling! Pang Pang!" He fills his voice with false cheer and waves hello from the bed, his torso tented by sheets of newspaper.

"I'm sorry we're late," Meiling says, taking containers out of the plastic bags she has brought, opening them up. "I made some green beans this afternoon. Spicy, the way you like them. And here's a tofu casserole—it's still warm, so you should eat it now."

"I'm not hungry. And you shouldn't go to all this trouble."

Pang Pang climbs onto the bed and sits down. Professor Li marvels for a moment at the way the boy touches his old, withered body without self-consciousness, burrowing into his side. Everyone else tiptoes, coddling him, as if death lingers just beneath his skin, ready to pounce. He doesn't blame them for their caution: a heart attack is like an earthquake. It reveals weaknesses and fault lines. It is never the end of the story. If it happens once, you live in fear, waiting for the aftershocks.

So he waits for the next attack. There is little else to do. His days used to be filled with activity, and now they stretch out before him, a blur of exhaustion and solitude. The body on the bed is almost unrecognizable, and sometimes he holds a hand up in the air and watches it shake and shiver, entirely out of his control. The nurses come to help him out of bed for trips to the bathroom, and those moments serve as humiliating demarcations of time.

There are visitors: former students, colleagues, and even minor officials from the city government. Each time someone new walks through the door, he imagines he can see the moment when the shock of his appearance registers on their face. He forces himself to sit up straight. He works hard to feign health and insouciance, trying to put his visitors at ease. It is hard to exude a sense of authority in his limp hospital pajamas, but he carries on, trying to hide his body's betrayal.

It is only Pang Pang and Meiling and Li Jing that he looks forward to seeing now. The breadth and the width of his world have withered away, useless, and now all that matters is the convergence of this small family that he can call his own. He is not the type of man to utter inanities about love or togetherness, but he wishes there were some way to tell Li Jing how grateful he is for the presence of his daughter-in-law and his grandson, for how they have become a part of him, without posture or doubt. At the end of his life he is surprised to find himself just like any other man, loving his family fiercely, needing them, knowing that it is they who give meaning to him, knowing that it is their happiness that matters above all else.

He looks down at Pang Pang and smooths his hand over the boy's hair, rubs his worn fingers against the boy's cheeks. Within the fragile, tiny skull an entire universe of secrets glimmers. Professor Li, more than anyone, continues to be startled at how much Pang Pang looks like Li Jing at the same age. But the boy is quiet and wary like his mother, both of them tending toward stoicism, burying their feelings deep within.

"Take a seat, Meiling," Professor Li says with as much authority as he can muster. "Tell me how you're doing. This has all been very hard on you."

"I'm not the one in the hospital." She sits down for a second and then gets up again, hovering over his body, folding up sheets of newspaper with shaking hands. "Good heavens, these *húangméi* days just last forever. Have your joints been aching from the humidity? Do you need more blankets? Are you in pain?"

She moves around the room, restless, brimming with anxiety, and her nervousness makes his heart beat faster; he closes his eyes and drags long, shuddering breaths through his nose. During all these years she has always been the calm one, the cool-headed young woman his son had married. Whenever Li Jing had one of his tantrums, Professor Li knew he could count on Meiling to be unflappable, with that cool, knowing tilt of her chin. But now she is hunched over and shaking, one of her feet tapping madly on the floor.

"You should go home, Meiling. Get some rest."

"I'm fine," she says, and then repeats herself. "I'm fine. I'll be fine."

She walks over to his nightstand and takes stock of the pill bottles and nutritional supplements. "You're almost out of bee nectar. I'll bring another box tomorrow. It's going to be a busy week, but I'll try to be here every night. It'll have to be after six, though. I hope that's okay."

"Are you heading back to work?"

"Something like that," she says.

He doesn't begrudge Meiling her job, but he can't help but think of his late wife, who had never worked, who had thought it her job to take care of him and of their son. Even when he was bussing tables fifty hours a week at a Chinese restaurant in Charlottesville just to pay tuition for one class, she had not worked. He would have never thought to ask her; she had given up more than enough to be with him.

When he met Josephine he was thirty-eight and had resigned himself to a lifetime of washing dirty dishes for a pittance. She was twenty-one, the daughter of a well-to-do Hong Kongese–American family from San Francisco, about to graduate from Smith with a degree in philosophy. He never quite figured out why she chose him, why she defied her parents to be his wife, what possessed her to sacrifice a life of relative ease for struggling alongside him. But she—strong-willed and chatty—would not give up on him when he had long given up on himself.

Josephine insisted that he go back to school to finish his bachelor's degree; she pushed him to go to architecture school, knowing that he had both the talent and the inclination. That master's degree took him five years to finish. By the time he graduated, she was already dead. A drunk kid driving the wrong way at night had totaled her little white car two years earlier. He had not wept upon seeing her in the morgue. He had not wept at her funeral. But he wept at his graduation, wearing his cap and gown and holding his diploma. He had wished more than anything that she was in the audience watching him, clapping her small hands together as his name was called.

He never remarried. At first, the idea of marrying anyone else had been inconceivable. Later, he tried to date an American woman, another student in the architecture school. She was beautiful and bright and even a little funny, but he also found her oblivious, abrasive, with far too high an opinion of herself. By then, he had gotten used to being both mother and father. He packed Li Jing's lunches, took him to the Salvation Army to shop for school clothes, attended parent-teacher conferences, and brought home quarts of hot and sour soup from the restaurant whenever Li Jing got sick.

Once they moved back to Shanghai, a rash of widows and spinsters tried to catch his attention. Some of them attempted to mother Li Jing, annoying both father and son in the process. By then the two of them had become a single, self-reliant unit that resented meddling and intrusions from outsiders. Professor Li decided that he had no room for a woman in his life, and he always assumed that his son felt the same way.

When Li Jing announced his engagement, Professor Li was furious. He would not have admitted it then, but some part of him felt as though his son were abandoning him. He complained loudly to anyone who would listen that they were too young to get married, that Meiling's parents were nobodies, and that she was just a pretty face, and one in ill health at that—who even knew if she could give him a grandchild! He was annoyed by her coolness, how imperturbable she was despite his disapproval, how she let it roll off her back without anger or tears. "She's an ice queen," he told his son to no avail. Meiling was nothing like Josephine, who was quick with her affections and quicker with her temper, and who, decades later, he still held as a lost ideal.

It was only in the last few years that he came to appreciate Meiling. Once they all began living together, he had the opportunity to watch her with his son and his grandson. Her beauty and her coolness hid the essential fact of her: she was what the Chinese called *nénggàn*: capable and practical, able to get things done without any fuss. Meiling's remarkable ease in handling any number of conflicts and tasks made it far too easy to underestimate her; it all looked like a sleight of hand. She was as good at running a household as she was at handling his son. Professor Li grew to be proud of his daughter-in-law, more than grateful that she was part of his family.

He wants to explain this to her, but what is there to say besides *thank you*? "I'm glad you're going back to work," he tells her now. "It's not good for you to be here at the hospital all the time. Your job is important too, your career. Make sure that you're looking after yourself, that you're doing what makes you happy."

"Hm," she says, noncommittal. "I just need to get some things straightened out."

"Have you seen Li Jing yet?"

"Not, not yet. We'll head down there after you finish eating. Do you want to come with us?"

"I saw him this morning for a little while, but I'll come down with you. That way you guys can talk. I'll translate."

Meiling shakes her head, coming over to the bed to thrust a banana in his lap. "It's okay, Dad. You look exhausted. We'll be fine, we have the electronic dictionary for translation. And besides, Dr. Feng tells me that his therapy with the American is going well, so hopefully before too long he'll be able to speak Chinese again."

"I'm glad to hear it, but I hope he's getting some results with Dr. Liu too. It's not just enough for him to speak English. The American better be making sure that he's improving his Chinese. Do you want me to talk to her? I don't mind. After all, you arranged for her to come here, and we're paying for her. She's really working for us."

"There's no need for you to talk to her. I'm sure Dr. Neal knows what she's doing. She is a professional, after all. I expect that we'll see an improvement in Li Jing's Chinese in the next couple of weeks." Meiling begins packing up his leftovers with one hand, holding on tight to Pang Pang with the other.

"You're taking such good care of all the rest of us, but I hope you're taking care of yourself," Professor Li says.

"I will," she answers. "I'll take care of everything."

ALL DAY LONG rain has streaked across the narrow window, the heavy air pressing down on Li Jing's body like a moist palm. On Sundays there are no therapy sessions, and so he stays in his pajamas, drifts in and out of sleep. Nurses come in and smile but flit out quickly, leaving him his lunch, coming back to take his tray away. He goes upstairs to see his father, but the English phrases stay reluctant on both of their tongues. Talking to his father seems unfair when he can't talk to Mei-ling or Pang Pang. He leaves the room when he notices his father's face white with exhaustion, sees the long, thin fingers shiver and grip the covers. Walking back to his own floor, every step gingerly, every corridor endless, he feels the possibilities of death and old age following him, casting the faintest of shadows.

Now he leans against his bed frame, watching the weak light dissolve into evening, listening for footsteps outside the door. Meiling and Pang Pang are supposed to visit soon, and he claws onto this certainty to try to keep anxiety at bay, wanting to see their bodies pass through the door, wanting their voices, wanting to talk to her. More than anything he just wants to sink into the comfort of her voice, hold her tight in the circle of his arms, tell her that everything is going to be fine. He misses her: misses talking to her, misses touching her. He does not know how to tell her this or make her understand.

He moves his mouth, his awkward tongue. "Meen je." He tries to say the syllables to himself, and he knows that they don't sound right. He has failed again. Not being able to say her name right feels like the worst betrayal, as if his stupid brain is determined to elide her from his syntax, from his memory. As if she weren't his to hold on to anymore.

But she is his. Only he has no way to tell her, no way to hold on now. Still, he knows everything about her: the way she likes to be held, from behind, his arms looping tight around her shoulders; how she has never taken to the ocean, preferring rivers and lakes instead; the way she has memorized hundreds of poems but can never remember phone numbers or addresses— But what is he to do with all this knowledge, now that he has no way of articulating it, now that he can no longer speak her name? How can he know her when he can't even say her name? His mind is like a whirlpool with no plug at the bottom, her presence diminishing, coursing down the drain.

The door creaks open and Li Jing sits up slightly but looks away and tries to compose his face, not wanting her to see his eagerness. The accident has shifted so many things between them, and what he hates is this newfound neediness inside himself, the way he feels like an open, aching wound whenever she is by his side.

"Li Jing," a voice rings out, deep and smoke-tinged and masculine. "Finally! You'd think you were some kind of treasure or something, the way they guard you here! No one would let me see you, so I had to do a little bribing, a little scheming. I tell you—there's really a high level of security at this hospital. You're lucky I'm so persistent!"

When Li Jing turns around and sees the man in the green polo shirt, he starts to smile, almost calls out. Lao Yang is the right-hand man to Mr. Wong, one of SinoVenture's biggest clients. Over the years, he has become a source of tips and gossip, a drinking buddy, even a real friend. There had been times when an intended business dinner had devolved into unstoppable laughter between the two of them, when they had gone on midnight adventures together, zipping around town in taxis and swapping stories until the sun came up. And it didn't hurt that Lao Yang has always convinced his wealthy boss to keep a good chunk of investments with Li Jing, boosting up SinoVenture's portfolio through good and bad times.

"Don't get up, don't get up!" Lao Yang puts a hand up and sets a cluster of brightly colored gift bags on the nightstand. "We don't want you to strain yourself. I just stopped by to say hello and pick your brain a little. You must be bored to death here! You don't look so bad, though. When are they going to let you out of this zoo?"

The sound of Lao Yang's nonstop chatter, interspersed with that hacking, persistent cough, is terrifyingly and wonderfully familiar. Li Jing closes his eyes for a moment and sniffs the scent of cheap cigarettes that has always clung to his friend, lets himself drift into the past, for just a moment, into twelve-course dinners in smoky restaurants, the pleasure of wrapping up a business deal over a handshake and a toast.

". . . I don't know if you've been keeping up, but things are looking pretty dodgy out there, especially for you guys. What's going on in the office? Without you, it's like a chicken with its head cut off. Whenever

I get ahold of anybody, they won't give me a straight answer. And the numbers are getting uglier by the day. I can't believe you didn't jump on the electronics factory that just won that huge bid. It's the kind of thing you guys are usually so good at, though I guess with you out of the loop, nobody else has the contacts, or the guts to make the move."

Li Jing's mind started racing as soon as Lao Yang began talking about business, questions clumping together, wanting to rush out, fingers aching to dial telephones and type e-mails and search for information. What have they been doing in his absence? Work has seemed like an abstraction for weeks, neatly divorced from the reality of the hospital. Meiling brought it up once, but she has avoided the subject since then. His mind, too, seems unwilling to dwell on it, and he finds himself shoving away thoughts of the company whenever they begin to bubble up. But now, with Lao Yang's presence, the possibilities for missteps and losses are clamoring through his head. Li Jing swings his legs off the bed and touches the warm, dusty floor with his bare toes, eager for . . . something, eager to set up appointments and make corrections and talk to people, eager to fix things, to put SinoVenture back on course.

The room is suddenly silent. Li Jing looks up at Lao Yang and realizes that the other man has finally paused, is waiting for his reply. He opens his mouth but nothing comes out. His body lurches forward, just a little, but no words of Chinese are willing to emerge out of his throat.

"What should I tell him?" Lao Yang repeats himself, shrugging, still at ease. "He's not happy, not happy at all. And I've been placating him for weeks now. I think he needs to talk to you, or at least get some reassurance that things aren't just going down the tubes. Do you want me to set up a meeting?"

Lao Yang is looking at him, and Li Jing manages to meet his eyes for a few unending seconds before looking away and shaking his head. "I . . ." he almost starts in English, but presses his lips together tight and closes his eyes. All he can hear is the blood rushing through his head, the ceiling fan; nothing else makes a sound.

After a long stretch of silence Lao Yang finally begins again. "Li

Jing? Do you . . . ?" His voice is lower now, more uncertain. "Do you want me to set up a meeting between you and Mr. Wong?"

Li Jing keeps his eyes closed and shakes his head again. He is sitting on the edge of the bed, hunched over, his fists pressing down hard on his thighs.

"What the . . . ? Are you . . . ?" The other man's voice rings out with disbelief. "You can't talk. You can't talk, can you?"

Minutes are ticking by so slowly that it feels as though this horror might never dissipate, this scene might never end. Li Jing opens his eyes and gives one shake of his head with finality before looking up. The two men stare at each other for a long moment, and it is Lao Yang who turns away first. "I see," he says. "I'm sorry. I probably shouldn't have come."

The door opens again, and Meiling and Pang Pang come in bringing blurs of color, the boy squawking out a sunny "Baba" before they both stop in their tracks. Meiling takes a quick step toward Lao Yang. "What are you doing here?" she calls out, sharp, her voice edged with panic.

"I'm sorry," the man mutters softly, dully, looking at Meiling and then looking back at Li Jing on the bed. "Meiling, I didn't mean to, I just thought . . ."

"You should go." She walks so that her body is now in front of the bed, as if trying to shield Li Jing from view.

"Is he . . . ?"

"You should go."

Lao Yang lowers his head. "I'm sorry." He says the words one more time, looking back at Li Jing, who will not meet his eyes.

When the door closes, the three of them all stay still. It is finally Pang Pang who walks to the bed and takes hold of his father's hand. Li Jing holds on to the small, sweaty palm and swings his legs back up onto the bed, lying down once again. *"I . . . He talks to Mr. Wong. They'll all know . . ."* he starts to mumble in English, but then he chokes it back down, swallows up the words.

"It's so hot and stifling in here. You must have been uncomfortable all day." Meiling's voice is bright and she walks through the room as if nothing were amiss, turning on a lamp, raising the window. The sound of the rain gets louder, the patter like too many sets of heartbeats on top of each other.

When he tries to explain, what comes out is still English. *"He's going to tell . . ."*

". . . What a mess," she mutters under her breath, not having heard him, gathering up a clump of dust and hair on the floor with her shoe, wrinkling her nose. "I'll have to talk to the cleaning person tomorrow. Don't worry, we'll get this room spotless in no time."

If she wants to pretend that nothing is wrong, then he can too, he can try to forget what just happened, he can forget Lao Yang's look of pity and surprise. He focuses on her face instead, trying to imprint it on his brain. Meiling has lost weight. Recently she has become as thin as she was when they were in college. But her face is older now. He can see that about her. He prefers this face, her features having lost the softness of youth, having distilled themselves into something more elegant. The planes of her face so clean they could have been carved out of stone.

"I brought dinner: green beans and a tofu casserole. Also a pork chop—breaded, the way you like it. And there's an egg tart for dessert."

Pang Pang makes a sound of protest and Meiling gives him the most fleeting of smiles before turning back to unpack the bag of food. "There's one for you too, Pang Pang. Don't worry, I didn't forget you."

The boy pulls out the tart and licks it before sitting down on the chair next to the bed. He looks over at his father and twists his mouth into a shy, private smile, then takes a bite out of the tart, smiling all the while. Li Jing freezes. The familiarity of the moment is almost too painful, but then something like a rusty hinge opens up inside him, and despite everything he forces the muscles of his cheeks to slip into an answering smile, sticks his tongue out and wriggles his eyebrows, making Pang Pang squeal. It has been too long, he thinks, since he has laughed with Pang Pang. Sunday used to be the one day of the week when he'd force himself away from the office, and in the afternoons it would just be the two of them playing soccer, gorging themselves on pastries and cakes on the way home, hiding the evidence from Mei-ling, too full for dinner and giggling in conspiracy when her back was turned.

Pang Pang gives another gasp of laughter now, takes one more bite of his tart. For a moment, something warm floods into Li Jing's chest, dissolving a little of the fear that had planted itself there, and he shares a look with Pang Pang before they both turn to Meiling, wanting her to see, wanting her to laugh with them. But she is still pacing around the room, arranging things on shelves, complaining about the hospital and its mess, the unbearable weather in Shanghai.

"Mom," Pang Pang calls out.

"One second," she says, "let me just finish wiping the windowsill. You would not believe how much grime is on here. It's a hospital, for heaven's sakes, you would think they'd do a better job of cleaning it up."

Li Jing watches her surreptitiously, trying to rein himself in, trying to hide his desperation, trying to forget Lao Yang's visit and stay still, without shaking too much. Next to Meiling, the rain gathers on the window screen before blowing away into the muddy blue sky, the wavering lights. She walks toward him and then his bed is sinking under the weight of her. She is sitting right in front of him, her shoulders hunched, her neck coiled tight, gripping a spoon full of rice and tofu, bringing it toward his mouth.

"You have to eat. Come on, open your mouth."

He closes his eyes and feels the spoon slipping in, metallic and smooth, onto the flat of his tongue. Each tasteless bite enters him like a stone; every swallow is humiliating. He wonders how she could be so entirely blind to the awfulness that must be on his face; he can feel heat just beneath his skin, burning him up. But he does not open his eyes. He lets her feed him as if he were an invalid, lets her wipe his face with her handkerchief, lets her smooth and pat his hair.

When he opens his eyes she is sitting still, her hands in her lap. Pang Pang leans against the wall in the corner of the room, listless, pushing buttons on the electronic dictionary, resigned to the stilted air. Li Jing picks up the empty food container, grips the spoon, and puts them on the nightstand, willing her to understand that he does not need her to feed him, that he just needs her to sit by his side, to stay still, to talk to him or let him hold her hand.

"Li Jing, I'm so . . ." Her fingers icy on his arm, her voice so soft he can barely hear her. "I'm sorry. He wasn't supposed to be here. I told the hospital that they weren't to allow any visitors. I didn't know he'd just show up.

"I . . ." She lifts her face for one moment and he can see a defeated smile smudged across the corners of her mouth. "The office, they keep calling me, and I don't know how . . ." She starts again but then jerks to a stop. "I'm sorry. It's fine. You have enough to worry about. You should focus on getting better."

"No." The English comes out before he can stop himself. He looks over at Pang Pang, at the device in his small hands, and breathes shallow, wanting the thing, with its tiny microchip filled with two languages, its crude engine of translation. *"You. Talk,"* he says, grasping, grasping. His brain gliding over everything he wants her to know, desperation making the words scattered, unstrung. *"Talk to me. Stay. Talk."*

"Li Jing?" She looks at him with a question on her face. Pang Pang holds out the dictionary in his hand. But then a loud, bright ring rushes out of her purse, and all of them flinch, listening as the unmistakable sound of a telephone peals across the room.

She stares at him for a moment longer, locked in, but the phone keeps ringing, dogged and shrill, and she wrenches her eyes away. "I'm sorry," she says, and she pulls the phone out of her purse and holds it up to her ear. "Hello." She pauses. "Yes, I'm here. What is it?"

It has occurred to him that since he has been in the hospital there might have been men dropping by with false cries of sympathy, with flowers, with shoulders to cry on. He has always been possessive when it comes to his wife, but then, the possibility of other men has always been present, from the very beginning. There were other admirers who circled around her when they first met. Boys bringing her small gifts or asking her for advice on papers and then sitting too close in the library. She told him about a boyfriend in high school who wrote her poems in the margins of textbooks. Later, during their junior year, he noticed a young assistant professor who would always ask her to stay behind after class.

"It's Sunday night." She stands up and walks toward the door, lowering her voice, turning away. He strains to hear her from the bed. "What can be so important that you're calling me on a Sunday night?"

The first time he asked her to marry him they were juniors in college. He proposed in a hot pot restaurant just off campus that they referred to as "our place." The restaurant was always foggy and overheated, it smelled like chili peppers and lamb stew. He remembers looking through the steam from the pot of boiling broth between them and seeing her face, her nose shiny with sweat. "I can't marry you." She shook her head with a calm smile, said something about her back, about the unknowable future. It was the matter-of-fact way she responded that infuriated him, that made a tightfisted ball of anger thrust up into his throat. He stormed off, leaving her sitting at the table with overturned bowls and glasses, chopsticks askew, the bill still unpaid, and he remembers thinking then, as he has thought from time to time since then, that she didn't understand anything. That she didn't love him nearly as much as he loved her.

"Tomorrow, I'll see you tomorrow." She's still whispering, trying to hide it from him, but she doesn't hang up the phone, just listens to whoever is on the other end talk on and on with her eyes unseeing, her jaw stiff.

Six months after graduation, three months after surgery successfully repaired her herniated disk, and four proposals later, she finally said yes. His father tried to talk him into waiting for a few years. Their friends were supportive but vaguely puzzled at the rush. He didn't know how to explain that she had brought a kind of certainty to his life, that in her he had found an organizing principle around which the rest of his life could be built. Their first apartment together was just a single room with a communal bathroom down the hall. But it was theirs, and she was beautiful, and he no longer felt the sense of aimlessness that had plagued him for as long as he could remember, that feeling of being unanchored in the world. When he touched her it felt like home.

"I'm sorry." She looks at him from the doorway, her hand pressed over the mouthpiece of the phone. When he fell in love he had opened himself up to the possibility of being abandoned again. From time to time, over the past fourteen years, he had felt a knife's edge of fear pressed against him, threatening him with her departure. Now that he is chained to this hospital bed, without language, without competence, that fear—irrational but unquenchable—surges through his body, making him shiver. She takes one step forward, and for a second he thinks she is going to hang up and rush into his arms, but then she says, "I'll be right back," and steps into the hall, closing the door.

CHAPTER 11

The rain keeps falling down, a relentless downpour that she's not sure will ever end. Alan had warned her about it: it's called the *huangmei* days—a flood season that batters Shanghai at the end of every spring. Rosalyn gives up trying to tame her hair and lets the curls loose, a knotted halo beneath her umbrella. In the rain it is easier to be inconspicuous. People rush along in accidental herds. She joins them with her head down, her poncho awkward around her shoulders, the water climbing into her shoes and splashing onto her legs. The steady pattern of rain is a soft, clandestine assault on her brain, wearing away her edges, grinding her down.

In her apartment there is barely any light during the day. On the streets it is always gray and wet, buses and cars splattering muddy water onto the sidewalks. At night there is no relief and the dampness hangs in the air with insistence. She wakes up at two in the morning feeling suffocated, the rain still hitting the streets outside the open window, and she can't fall back asleep, loneliness prowling the inside of her skin like an army of ants, unsettling her, the strange bed so empty beneath her body.

On Friday night she goes to see Clarissa's boyfriend's band play in a packed club, stands in the back of the room sipping beer and wishing she had brought earplugs. The band plays competent grunge rock in oversized T-shirts and tattered jeans to a listless crowd. Chinese rock shows, she discovers, are much like their American counterparts: insanely loud and not particularly glamorous. Afterward, Clarissa's boyfriend Shin—"Call him Steve," Clarissa says—slumps into their booth, sweaty and aloof.

"Great show," Rosalyn says.

Steve grunts in response, barely turning his head.

"He doesn't speak any English." Clarissa pats Steve on the knee and says something in Chinese, laughs her sharp, stuttering laugh while he lights up a cigarette, his eyes latching onto a spot in the ceiling. The smoke expands in the air and when Rosalyn breathes it in it seems to stain everything.

Saturday morning she meets Clarissa for dim sum, sits next to the window on the second floor of the restaurant, and watches the world outside, which seems to have been drained of all color and light. Clarissa—on a diet—orders for the two of them. Sparse plates appear on the table: a few stalks of broccoli, four tiny shrimp dumplings, a small heap of Singapore noodles. The waiter looks at them with pity, refilling their glasses with iced coffee. Despite the meager offerings Rosalyn is grateful to not have to point and gesture her way through another meal. When she sits back and closes her eyes, Clarissa starts talking again, asking pointed questions about Danny, trying to dig for dirt.

Danny has been on tour with his orchestra, absent since the night she met Clarissa. But his presence looms blurry and persistent inside her, making it impossible to remember what he is actually like in person. He sends her e-mails from the road, regaling her with well-crafted anecdotes about travels through southern China, dotting his paragraphs with misty pronouncements on the beauty of music. Flattered by his attentions, Rosalyn writes him long, thoughtful notes in return.

Somehow, writing makes everything easier, and she teases and cajoles, charms and flirts with abandon; his return, which they have both begun referring to with increasing frequency, takes on a sense of possibility that she isn't sure is entirely warranted.

The rest of the weekend passes by with more shopping, dinner with Maia and Patrick, drinks with everybody, and a long, meandering walk through the city. On Sunday night she rattles around the empty apartment, the humid air curling against her body, licking her skin. The TV blares loudly and she shuts it off. Every book she brought looks scrambled and she flips through one after another, slamming the covers down. The only thing that holds her attention is the silver plastic of the telephone. She paces, stares at it, picks it up but then puts it back down again.

She tries calling her sister but only gets Alice's voice mail. She tries calling Carlos but no one picks up. In the courtyard, somewhere, a man and a woman scream at each other in Chinese for what seems like hours. Rosalyn closes her eyes, absorbing each vehement sliver of their argument like a stab in the heart.

Sunday night in Shanghai. Sunday morning in Oklahoma City. The eleven-hour time difference flips over in her mind as easily as a sheet of paper. Sunday night in the house on Hardenburg Lane. During the last few months, after it became clear that it was only a matter of time before he would leave, they would sit together on the couch sometimes, on Sunday nights. Ben would work on the crossword. She would flip through medical journals and women's magazines. On those nights she tried not to think about Monday or the future. She just liked having the long, lean shape of him next to her, the sound of his pencil scribbling on the newsprint.

She dials the number. He doesn't pick up. He doesn't live there anymore. She listens to the beep of the answering machine, the memento of his voice that she hadn't wanted to erase: "Ben and Rosalyn are not here right now. Please leave a message. We'll call back as soon as we can."

"HOW ARE YOU?" On Monday Rosalyn Neal walks into his room with a half smile, with gray shadows beneath her eyes.

"Fine," he says. Early in the morning they attached electrodes to his skull, the wires coming out of him like skinny, malicious tentacles, feeding information back to a machine. He tried to repeat their phrases, tried to gurgle out the oddly shaped syllables of Chinese, and he listened to the scuttling rhythm of the machine, wondering what it revealed, wondering if it would be able to expose which synapses were broken, how he might find his way back to all the words he lost.

"Please follow the trajectory of my finger," she says. They always start their sessions this way. He focuses on her finger, moves his eyes back and forth.

Day after day of the hospital bleeds into each other. The ceiling fan spins the same air in circles. It's deceptive, the breeze created by the fan; it brushes up against your body again and again, but never cools the room down or makes anything easier.

She sits down by his side and lets her head drop to her chest. He watches her, but she does not break the silence. Her legs are bare beneath her white doctor's coat, and he can see her muddied feet in between the gaps in her cheap plastic sandals. Her pale calves curve up, smudged by freckles and splattered with rainwater. Fields of short, golden hair poke out of the skin, occasionally glinting iridescent. She has been chewing on her fingernails, and it is painful just to see the strips of cuticles that have been torn away, shredded folds of raw skin poking out. He can't see her face, but can feel the heat radiating out of her round, soft shoulders, can watch the parabolic lines of her body, the solid mass of her beside him.

"God, I'm sorry. I'm a little out of it." She rolls her shoulders forward and back. "It's been a rough weekend. I think the rain is getting to me."

He makes a consenting sound in the back of his throat. They sit and listen to the occasional steps outside the door. He finds himself relaxing back against the bed. The silence is comfortable now, without resentment, without tug or pull, and he luxuriates in it, letting its warm, slippery waves wash over him.

"Will . . . be . . . easier."

It is the first sentence he has spoken without being prompted. They both stay still for a second, letting the sounds loose in the room, letting the tail of the sentence flutter, letting the vibrations fade.

"It will be easier," she says. "But after that it will be something else."

He stutters but then wills the English words to focus in on themselves. "Maybe . . . maybe good thing. Good some thing."

"Maybe."

He sits up more in the bed. The sound of a nurse's cart creaks down the hallway. The rain outside gets heavier, knocking against the window. Her scrubbed face, with its simple geometry and its freckles, has been made plain by defeat.

"What's . . . wrong?" he asks her.

"It keeps raining. We're barely making any progress. I don't know anyone here." Her voice loops thinly through the phrases. "I miss home."

"Sorry."

"It's okay."

"I miss too."

"I know."

She turns to look at him and her hair casts shadows across her face in coils, her eyes are heavy-lidded and rimmed in red. The air feels looser, less suffocating, and his throat begins to open, as if some obstruction is melting away.

"It . . . is hard."

She smiles a weary smile. "Harder when you can't speak."

"Yes. Everything . . . harder."

"It's exhausting, isn't it? Every second of it. I walk around and everything is difficult. I'm constantly nodding, or shaking my head, or making some ridiculous gesture, just hoping that I can get through whatever I have to do. Most of the time it's fine. Most of the time I like it, even. But sometimes I'm just too tired to make the effort. Sometimes I just want to say something and be understood."

"I know . . . Now . . . and before. When I was small." His words like beads threaded unevenly on a string. "No . . . Chinese."

"I don't know how you do it," she says. "I have a remarkable amount of new respect for patients with aphasia now. I knew it was hard, but I didn't know it was this hard. How did you get through it when you were a kid?"

"Easier . . . then."

"Maybe it could be easy now, too."

"Maybe."

She brightens and leans in so that he can see her face clearly, can stare into the brown eyes with tiny pinpricks of green in them. "We'll just need to work hard together on your language rehabilitation," she says. "Then you can teach me Chinese."

"Okay." He chuckles and it sounds like a series of small, throat-clearing coughs.

"Promise?" She smiles, but her smile still rings out like a minor chord. Her face has gathered all her sadness beneath its skin and now flickers, diffusing melancholia around her head like a veil.

"I . . . promise."

Her fingers are lying right on the side of the bed, and he reaches for her hand, kneads the inside of her wrist, feeling her flesh between his fingers, and covers her shredded nails and cuticles, closing his palm.

CHAPTER 12

When Meiling sits down at his desk early in the morning, the rain is already coming down in sheets. The sky is dark with storm clouds, and the buildings outside the windows look like fortresses, forbidding and glum. The office is still empty, and so she makes herself a cup of tea and eyes the ugly plastic of telephones and fax machines and computers on every desk, thumbs through reams of papers dense with numbers, and empties out the ashtrays cowering under printouts and magazines, tipping them over, watching the powder drift down to the garbage cans.

What is she doing here, really? The air conditioner turns on with a boom and then begins to hum. She made an effort to get in early this morning, wanting to beat out the fresh-faced analysts, the chatty receptionist, and Vice President Wu, who still looks at her presence here with suspicion. By herself she can try to measure out the space, wander around unobserved, familiarize herself with operating systems and arcane equipment. Yesterday afternoon she stood in the copying room confounded for ten minutes until the receptionist walked by and helped her retrieve her printouts.

Meiling wore her darkest suit to the staff meeting two days ago, kept her shoulders back and barely smiled when she told them she would be carrying out Li Jing's orders during his absence. Vice President Wu had obviously prepared everyone for the announcement. Meiling was grateful not to have to explain too much.

"All of you should just keep doing what you do best." She tried to rally them and put them at ease at the same time. "Li Jing will be calling all the shots. We all know he would be back here eighty hours a week right now if I let him, but he still has a long way to go to recover from all of his physical injuries, and so I will be acting as the intermediary between him and all business matters."

Did any of them believe her? It's hard to tell, and she supposes it doesn't matter in the end. They nodded and affected the appropriate looks of deference before heading back to their computers and telephones.

"Let's talk about this report on the airline industry in a few days." The head of the research department handed her a thick sheaf of paper.

"I need approval for the semiannual reports and all the different versions of the chairman's letter from Li Jing by Friday," the production editor said. "The letters have already been drafted, but need to be personalized. Since most of the funds underperformed, we're going to have some explaining and reassuring to do."

It's eight in the morning, the Shanghai and Shenzhen markets are set to open in an hour, and people start to trickle in through the door, turning on their computers, checking their voice mails. She nods hello but retreats to his office, stares at the long list of to-dos she worked on with Vice President Wu the day before. "We'll get you started with this," the vice president said. "Li Jing . . ." The woman paused meaningfully and then cleared her throat. "The two of you can decide what you want to do in terms of holdings and purchases. I'll check in with you tomorrow, and we'll make our move then. Xiao Zhou—I'm really glad you're taking this on, and glad that he's . . . back in the loop."

"I think"—Meiling looked down at the list—"that you better call me by my full name when we're in the office. Or you can call me Ms. Zhou."

At first glance there seems to be nothing that she knows how to do. She stares at her own handwriting as if the words have been written in a foreign language. But as she pores over the list she realizes that she has heard all of it before. These words—words like *dividend* and *derivatives*—have been part of his world for years, and now they ring with familiarity in her ear. She doesn't know what they mean, each word a part of a new vocabulary, but the syllables are worn and comfortable, and she convinces herself that there's no reason she shouldn't be able to figure it all out. She traces her finger over the list and sorts the tasks into categories: meetings, personnel, approval, analysis, buying and selling. When she calls his assistant into her office to schedule appointments she is ready, her calendar blank and open. After they finish she asks the assistant to hold all calls, and slumps back against the chair, crossing a few items off the list.

She'd told the secretary at the publishing house that she would not be returning in the foreseeable future. Her boss, Lao Chen, had called her back, but she hadn't picked up the call. She didn't want to be talked out of her decision or be reminded of what she was giving up. There were manuscripts in production, authors who'd counted on her to see their books through. But for now, the wild swerving markets, the prices down to one-sixteenth, the intricate relations with investors and officials and businessmen—this strange narrow alley encompasses her whole world.

Fourteen semiannual reports now on her desk, piled next to research documents, telephone messages, names of skittish investors, companies to check out . . . what else, she can't even begin to understand. There is another stack of paper—charting the names and shares and values of certain holdings, and on the top sheet Vice President Wu has put three question marks in black marker next to each other. *For Li Jing—Hold? Sell?* it says underneath, and the urgency of the lettering stamps into Meiling, making her heart rattle, making fear flood in.

She starts by reading the reports, hoping for clues. The paragraphs look like deformed poems. "Bond investors were hobbled by a shift in sentiment," they say. "The market descended due to the lack of liquidity." All morning long she studies page after page, rereading difficult passages, marking down phrases to look up. She is reminded of being in school, and this reassures her, gives her a way to burrow into the information. She remembers how understanding the words *electrons* and *oxidize* in chemistry opened up a new world of atoms and compounds to her, and so now *diversification* and *mid-cap* usher her into the world of stocks and finances, exposing their cavities and crevices.

At two-thirty Meiling is jerked out of her concentration by a small knock at the door. Li Jing's assistant peeks in with an apologetic look. "Can I get you some lunch?" the woman asks. "Li Jing ate at his desk unless he had an appointment. I can order something and pick it up if you'd like."

Meiling stands up, suppressing a yawn. "I think I'll go out."

Outside, in the rain, she realizes that it was a mistake to leave the building. But she doesn't want to admit defeat and go back to the office, so she wanders, walking past restaurants with extravagant place settings, full of businessmen in suits. When she finally settles down, wet and exhausted at the back of a grocery store, she eats a bowl of ramen and scalds her tongue on the hot, oily soup. Trudging back to the office, she glances at her watch and is surprised to find that she has been gone for over an hour. She keeps her head down and dodges through the halls, not meeting anyone's eyes.

The door to Li Jing's office is half open, and when she pushes through she finds a young man sprawled on her husband's chair, fingering the pages of her husband's Rolodex, chatting on the phone. His feet, she notes, are ridiculously propped on the desk in front of him, the worn heels of his shoes exposed.

"Excuse me." She takes a step forward. "It's Mr. Zhang, isn't it?"

The young man stares at her for a moment, his glasses perched at the end of his nose, and then tries to gesture her away with his chin, pointing to the receiver with his other hand.

Her first instinct is to step out of the room, but she stiffens instead and walks closer to the desk. Li Jing had talked about this particular young man, she remembers now, telling her about the "whiz kid" he recruited three years ago from their alma mater. He had laughed when he spoke about Zhang's eagerness and ambition. "He's a little bit like me, too smart for his own good," Li Jing had said. But he also spoke disdainfully of the way Zhang tried to get ahead; he wasn't sure whether the young man could be trusted in the long run. Back then they were just making conversation on a long drive, Pang Pang sleeping in the backseat, Li Jing rambling on. "I'm going to have to keep a careful eye on him. But he's a hell of an analyst already. Someday soon he's going to make a move and try to throw me over. I'm not sure whether I should scorn that kind of ambition, or admire it."

"Xiao Zhang." She stands over him now. "Perhaps you can continue your conversation at your own desk."

He looks her up and down and holds up one finger, spins around until all she can see is the black leather on the back of the chair. "I knew I could count on you. You name the day, I'll pick the place."

After he hangs up the phone he turns back to her. "Mrs. Li! We haven't had a chance to talk. I'm Zhang Qing, the associate management strategist. I want to extend my sincerest condolences about Li Jing's accident. If there's anything I can do"—the young man presses both of his palms over his heart—"I would do it in a heartbeat. Li Jing is like a brother to me."

"Thank you." Meiling throws him a tender smile as if he were an unruly child. When he gets out of the chair, she settles herself in, the seat still warm from the heat of his body.

"But let's not be formal," she says. "Call me Zhou Meiling. Or Ms. Zhou."

"Yes, Ms. Zhou."

"And Xiao Zhang. Would you mind making your calls at your desk in the future?"

"Of course!" His smile widens. "That's what I usually do. But this call in particular is a very important call for the company. I needed some privacy, and since you were out at lunch . . ."

"What was the call about?"

Zhang Qing fingers the edge of the big wooden desk. "That's not for you to worry about, Ms. Zhou. Leave that to us. We're the ones who get paid to worry about it."

The phone rings. She tears her eyes away from his face before picking up the receiver. "I thought I told you to hold all my calls," Meiling says when she hears the voice of the assistant.

"It's your son's school," the assistant says, putting the call through.

"Ms. Zhou. Is this the right number for you?" A man's voice fills the earpiece, sending waves of panic through her body.

"What happened? Is Pang Pang okay?" The words rush out of her throat.

"He's fine, but . . ."

Out of the corner of her eye she can see Zhang Qing pick something up off the desk and head for the door. When he slips out she sees the Rolodex in his hands before the door swings closed and she is shut in with the telephone receiver in her hand.

"Are you coming to pick Pang Pang up today?" the voice on the phone says. "Or is the nanny picking him up?"

"The nanny . . ." she says weakly before remembering that it's Wednesday, the nanny's day off. She looks at the clock. School ended thirty-five minutes ago.

"He's waiting, and it's getting late. We wanted to make sure someone's coming."

"Oh!" She stands up so quickly that she almost trips and falls. "I'm so sorry. I'm on my way. I'll be right there."

PANG PANG WAITS under the awning of the school and searches the hooded faces posed over bicycles, looking at the people standing under the umbrellas while the raindrops drum and bounce off the domes, shake through the leaves on the oak trees, skid across the roof tiles, and sink into the streets where they gather, a brown swell of water that rises onto the sidewalks.

His friends wave goodbye and scoot their bodies under the protection of parents or grandparents, riding away on the backs of bicycles and mopeds, in taxicabs whose tires coast across the flood, making symmetrical waves behind them. Everyone walks away holding someone else's hand, the water covering up their feet, a few kids laughing and jumping up and down, splashing the muddy drops everywhere.

"Pang Pang." His teacher comes over, looking at his watch. "Is your mom coming to pick you up?"

There are only two other kids still under the awning, and both of them fix their eyes on the other end of the street, studying every passerby, letting their shoes get wet.

It's Wednesday, which means no lessons, but he has to practice his English phrases before going to class at the language center tomorrow afternoon. His mom was supposed to pick him up, but last Wednesday Nanny Chang had come instead. The day has been one long blur without sunlight, the rain and the humidity seeping into his brain, making him confused and tired.

"My mom's picking me up." He nods at his teacher and takes a step forward, craning his neck to look for her to pull up in a cab, the way she usually does on rainy days.

The raindrops pelt him across the face, blurring his vision. The trees stand in their little fenced-off squares, their trunks as lonely and thin as he is. Pang Pang wonders if he will have to go to the hospital tonight, but corrects himself: he wants to go to the hospital tonight. In English class yesterday their lesson was based on a family that spent a Saturday afternoon together—he wants to run to his father's side and say, *"To the amusement park!"* He wants to say the words *roller coaster.* He repeats the two snippets of English out loud, swiveling his head around, looking for a familiar face, waiting for his mom.

They had gone to the amusement park together once, all four of them, and it had been so much fun. His mom and his grandpa hadn't wanted to go on the scary rides, so his dad took his hand and the two of them rode the roller coaster and the pirate ship, screaming and laughing. Pang Pang knows that if he studies English, if he studies it really hard, soon he and his dad will be able to talk to each other again. He imagines that when he goes to his father's side and lets loose a mouthful of English they'll both smile again and his father will say things back to him. All this silence between them would be gone as quickly as the roller coaster plunged down its tracks.

The other two kids are gone now, and the water creeps up, covering the steps of the school. It's getting late, and he wonders where his mom is, or if Nanny Chang is coming, and sees his teacher look at his watch before heading inside, toward the telephone in the front office. Pang Pang steps down into the water and it rushes up through the plastic of his sneakers, soaking his socks, running up his bare calves. The whole street is flooded, brown water with bubbles in spots, swirling, rushing toward the drains. It smells like rotten fruit, like decay and fish scales, and he grimaces at the thickness of the liquid on his skin. He watches the garbage on the surface of the water ebbing up and down: an orange rind, a sheet of newspaper, a pink, grimy plastic basket upside down like a hat.

Nervous, nervous, he looks back at the school, afraid his teacher will come out at any second, and pushes his legs against the current, waddling through the water as quickly as he can, wiping the rain from his face and splattering brown drops onto his shorts, until he is around the corner, another street flooded. All the streets are flooded and the rain won't stop. You can't see the ground, you can't see the sidewalks, water climbs up the walls and storefronts have to shut down their gates and people in galoshes and bare legs skitter across the road, sending up little splashes around their ponchoed bodies. Bicycles with a third of their wheels submerged ride past, making a thin trail behind them like the path of a snake. Cars toggle through, half driving, half floating, slow, slow as a pleasure boat on a sunny lake.

Walking home usually takes about fifteen minutes and he always has so much stuff to tell his mom—about the new girl who wore her hair in two long braids, about the math test he'd gotten a 95 on, about how they played soccer during recess and he scored a goal with the move that his dad taught him—that sometimes he is surprised when he looks up and they are already home, walking past the curved driveway and coming upon the glass doors of their building. But today, the trip home seems to take hours, the water weighing down his shoes, the blocks stretching long and endless. Pang Pang shrugs the straps of his backpack higher onto his shoulders and keeps trudging forward. Up ahead, there is a fat man laughing on the sidewalk, carrying a young boy on his back as easily as a turtle carries its shell.

When Pang Pang walks through the gate of their development he knows that he is almost home. He looks back and the whole world is curtained with rain, water climbing past the sidewalks, up the walls. He walks up the cul-de-sac, through the front door of the building, and waves hello at the doorman, who gives him a funny look. But he just keeps walking—he has a key in the secret inside pocket of his backpack, and as soon as he is out of the doorman's sight, he slips his backpack off his shoulders and drags it behind him, letting it smear the carpet with a gray trail, dragging it into the elevator.

He wants a long bath. He wants to sink into the couch and watch TV. He wants to yell at his mom for forgetting to pick him up, then he wants her to bring him soup and candy and roasted pork buns and french fries. He turns the key in the door and walks in without wiping his feet on the mat. "Mom," he calls out. "Mom, where are you?"

The empty apartment refuses to answer back. Pang Pang stomps on the green carpet, wet footprints everywhere he goes. In the kitchen plastic boxes litter the counter. In the bathroom there is only his face staring back at him from the mirror. The doors to the three bedrooms are wide open, all the beds immaculately made, but there is no one there, and Pang Pang creeps back into the living room with all its familiar things, his heart pounding, his legs shivering from the cool of the air-conditioning. He walks out onto the balcony and edges next to the railing, his fingers gripping its smooth cylinders, feeling the rain again as it bathes his face, trickles onto the back of his neck, smothers his feet. Looking down onto the city he sees gray murky waters on every street, welling forth like little creeks, and at the site of the Swan Hotel the wreck of the building is still there, piled into a hole in the ground, slabs of cement caving into an open grave.

IV

FIN DE SIÈCLE

The hospital doesn't want to discharge Professor Li, but when he insists on it, they simply have no way of keeping him there. He argues with doctors, badgers nurses until they hold their hands up in front of their bodies, demands meetings with administrators, yells to anyone who will listen that he needs to be home. His son is getting discharged, after all, and his son can't even speak! Why should he have to stay, he who is holding his body straight, affecting robust health and good spirits with every ounce of strength he can muster?

Finally, the hospital acquiesces. As usual, Professor Li gets his way. He and Li Jing are discharged on the same morning, and Professor Li is sent home with eight bottles of pills and countless cautions not to exert himself. Meiling flags down two taxis, bundling herself in with the professor and his wheelchair. When they are finally settled, she shouts through the windows at Pang Pang and Li Jing in the other car, making sure that Pang Pang tells the driver where to go.

"Thank you for getting me out of there," he says.

She slumps against the seat. "I should have listened to the doctors and made you stay, but I'm sick of hospitals, and I didn't want you to have to be there by yourself."

Her chest is so thin that he can see the bones, right there, through the material of her dress. He's filled with a surge of tenderness for her, and he wonders, staring down at her face, if this is the way Li Jing sees her too, if part of her draw is the vulnerability one can occasionally glimpse beneath that perfect, stoic exterior. He wishes he could say that to her, say, "Let him see how you feel," but he knows this would be an affront to her dignity and poise. She would insist on being quietly and brutally efficient, but she would not understand that what Li Jing sees in her efficiency is indifference, and what he needs to see is her weakness.

"Meiling." He doesn't know what to say, but he wants to try. "How are things between you and Li Jing?"

"Fine."

"Have you gotten a sense of what his sessions with Dr. Neal are like?"

"It seems to be going well. She got him to talk, after all, and the hospital says they're working on his Chinese too. No one else is getting any results. I'm really glad we brought her over—I think she's good for him."

Before Rosalyn Neal arrived in Shanghai, Professor Li had asked Meiling for a copy of her credentials. He had known where she attended medical school, where she did her residency, the titles of articles she'd written, but he had not known that she would show up with that big American smile of hers, he had not known that she would turn out to be pretty, in that big-boned, American way.

"Meiling, I'm worried about her, about the two of them together." He wants to be more subtle, arrange the situation through hints and ambiguities, but he knows that the American would play by no such rules. He knows that he is running out of time.

"You really shouldn't worry." She sighs. "Just worry about getting better."

It all comes out in a rush. "I went down to the ninth floor, to Li Jing's room, just as he was finishing up with Dr. Neal last week. They didn't know I was there, and I saw them, the two of them, holding hands, their heads bent together. I wasn't going to tell you, normally I wouldn't tell you. But he doesn't want to listen to me right now, and I'm too tired, too old to make sure he's on the right path—" Professor Li gestures down at his inert body, shaking his head. "Li Jing is not himself right now, and none of us know anything about that woman."

"Dad, I appreciate your concern, but there's no need to worry. Really, I just want you to worry about being better." Try as she might, she can't hide the slight edge of condescension in her voice. "Dr. Neal is a professional, and she knows what she's doing. If she and Li Jing become friends, then I'm sure that will help him even more."

"But what if . . . what if they become more than friends, Meiling? Don't tell me I'm being old-fashioned. I know the difference between friendship and something else."

She brushes her palm across his forehead. "Thank you so much for thinking about me, for looking out for me. But I'm not too worried about this 'something else.' Even if Dr. Neal were after Li Jing, which I highly doubt she is, he would never do anything like that."

"Yes, of course, but what about her? I don't trust that woman at all. She's from America—who knows what she wants with Li Jing."

Meiling's laughter is far too rare these days for Professor Li to mind it, even if she's laughing at him. "Sorry, Dad. I didn't mean to laugh. It's just the way you said *America*, as if it's a poison. I thought it was supposed to be the Chinese ladies who go after the American men, instead of the other way around."

America. He rolls the English word on his tongue. *Měiguó.* In Chinese, the two syllables mean "beautiful country." He himself knew the allure of America. He has seen her openness, her way of taking in strangers and giving them comfort, her soft flesh that seems to absorb all pain and loneliness. But he has seen the other face of America as well, her perpetual fancy for the new and exotic, how ruthlessly she throws off those who hold on too tight, the impenetrable fortress of her heart. He had spent far too many years in America. America had buoyed him in youth, strung him along, and killed his wife with its carelessness. When he came back to Shanghai he knew he was finally coming home. Shanghai showered him with commissions and accolades, doted on his son, made him—finally—into who he was supposed to be. Despite what his American friends had called a "lack of democracy and freedom" in China, Professor Li found himself far more content than he had ever been in America. "If I stayed in Virginia I might still be a waiter," he'd say again and again. "If I was lucky, I might have gone on to own a Chinese restaurant. I would have never become a practicing architect. How's that for freedom and democracy?"

"Why wouldn't Dr. Neal be interested in Li Jing?" There's a touch of annoyance in the professor's voice now. "He's a very successful man. You fell for him, after all. Is it so inconceivable that other women might fall for him too?"

"Of course not."

"And you, you're barely paying any attention to him!" Professor Li lets his anger with Meiling slip out. At her small huff of surprise he waves his hands in dismissal. "I know all the things you're doing for him, Meiling, and I know that you've been taking on too much at his company. You've been amazing and I'm not trying to be critical, really, I'm not. But you've barely spent any time with Li Jing, you don't ask him how he is, or what he's feeling—"

"I can't!" Her voice flares high and accusing. "Have you forgotten that we don't speak the same language? Have you forgotten that he barely says anything to me? What am I supposed to do, sit and wait by his side and beg him to talk about his feelings? Does it look like I have nothing else to do? Between keeping this family together, and running back and forth to the hospital, and making sure things don't fall apart at SinoVenture, it's not like I have plenty of time."

"I know, Meiling, I know, and I'm sorry." Professor Li crumples.

Meiling scoots over in the backseat, repentant and apologetic. "What am I doing? You need to rest—"

"No, let me just say this." He looks into her eyes, trying to explain. "It's just that he spends so much time together with that woman, and they can talk to each other. It's dangerous, don't you see? The two of them, together. Who knows where it'll go?"

Meiling gazes off and out the window, the afternoon haze making everything blurry, tinged in gold. "I appreciate it, Dad, I do. But she is his doctor. They're supposed to talk to each other."

"Not like this, they're not."

"You know that I've never had any cause to worry about Li Jing's fidelity, and for a man in his position, who could have had any number of affairs by now, that's very rare. You shouldn't think that way of him. I don't."

Professor Li almost envies Meiling her assurance. He almost smiles at her naïveté. But in this, he knows, she is not wrong, not yet anyway. Her unwavering belief in his son makes Professor Li wish, for a bright, painful moment, that he could have had more time with his Josephine, that they might have gotten a chance to test their devotion to each other across decades and continents.

The taxi comes to a stop in front of their building. Already Li Jing and Pang Pang have gotten out of the other car and are walking toward them, heading for the trunk.

"I just thought you should know." He grabs her hand to stop her from getting out of the car. "I know you think you have it all figured out, but they were holding hands, and I know he's feeling scared and distant from you right now, and Meiling . . ."

Then the car door is open and the wheelchair is waiting for him on the curb. His son helps him out of the backseat and he settles, with a thud, down on the wheelchair. The four of them head into the lobby. When the elevator door opens it is Pang Pang who pushes the wheelchair past the threshold, and then they are going up, they are almost home.

THE LEFTOVERS FROM dinner still lie open-faced on the dining room table. Pang Pang is in his room and a light peeks out of the bottom of the door, but Meiling doesn't bother to check in on him; it's too early for him to go to bed. They have put Professor Li to sleep, and the sound of his snores trickles into the hallway, rough but comforting. The weeks of rain have finally ended and now heat filters in through the windows. The cars downstairs honk away, the lights across the horizon flare on, and she walks out onto the balcony to stand next to her husband, watching the city hum at twilight.

There is a slight breeze and she can feel it batting at her face, see it slapping at his shirttails. He does not turn to look at her, but takes her hand and presses it under his on the railing. In the dimness she can just make out the site of the Swan Hotel; it is the only stretch of darkness in the city, no light flickering out of it. She shivers a little, standing there, remembering the line that split the building, the way it grew wider and pushed itself outward into veins that crawled across the façade. His hand is hot on top of hers, his body next to her. She thinks that as long as she holds on to his hand she can close her eyes and not be afraid.

He leads her into the living room and she does not open her eyes. He draws her into his body and rubs her back with his other hand. She does not let go of him, she does not open her eyes. He takes her by the shoulders and walks her down the hallway to their bedroom, taking off her slippers, pushing her stiff torso onto the mattress. She does not open her eyes. She thinks this is an illusion, a dream, that she'll wake up at any moment remembering all the things she has forgotten to do. There will be no one to help her, no one to take care of her, no one to hold her hand. She presses her eyes even more tightly together to concentrate on his fingers on her face, on the sag of the bed as he sits down, on the smell of him, salty and warm and close, so close that she can feel her breath whisper across his skin.

He kisses her. He kisses her and his stubble rubs raw across her chin. He puts one hand on her jaw, one hand in her hair, and his lips are still on her, his tongue thick in her mouth. She opens her eyes. He's still there, his black pupils huge and radiant, boring into her. She stares back, recognizing him, recognizing something in him that had been absent. She does not close her eyes again.

She presses harder with her lips, clutching tight, rolling onto her back. Kissing occupies his mouth, negates the possibility of speech, and she groans from the bottom of her throat, bites down on his lip when the full weight of him sinks into her body. His lips find her neck, his tongue follows the lines of her collarbones, and when she realizes his fingers are at the buttons of her shirt she wriggles her shoulders back and goes to undo them herself. "Come on, be patient. We have all night," she says, laughing a little.

At the sound of her voice he freezes, and then backs away from her, not looking at her face.

She undoes her buttons and takes off her shirt, her bra, unzips her skirt and sheds her underwear. She keeps her mouth shut but presses her body against his, wrapping her arms around his waist, trying to imprint her desire onto him without murmur or sound. Everything is different now, but everything is the same. He smells the same, the contours of his body so familiar. He tenses up like he always does when her fingers touch his thigh. He lets himself fall back to the mattress. But his hair is longer now, his arms softer to the touch. She straddles him and watches him search her face. She puts his hand on her breast and moves her hips over him.

He jerks under her. A noise throttles out of his throat as if he is choking and then his entire body shudders and tightens in release. She closes her eyes and scoots off his body, sinking down next to him, touching his arm. He covers his face with his hands and silence stretches between them for a long moment, a car alarm outside the window churning the same siren around and around.

"The doctor said this might happen at first," she says, her voice soft.

He twists his body away so that she is no longer touching him. He buries his head in his hands. She wants to say something else, talk it away, tease him about needing more practice, offer her services as coach and partner. It's what they would have done before—they would have laughed, but everything is different now. Her throat stays closed; she has no words for him. She pries his hands away from his face and he is grimacing as if he cannot stand being looked at. So she smooths her arm over his torso, tries to wrap herself around him, but he jerks his body away, rolls off the bed in one desperate motion, and walks stiffly to the bathroom before closing the door and turning on the shower. It's past twilight, and now the room is thick with night. She sits in bed, naked, and watches the golden silhouette of the bathroom door, listens to the cascade of water hitting flesh and tiles.

CHAPTER 14

Walking back into the hospital feels like trying to crawl back into skin that he has already shed. But it is familiar: the constant smell of herbs and bleach, the worn carpet beneath his feet, the hallways dotted with slow-moving people in thin pajamas.

Despite everything it has been good to be home. But Meiling left so early in the morning that the water in the kettle was cold by the time he got up. Once Pang Pang left for summer school, he no longer knew what to do with himself. His father dozed in his room all morning long, while the nurse sat in the living room, watching one television show after another.

"How are you?" Rosalyn Neal sits down across from him in the narrow, stuffy office, her freckled arms propped on the desk like pale tree trunks. Alan stands in the corner and gives a nod, his hands clasped tight in front of him.

"I am . . . fine," Li Jing says.

Out of the sickroom, out of bed, out of hospital pajamas, sitting in her office, he pulls his shoulders back and runs a hand over his hair, fingers the too-long pieces at his nape, wanting a haircut. For the first time since he has met her Rosalyn is not wearing her white coat, and he notices that her green shirt colors her eyes a different shade; they look like mossy, deep lakes, the light shifting over them.

He has been looking forward to seeing Rosalyn, wanting her loose-limbed chatter in English, her easy sense of humor, the way they can talk, the two of them, without fighting a battle over every word. Over the weekend, the quiet in the house rubbed him raw. Every short exchange with Meiling was taut with unspoken accusations, mediated through his father or the electronic dictionary barking out its staccato sounds. When they touched each other rolling over in bed or by accident in the kitchen, he snatched himself back, not wanting to press himself on her, not wanting her to see his face. She barely noticed in all her rushing around. Her days seemed to be spent on the phone and in taxis, arranging this or that, and it made him feel as though his failure to speak was just another inconvenience to her, something else that needed to be fixed.

She has taken a leave from her own job to manage things at Sino-Venture, and though he is grateful, there is something humiliating about it too. She did not even talk to him about it or ask him any questions before meeting with his staff. He wanted to help, to explain, to offer to do . . . something, read through reports or analyze trends, but the truth is, what he excelled at, before, was the cultivation of *guānxi*— the complex relationships he built up with sources and clients, the endless hours of networking and gossiping and flattering and drinking that yielded new accounts and investment tips. How he talked to people, how he charmed them and manipulated them, made him good at his job. And now, now that he has been rendered dumb and mute by a hole in his brain? How can he do anything, how can he even be of any help to the company that he built—now that he can no longer speak?

Every time he thinks of work he is reminded of the scene with Lao Yang, the way he had just sat there in the hospital room, silent and helpless. No doubt all the investors know all about it now, the staff too, and who would want their money to be invested by a man with brain damage, a man who been made pathetic, completely inept?

The portfolios had been in disarray right before the explosion, and he imagines that things had not miraculously improved during his absence. At times he is tempted to glance at a newspaper or log on to his e-mail, but what does it matter in the end? It's not as if he can march back into the office and shout out commands, meet with investors, wine and dine city officials, put out the fires constantly cropping up in his line of work. No, he can't do any of it. If anything, he'd just lose the respect of his staff, sink the reputation of the company, make things worse. It is better to let Vice President Wu and the other senior managers handle things at SinoVenture, let Meiling help out too—she is as capable as anyone he's ever met. He feels the slightest pangs of guilt at the thought that she is taking time away from her own work to help out with his company, but the guilt is snuffed out by the waves of self-pity that rise up in him every time he looks at her face, the way it is shuttered, not giving him a glimpse of her feelings.

"So." Rosalyn leans in. "Alan is going to help us work on translating English into Chinese today. Instead of working on spontaneous speech in Chinese, we're going to try to link up English and Chinese, to see if English production will spur your Chinese. Actually, this'll be a great chance for me to learn some Chinese too: I've been studying my tones. Sit back, and we'll both try to repeat after Alan."

Alan pronounces each word in English and speaks its equivalent in Chinese, dragging out the syllables. Li Jing mimics the shape of Alan's mouth, contorts his lips and teeth to find the right sound, but what he manages to say doesn't click into place.

"Today," Alan says.

"Today."

"*Jīngtiān.*" Alan again.

"*Jiaan . . . Tane.*" Flattened phonemes, without tone, carry no meaning.

Rosalyn joins in, tries to repeat the Chinese syllables too, and when he hears her struggling to find the right sounds it makes things easier. When she giggles and shakes her head he laughs too, wagging a finger at her. They both look at Alan, but cannot drag a smile out of him. The translator goes on with the exercises and excuses himself at one-thirty precisely, closing the door behind him without a sound.

"Well." Rosalyn sits back and puts her face in her hands. "Chinese is tough to crack, but Alan might be even tougher."

"Maybe," Li Jing says. "Very serious man."

"I know. He puts me to shame. Every time I'm around him I feel like I need to act every inch the professional. I keep getting the feeling that he's checking up on me, making sure I'm doing everything I'm supposed to be doing. I've been feeling a bit more pressure here at the hospital. They'd really like to see you start to recover your Chinese. I only have another four weeks of my fellowship left. I don't want Alan—or anyone else—to think that I'm just goofing around."

He turns his head to the side, thinking about a future without seeing Rosalyn every morning. Four weeks is not a very long time, and the possibility of her absence tugs at him in unexpected ways. The only times he feels vaguely at ease are when he's sitting across from her, listening to her talk. At home—*home*, he laughs at the word in his head—everything looks so pristine and unblemished and empty that he finds himself filling up with rage and panic, wanting to lash out, wanting things to break.

They work on the by-now-familiar set of exercises in English. The sound of his childhood comes back to him, and the words get easier and easier to say, forming themselves into sentences. He's beginning to enjoy this part of the sessions, where it feels like he can stretch his thoughts, where unexpected words float out of him, making Rosalyn smile. Speaking English, for years, had felt awkward, as if he was lumbering through it, but now English feels like a salvation, and he throws himself into mining his brain, looking for half-forgotten words, every one of them a way out of silence.

At the end of the session she waves goodbye. "See you tomorrow, Mr. Li."

"James." He breathes the name out like a secret. "It's James."

"Excuse me?" She turns her head and curls fall loose across her cheek.

"James. My name. My . . . American name. Li Jing. James Li." He points at her and then turns his finger on himself. "Dr. Neal. James Li."

A smile flares bright across her face. "Well, it's nice to meet you, James." She extends her hand to him and laughs a throaty, low laugh. "Please call me Rosalyn."

"Rosalyn." He closes his mouth around her name. The sound of it like a ripe berry staining his tongue. When he gets up to leave, she is still chuckling, looking at him in wonder, and the sound of her laughter fills him with something warm and honeyed, clearing away the anxiety in his chest.

"Goodbye, Rosalyn." He says her name just to hear it again.

"Goodbye, James."

He has already taken two steps out the door when he hears her call out. "James!" The single syllable slides past him, as smooth as an eel. The name sounds strange to his ear, tinged with irrelevance after not being used for more than twenty years. He takes another step down the hall before turning back, seeing her behind the big wooden desk again.

"Where might a girl go for some lunch around here? I'm sick of the cafeteria. Do you have any suggestions?"

She wears a playful smile and raises her eyebrows. He looks at her, wondering about all the different expressions that ripple across her freckled face so easily, as if there were no thresholds in her heart. He does not answer her right away, and now there is a sliver of uncertainty in her eyes. The corner of her mouth wavers, and the slight motion of it shoots a pulse through his veins.

He gestures her forth with a wave of his hand, not wanting to speak. She takes two small, tentative steps toward him before striding forward with her face looking completely exposed. He stands tall and holds the door open for her, and she walks out under his arm before stopping her steps. Her long skirt keeps spinning in a circle for a moment longer, as if something were spinning out from the heart of her. She stands there, smiling, waiting for him to catch up.

Outside the hospital heat hisses down on the pavement, making the city seem new, desertlike, every drop of moisture lifted out of the ground and burned away. Stacks of bicycles lie on their sides, bursting out of the rack, their metallic bodies glowering in the sun. She cranes her head around to take in the streets, gawks at every abandoned construction site, every thin tree trunk rising up out of the ground. He walks next to her and tries to see the city from her eyes, notices the buildings in the distance wavering in the sun, the oyster-colored sky.

"Noodles?" He walks past three long, narrow windows and stops in front of a door. The windows are frosted over, so opaque that you can't see inside. At her nod they walk into the restaurant. The smell of sesame oil, chili powder, and a hint of garlic shimmers in the air. Tables litter the room, peopled and dense, but Li Jing navigates Rosalyn through with ease, turning sideways and edging past bowls of broth. They sit down next to the wall in a small booth, their legs so cramped under the table that he can feel her knees nudging against his own. A waitress whirls up to their side and Rosalyn gestures with her palms open and touching in front of her face, asking for a menu.

"God, I hope they have a menu in English." She looks back at him, wrinkling her nose. "Chinese menus are the bane of my existence. I'm always in all these places with amazing-looking food, except I never know what anything is, and I can never get ahold of the things I want to eat!"

The waitress comes back, throws down two tattered menus, and stands by the table, her arms folded over her chest. She can't be more than twenty, but the severity of her hair—pulled up and away from her face in a tight, black bun—gives her a mean, spiteful look. She taps one foot fast on the floor.

"I think we're going to need a minute," Rosalyn says.

The waitress rolls her eyes and turns to Li Jing. *"Kuài yīdiǎn,"* she says. *"Nǐ mén yào chī shén me?"*

He lurches forward and stares at the menu wildly, recognizing the characters, picking out two bowls of roast duck noodles. But when he points to the line on the page and hold up two fingers, he sees that the waitress is looking back at the kitchen and gesturing to someone, her face turned away, barely paying attention to him.

"Nǐ mén yào chī shénme?" she says again. *What do you want to eat?* He is still pointing at the menu, but she hasn't turned around, and he grunts, holding his hand out to get her attention, before pulling it back, fast, as if it had been burned.

The waitress finally turns back and glares at him with her hand on her hips. *"Shénme?"* she says. *What?* But his fingers are frozen, they will not move to the menu again. All along something has been lurking inside him, this black, ugly, shapeless feeling that burrowed beneath the ribs, biding its time. Now it expands, stretching out livid tentacles, threatens to swallow up all of him, from the inside, and he starts to shake, not looking up, not wanting to give himself away. He is not ready for this, has not thought about the necessity of speaking to order food, ask directions, go anywhere, do anything. When he opens his mouth he can only gape and close it again, knowing that it is a black hole where words are swallowed but nothing can emerge. The menu is on the table in front of him, the edges ripped and dissolving, and he stares at it, watches it darken, watches the black haze over his vision. The thing inside him surges up, from deep in his stomach, sending up panic, knocking over reason and calm. He can hear his own breath, ragged and desperate; he can feel a scream thrashing around his chest, wanting to come out.

But then he hears laughter, her laughter. The sound of it seeps into his body, porous and soft like cumulus clouds in the bluest sky. He opens his eyes and watches the shake of her shoulders, the bounce of her hair, how she tries to share the moment with him in a wink, making it easier on him. "Oh dear!" She puts her hands on the side of her head and then puts them on the table, stretching them out, leaning toward him in conspiracy. "Look at the two of us." She stares at him, animated, unembarrassed. "This is just delicious, and I know, I know, that is a terrible pun. It's my fate, clearly, to be in one of the best food cities in the world, and not be able to eat anything. Do you think she's going to take pity on us and just bring us a couple of bowls?" Rosalyn looks up at the waitress and waves absurdly, laughing all the while.

Before he can react she is sliding out of the booth, arching her neck to look at the other diners. She grabs the waitress by the arm and points at bowls of noodles on other tables, then points back to their table, giggling, making an exaggerated, hapless face. All the other diners stare at Rosalyn now, talking over each other as the restaurant breaks into anarchy. "Well, that's one way to get the job done," a man by the door says, raising a glass to Rosalyn. "The *lǎowài* knows what she wants," someone else chimes in.

The waitress smiles reluctantly and nods before taking off for the kitchen. The other customers point and smile, and Rosalyn takes a curtsy before sliding back to sit across from him. "You didn't realize that eating out with me would be such an adventure, did you?" she asks, her face still giddy, her voice too loud. "I figured it was time to take things into my own hands, so to speak. I hope I haven't embarrassed you."

He shakes his head and considers her for a second, marveling at the way her laughter has taken him completely out of himself, the way she so easily won over everyone, taking the attention off him, making things easier. He spreads his hands on the table and stares at her hard before closing his eyes in a smile. "Good," he says. The anxiety that had gathered in his chest dissipates as he laughs out loud, shaking his shoulders. "You order. You pay."

There are syllables drifting in the air, other people's conversations, but sitting across from Rosalyn those streams of Chinese stop taunting him and dissolve like steam rising out of the food. They are both still smiling when the waitress comes back with two giant bowls of noodles, the strands swimming in a clear, savory broth. When he bends his head down to slurp the soup, the heat of it smooths over his face like a fog, filtering the world and all its sounds, softening its blows.

CHAPTER 15

As the weather warms up Rosalyn begins to spend less and less time in her little apartment on the ground floor. There is no air-conditioning there, and she has come to think of her small, dark bedroom as a cell. Every morning she wakes up with the loudspeaker in the athletic field blaring its insistent music, her body slick with sweat, her mind tumbling over sinister dreams, druggy with aborted sleep. Having stayed out late the night before, she falls back under the covers again, wanting a few more hours of rest, wanting silence and oblivion.

The weeks slide past her easily, filled with activity. On Tuesday nights she meets Danny and Clarissa and Patrick for dinner and music, usually a jazz band at the Portman, or occasionally at the Cotton Club. The music is adequate enough to cast a hue over the room. She hums under her breath when the band strikes up "You're My Thrill" or "Strange Fruit."

Saturday afternoons are set aside for marathon shopping trips with Clarissa, and they meander through Shanghai's endless array of shopping malls, flea markets, department stores, and boutiques, leaving trails of salesgirls speaking broken English in their wake. Clarissa tries on everything and discards piles of unfolded clothes on the floors of dressing rooms. Rosalyn still cannot get used to the way the salesgirls descend on them, grabbing their hips without permission to get their measurements. When told the price she learns to automatically divide the number by seven. With the exchange rate, everything seems like a bargain, and she comes home with arms full of shopping bags; in the apartment, dresses are strewn everywhere, the price tags still attached.

Saturday nights are devoted exclusively to barhopping and clubbing. There is always a new place opening with a flourish, touting fancy cocktails and hip DJs. Rosalyn likes watching couples smother each other in the dark nightclubs, hidden by the crowds. She makes a study of the Chinese women with painted eyes, the way they stare at the door, looking for the next gullible foreigner to seduce. She has never seen this kind of life before, not up close, and something about it thrills her, the way people glitter and shine under the disco lights, how their faces can look hard and soft at the same time.

Last night was a Thursday night, or "dinner club night," as Danny said when he called to remind her earlier in the day. She met up with everyone at a Franco-Thai restaurant in the French Concession. She ate snails cooked in curry and drank chocolate martinis garnished with orange peel. After five courses and too many drinks they headed over to Maoming Road. By the time they hit the clubs Rosalyn was drunk enough to step onto the dance floor. She could not remember the last time she had gone dancing—Ben would never dance with her—but it didn't matter. Under the dim, colored lights she flailed her limbs with abandon, letting her hair run wild, grinding up against strangers.

Danny nudged up next to her and she laughed at the sight of him. He was too awkward and self-conscious to really dance, but he shrugged his shoulders and moved his hips with good humor, shyly sneaking one hand out to grip her wrist. She smiled a flirtatious smile and twirled herself in his arm. He looked at her with a kind of awe, and tried to pull her closer. Rosalyn tensed before letting her body crash into his.

The feel of his hand on her back sobered her up, and she squeezed her eyes closed when he tucked her head into the crook of his neck.

Danny. Her tour guide. Her friend. The one who introduced her to all the other expats, to this new kind of life. She likes doing things with Danny. They went sightseeing together. He helped her pick out a camera in a dizzying electronics store. When she mentioned that she wanted to go for a jog he came over the next day in sneakers and shorts, bringing her a surgical mask so she could filter out the city's polluted air while they ran through the streets. He was attentive and kind and nervous and sweet. He was also the first man she had dated as an adult, and she found the rituals of courtship strange and alluring at the same time.

He brought her flowers. Gave her a box of moon cake. Took her to romantic dinners at dimly lit restaurants around town. Called her "just to say good night" before she fell asleep. He paid for movie tickets and endless drinks, opened doors and hailed taxicabs. He was just shy and awkward enough to be sincere. "You're . . . wonderful," he'd stammer when nervous, or when drunk, and his stammer put her at ease. She wanted to pat his head and kiss him on the cheek.

She tried to ask Clarissa about him, feeling unsure of herself.

"You have no idea how lucky you are!" Clarissa talked as though she'd been waiting for an opening. "Most white guys in Shanghai have a serious Asian fetish. Look at Patrick. He's with a different girl every night. It's slim pickings here for girls like us—the Chinese guys are intimidated by you, and most of the white guys have no interest in dating you. Why would they, when there are boatloads of Chinese girls lining up for a crack at a green card? Danny's one of the few good ones left, and he really likes you. Go for it. He's a catch."

Rosalyn thinks about Danny as she heads toward the hospital in the late morning. She's running late, but she takes her time, takes the long way so that she can walk through the winding market in the alleyway where old ladies haggle over the price of bok choy and spend hours picking out asparagus. She stops to watch the fishmonger scale and gut a carp, the knife flying, the man's fingers sinking into the belly of the fish, pulling out the entrails. She emerges on the other end of the market and hears the strains of a waltz, the melody delicate but the volume robust, the notes distorted, coming out of a boom box set on the ground.

Couples flicker around each other on the wide sidewalk, turning in the shadows of apartment buildings, dancing careful steps, murmuring counts to keep track of their feet. Their arms are locked together in dance holds, their torsos straight and their shoulders broad. They wear pajamas and housedresses, faded T-shirts and flip-flops. Most of the dancers are women with lined faces, glimmers of silver at the roots of their hair, and they are partnered together, trying to sync their movements up to the music, trying not to collide into each other or step on their partners' feet. When the music ends they stumble and stop, laughing, clapping and calling out to each other. When the music starts up again the waltz begins once more. Rosalyn watches the couples whirl and glide on the pavement, oblivious to the traffic swishing by, to the bicycles ringing their bells. The sun beats past the haze, throws a hard glare over the dancers' bodies. Their faces wear the most serious and focused of expressions, but their contentment is palpable. She lingers for a moment longer, watching, wishing for something unnameable, wishing she could be a part of this world that she has caught the occasional glimpse of. But then she glances at her watch and drags herself away, off to another day at the hospital.

"SORRY I'M LATE." Rosalyn opens the door to the smoking lounge, still dreamy from her walk. The other doctors look up in silence. Alan is already in the corner and she walks over to stand next to him, tossing a contrite smile to the rest of the room.

"Dr. Neal," Dr. Feng begins, but it's Alan who cuts in smoothly and unrolls the phrases of English. "We've been talking about Mr. Li's case for the past fifteen minutes. Since we haven't had one of these consultations in a while I thought it'd be useful for all of us to hear what the others are doing. Each of his doctors has reported on their progress with Mr. Li."

"Oh good," Rosalyn says. "Did I interrupt someone when I came in? Or would you like me to give an update now?"

At a nod from Dr. Feng she glances around the room. Faces look up at her through tendrils of cigarette smoke, their expressions hard, openly hostile. She wishes that she had gotten here early, looked through her notes before being asked to present her work. She has always prided herself on being prepared, but since she's been in Shanghai, with James as her only case, she has allowed herself to become lax, as if absolved of any responsibility.

"Well," Rosalyn says, eyeing Alan, who clears his throat before starting his translation. "I think Mr. Li's language therapy is going very well. Since four weeks ago, when I made a breakthrough and Mr. Li began actively communicating again, I've been working with him in the areas of word recognition, sentence comprehension, and spontaneous production. He has improved dramatically in all of those areas."

They let her go on and on about assessment methods and fMRI results. She deliberately fortifies her speech with technical terms, but Alan doesn't miss a beat, just utters sentence after sentence of Chinese without any change in inflection. The other doctors sit aloof, waiting for her to finish. When Rosalyn finally trails off, the young physical therapist utters something sharp and accusing, but Alan does not translate its meaning, nor does he meet her eyes. Everyone else sits in silence.

"Why don't we break for tea," Dr. Feng says.

Thirsty, hungover, Rosalyn edges toward the water dispenser only to realize that everyone else has grabbed their own ceramic mugs out of the lounge's closet. Even Alan has a glass jar that he pulls out of his bag. The paper cup dispenser is empty, no one offers her a sip out of their mugs, and so she walks back to her spot by the wall, cotton-mouthed, defeated.

They are right to look at her with suspicion, she thinks. If she were in their shoes and saw some ham-fisted foreigner coming into her hospital to headline a case, she'd be angry and dismissive too. They had probably heard about her behavior in the sickroom, heard about her lack of rigor, her occasional solipsistic breakdowns in front of her patient. She could defend herself by arguing that a personal connection can often jolt aphasic patients out of their self-imposed shell, that the use of humor is recommended as a strategy in linguistic therapy, but the truth is that she has been lonely and lost here in Shanghai, that she has treated her patient more like a friend. Her lack of professionalism is indefensible, and what's worse, she doesn't want to change her dynamic with James. It has become increasingly difficult to think of herself as his doctor, now that he has become this person, become just himself to her, and she will be the first one to admit that she doesn't know what she's doing anymore.

"Dr. Neal." Dr. Feng sighs out the name. She looks at Rosalyn, not unkindly, but disappointment rolls off her body in waves. "We are rather concerned," she says, "with Mr. Li's lack of progress in Chinese. While we are pleased at your work with him in English production, he has yet to hit any assessment benchmarks in Chinese, which was his dominant language before the accident. You have been in Shanghai for almost six weeks. There are only two more weeks to go in your fellowship. To us, it seems like there's not a lot of time left . . ."

Dr. Feng's use of the first-personal plural plucks at Rosalyn's nerves, making her aware of her solitude.

"We were wondering . . ." Dr. Liu, the Chinese speech therapist, takes a drag of his cigarette before stubbing it out. "Is it possible that your work with Mr. Li in English is detrimental to other aspects of his therapy? I looked up some of your research, Dr. Neal, and you yourself have hypothesized that in cases of multilingual aphasia where the languages are lateralized in the same part of the brain, recovery in one language may hinder the patient's abilities in another language."

"Might Mr. Li's English be improving at the expense of his Chinese?" Dr. Feng says.

Alan takes no sides, is careful not to inject feeling into anything he says. He stays as shallow as a mirror, deflecting everything away.

"But I . . ." Rosalyn says, grasping. "Of course your concern is perfectly valid. In my experience, however, multiple languages are usually only lateralized in the same location if they were simultaneously acquired. Since Mr. Li didn't learn Chinese until he was ten years old, it's unlikely that the kind of cross-pollination I wrote about in that paper would have occurred. In any case"—she turns to Dr. Feng now—"while I have been working with Mr. Li, and with Alan, on transposing meaning from English to Chinese, I do realize that I can do a better job of working with you and Dr. Liu to help accelerate his progress in Chinese."

"Even an incomplete recovery of his Chinese will, ultimately, be more useful to Mr. Li than any fluency in English, don't you think?" Dr. Liu says.

Alan's voice clips through the words, and then the question hangs over the room, everyone's eyes on Rosalyn. She forces herself to nod. "Of course," she says, looking away. "Our ultimate goal is to help Mr. Li improve his complex speech production and adapt his language skills to a productive and satisfying life with his family. I understand your concerns, and I can assure you my work in the next two weeks will reflect a renewed sense of focus on the integration of Chinese into his speech."

THERE ARE NO constellations in the sky. Airplanes are the only meteors streaking overhead. But Shanghai is never dark. Billboards and headlights flood the streets with light; twenty-four-hour convenience stores glare brightly, casting a sheen over the sidewalk. The city transforms itself after hours. At midnight, it is as if the alleyways and dead ends have been rearranged, as if they've been shifted around so that you're lost all over again. There are new corridors to walk through, intricate, ephemeral hubs of activity down new paths. Uncanny Shanghai. There are countless sets of universes within the city, shifting, temporary. How could anyone hope to know her? Her face changes by the hour.

On Maoming Road, the buildings bloom, pouring off pools of light through their windows. Music hangs low and thumps past the court-yards, and the scent of magnolias, soft and sweet, drifts through the air. Taxis idle one after another by the curb. Crowds of people mean-der through the streets, men with tight shirts and slicked-back hair, women staggering in heels. Laughter and the clink of glasses surge out of bars and nightclubs. Rosalyn opens the door of the cab and watches the little kids with open cases strapped to their torsos call out in English: "Cigarettes! Cigarettes!" Before she even gets out the children run up and swarm around her, chattering like birds, stretching out their palms.

She is glad to be done with the horrible day, with the accusatory doctors meeting in the morning, with another session where James's Chinese sputters incoherent and disappointing, with the sight of an e-mail on the screen from her lawyers, saying that the divorce has been finalized. She has not worn her wedding ring in months, but kept it in a zipped compartment of her wallet. At her desk, staring at the com-puter, she took it out and squeezed it tight in her fist, feeling the metal cut into her palm, hating everything it was supposed to represent, hat-ing Ben, the way he made her feel as if she were responsible for her body's betrayal, the way he talked about their parting—"We just want different things." She hasn't let herself feel angry at him in a long time, still holding out hope that he would change his mind, but with the finality of the words on the screen, with the cold metal of the ring against her heated skin, she seethed, wanting to destroy that part of herself that still loved him, wanting to leave him behind for good.

The evening began with dinner for two at a Japanese restaurant. Little boats of raw fish coursed around on a conveyor belt. It was the first time she had ever eaten sushi and the slimy texture of the fish felt aw-ful in her mouth. When Danny leaned in close and touched her cheek, she could smell his cologne along with the scent of wasabi and fish. She wanted to throw up, and she dodged away from him, feigning a cough, cupping a hand over her mouth.

He mistook her nausea for coyness. She kept draining the tiny cups of sake, avoiding the fish, which went around and around until they wore a sheen from the lights and the cigarette smoke in the air. But why not Danny? She looked down at her lap and tried to gather her courage. Why not someone new? An image of James flickered up, the ease of talking to him, despite everything, flooding her with warmth, but she brushed it away, tried to focus on Danny's smiling, worshipping face.

She has stepped out of her life, tried to leave it all behind, but now she sees that what she needs to leave behind is that older version of her, the one who spent years being afraid, the one who was still in love with Ben, waiting for a future that no longer exists. She is in a foreign country now, surrounded by a new set of people, and her old self, her old life with its responsibilities and codes, its clear way forward—none of it counts anymore. She can be a different person here, in Shanghai, someone brave and careless. Out of the cab now, running fast across Maoming Road, she stretches her arms out and throws her head back.

Danny catches up. "Come on," he says, "Patrick's waiting for us at Babylon."

She squeezes herself through the crowd at the club and walks halfway up the staircase, recognizing familiar faces, giving a nod or two of hello. She sees the same faces all the time, without knowing their names, but they all end up back on this same stretch of the city eventually, wasting their nights away. A spotlight sweeps over the dance floor, illuminating tall, golden-haired Europeans in polo shirts, women with long, sparkly earrings dangling out of short black bobs of hair. There are baseball-capped frat boys gulping beer, middle-aged American tourists looking lost and nervous. She watches a young Chinese woman deliberately spill her drink on a balding man in a sweatshirt. The man looks startled when the young woman bends down to brush away the liquid, her fingers moving across the crotch of his pleated pants.

"Patrick's in the back room." Danny comes up behind her, screaming to be heard. Two glasses are balanced precariously in his hands. She bends down and drinks from one of them, and someone pushes past Danny, sending him hurtling toward her, making the vodka spill out of her mouth and across her chin. Rosalyn lurches under his weight for a second, letting him lean against her, and then takes the glass out of his hand, draining the rest of the drink.

"Can I have another one of these?" she says.

Danny looks at his own drink, still full, and starts to protest, but she is already walking away.

"Patrick!" She swerves through a pack of people and spots Patrick on a sofa, his legs spread wide, surrounded by women. He holds out his arms, and she pitches herself into his lap, giggling, struggling to sit up straight, shoving the other women aside.

"What do you say we go dance?" Patrick says, pushing her onto her unsteady feet.

Out of the corner of her eye she can see Danny furrowing his brows, looking concerned, so she gives him a little wave, blows him a single kiss. She makes her way onto the dance floor with Patrick, stares up into the lights slithering across the ceiling on tracks, flashing away. Bodies crowd against her and she can feel their sweat and perfume sinking into her skin. She rolls her shoulders and moves closer to Patrick, and then away from him, gives him a little shrug before turning and dancing with the stranger who has been trying to press up against her hip. The music changes now, from the unrelenting attack of drums and bass to a Latin melody, speeded up, the horns blaring bright, making everyone whoop and throw their hands up in the air. She threads through the crowd and back to Danny, lifting another full glass out of his hand and taking a gulp, putting her cold tongue against the side of his neck.

"Dr. Rosalyn! What's gotten into you tonight?" He looks thrilled with the attention and drapes his hand bravely over her shoulder, dangling his fingers near her breast.

She wriggles into him, stamping out every gap and crevice between them with her flesh. "I just want to have a good night," she slurs into his ear, and then darts her face away when he tries to kiss her. "Come on! Don't you want to dance?"

"Danny and Rosalyn, sitting in a tree." Clarissa's low, mocking voice cuts in, "K-I-S-S-I-N-G." She waltzes up to them with bare shoulders and long, sparkly necklaces wound about her throat. Her boyfriend Steve is a step behind her, and his hands, Rosalyn notices, are carelessly stroking Clarissa's ass through the thin fabric of her dress.

"Clarissa!" It is a night for throwing herself at people. Rosalyn hugs Clarissa hard and takes a sip out of her wineglass. "I'm so happy to see you. Come on, let's get out of here. It's a good night for a pub crawl!"

She hears Clarissa stage whisper to Danny: "How much has she had to drink?" Patrick finds his way back to her side and lifts her up, off the ground. "You," he says, laughing, "are high as a kite tonight!" They follow her out the door and to another club, this one even more packed, the bartenders bare-chested, girls in sequined bikinis dancing on platforms in the middle of the floor. She beelines for the bar, fighting through the crowd, but she likes the feeling of being squeezed from all sides, the music so loud that it makes her forget everything else.

"Rosalyn! Rosalyn!" Danny comes up next to her, yelling in her ear.

"What are you drinking, Danny?"

"Maybe you should slow it down a little," he says. "You seem—"

"Two vodka martinis!" she shouts at the bartender, and watches the flex of the man's muscles as he bends down for the vermouth.

Out on the dance floor she throws her head back, exposing her throat. Clarissa runs up and dances with her; she has lost her boyfriend somewhere along the way, but she doesn't seem to care. The drumbeat is steady and insistent, moving past skin and sinking into bone. Danny is next to Rosalyn, once again, and she grabs the front of his shirt and pulls him toward her, hugging him tight.

"Danny!" she says. "You're wonderful. You're the best."

The music breaks for a second and then there is a voice, shrill and accusing across the club. "Pat-trick!" The syllables are stiff, broken into discrete blocks of sound; a tall, emaciated woman stalks forward, heading straight for the dance floor. "Oh shit!" Rosalyn hears Patrick say next to her, and then before she knows what's happening Clarissa has grabbed her hand and they are running out the door. "What the hell!" Rosalyn says, already out of breath. Danny and Patrick are running behind them, trying to keep up, Patrick's burly body heaving up and down with every step.

"Long story," Patrick gasps once they're outside, but he keeps running.

"Oh Patrick!" Clarissa is laughing hard. "Don't tell me you didn't know about that woman. Doesn't she go by that awful name—'Black Jade'? What did you do? Did you not pay her? You didn't, did you? Tell me, please, that you knew she was a prostitute!"

"How was I supposed to know?"

Patrick stops running and holds his stomach in his palms, huffing and winded. Rosalyn takes one look at his flushed, beleaguered face and starts laughing too. She starts running again, down the middle of the street this time, dodging past headlights, causing a cacophony of horns. Danny and Clarissa and even Patrick follow her, giggling, running between cars, screaming at the top of their voices. Her heels are steady on the ground; the air brushes hot and humid against her face. She keeps running, faster, faster, thinking of Shanghai, the glorious city, its endless allures.

CHAPTER 16

During the afternoon Meiling lets the details of her former life seduce her, lulling her with their comforts. She spends an hour at the salon, sinking into feminine chatter, warm water raining down on her head, scissors snipping away her hair until her face is exposed again. Walking into a familiar boutique she inhales the subtle scent of gardenias in the air, slips dresses of silk over her skin, stares at herself in the long, sleek mirror while salesgirls cluster around, complimenting her everything. On her way home she asks the taxi driver to close all the windows and turn off the radio, the loud hum of the air conditioner brushing all other sounds away. She leans back against the seat and touches her face with manicured fingers, closing her eyes, trying to remember everything she has learned over the past few weeks, trying to recite her script.

Stock quotes. Quarterly projections. Growth rates. Investment strategies. The words sprint around her skull, and she tries to pin them down with meaning, tries to memorize their every possible trap and implication. Vice President Wu drilled her, again and again, on each facet of the business, preparing her for all possible questions. "We must hold on to Eastern Star's account," Vice President Wu said. "They're one of our biggest investors. Xu Luotong, their CEO, has been clamoring to see Li Jing for weeks. If he pulls out after this meeting, then I'm afraid that we'll have to lay off staff during the next quarter."

Why couldn't the vice president, Meiling asked naïvely, go to dinner by herself? There would be no fear of embarrassment then. No chance of slipping up.

"Xiao Zhou." The vice president gestured at her own plain face and then back at Meiling. "Look at me, and look at you. Charm counts for a lot in this business. Why do you think Li Jing was so successful? Sure, he worked hard, and he was smart, but he was also charismatic—people gave him tips because they liked him, and he could always talk a rich person into handing over their money. Now, I'm not saying that you're just a pretty face, but surely that doesn't hurt. Me, I've got the kind of face that belongs behind the scenes. I'll come along this time, but I hate business dinners, and I'm no good in that kind of situation anyway. I'm counting on you tonight."

Meiling remembers the nights when he would come home at three in the morning, exhausted from trying to outwit other businessmen while drunk, the slow collapse of his limbs next to her. She remembers how he would get up three hours later, put on a clean shirt while she was still asleep, and head out again for another long day at the office.

The car is coming to pick her up at six-thirty. Dinner would begin at seven o'clock. The restaurant Quanjude for their famed Peking duck. Every bit of charm and cunning she could coax out of herself.

As soon as she gets home the nurse stands up from the sofa and stomps out, giving her an exasperated look.

"I'm supposed to get an hour's break. It's already 5:13. I won't be back until 6:13, not a minute before." The door bangs shut and Meiling sets down her bag with a sigh. In the living room Pang Pang and Li Jing are sitting on the floor, both of them cross-legged and holding video game controls in their laps, their eyes trained on the television, not even giving her a glance.

"The Lakers ahead by seven!" The voice on the television calls out in

Chinese, thick-throated and robotic. She rubs her head and squeezes her eyes shut. The video game console had been a reward, a bribe, and an apology to Pang Pang. She had also, in her guilt, bought him a laptop, a miniature car with an electric engine, and signed jerseys from Pang Pang's favorite players on the Shanghai Sharks. She knows that gifts won't make up for her neglect, but she doesn't have the time to look after him right now. She is not, after all, the one who stays home all day, with no job to go to, nothing to do.

"Slam dunk!" the game screams out. She can't understand why the volume is always turned up so high—it's not as if he's lost his hearing. The telephone begins to ring, adding to the noise from the television. Neither Pang Pang nor Li Jing looks up from the screen, and the racket of the video game and the metallic ring of the phone bleed together, scratching hard against her nerves. Finally Pang Pang looks over at the phone and then looks at her, plaintive, as if to say, "Make it stop," before turning back to the game, jerking the control hard in his hands. She stares at Li Jing, feeling this venom that she can almost taste. He is wearing a thin T-shirt, with a frayed V-neck collar, and she narrows her eyes at his long, disheveled hair, his thickening waist above the cross of his legs.

So he can't speak. The phone finally stops ringing and she wrings out a washcloth in the kitchen and starts wiping down the counters, clearing away toast crumbs and stuck-on bits of apple peel. He could still make the bed, couldn't he? He could still do laundry. He could re-hang the blinds that had fallen down last week or change the lightbulb in the front closet. He could still pick up after himself. She throws the washcloth into the sink and clips through the hall, trying to shake off her anger, trying to calm down. But the sound of the video game rushes in, blaring, relentless.

If she could just go to the bathroom and turn on the shower, then she could drown out all the noise in the apartment, listen to the sound of water spraying out from the showerhead. But when she passes by the door to Professor Li's room she hears his voice, feeble and desperate, calling out her name, reeling her in.

"Dad? Is everything all right?"

"Ah, Meiling. Sit, sit. I want to talk to you," Professor Li says, holding out a shaking hand. "Come now. Sit."

"What can I get you?" She flicks a look at the antique clock on the bookshelf but stays in the doorway.

"Come now," he says. "There are things I want to talk to you about."

Half past five. The car is coming in an hour. She walks over to the side of the bed but does not sit down. "What is it, Dad?"

Every time the professor takes a breath it sounds like a gasp. "Listen," he says, putting a hand on her arm, pressing down. The pressure from his hand is so light, so tremulous, that she shivers, involuntarily, afraid for him. "Meiling," he starts again, "Li Jing needs you right now."

"I know, I know," she says, her eyes darting to the clock again, watching the minutes tick by. Professor Li wheezes and starts to cough. She sits down behind him and pats him on the back, rubbing her palm in circles, helping him sip from a glass of water.

"No, you don't understand." Professor Li tries to look her in the eyes, but Meiling is turned away, her hair hiding her face. "You think you know what's happening. Both of you think you know how the other person is feeling. But you don't. Can't you see? Li Jing needs you to slow down. He needs you to sit next to him, talk to him, or try to listen, as hard as it might be. He needs to feel like you're not just martyring yourself for him, and that he's still your husband, not just another person you have to take care of. I see you two growing further and further apart, and I wish—" The professor speeds up his speech and tumbles over the words. "I wish you could see that. I want you to fix it."

On the bookshelf there is a photograph of Professor Li, Li Jing, and Pang Pang that she remembers taking a few years ago. Pang Pang had been in Li Jing's arms, and all three of them were looking at each other instead of at the camera, wearing the same smile on their three faces.

"I'm sorry, Dad. But I really have to go," Meiling says, getting up.

He seizes her by the wrist and tries to pull her down. "I'm worried about you and Li Jing."

"Tomorrow. We'll talk tomorrow." She pries his hand off her wrist and puts it gently on his chest. "But don't worry. Everything is going to be fine."

"The American . . . the doctor." His voice is a quiet, weak rasp, the words slipping away. He watches her move toward the door, shaking his head.

"I know." She turns the doorknob and steps out of the room. "You don't have to worry about that. I know you doubted her, but she's getting excellent results with Li Jing, don't you see? She's been the only one to have an effect so far. We should consider having him spend more time with her, or see if she's willing to stay in Shanghai for a little longer. You don't have a thing to worry about, Dad. I'm going to take care of it. We're all going to be fine."

HE HAS NOT forgotten that his wife is beautiful, but it has been hard to notice her face since the explosion.

The first time he saw her face in the university library it did not occur to him that she was beautiful. What occurred to him was that her face moved him. Even back then she was not unaware of her looks or their effect on other people, but she always took them for granted, with a casual self-possession that made her admirers in college—him included—feel mildly absurd about their pursuit. After she began working, she was constantly around poets and editors, these thin, gloomy men whose eyes lit up at the sight of her. Once a poet dedicated a book to her by name. Despite her reassurances, Li Jing was angry about it for weeks. There had always been, he thinks, a slight asymmetry between them, he had always needed her more. But it didn't seem to matter so much. At least, it hadn't, before.

She walks out of the hall now and a whiff of her perfume prickles his nose. The subtle scent is familiar. He has gotten so used to the smell of it—cool and expensive—that it seemed a part of her. Until now, he hadn't realized that she stopped wearing it after the accident. Why had she stopped wearing her perfume? Why was she starting again?

"I have to go out tonight. I won't be home until late," she calls out from the kitchen. He doesn't turn to look, just keeps focusing on the TV screen and the video game control in his hands, inhaling the smell of her, listening to her voice. At the lack of response, she walks into the living room and stands next to the television. "There's food in the fridge left over from last night. And there are dumplings in the freezer too."

She's wearing a new dress, this cream-colored thing that falls smooth and sleek like water to her knees, outlining her body without giving anything away. He thinks about how she always looks like this when she is trying to impress, how she picks out the most austere and expensive fabrics to cover herself up so that everyone ends up staring at that marvelous face. Her hair has been trimmed and brushed back. In high heels she stands differently, with her back arched, her small breasts jutting out. He stares at her mouth, her long neck, imagines those small breasts tipping into dark nipples, traces his eyes down her torso, past her boyish hips, to her absurdly narrow feet, wearing round-toed, cream-colored shoes. It is a body he knows so well, a face that still moves him. She lowers her eyes for a second and he can see pale, glittering powder on her eyelids, carefully drawn eyeliner, her lashes thickened by mascara, and he has an insane urge to run up to her, hold her tight, and ask her to please just stay here, just stay with him.

"Where are you going?" Pang Pang barely looks up from his game.

Where *is* she going? Why is she so dressed up, wearing perfume? He thought she had been working at SinoVenture, but perhaps she's gone back to her old job without telling him? Perhaps she's meeting besotted poets and pedigreed editors trying to impress her with their insights and barbs? The questions flare up inside his chest, the ragged edges of jealousy slice into him, and he grunts, almost breaking into English.

Part of him always found her presence in his life precarious. Even at the very beginning, she felt like a treasure to him. She was so fragile, with her back, and so brave, her face white with pain but not making a sound. Her heart, which she gave freely, felt like a delicate, easily spooked thing, like a bird. He held it in his clumsy hands, not quite believing his luck. He used to try to read the books she edited but could make no sense of the strange metaphors, the wildly varying rhythms. When he followed her to art museums he almost always wound up sitting somewhere, bored by the displays, waiting for her to finish. She told him she liked their differences in temperament. She teased him about his lack of appreciation for the arts but did not seem to mind. He always wondered, though, whether she'd prefer to be with someone more like her. Someone with whom she could talk about poetry and foreign films.

"I'm . . ." She meets Li Jing's eyes for a second before looking away. "I'm meeting with some business associates, so I have to look like a grown-up tonight."

"Dad." Pang Pang motions toward the TV. "What's the matter? You're not even playing anymore."

She opens the front closet and takes out a purse, then stands still for a moment, taking a deep breath. He gets up, before he loses his nerve, and reaches out, touching her upper arm.

"Dad! You can't just leave the game in the middle of—"

"Where are you going?" The words fly out of him, round, boneless. It takes him a second to realize he has spoken in English, and now he is grasping, desperately wanting to find the Chinese.

She stares at him with her mouth half open. His hand is still on her arm, and now he raises it to her jaw, touching her, gently, as if she were a live wire. *"Where . . ."* The words still come out in English, and he searches for their Chinese equivalents in his brain, the two syllables that mean place, which place, *where.* The words are in there, in some dark room with no accessible paths. He can feel them, the shapes of the sounds, but he can't draw them out or make her understand.

"Please . . ." he says, but then drops his hand and backs away.

She stands still for a moment, and then closes her eyes, smiles a tired smile. "It's all right," she says. "I'll be back late, and you just . . ."

Another phone rings, her cell phone this time, the sound of it ripping something apart between them. She digs the phone out and stares at it, dumbstruck, but then throws it onto the table and glances at the kitchen clock. Pang Pang has disappeared from the living room, and the video game flickers on the screen, abandoned, repeating the same abrasive snippet of crowd noise over and over. He tries to reach for her, once more, but she is already walking down the hall, disappearing behind the bedroom door.

He leans against the wall and closes his eyes. He sees himself again, reaching out for her, and her flicking him away, like an annoyance, like a gnat. His forehead breaks out in sweat, and he grips his head, runs his palms over his face, pressing down with his fingers, leaving marks. He is almost panting, and his hands curl up into fists and drum hard above his eyebrows, wanting to let out this feeling that has filled up his insides, this anger and confusion and blackness that will not let up.

The cell phone's ring again: thin, trilling, insidious. She runs out of the bedroom, muttering under her breath, picks it up. "Hello," she says, "what is it?"

"Dad!" Pang Pang comes back into the living room and grabs Li Jing's elbow.

"I . . ." He tries to keep his eyes on her but Pang Pang keeps tugging at his arm. *"Hold on,"* he turns around and starts to say, but at the boy's look of confusion he shakes his head, hard, trying to shake the English out of his brain.

"Dad? Are you—?"

He tries to concentrate on Pang Pang's voice, the thinness of it, how scared but brave the boy sounds. Pang Pang pulls him over to the laptop sitting open on the dining room table. "Do you want to try this?" the boy says. "I made Mom buy this new software that's like the electronic dictionary, but better. The box says that it can translate more than a hundred thousand words."

The pulsing in his head lets up a little, but the feeling in his chest, bursting and ugly and so massive that he can barely breathe, does not decompress or go away. He stands there, still craning his neck around to look at Meiling. Pang Pang thrusts the laptop forward, and before he knows it he is holding the flat, smooth shape of the machine, feeling its heat on his palm.

Meiling paces the living room, her voice tauter, more vibrant somehow. "What do you mean?" she tells the telephone. "I can't believe you're telling me this now."

The buzzer flares up, making everyone jump. He stays rooted to the same spot, and she goes to the door, the cell phone still at her ear, yelling, "It's too early for the car" into the intercom.

The response comes back. "It's me, the nurse."

Meiling buzzes her in and then goes back to her call. "No, it's going to be fine." Her voice is low now, tight and dangerous as she walks across the living room with deliberate steps. "I'll wine and dine him, I'll charm him. Don't worry—I can handle him."

All he wants is to just hold on to himself, to stay calm, to not give in to the anxiety trying to knock him over and tear him up. But it is impossible not to hear her voice in his head again: "I'll wine and dine him, I'll charm him." A part of his brain insists that there is nothing amiss, that it's probably just a business dinner, but everything else is blaring so loud that all rational thought seems to be slipping away and fear comes flooding in. He grips the laptop and holds it tight in front of his chest, as if it were a shield, but his hands feel strange, the fingers thick and filled with energy, all his blood pulsing toward them. There is noise everywhere—now there is a knock at the door, the sound from the video game keeps piercing through, and Meiling's voice is still sharp, but muddied, on the other side of the bedroom door. The sounds blare together and condense into this pulsing, a blackness inside his body, flaring out of control. His fingers are hot and shaking, gripping tight, filling with blood, wanting to break something, wanting violence.

He lifts the laptop above his head and throws it to the ground.

But the carpet smothers the impact; the machine stays intact upside down. Pang Pang starts to bend over and pick it up, but Li Jing is quicker, swooping in, picking it up again, hurling it at the wall. It makes a crunching, vaguely satisfying sound this time. The plastic body clatters and breaks; pieces of the computer snap off and fall to the ground. The feeling inside him is at once quenched and more voracious, and he lays his palms on the thing again, holds on to it but smashes it into the wall once more, stares at the fractures splitting the smooth, black plastic of the screen, and then brings the laptop down, across his thigh, trying to break it in two.

She runs out of the bedroom, slapping her palms against the wall, calling his name. "What are you doing?" she screams, all this accusation and rage sharpened into a single point. "Are you insane? What did you just do?" When he looks at her he sees a mixture of disbelief and anger on her face, he sees her throw her hands up in the air. They have been on opposite sides all along, since the accident, fighting each other, but he hadn't seen it before, hadn't seen how much she resents him for all this. Now, with one more look at her face, he thinks he understands everything, understands her contempt, understands how pathetic and useless he has become in her eyes.

The laptop is laying agape at his feet. His mind seals up, full of rage, impenetrable. He is locked in, without language as an escape valve. He can't pry the lock open, can't find a crevice or a handhold. Nothing can touch him, nothing can let up the pressure inside his body. He stares at her for a moment, watches anger and fear tear across her face, and aims a vicious, hard kick at the battered thing at his feet, sending plastic flying through the air, tiny, splintering pieces darting away from him.

Pang Pang lurches and breaks into a cry.

"Oh god." Li Jing turns around to look at Pang Pang, his shoulder slumping in horror. *"Paan . . ."* He tries to call out the boy's name, tries to apologize or explain, but Pang Pang has already run to his mother's side. Meiling pulls the boy into her, sheltering his head under her arms,

and turns back to Li Jing with a look of ferocious accusation, daring him to speak again.

A wheelchair creaks into the living room. "Li Jing . . ." His father's voice, a hoarse whisper, and then the sound of him gasping for breath, a squeal of rubber as his body makes a slow slide down the chair.

Before Li Jing can call out, Meiling is already moving over to the wheelchair, grabbing Professor Li under the armpits to pull him up to sit.

"*Oh god.*" Li Jing says again, grabbing his head, letting the English pour out of him. "*Dad, I'm sorry. I'm sorry. Tell Pang Pang sorry. Didn't . . . want scare him. Tell Meiling sorry. I'm sorry, Dad. Are you— okay? I'm so sorry.*"

Professor Li's mouth gapes open and closed, spit dribbling out of it. Meiling arranges his body on the wheelchair and starts to push it down the hall without looking back, her entire body stiff and furious. Li Jing lifts his head, looking for Pang Pang. The boy has pressed himself flat against the wall, his shoulders hunched up near his ears, his head tiny and skittish but still. As soon as he meets his father's eyes, he looks away and runs off, as if he is afraid of being caught. When the door to Pang Pang's bedroom slams shut, Li Jing crumples to the floor with a soft cry that no one will hear.

HE LIES ON the carpet, curled up into himself. His hands are grasping his bare, bleeding feet, and a long, deep moan slides out of his throat—he sounds like an animal in pain. Meiling stares blankly at him, looking at his ankle, the strands of black hair matted on the skin, the pink row of marks left by the elastic cuff of his sweatpants. This, she thinks, cannot really be happening. She takes two steps into the living room and snaps the television off so that all she can hear is his moan, Pang Pang's darting sobs, and Professor Li's wheezing breath coming from down the hall. When her cell phone rings, again, she wants to grab it and throw it against the wall. She wants him to know that she can break things too. But she reaches for the phone and turns the ringer off instead. She collapses and sits on the arm of the sofa, holding her heart, feeling it drum beneath her palm.

The knock at the door comes again. When she goes to let the nurse in she tries to shield the living room from view. "The professor," she says to the nurse, "he's . . . let's go to his room." She cannot even look at Li Jing's body on the living room floor, balled up, his knees pressing into his chest.

In Professor Li's room she helps the nurse lay him down in bed, tenderly wipes his cold, clammy face with a wet cloth. The clock on the bookshelf tells her it's six-thirty, and she turns away from it. "I'm terribly sorry," she whispers to the nurse, and for once, the other woman looks at her with sympathy.

"It's all right," the nurse says. "I'll watch out for him. You go on ahead."

Meiling walks through the living room, letting the sofa shield Li Jing's body from view, and steps out onto the balcony, where she dials Vice President Wu's number to tell her they'll meet at the restaurant instead, hanging up before the other woman can protest.

Out across the city the day is just beginning to fade, and a sliver of the setting sun shines out from between buildings, dull and orange, casting a strange glow on glass and concrete. The balcony is so high up that standing there gives her the feeling of vertigo. She can only look up into the blank sky, cloudless, can only look across at other buildings, other balconies, shirts the size of postage stamps hung to dry. She does not allow herself to look down, but she knows the Swan Hotel is there with its debris, its emptiness that reaches up into all of them. The rest of the night stretches in front of her, but she tries not to think of it now. She walks back to Pang Pang's room and sits down on his bed, puts her hand on his head. "Shall I read to you?" she says.

He gives a small, shriveled nod, not making a sound.

She kicks off her shoes, gets into bed with him, and he burrows into her, wraps his arms tight around her waist. He is still so very little, her darling boy, and though he looks like Li Jing he reminds her so much of herself at his age. He has always been quiet, and it is Li Jing who used to draw him out and make him shriek in laughter. Over the past month he has gotten even quieter, and it makes her heart sore, thinking of it now, thinking how little she has heard his voice recently, how little time she's spent with him.

Meiling opens up the well-worn copy of *The Monkey King* and reads Pang Pang's favorite chapter, making her voice animated, drawing out the words in suspense. She lets herself drift into the story, cries out when the monk is captured by bandits, and finally, when the monkey king rescues the monk by disguising himself as a maid, she presses a kiss on Pang Pang's head and closes the book shut. Pang Pang grabs on to her arm but doesn't say a thing, just holds on tight, his little fingers digging into her.

"Pang Pang." She cannot let herself cry right now. "I have to go. But I'll be back soon, I promise."

In the bathroom she checks her reflection, brushes her hair again, fixes her makeup and sprays one more puff of perfume on her neck. Her face is stiff and dry, with thin lines faintly coursing across her cheeks. She dabs at herself with a powder brush and twists her mouth into a smile, making the corners of her eyes lift, but the lines seem even more pronounced now, and so she shuts off the light and stands in the dark, in front of the mirror for a moment, before letting herself out of the bathroom. It's almost seven, and as she walks down the hall she focuses her gaze on the orange sky outside the balcony doors, she does not look at his body on the living room floor. She takes a step toward the door and something crackles under her heel. When she picks it up she sees that it's a small square of plastic marked with the number 4 and above it, the ¥ sign. She tucks it into her purse and grabs the doorknob, stepping across the threshold, trying to flip a switch in her head. Dividends, she thinks, expense ratios and market trends. Profits, returns, she thinks, exchanges and futures.

CHAPTER 17

Meiling walks into the private banquet room at the restaurant a different woman: at ease, unafraid, full of bravado, clothed in silk and perfume, shrouded by charm. She inhales the cloud of smoke and smiles in pleasure. She orders two bottles of the most expensive wine at the restaurant. When she greets Mr. Xu she smiles coyly but shakes his hand hard. Two of his associates rise at once, bowing to her, and she nods and stands there, waiting, showing off her legs, until one of them pulls out her chair.

Strange, how she can leave that wreck of a scene back at the apartment behind her, how she forgets about Li Jing and Professor Li and even Pang Pang, locking them away to focus on the task at hand as easily as pressing a button on the remote to change the channel. Mr. Xu is a small, gruff man in his fifties. When he looks at her she can see his suspicion of her youth and her sex. It makes her want to laugh. She is determined to win him over now. She never did take well to being underestimated, and she always did like a challenge.

"I don't mind telling you this," Mr. Xu begins without preamble.

"Why not lay it all on the table? One of the guys at your company— Zhang Qing—called my vice president last week. He told us that things at SinoVenture are a mess. That Li Jing's as good as finished. That he's starting his own fund, and we should pull out and go in with him."

She fills everyone's wineglasses with steady hands. "Yes, I'd heard that Xiao Zhang has been trying to stir things up," she says. "But let's get to that in a minute. Let's drink a toast first, shall we? To the future of SinoVenture and the future of Eastern Star. May they both glow brightly and grow prosperous."

She takes a long sip of her drink and waits until all eyes are on her. "Mr. Xu, did you know that twelve of our fourteen funds are up more than 3 percent just in the last two weeks? That's about $150,000 for Eastern Star, and it happened, as I'm sure you know, during a time when the market was off by more than 5 percent."

"Well, that's just to make up for the money you lost last month," he grumbles, but his eyes dart to her face, alert now, interested.

"Of course, if you pull out of SinoVenture now, and join up with Xiao Zhang, it's possible that you'll get the same type of returns. Possible, but not particularly likely. Xiao Zhang is a very ambitious young man, but he's still terribly green. Let's be honest, he doesn't have a company or a reputation, so he would essentially be gambling your money with nothing to lose. We, on the other hand, are playing with our reputation and the shirts off our backs. And believe me when I say that we definitely want to hold on to our shirts, and our clients as well."

She knows that her smile is a sly one, one that promises sex and disdain all at once. She has long since learned that this particular smile is potent, but how strange, now, to be using it, talking of share prices and investments.

Mr. Xu is not so easily won over. "Your last month was a disaster," he says. "I couldn't get ahold of a goddamn person. That's not any way to run a business."

"Last month was . . . a difficult time for us." Meiling lowers her eyes. "But that's all over with. SinoVenture is back on track. It would be to everyone's benefit, especially yours, for Eastern Star to stay on board and reap the rewards. Nothing like last month will ever happen again."

He gives her a penetrating look. "What's going on with Li Jing? Be honest. No one's seen him since the accident, and the rumor is that he's lost his mind. Now tell me: what happened? Why isn't he here?"

"Mr. Xu." She leans in, conspiratorial. "Surely you understand that as his wife, my first concern is for his health. Li Jing is going to be fine, and those rumors are just that: rumors. But it's true that he suffered some serious injuries, and he needs time to recover. If I let him out he'd be back in the office around the clock—you know that! But that punctured lung isn't going to heal itself. So I put my foot down, and I told him he's staying home until I let him out."

"And until then?"

"Until then, I'm in charge." Meiling pulls her shoulders back and looks straight at Mr. Xu. "Of course, Li Jing is advising me from home, he's making the calls. But I'm executing everything at the company."

Mr. Xu cocks his head to the side. "Well," he says, "as long as someone is in charge . . ."

"Most definitely. I understand your concern—things were a little rocky right after the accident. But as you can see from our numbers during the last two weeks, we're getting back on course, everything is running smoothly again, and the funds are heading up."

"Well done, Xiao Zhou. But you know, I wish you had gotten in touch with me and told me what's going on. The most frustrating thing was not being able to get in touch with anyone at SinoVenture. Li Jing and I have known each other for a long time. I could have helped."

"You're right, of course," Meiling demurs. "You have so much experience in these matters, Mr. Xu. Tell me, would it be an imposition if I called you for advice sometime? Of course I'm talking to Li Jing about everything too, but it would be so helpful to learn from a man like you."

"Anytime, Xiao Zhou. Anytime."

"And will you do one thing for me?"

"Of course."

"The rumors . . . they're just that, rumors. But if they get to Li Jing, he'd be very upset. Will you see"—she widens her eyes and bites her lower lip—"if you can get them to quiet down a bit? Li Jing is going to be fine, but I want him to recover in peace."

Mr. Xu nods gravely. "You're right to want to protect him."

She knows she has Mr. Xu now. She leans back in her chair with the assurance that Eastern Star's capital is not about to go anywhere. When he asks about the losses suffered by high-tech stocks, when he worries over the diversity of the international portfolios, she hones in on statistics and yields, extracting each piece of information at will, dispensing share prices down to the sixteenth, anticipating every doubt and demand. She has gotten through the tough part already. She has won him over and now she is just showing off. Looking across the table she catches Vice President Wu's eyes and lifts her eyebrows ever so slightly in triumph. The vice president does not recognize her look and continues wearing a dogged, anxious expression on her face. It makes Meiling miss Li Jing, the way he could read her face so well, how much they used to be able to understand with just one look between them. But then she pushes thoughts of him out of her head, pouring another glass of wine for Mr. Xu with a smile.

"I'm impressed," Mr. Xu says. "Li Jing prepped you well. I hope he knows that he's lucky to have you on his side. Pretty soon, though, you won't even need him. Heck, forget Zhang Qing. You're the one Li Jing should watch out for. If you ever decide to go into finance on your own, then I might be tempted to leave SinoVenture."

She comes home with a buzz in her head. She desperately wants to tell somebody how well she had done. It is past midnight by then and all the lights are shut off. She walks to each bedroom, opening the door quietly to slip in and stare at all three of them, sleeping in the same open-mouthed way. Pang Pang's blanket is askew; a copy of *The Monkey King* is still open on his chest. She closes the book and tucks the blanket around his shoulders, wanting to press a kiss to his forehead but pulling back because she doesn't want to wake him up. Professor Li's snores are shallow and irregular; but he sleeps on, the nurse dozing at his side. Meiling watches him, still not used to how weak he looks, still not used to the liver spots that seem darker now, trembling with age and decrepitude on his cheeks. In their bed, Li Jing is clutching her pillow tight, still in his T-shirt and sweatpants, asleep, but thrashing about occasionally. His jaw is shadowed with the beginnings of a beard, a strip of his stomach is exposed, pale and soft. She cannot bear the thought of getting in bed next to him and goes back out into the living room, kicking off her shoes, not bothering to set them in the closet. When she looks around she sees torn food packages piled in the armchair, video game controls sprawling across the floor, and then the open wreck of the computer on the coffee table, its belly ruptured, its copper hardware exposed. She looks away and closes her eyes but the memories rush in, insistent and unsparing. She lies down and tucks an arm beneath her head, wanting sleep, wanting to forget.

IN HIS DREAM the words slide out of his mouth, endless; sentences unspool and gather at his feet. He watches thoughts gather in the nape of his neck, these puffs of air, and then they pass through his throat, turning liquid when compressed through his larynx, finally becoming a solid, physical thing with a flick of his tongue, streaming out, piling up on the ground beside his feet.

He wakes up with the taste of speech on his tongue. What comes out of his mouth is *"I'm so sorry."* He does not think there could have been any hope left in his body, but there, in the split second before he hears the sound of English, he had felt a desperate, pathetic sense of hope, thrashing in his stomach, surging up.

English. The language of his childhood, eroded by time, the words siphoned off over the years until he didn't think there were any left. He had been a voracious reader as a kid. By the age of ten he had read *Robinson Crusoe, The Jungle Book*, dog-eared all the Tolkien in the

Charlottesville library. Later, in high school, he came across an English edition of *The Lord of the Rings* at a bookshop on Huaihai Road and bought it on a whim, remembering the nights when he would fall asleep reading it on the couch. When he opened the book the configurations of the alphabet looked so strange, strings of letters jumbled and unwieldy. He brought the book closer to his face, stared at the black marks across the pages. Words jumped into coherence: *Forest. Invisibility. Love.* Other words he could figure out by curving his mouth around one letter after the next, sounding them out, stringing them together. But the ease of reading was gone, the way his eyes used to gallop across the page, rushing through each paragraph to find out what would happen next. He put the book away on a high shelf and never opened it again. His English was hopeless, he thought. A few words of it would always wash ashore for him, but most of the written words had sunk out of his reach, irretrievable.

At times, before, he almost felt it as a wound, the loss of a language, all the words fading out of him through lack of use. The sound of it stayed with him, and he could muster up a smooth, unaccented English, pausing occasionally to hide his lack of total fluency. But he knew he was a fraud: he couldn't even read a newspaper, couldn't even read the same books he practically memorized as a kid. It was gone, he thought, all those words that he accumulated when he was young, pushed out by the Chinese that had come barging in when he came to Shanghai.

On the first day of fifth grade at the Hongqiao No. 2 Elementary School the teacher made him stand up in front of the class and introduce himself. *"My name is James,"* he said in English, and everyone giggled, clasped their hands over their mouths, tugged at the little red scarves around their necks. They looked like him, these kids; they had black hair and black eyes and round faces and smooth, skinny legs. But when they spoke he heard hard, stuttering words, words that seemed faintly familiar from Chinese restaurants or from his father's voice on the telephone late at night. He could make no sense of any of it. It frightened him not to know the language, and he felt utterly alone. He wanted to sit down and cry, but then the teacher put him next to a boy with a spiky haircut who nudged him and showed him a toy tractor under their desks. The boy smiled and said, *"Nǐhǎo."* He looked back and mimicked the sound: *"Nǐ hǎo."*

From then on Li Jing felt as though he had to wrench his brain open and fill it up with as much Chinese as possible. He gathered sounds from conversations or radio programs, tried to match them to the precise turns and exacting strokes of every Chinese character in his schoolbooks. English became useless. He shook loose all the words he knew, evacuating them to make room for Chinese. An easy, thoughtless abandonment.

Much later he wondered about the absence of those first words, the English, the way they seemed to disappear, as if their imprint in his synapses had been far too shallow to retain. How wrong he was. The words were there all along: embedded, burrowed into deep grooves, stifled by time and distance. It was English that had dug itself into the soft flesh of his mind, stayed intact through decades of inactivity, hidden itself beneath the Chinese that wove its dense, difficult webs. And now—he tries to think back to his dream, remember what language came out of his throat so easily—now it is English that swells triumphant, its every sound spitting contempt at the Chinese that displaced it for the past twenty-two years. English, with its grooves in his brain, its grip on his tongue, now the bully, trampling those damaged characters of Chinese, silencing their syllables.

Had he been speaking Chinese in his dream? Somehow it seems important to know, as if it could unlock his tongue. He shuts his eyes and burrows into the mattress, trying to lie as still as possible. If he can just stay still, then maybe he can fall back into the dream, the warmth of it, its ease, the way words came out of his throat, the way he didn't have to lock everything away inside his chest. In the dream speaking had been so easy, so freeing. He wasn't afraid anymore. He just wanted to say *I'm sorry.*

From down the hall a sound comes to him, a muffled yell, and then a bed creaking, heavy breaths, the bed creaking again. He springs up because a sharp pain is shooting from the base of his spine to his skull, because he knows something is wrong, and by the time he gets there his father's face is already bloodless and the nurse is on the bed, straddling him, pushing down into his chest with one hand on top of the other, trying to pump blood into his heart. A sound tears out of Li Jing's throat like flesh tearing across gravel. He stares at his father's open mouth, and takes a step forward, squeezing his father's hand, which is dangling off the side of the bed, which is cold to the touch, which does not squeeze back or even shiver.

The nurse is still kneeling on the bed, still pumping, her wide hips moving up and down in the air, determined, but obscene too. She turns around but keeps moving her hips and arms. "Go!" she hisses. "He's had a heart attack. Call an ambulance. Do it now!"

When he stumbles into the living room he sees Meiling lying on the couch. The side of her face looks smooth, still made up, and her stockings are lying on the carpet like a ruined cocoon. He picks up the telephone still staring at her, dials 120, but when the operator comes on the line he gurgles and then spits out a useless phrase of English. *"Help,"* he says before he can catch himself. *"My dad . . . heart attack."*

"I'm sorry, what did you say?" The operator's voice seems unperturbed. "Can you repeat that, sir? Try to be calm. Speak clearly."

But it's already too late, and he does not know how to repeat the phrase, not in the right language. He moans and leaves the phone on the kitchen counter. On the couch, her face is still quiet, like some painting, but how could she be oblivious to all of this? In the second before he wakes up Meiling he hesitates, wishes he could let her stay asleep. But then he is shaking her hard, hard enough to bruise, and when she opens her eyes he is already dragging her by the arm, down the hall, to the open door of Professor Li's bedroom, to the sight of his father lying there, without a breath, without a heartbeat.

V

LIMITS AND DIVISIONS

He remembers the first time he heard Rosalyn's voice. He didn't want to listen to anyone then, but he remembers noticing that throaty quality she had, the way her inflections swung wildly, like music, like something he couldn't quite make sense of, its trills and melodies inaccessible for a few sentences until it settled into him, mapping out its limits and divisions.

She is talking again. During their sessions it seems as though she is always talking. He locks on to her voice, its particular pitches, and listens, waiting for meaning to rise out of the muddle.

"I'm so sorry," she says. "I don't know what to say. I didn't know him well, but I liked your father very much. I'm so terribly sorry."

He does not want to think about his father, the finality of his absence, so he watches Rosalyn instead. He has been taking note of her quirks and habits during their sessions. She speaks in a hard, bouncing rhythm when she slips into medical jargon. She gestures constantly when trying to explain. She leans forward when she's focused but throws her entire body back when she laughs. She tends to tilt her voice up at the end of declarative sentences, occasionally tacking on "you know" and then looking you straight in the eye, taking you into her confidence. "How terrible for you and Meiling," she is saying now, "to find him like that in the morning. Dr. Feng told me there was nothing anyone could have done. But still, it must have been awful."

Boisterous America. Her chatter saving him from having to articulate his own grief. At the funeral the sun blazed down, scorching the grass, his leather shoes, the carved gravestone with its rows of intricate characters. People stepped around him, met his eyes and looked away; when they spoke to him he shook them off and turned his back. He had no tears, had nothing left, and so they rushed to Meiling with their sorrow, forming a line so that she could receive them one after another, gave her their frothing, useless words of sympathy. She gave them absolution.

He, the invalid, the imbecile, stood alone by the gravestone.

Li Shenjian. 1927–1999. Husband. Father. Teacher. Architect.

A blood clot in an artery. Another heart attack. This time, there was no rescue, just a rumble in his father's chest, a slow choke hold, a lack of oxygen.

While his father was dying he had been in the next room with his pathetic jealousy, his useless rage.

"You don't have to be here today, you know?" Rosalyn again.

"I know," he says, but does not tell her it is a relief to be sitting in front of her.

He shuts his mouth hoping she'll say more. He likes it when she talks, likes the way her face careens from one expression to the next, likes listening to her stories. It's easy to get lost in her voice, in the English that drifts warm and loose from her throat. If he can just focus on her, on accumulating all the precious words of English and slotting them away for use in his brain, then he doesn't have to remember the sight of his father panting with effort, rolling his wheelchair to the living room, doesn't have to imagine his father's heart pounding in fear, stretched past the breaking point. The operator's voice: "What did you say?" His father's bloodless face with its gaping mouth.

"My grandfather died right when I went off to college," she says after he stays silent for too long. She's in her storytelling mode now, and he can feel his shoulders relax, he rests his chin on his palm. "In some ways, I was closer to him than I was to my parents. He was the only one in my family who didn't treat me like a freak just because I got perfect test scores and wanted to go to medical school. Everyone else told me I'd be lucky to be a nurse, but grandpa told me that I was going to be a doctor.

"I was the one who noticed when he started forgetting things. The Alzheimer's was quick, and soon he didn't know any of us, not even me. And he'd stopped speaking English—he had grown up in Ireland, and near the end, he'd say everything in Irish Gaelic and get upset when no one understood. I told myself I was going to learn the language so I could talk to him, but it was too late. Two days into freshman orientation he passed away. We didn't have the money for me to make it back home for his funeral.

"So when I went home for Christmas Mom told me he'd left me something. They hadn't touched it, probably thinking that it was an heirloom, or a book of some kind—he was always finding me books at the junk store. But then when I opened the box there was just a half-full bottle of Irish whiskey and a little silver flask. The note said, 'Stay warm, Rosie. Don't let the Yankees get you down.'"

She laughs a little and it makes him wants to laugh too, even though he isn't quite sure what the word *flask* means. He clears his throat instead. Her hand flies up to her mouth, clasping it shut, and she says, "Oh god, I'm so sorry. Your father just passed away, and here I am, laughing. God, I'm such an idiot."

"No." How can he make her understand? "No, please talk. Laugh. I like it."

Her skin has a transparency to it, her every emotion visible. Now she is tender. Now she is sure of herself. "I've done enough talking," she says. "Why don't you talk instead?"

They both keep still for a minute, and he is reminded of their first few sessions together, how silent he was then, how much he wanted her to go away.

"My mother. Died. I was eight, you know?" He didn't know what he was going to say until the words come out of his mouth. Didn't know how easy it was to take on the cadences of her speech. "I remember," he says. "I am . . . remembering her."

A picture of his parents on their wedding day shows them in front of a San Francisco courthouse, squinting into the light. His father already had lines above his brows and at the corners of his eyes, but he was lean and handsome, wearing a borrowed seersucker suit. His mother was a head shorter, young and too intense-looking to be called beautiful. Even in the photograph she looked uncomfortable in her silk *qípáo*, tugging it across her hips, one shoulder bunched up near her ear.

For years he would have said that the photograph was all he remembered of his mother. It wasn't just her that faded out of him and left him grasping, it was all of it, those first ten years of his life. He could never remember much of his life in America, could only see its dim outlines, an occasional flickering detail. Other people could name their childhood playmates, remember scores from particular soccer games, reminisce about grade school teachers and the punishment they doled out. For him, those things were like underexposed photographs, the colors too pale to make out, the shapes blurry. It was as if in losing the language that all the memories had come encased in, he lost the memories themselves. Without phrases of English to anchor them, the memories dissipated, leaving him in the dark.

Everything that came after, in Shanghai, seems so vivid in contrast. He can remember holding his father's hand as the airplane descended into Shanghai: the city was so sprawling, bigger than anything he had ever seen before—he couldn't imagine who lived in all the tiny gray houses, how many people walked down the infinite turns of streets. He can remember taking the bus to the cemetery for the first time: his father had brought back his mother's ashes in a pale wood box, and they went to the management office of the cemetery together, his father buying a plot right then and there from a man whose stomach ballooned out beneath his plaid shirt. Every year since then, they went to the cemetery during the Qingming Festival to sweep her grave. Next spring, he will have to sweep two graves for the first time. Over the years he has gotten used to his mother's absence, but it is as if his father's death has reopened the wound, and now the loss of both of them has left him completely exposed.

Strange how he has been thinking of his mother more than he had in years. How in the weeks since the accident, since he has started speaking English again, he has unearthed little pieces of her, moments rising up into consciousness, making him gasp with their clarity. He remembers her cooking dinner with a red shawl wrapped around her shoulders, dancing across the kitchen with a spatula in her hand. He hears the sound of her yelling at his father, a phrase of Cantonese slipping out, cluttering her vivid, full-throated screams of English. And he remembers that little suit she bought for him from Woolworth's, much to his father's consternation because it was more than they could afford. The suit was made of a light blue polyester, with brass buttons. By the time he wore that suit to her funeral it was already too small, the trousers ending somewhere around his calves, his white socks exposed.

Rosalyn has put her elbows on the table and braces her face in her hands, peering at him. "Tell me more," she says.

The memories have risen out of him, tentative, shifting. When he hears his own voice it is as if he is recovering them all over again, the details sharpening and becoming clear. The images are set now, articulated, exposed to air. He is no longer afraid of their loss, now that he has given them a voice. He looks at Rosalyn, her open and waiting face. For so many years, America has receded away, as if evaporated into the air, but now it is drifting closer in spots and patches, details retrieved through his hesitant English. Edges of memories feel close enough to touch. "I am remembering," he tells her, relief and certainty flooding his chest.

"Did your mother speak Chinese around the house when you were a kid?"

He shakes his head, trying to unlodge his mother's voice. "I don't know."

"Try and remember."

"Difficult," he says. "I . . . remember in father's voice."

There were only small snippets of things that were his and his alone: the unraveling corner of a patchwork quilt, the brown velvet couch where he stayed up waiting for his dad. "Don't know," he says again. "Trying to hear her. Maybe? Maybe she spoke Chinese too?"

Maybe he had heard his mother cooing in Chinese as a baby. Maybe he embraced it so quickly years later, in her absence, as a way of finding her. There is no way to know. If only memory could be steadfast, something he could count on. But it shifts constantly and dangerously. Now that his father is gone there is no solid shape to his past anymore, no witness, only this space inside him that gapes empty, pushing everything closer to the surface of his skin.

"How are you, really?" she says. "How are you feeling about your father?"

Alone, he wants to tell her. He feels unanchored, as if he were adrift on an open sea without a compass, without any shore in sight. In his entire life he doesn't think he has ever said the words *I love you* to his dad; they were not that kind of people. But for as long as he can remember it has always been he and his father against the world, and since the accident, despite everything else, he had been able to take comfort in the fact that he got his father out of the Swan Hotel in time. The hospital had felt a little less lonely because he knew his father was in the same building. Being at home all day was easier to bear because they'd still play a game of chess in the afternoon or murmur in English on the nights when Meiling came home late. But he had dragged his father out of the Swan Hotel only to deal the blow himself a few months later. His guilt over his father's death beats relentlessly on with every pump of his own heart.

He shakes his head, trying to shake it off. "I don't know."

"Talk to me, James. I want to know if you're okay. You're not going to be like you were before, are you? Come on, say something."

He has burrowed deep into himself but the tone of her voice, almost childlike, makes him look up. He tries hard to grasp for more words in his head. This time he does not wade through the murkiness of Chinese with its inevitable failures. English is what he is looking for now, and though his diction is so limited, so corroded by time, a word bursts out of him, taking him by surprise.

"Shrink," he says.

"I'm sorry?"

"You, my shrink?" There, he finds it. Someone paid to listen to you talk. A doctor of the mind.

"I don't understand."

"You, my shrink?" He smiles to show her he is joking.

"Are you saying that I'm acting like a psychiatrist? Are you making fun of me?"

She freezes her face for a second with her mouth open, her tongue pink and wet against her lips. Then she is laughing, rolling her head back and snorting out her nose, shaking her shoulders, clasping a hand over her heaving chest. "You're hilarious!"

She acts as if he really is hilarious. Despite everything he believes her. "You are . . . like . . . shrink," he says, and it makes her laugh more.

That singular word, *shrink*, dislodged after decades. Where had it come from? A television show? A novel he read? Some kid in elementary school spitting out the syllable during recess, its sleek, diamond-cut sound embedding itself into his brain? If he could remember this word now, then what else could he remember? Those other words, those Chinese words, are they in there somewhere too, in hiding? Could he learn to speak them again?

Rosalyn's laughter trails off. "If I sounded too much like a psychiatrist just now, then I'm sorry. I didn't mean to do it. I don't want us to have that kind of relationship. I just wanted to ask how you're feeling. I just want to be a friend."

He's not used to someone who offers herself up so easily. Are all Americans like this? This constant rush to confession? This saying exactly what they mean? Rosalyn smiles as if she wants his approval, with her hair loose, her shoulders curving in. She did something to the room, saturated the air in it with this openness, this sense of possibility. The two of them are having an actual conversation, he thinks. He made her laugh!

"I . . . am fine. Don't need shrink." He tries to keep the joke going.

"I think you're right, James. I think you're going to be okay."

She looks confident enough for the both of them, and something unclenches in his stomach.

"Thank you," he says, sincere.

Her eyes flick away from his face and look down.

He notices things much more now. Without speech he has been reduced to being an observer. He has learned to watch people, notice the tension in their shoulders, the changing color of their ears, the contradictions between their faces and their words. Before his father died Li Jing had seen how tense and afraid he was by the way he twisted his fingers against each other in his lap. When he looks at Meiling he sees her disgust and her anger that she tries to hide, how she holds her face as still as possible, keeping her emotions under lock and key.

Rosalyn, on the other hand, is an open book. She looks at him and her face exposes everything. He doesn't even have to ask.

"James," she says, struggling to smile. "I'm going to have to leave soon. My fellowship is coming to an end, the woman whose apartment I'm living in is coming back. I think you've done so well, and that you're on your way to a partial recovery. I'm going to work really hard with Dr. Feng and Dr. Liu on a plan of action for you. Anyway, it's time for me to go home."

He hears her say the word *home*, sees her eyelids fluttering, the room darker now. She has no desire for America.

"I wish I could stay longer, James. And not just because I want to follow through with my research." She has a habit of making everything easy for him. "You're my favorite patient, you know?"

"Your . . . single patient. Your only patient."

She laughs valiantly but her chuckle is a dry, raspy one, unsustainable.

The trouble with English is its distance, the limited number of words he has easy access to, the way he is always searching, trying to remember words from so long ago. He knows what he wants to tell her, the ache of it in his stomach, and stares at her bitten nails on the wooden table, trying to explain—

She says it for him. "I'm going to miss you."

CHAPTER 19

Up on the roof there are no fences or thresholds. There is only a line at the edge of the shingles, dividing solid ground from the steep drop of air. Pang Pang slides down a little more so that he can see over the side of the roof into the narrow street below. From three stories up he watches figures moving across the sidewalk, their heads little black circles going forward, walking back.

Despite the heat there are goose bumps on his arms. The tall buildings on the next block form a wind tunnel, and the wind keeps whipping through his hair; he can hear a faint, whistling sound. Other buildings block his view, but through their gaps he can look into the horizon, seeing high-rises, clustered together, menacing even from so far away.

A pigeon swoops around the roof and lands close to him, pecking at its own feet. It coos once, flaps its turquoise feathers, hops a few steps forward, approaching Pang Pang. He tries to keep completely still. "Hello, Mr. Bird." He stretches out a hand.

There is a solitude to being on the roof. Here, he can be alone and watch over the city. Things kept happening recently, things that flared out of control when he wasn't paying attention. Then he'd see his mom coming toward him. She'd crouch down so that they could see eye to eye. She'd have that nervous look on her face, then she'd tell him something that struck him like a brick on the head or something dropped out of the sky.

Bad things happened, Pang Pang thinks, when he wasn't paying attention, because he wasn't paying attention. He had gone back over them again and again, combing through the details, searching for clues. That afternoon when the Swan Hotel crumpled down as he watched from the balcony. The night his father threw the computer against the wall. Each time he had been so afraid, and then when it seemed all over he was so relieved that he stopped paying attention right away. It was this turning away, he decides, this lack of vigilance, that made things even worse. When he thinks about it now, he realizes that he should have known that something else lurked just around the corner. The moment he let his guard down things erupted again: his mom coming home, saying, "Your dad's been in an accident" as if they were in a movie; and then, again, that morning, the sound of heavy footsteps coming down the hall, two men in uniform standing over his grandfather's bed.

The pigeon hops toward him, and then hops back away, wary of getting closer. "It's all right, Mr. Bird." He knows just how the bird feels; it's smart not to let its guard down. "I won't hurt you, Mr. Bird. I'll just sit here for now, and you can sit wherever you want to sit. You have to be careful. You know that, don't you? You have to pay attention so that nothing bad happens."

There are shouts ringing out from the window. The summer school instructor, with her thin, young voice, calls out, sounding like she's about to cry. "Please come back inside," she says, "but be careful. Crawl slowly, carefully if you can." But he just wants to stay outside in the sun by himself, stare out at everything around him, learn to pay attention to all these scenes and people and details at once, practicing his vigilance so that nothing bad would happen to his family again. The pigeon flies away in a flurry of feathers, gliding over the sharp roofs of the brick houses across the street, shooting into the heart of the city. "Goodbye," Pang Pang shouts, and stares at the shape of the bird, watches it disappear despite the sunlight that shunts straight into his eyes. "Good luck, Mr. Bird. Stay alert. Be careful."

If he could just stay out here he'd be able to keep watch over it all, see into the city to the west and look across the river, toward all the office buildings and the Oriental Pearl Tower in the east. All he wants to do is stand guard against whatever is coming. He practices staring out onto the horizon but keeping the streets in sight too.

"Pang Pang! Oh Pang Pang, what are you doing out there?"

When he hears his mom's voice he swivels around so fast that his teacher gasps and his mom lurches forward out of the window, reaching two arms toward him, falling short and then crying out. He scans over the rooftops and clotheslines, looks up as if checking for meteors and stars, and then turns over so that he is on his stomach, tilts his head toward the drop just over the edge of the roof, seeing all the lampposts and bicyclists below. Then he starts crawling back toward the window, slowly. His mom is still crying out, "Be careful!" He doesn't want to go back inside, he won't be able to see as much when he's inside again, but his mom is waiting there, and the promise of her arms around him makes everything else recede.

PANG PANG DOES not cry when he comes back in from the window. Meiling is the one who breaks down sobbing until she feels his small hands on her arm, patting her awkwardly, saying, "Nothing bad is going to happen again." She thinks, for a minute, of just taking him to the airport and getting on a plane to Sichuan. They could go to her parents' house, take mid-afternoon naps or go swimming in the river. Her parents are not the type to ask any questions, but they would fuss and flutter, bringing bowls of soup and pieces of fruit, spoiling Pang Pang with treats and toys. The promise of running away sounds heavenly. She lets her shoulders sag and closes her eyes. When she opens them again she looks at Pang Pang's face. His jaw is set as sharp as a small shovel, and he looks so determined to be brave that she can only hug him and try to smile.

Her cell phone begins to ring with demands and reminders from the office. She doesn't want to take Pang Pang back to the apartment, where the door to Professor Li's room has stayed shut, where Li Jing sits in the living room silent, as if still in a state of shock. So she drops Pang Pang off at Nanny Chang's house and explains what happened. The nanny collects her fee and smiles, showing the gaps in her teeth. "He'll be all right," the nanny says. "He's just a kid. He doesn't know any better."

When she is in the taxi she begins to cry again. Pang Pang does know better; she can tell that every loss registers like a piece of shrapnel beneath his skin, hidden but insidious, burrowing toward his heart. Then the driver is asking where she wants to go, and without thinking about it she says, "Pudong," she begins to gather herself, preparing for the afternoon ahead in her other life. She thinks of it as work now: not *his office*, or *her stepping in*, but just work, the business sections to scan in the morning, the endless e-mails on the computer screen, the phone ringing all day long, the lunches and dinners with men whose names and positions she can barely keep track of. It offers comfort, strangely. It keeps her too busy to think about things, to remember the past, to mourn or worry endlessly. The stock market hurtles forward at break-neck speed, the pace of it obliterating all past and future, and she is forced to focus on the moment, everything—money, shares, time— becoming numbers, abstract and almost beautiful, weightless.

Her brain has thrown itself into this new work with surprising vigor, routing itself into new pathways, allowing her to discover aptitudes she didn't know she had. Every hour is filled with decisions, the choices emerging, doubling, splitting infinitely. To keep up means no second-guessing, no time to reflect. It is always a binary of zeros and ones: up or down, buy or sell. She operates in a realm of balances and equations, of adjustments and variables, tinkering with each investment until it clicks into place like a line of poetry. When to buy, how many shares, and when to sell have become a new kind of rhythm, a puzzle to figure out, the exactitude of the answers not entirely unlike the break of stanzas, the substitution of one word for another, the choice of a colon instead of a comma. The creation of perfect scrolls of numbers or words.

She made money. She lost money, too, but mostly, she made money. Vice President Wu has been impressed, has said, with a meaningful look, that Li Jing has put the company in good hands. They stopped talking about him weeks ago. The other people in the office don't ask after him anymore. Investors and businessmen ask directly for Meiling, now, when they call. Whatever might have been known or rumored about Li Jing's condition fell away in the face of profits and Meiling's competence. Her assistant had printed up a box of business cards for her, and when she saw them on her desk, she dropped the file she was holding, sending pale pieces of paper fluttering all over the room. Still, she has tucked a small stack of cards into her purse: *Zhou Meiling, Interim President.*

Her cell phone rings, and it is Dr. Feng on the other end, reminding her that Dr. Neal will soon go back to America, reminding her that Li Jing is no closer to speaking Chinese than he was almost eight weeks ago. When she hangs up her legs begin to shake. The cab pulls off the elevated highway and begins to turn onto the bridge to Pudong. In the distance she can see the familiar sight of all the skyscrapers chaotic against the horizon. She leans forward, restless, and tells the driver that she's changed her mind, that she wants to turn back. Without acknowledging her the driver slams on the brakes and then turns wide and breathless into the opposite lane of traffic, drawing honks and curses, scraping by another car with a few centimeters of room. Meiling dials Alan's number, asking him to call Rosalyn Neal on her behalf, asking him to meet her at the hospital as soon as possible.

When she walks through the automatic doors, the smell of the hospital crawls up her nose and she is overwhelmed by the memory of pain and disaster and death. She goes out of her way to avoid the emergency room and the row of doctors' offices on the third floor. She cannot face the possibility of what would have happened if they had brought Professor Li here more quickly; she cannot face all the doctors and nurses who have become so familiar to her now.

There's no one in Dr. Neal's office, so she stands outside the door, not leaning back against the wall, not touching anything. From down the hall she hears a voice call out, and when the sound flies foreign past her ear she looks up to see the American woman trotting toward her, tucking her red hair behind her ears.

Dr. Neal waves her into her office, says something bright, shaped like a question.

Meiling shrugs and shakes her head. She sits down and they both look at the clock, waiting for Alan, before turning to each other with sheepish smiles.

"Mrs. Li." Dr. Neal opens her palms and gestures toward the water cooler, pulling out paper cups from her desk drawer.

Meiling shakes her head no but says thank you. And then they sit back, awkward, both of them darting their eyes. Meiling sneaks peeks at Dr. Neal, at her pink skin dotted with freckles, her bright blue shirt, cut low enough to show off the shadow between her breasts, her half-painted, half-chewed fingernails tapping away on the desk. This the woman she is forced to put her faith in.

"Neal *yīshēng*," Meiling says. The syllables for *doctor* awkward in her mouth.

"Rosalyn." Dr. Neal points at herself. "Raahselynn."

The name, stretched out, sounds like something sinister, a slow drift of vowels, a ghost. Dr. Neal presses her hand to her heart. "Raahselynn. *Call me Rosalyn,*" she says.

"Rai-Si-Ling." Meiling can hear the sounds change shape in her own mouth, their tails cut off, their duration truncated. She tries it again—"Rai-si-ling"—trying to glue the sounds together, imitate the soft, wet shape of the name.

"Rosalyn Neal." The woman says her name again.

One long blurry sound without demarcation, without corners or edges. "Rai-si-ling." Meiling mutters the name to herself this time, aware of the way it breaks into pieces on her tongue.

For so long she had thought of the woman as Neal *yīshēng*, as Li Jing's doctor, like a character on the fringe of a play who has a function but no name, who passes through the scenery, utters her lines, and then disappears into the wings. But now here she is: Raisiling Ne-al. The syllables of her name pin down the soft, smiling face with its exotic features and foreign expressions.

"Raisiling." She points at the doctor and then points back at herself. "Zhou Meiling."

"Zoman-Lee."

"Zhou Mei Ling."

"Zoemay Lynn."

Chinese, with its tones, its divisible sounds, its sharp, inflective syllables, allows for no imprecision. Her name, on Rosalyn Neal's tongue, loses its clarity and collapses in a heap.

"Zoemay Lynn."

"Raisiling."

When Alan comes in they are still repeating each others' names, miming "Thank you," miming "You're welcome." With nowhere to sit he finds a corner and waits for them to begin. Meiling turns to him, asking if they might find him a chair down the hall.

"I was sorry"—Alan waves no and settles in—"to hear about Professor Li."

"Thank you," she says, turning away.

"Dr. Neal. Rosalyn," Meiling starts again, all business now. "Your time here is supposed to end in a little more than a week."

"I'm afraid so. And I know that Li Jing has still not made very much progress in Chinese. He's able to repeat words and fragments, but spontaneous production remains difficult. This is typical of patients with nonfluent aphasia, but there are exercises that can be pursued, especially translation exercises, that might offer up additional possibilities for bilingual aphasics. I've been working with Li Jing on some of these exercises, and I'm leaving extensive notes for Dr. Liu."

"But you're the only one getting through to him! Even Dr. Feng admits that Li Jing seem to respond the best to your work with him."

"That's because for now, speaking in English is far less frustrating for him."

"Then it'd be better for him to keep speaking English, don't you think?"

"That's . . . debatable. It might be better for him to focus on Chinese—"

"I don't know what we're supposed to do once you leave."

When Meiling listens to Alan speak, the conversation sounds calm, leisurely, as if they're discussing the mildest of topics, as if they're chatting about the weather over tea. But she can hear her own voice getting high-pitched and wobbly. She tries to rein it in, turning to Rosalyn again.

"Everyone says that he needs individualized attention. Who will give him that, if not you? Do you need to go back to American right now? What if you stay?" Forced to beg, Meiling sits up even taller but keeps her eyes downcast, not wanting to let Rosalyn see the desperation on her face. "We can make it worth your while."

Alan looks at her sharply before translating her words into English.

"Meiling." Rosalyn garbles the name but Alan says it smoothly, carefully. "There are excellent doctors here who will continue to work with him. Being here and working with Li Jing has been an amazing experience, one I wouldn't trade for the world. But I have to go back to America. The fellowship is over and I have to give up my apartment. Logistically, leaving is the only thing that makes sense."

Meiling sees an opening and pounces. "The length of the fellowship was arbitrary. I asked the hospital to arrange it as they saw fit. Now I can just pay your salary directly. I can find you an apartment. Or, you can come and stay with us. We have an extra room now—you'd keep working with Li Jing, in much the same way you have been."

She had decided to ask Rosalyn Neal to stay in the cab ride back to the office. Her mind focused in on the possibility of it, latched on, and refused to let go. If Rosalyn Neal stays in Shanghai, for just a few more weeks, another month or two, then there is a chance that Li Jing could still improve. But if she leaves now, then he will just sit silent in front of Dr. Liu, in front of the television, across from her at the dinner table, with no one he could talk to, no hope of recovering anything at all.

"I don't know, Meiling," Rosalyn says. "That's rather . . . unorthodox."

"Stay. Please stay, Rosalyn. I think my husband needs you," Meiling says.

When Alan looks at Meiling again she simply shrugs, giving him a sad smile. She has run out of options, and asking Rosalyn Neal to stay for a few more weeks seems, at least, like not entirely giving up on the possibility of Li Jing's recovery. Somewhere in the back of her mind, she wonders if she is trying to assuage her own guilt, to pass Li Jing off so that he is someone else's responsibility, so that she doesn't have to deal with him. But the thought floats away like smoke. She stares again at Rosalyn's plain, freckled, American face.

"I don't think . . ." Rosalyn starts, and then trails off.

"Don't say no right now," Meiling says. "In fact, don't say anything at all. It's a big decision, but we would all be so grateful if you stayed, Dr. Neal. I really do believe that my husband needs you, Rosalyn. I think you, too, could get a lot out of the arrangement. Take your time, please. Think it over."

CHAPTER 20

"Please follow the trajectory of my finger."

She swings her index finger back and forth. He leans back and looks up at the ceiling instead. She follows his glance and looks around: her sad little office, with the fluorescent lights, old medical texts lining the walls. She had doodled in them occasionally, finding diagrams and coloring them in, correcting some of the more inexact illustrations, filling in details from the last thirty years of physiology. Now that she is about to go, the doodles might be the only traces she leaves behind. Nothing else: no results, little research. She has nothing to show for herself.

"When," he says, "do you leave?"

"A week. My flight's scheduled for next Tuesday. I'll be home by the sixteenth."

Home. Alone in that silent house on Hardenburg Lane. Even when she turns on all the lights the darkness never lets up at night.

She looks at him, admiring his face, trying to impress it into her memory. He has cut his hair and his bruises have all healed, but there is still a tightly wound energy beneath his skin, something darker, more compelling waiting to be found. It is hard to look away from him now. When she sighs and passes him a stack of worksheets for sentence completion, he shakes his head, tells her that with a week left, they should skip therapy and wander around the city instead. His speech still trickles out, slow, but he is far more certain of himself. When he gets up out of his seat and waits for her by the door, she does not hesitate to grab her bag and walk out of the hospital by his side.

As soon as they leave the air-conditioned cool of the hospital Rosalyn begins to sweat. It's almost the middle of July, and the sun hammers down, vicious, the light almost pulverized. She doesn't know how all these women in Shanghai can just float by in little wispy silk dresses in this heat, their faces dewy and flushed instead of streaked with sweat. Today she has broken the unspoken dress code at the hospital with her shorts and a sleeveless cotton blouse, but it doesn't seem to matter. At the hospital, she thinks, there is a tacit understanding that she's a lost cause. None of the other doctors seem to have much to say to her anymore.

She squints as they walk down the street. She has forgotten her sunglasses, and holds a hand out, shielding her eyes. He grabs her arm and pulls her to the other side of him, allowing her to walk in the shade. She notices his touch on her skin. She does not ask where they are going and he does not tell her.

"I'm being a terrible doctor, letting you boss me around like this," she says. "Promise that when you get home you'll practice writing in English for a while? If nothing else, that'll give you more phrases to enter into the dictionary, and it'll make me feel less guilty!" He laughs and she keeps talking, knowing that he likes it. "Of course, if I'd known we were going on an adventure today, I would have worn different shoes."

They go to lunch at the noodle restaurant near the hospital that they had gone to before. The same waitress comes up and says hello, settles them into the same booth and brings out two steaming bowls of noodles without being asked. They chat about the hospital and the weather, suddenly shy, her departure changing something between them. He pays, waving off her money, and they are lulled back outside, the heat and humidity easier to bear now.

"I don't know what I'm going to do once I leave," Rosalyn says. "There are no great Chinese restaurants back home, you know, and I've gotten used to eating so well."

"Not hard. Cook. Just a bowl of noodles."

She stops walking and glares at him. "Really? So you'd be able to make it, just like that, just like at the restaurant?"

"No." He makes a face. "But I learn."

"Maybe. But I wouldn't be able to. I can't cook a thing, and I have absolutely no interest in learning." She starts walking again. "The one bad thing about where I live is that it's far from town, and there aren't any restaurants nearby. We've eaten a lot of frozen dinners over the years. About fifteen miles away, there's a little Tex-Mex place called Isabella's. It's nice there, homey, like the place we just went to. We used to go there a couple of nights a week and Isabella always treated us like we were family."

"You and . . . ?"

"Ben. Me and Ben." She has wanted to tell him about Ben. It seemed important, somehow, to say it before she left. "My husband."

"You are married?" He asks the question smoothly, without his usual hesitation before speaking, the surprise of it jarring him into easy articulation.

"Was married. I was married. I signed my divorce papers right before I came to Shanghai."

"Sorry."

"It's okay. It was probably for the best. We wanted different things," she says flatly. "It's hard right now, but it was the right thing to do."

They walk up to an intersection, swinging their arms, and it feels, now, like the distance between her arm and his body is pulsing. The light turns red, and they are standing on an island between opposing lanes of traffic. It seems a long way to the other side of the intersection, a long way back as well, though she does not look back. Cars rush by, the air humming with speed, and it makes her feel like her body is a delicate, precarious thing, balanced on this thin strip of concrete. Next to her, he seems so certain and solid that she wants to touch him, wants to hold on. But then the light changes and they keep walking, dabbing their faces with their hands, passing the heated hoods of cars.

He takes her on a bus because, he explains, he can no longer say the names of streets to taxi drivers. When the bus turns wide she loses her footing and crashes into other passengers, giggling and drawing stares.

"Not used to buses?" he says in a low voice, and puts a hand on her shoulder to steady her, his mouth hot at her ear.

"I guess not." She looks up into his face, smiling. "It's a good thing you're around, keeping me on my feet."

The bus accelerates onto an elevated highway that belts straight into the heart of the city, skyscrapers on either side of the road so close you could almost reach out and touch them. Once it pulls off the main road it stops behind a long line of cars, and in the distance, she can hear the sound of a train passing by, and then fading away. They start moving again, and out the window there are women in high heels pumping hard on dusty bicycles, their thin skirts flapping in the wind. Rosalyn lets her eyes glaze over in the heat, lets herself sink into her thoughts. Two months in Shanghai, and what does she have to show for herself? She had been full of plans on the plane ride over, had studied her phrase book as if cramming for an exam, had been determined to refine her computational model with a new set of data, expecting insights and breakthroughs, plotting notes for a new article. Only the time has trickled away so quickly. She has meandered through the days chatting with James instead of compiling data. At night, she has gone out to dinners and bars. His Chinese has not improved; her computational model has barely been touched. She does not know what she has been doing with herself, and now an airplane six days away is waiting for her.

The bus turns again and she lets herself brush up against him. With so little time left it's all already a lost cause and there can be no consequences for her actions. When they get off at the ferry docks she stares up at a large ship the color of rust and grabs his arm, clutching tight.

"Where are you taking me?" she says, laughing.

"To park in Pudong, across the river." His English gets better all the time.

He pulls her onto the ferry and lets his hand rest on her wrist. They are penned into the bottom deck with a huge crowd, and they fight their way to the rear of the boat, watch white water froth in its wake. The metal gates of the dock close up as the boat pulls away. There are so many people that they are forced to stand close together, and she shifts weight off her right leg and leans into his body.

"Why divorce?" he says, his eyes steady on her face.

As they leave the shore behind, Shanghai comes into focus, and she can see the baroque buildings of the Bund farther up the bank, the dense crowd on the promenade smudging into bits of color. Skyscrapers poke out all over the city, without rhyme or reason. The sun is distorted behind clouds and its dull light hovers over buildings, casting muddy rays on their façades.

"Reasonable reasons," she snorts. "Irreconcilable differences."

Shanghai in the heat of summer: all its dust kicked up and refracted. A dirty outline. The air thick with exhaust.

"We always planned on having kids, but we wanted to wait for me to finish residency and for him to finish graduate school. Makes sense, right? Well, when it was finally time, when it felt like our lives—our real lives—were finally about to start, I discovered that my fallopian tubes were blocked. Conceiving naturally was impossible."

She keeps looking at the city on the west side of the river, watching it move farther and farther away, not turning her head to meet his eyes. He puts a hand over hers on the railing, gives it a squeeze and waits for her to begin again.

"I wanted kids. So did he. So we went through a round of in vitro that resulted in a miscarriage, and another round that left me exhausted and resentful. In vitro is an awful process—debilitating and expensive—and it doesn't even have a high success rate. For us, it seemed like it wasn't going to happen, so I focused on adopting—it didn't matter to me whether our kids were biological or not. To my surprise and maybe even to his own surprise, Ben wasn't okay with just having adopted kids. He's an only child, and he wanted the kids to be ours. He kept saying that we should keep trying. But I . . ." Her voice cracks and she tightens her hold on his hand. "I didn't want to anymore, and I thought it would still be okay. I thought that ultimately, he would choose me."

There are smaller boats in the river. Long, skinny boats piled high with coal, men with poles standing at the stems, gazing out from beneath their wide-brimmed straw hats, not needing anyone.

"We talked about it for months. It was awful, all the back and forth, me feeling like I wasn't good enough, that it was my problem, my body letting us down. I really thought we were going to figure it out, but it turned out that I was wrong. He wasn't the one whose body was being tortured by all these treatments, but he wanted me to keep doing it, and I refused; neither of us would budge. Still, it was a shock when he asked me for a divorce. He kept saying that it was the only sensible thing to do."

James makes a choking sound in his throat, but she doesn't turn to look at him. If she looks at him she might never be able to get out what she wants to get out.

"It all seemed so horrifyingly civilized, which made it worse. I couldn't be angry at him, not really, because supposedly, we had made the decision together. So I had to watch him move out like I had some say in it too. When it came time, I hugged him goodbye, and then he was gone. And our future, the one we talked about all the time? That was gone too. Suddenly that life, the one I had been picturing in my head, the one that was going to be secure and happy and long-lasting, didn't exist anymore. After the divorce I felt like the past ten years of my life had been erased: I don't really know what I'm supposed to do anymore. I don't even know who I am."

He pulls her into his arms and holds her. She does not cry, but it is comforting to have his warmth against her skin.

"I'm sorry," he says. "It sounds hard. I didn't . . . we didn't know, if Meiling could have child. Her back problem. Doctors said maybe no children."

The ferry clanks into the other shore and lurches from side to side. She opens her mouth again with the unfairness of all of it. "But she did have a child. You have Pang Pang now."

"We didn't know if it was possible."

"He looks so much like you. That's what Ben wanted, a child who looked like him. You didn't have to choose, after all," she says, with a trace of bitterness. "You have a beautiful son."

He lifts her chin and looks straight at her. "I chose," he says. "It was hard, but I chose . . . Meiling, without child. Then, we were lucky. But I chose."

The other passengers begin to disembark, and they are left standing alone along the rear of the boat. She looks at him, her face quivering, and he hugs her tighter, so tight that it is hard for her to breathe. She wants to stay there, in his arms, but then the ticket taker walks by and shoos them off the boat. He keeps an arm around her and whispers, "Sorry" in her ear. They walk to an empty park right on the water, with spectacular views of the city, trees everywhere. She opens her mouth again, looking up at his face, wanting him to understand: "I don't know how to go on or who I am without him. Ben was the only person I've ever loved."

ON SATURDAY DANNY comes to pick her up with yellow chrysanthemums bunched in his arms. "Rosalyn," he laments in her doorway, and then pulls her into his arms. "I'm going to miss you so much."

"I'm going to miss you too," she tells him, and is surprised to find herself sincere, with tears in her eyes. Danny tells her he'll just leave his moped outside her apartment and begins to hail a cab. She pulls him back toward the bike, gesturing for him to get on.

The first time she'd ridden on the back of the moped with him she had been exhilarated by the city. This time there's a feeling of melancholy as the wind blows softly across her face. She wants to take everything in, remember every street, every storefront. And she wants the smell of it too, and the sounds roaring in her ear.

They pull up to Yuyuan Garden and walk through the night market in the old city. The labyrinthine pathways are lined with stalls selling antiques and trinkets, and the lights dazzle, the crowd is loud and electric. An old temple rises out of the middle of a pond, and Danny takes her hand and walks her over the winding bridge to the temple, ushering her through the door of one of the oldest restaurants in the city. It makes her remember the feel of James's hand in hers, on the boat, and she lets go of Danny and crosses her arms in front of her chest.

Clarissa and Patrick are there already, in a private room on the second floor. Patrick shakes his head—"Don't go, honey," he says—and Clarissa hugs Rosalyn fiercely. "What am I going to do without you?"

"Oh, Clarissa," Rosalyn says. "I'm going to miss you. I'll e-mail. I promise I will."

Out the window the sky is full of clouds dissolving the moon. At the table, her friends raise their glasses with their faces glum, each of them lost in their own thoughts. The waiter knocks on the door and courses of food begin to appear. Danny, as usual, has ordered a feast. But they sit dully, the four of them, barely talking, barely making a dent in the meal. The waiter keeps running in to refill their glasses with champagne, asking, "What do you need?" in an awkward, worried English.

Danny tries to rally them. "This is supposed to be a celebration," he says. "Come on, have another glass of champagne."

None of them stir and then he gets up to stand next to the window. After a few minutes of silence, he seems to deflate too.

"I hate that you're leaving." Danny's voice carries a plaintive tone she's never heard from him before. "All along, I knew you were going to leave. But some part of me was hoping you'd stay. It's going to be lonelier without you here."

"Danny—" Rosalyn walks up behind him and puts a hand on his shoulder. "I'm sorry. I'm going to miss you too, you know? I'm going to be lonelier without you, without all of you, but I have to go."

Clarissa sighs at the table, looking up at Rosalyn. "Everyone always has to go. Everyone always leaves this place. People pass through here, and you get attached to them, but then they just leave you behind. You'd think we'd be used to it by now."

"What do you mean?" Rosalyn says. "This is your home. Of course it's sad when friends leave, but you don't need me, Clarissa. Your life here is amazing. All of you—it's like you've been given the keys to the city. Everything is at your fingertips."

"It's not a bad life, I'll admit. But it's not home," Patrick cuts in. "It'll never really be home."

Rosalyn pours more champagne into everyone's glasses and raises hers in a toast. "What's so great about home anyway? Home is too many hours at work and grocery shopping at midnight. It's watching cable on the couch and all the stores closed on Sunday. It's going to the same bar you always go to, the one where they barely know how to make a cocktail and where everyone's watching college football. Fuck home." The others raise their eyebrows but raise their glasses too, watching Rosalyn sway, maudlin and tipsy. "Here's to Shanghai!" She downs her drink in one gulp. "Where I met wonderful people who took me under their wings, where I finally started having fun again, and where I felt . . . special, like I got to have a brand-new start and make my own way in the world again. Here's to all of you!" Rosalyn's glass is empty and her face is flushed. "God, I'm going to miss this place so much. I'm really going to miss all of you."

There had been times when she was unsure of all of them, when she wasn't even certain that she liked any of them. Clarissa complained about her boyfriend constantly and treated waitresses and salesclerks like servants. Patrick showed up every week with a different girlfriend; when he got drunk he would joke about the Chinese in a way that made everyone around him ill at ease. And Danny, sweet Danny, who was kind and attentive and completely devoted to her, but whom, she has acknowledged from time to time, she found a little dull. But now, on the verge of her departure, she is filled with affection for them. She stands by the window and smooths her hands over her white dress, smiling, holding the black night at bay.

"Really," she says, "living here has been amazing. I'm so sad to be leaving all of you. I don't want to go, I wish . . ."

Clarissa looks up, accusatory and affectionate at the same time. "Then don't go! Why don't you stay here for another month or two?"

"Yeah, don't go," Danny and Patrick chime in and walk over to stand on both sides of her, trapping her with their arms as she laughs, shaking her head. "We're kidnapping you and keeping you here," they tell her. "We're not going to let you get on that plane."

"What is it"—Rosalyn is still laughing—"with everyone wanting me to stay? My patient's wife wanted me to stay too. She offered me a salary and a room in her house."

"So take it!" Clarissa says. "That's perfect. You can stay here for the rest of the summer."

"It's crazy! I'm not going to go live with my patient."

"Why not?" Danny says. "You'd just be working for them directly instead of for the hospital. It makes sense that she would want you to stay."

"Okay, now you're all ganging up on me." Rosalyn sticks out her tongue. All three of them glance at each other, looking happy and conspiratorial.

"You have to admit that your stay seems fated now—you've got a place to live and work to do. Come on, stay! We'll have such a good time!" Clarissa says.

"Rosalyn." Danny smiles, his sincerity transforming his face, making him handsome. "Stay. Really, just for another few weeks. What's so important that you need to get home in a hurry? What's waiting for you there?"

VI

HOME

All it takes is one taxi ride. Her black nylon suitcases. A few overstuffed shopping bags. Her purse with its fraying strap. Rosalyn leaves the small, dark apartment on the first floor, smiling and nodding goodbye at the neighbors. The taxi flies past her breakfast stand; past the toothpaste factory down the block that permeates the air with a sweet, sickening smell by the end of every afternoon; past all the clotheslines in the sky, waving their cartooned underwear, their unraveling tanktops; past the walk-up apartment buildings, spotted from peeling paint, water stains running down from the gutters like exposed wounds. Once the car pulls onto the highway she loses sight of her little neighborhood. The familiar blocks are swallowed up by miles of thrusting concrete. She touches her cheek to the window, feeling the heat gathered on the other side of the glass. She has ridden in so many taxis since she has been in Shanghai, more than she had in her entire life. It will be another few weeks before she leaves this city behind.

The car drives past metal gates and pulls into a forest of condominiums. Rosalyn catches sight of the three of them waiting for her on the sidewalk. Lined up and sober, they look like a photograph of a family from a real estate brochure. For a moment she wants to tell the cabdriver to keep going, but then the door is already being opened, Meiling is grasping her hand, and James has lifted her suitcase out of the trunk, pulling it across the walkway and into the lobby.

"Rosalyn," Meiling says, changing the sound of her name into something new and strange, and then turns to her son, nodding for him to go ahead.

"Hello how are you." Pang Pang mutters the phrase of English dutifully but looks off into space. "Good morning. Good night. Thank you. Goodbye."

They take a long, silent elevator ride up to the thirty-fourth floor. When they walk into the apartment James and Meiling head down the hall, pulling her suitcases and bags. But Rosalyn stands in the doorway, looking around the space, hesitating, as if—as if taking a single step into their home meant crossing a line in the sand.

She crosses the threshold and walks in. The apartment is furnished in clean, sleek lines, the pale leather sofa mod and spotless, the cream-colored walls carefully dotted by inky landscapes. Shelves of books are lined up and meticulous behind glass doors. The only burst of vivid color in the room is a bowl of yellow roses on the coffee table. It looks like a museum or a showroom, curated to perfection, devoid of personal effects. There seem to be no traces of the people who live here, no photographs or a coat flung astray.

She smooths her fingers over the shiny blond wood of the dining table and then tries to scrub away the smudges with the hem of her shirt. An image of her own living room, back home, flashes through her mind. She sees the enormous sofa with mismatched pillows, the wall of crayon drawings and paintings from flea markets, shoes kicked off and overturned peeking out next to the coffee table, and it makes her long for her house's shabby warmth. Here, the living room's cold precision, its meticulous polish, makes Rosalyn shiver and turn to James in silent dismay. He shrugs at her look, as if to say, "I had nothing to do with any of it."

The boy has been standing at the doorway to the kitchen all this time and now he comes up to Rosalyn, holding out a glass of water but not meeting her eyes. She bends down to take it from him. "Thank you," she says, and he looks up with a tight and nervous face, he sweeps his eyes over her, taking in every detail. When Meiling comes to stand next to him, she touches his head, lightly, and he looks up at her for approval. Looking at mother and son, Rosalyn can feel her own heart filling with something sour.

Meiling motions for Rosalyn to follow her, and they walk into a large bedroom, Rosalyn's suitcases and bags already on the floor. The walls are a rich, slate gray; the bookcases, their mahogany skeletons stuffed full, stretch to the ceiling along one length of the room. An ink tablet sprawls over a corner of the desk, next to a jar of calligraphy brushes with pale tops, stiff and watchful. It would have been Professor Li's room, then, repurposed for her, Rosalyn thinks, hiding her shudder. "Thank you," she says, and sits down on the bed, creasing the silky blue covers.

Meiling starts to leave and then remembers. "Al-an," she says, and then repeats it again. "Al-an."

"Alan?" Rosalyn watches Meiling dial and say something fast into the cell phone, pause, and then delicately laugh. The phone is handed over to her, and then Alan's familiar voice is in her ear. "Dr. Neal. How are you getting on?"

The last time she saw Alan had been the Friday before she was set to leave. He had presented her with a beautiful tea set. She was embarrassed that she hadn't gotten him anything in exchange. She hadn't decided to stay on in Shanghai then, and they sat, awkwardly, in the office she was about to vacate, exchanging pleasantries, saying goodbye. At the end of a polite twenty minutes he got up; she went to hug him just as he stuck out his hand, and she'd cringed, thinking of it later, thinking that it was a scene straight out of some awful movie about a big, boorish American in China.

"Alan." She draws out his name. "You probably thought you'd seen the last of me."

"Ms. Zhou called to tell me that she asked you to stay on, in her home, and she asked me to help all of you out with some translation."

"Thank you, Alan. But tell me, how is this going to work?"

"For basic things, you can use one of the electronic dictionaries in their home. But if you run into anything more difficult, then you or Ms. Zhou can just call me, and I'll do my best to translate as soon as possible."

"Thank you Alan. I'm terribly grateful."

"Ms. Zhou also wanted me to ask if you're free tomorrow evening for dinner. She'd like for us all to dine together. That is, if you're not doing anything else."

"That's very sweet. I'd love to, but my friend Danny's orchestra is performing tomorrow night. I've already promised him I'd go."

"Shall I tell Ms. Zhou that you're not available then?"

"No, actually. Ask her if she wants to come."

Meiling stands in the doorway, looking down at her feet. Rosalyn passes the phone to her and busies herself opening her suitcase, putting dresses away. Meiling's voice is supple but a little reedy, with a musical quality, and a sense of restraint, too, as if there's something she's not quite saying. Then the phone is back in Rosalyn's hand and Meiling is smiling at her, twisting her mouth, acknowledging the absurdity of the situation with a sheepish shrug of her shoulders.

Alan explains that Meiling is inviting Rosalyn to go shopping and visit a spa with her in the late afternoon. Then they'd join up with Li Jing for dinner, and head over to the performance after that. Rosalyn nods emphatically, making a thumbs-up sign. With Alan's help they arrange the details of the outing. When Meiling leaves the room, Rosalyn falls back against the headboard and closes her eyes.

She can hear the faint thumps of Meiling's steps, can hear a faucet running in the bathroom. There is a clock ticking out the seconds, and the air conditioner hums loudly, evenly, blocking out the rest of the world. There are motes of dust in the air, drifting toward the window like a flock of tiny, glittering birds. Someone coughs violently down the hall, and it sounds like James; she listens to the coughs fade away, and then muffled footsteps, and then the slam of a door. James, on the other side of wall in the living room, or across the hall. He is so close now, just a few feet away.

On Friday she had said goodbye to James, thinking that she was never going to see him again. They gazed at each other silently, and she thought about all the things they'd said, and all the things they might have said. James had become, for her, a friend, but also a possibility, an open question, a reassurance that she might, in time, fall in love with someone else. They wandered out into the city, sat on benches and in cafés, walked under scaffolding made of bamboo, darting through electric sparks flying out from construction crews. When he had to leave, finally, she asked him to hold her, and he hugged her hard, touched his lips to hers and drew back before she could react. He walked away and she watched him go, finally losing sight of him in a crowd.

When she got back to the apartment she began preparing for the trip home. She looked at all the glittering dresses she had bought, and wondered how they were going to fit in her suitcase, or when she might ever wear them again. She sat down in front of her laptop to avoid packing; she had downloaded e-mails at the hospital, but had not had time to read them. Carlos wrote asking when he should pick her up at the airport, and she thought about what she would do during her first few days home, thought about taking long walks on the plains, about grocery shopping and bill paying and going into her office, about calling Alice and talking to her niece and nephew. She thought about the house too, thought about its empty corridors, the bare bookshelves. She wondered if she should sell the house and move to a smaller place, but the thought of leaving their life behind, wiping out all traces of it, felt unbearable. She shook it off and focused on the computer screen once more.

There was no use in getting melancholy about the life that she was returning to, which was, after all, her real life, instead of the escape she has found in Shanghai. At the bottom of the e-mail Carlos had put a series of dots and in her head they sounded like a series of warning bells. She scrolled down and there was another block of text below the dots. The word *Ben* flashed up, catching her eye. Of all the words on the screen that combination of letters still produced some instinctive moment of recognition in her. She wanted to shove her computer away but kept reading instead.

I ran into Ben and a girl the other night at the Lighthouse. He introduced her to me as his girlfriend. He was embarrassed, and it was awkward, but he asked about you, asked how you were and when you were coming back. In some weird way, I think he was looking out for you. He wanted me to tell you so you wouldn't be surprised by the fact that he's with someone else now. I'm sorry, Rosalyn. I wasn't sure if you'd want to know . . .

She tried to prepare herself for the plane rides and the empty house waiting dark and restless at the other end of the earth. She tried to imagine running into him—into them—on campus or in a parking lot or at the drugstore, the faceless girl buying vitamins, buying a new toothbrush. Ben would be thoughtful and stammering, he would hug her hello but let go too quickly. He would be glad to see her, but he would also look after the girl, make sure she is not slighted by all their history and all the nameless things between them. He would put his hand on the girl's elbow or shoulder, as a subtle sign to all three of them that this is where he belongs now, with the girl, two against one. What does it matter if he found someone else first? Only it does matter, it does.

When she decided to stay for another four weeks, she e-mailed her parents and her sister, her friends and colleagues. Somehow, she had expected howls of outrage, but all that came into her inbox were notes of envy and congratulations, her sister's "Wish I was there with you," Dr. Reddy's "See you in September!" The truth was that no one was waiting for her to get home; no one depended on her or counted down the days until she returned. All she had to look forward to were nights at the bar and microwave dinners, encounters with her ex-husband and his new girlfriend in the drugstore, under the fluorescent lights.

"Ma ma!" From down the hall the boy's voice rings out, and then there is a sentence of something slippery and smooth, like a fish slipping out of your hand. Meiling calls back, and her voice is quieter, muffled, so that even if Rosalyn could understand Chinese she wouldn't be able to hear the words. There is a click, and then the television is on, a news-caster's steady voice, and then a cartoon sound track, and then a pop song. She can hear their lives hurtling forward, lying here in this bed. The door is closed and the sun is so bright that she can see it through her eyelids, and surely, she thinks, this was a mistake, the way she has stumbled into their family so carelessly. Surely, they would have asked more questions, asked for her Social Security number, asked about her allergies and for her blood work, interrogated her on her methods and intentions. But she is here, in their home, in Shanghai still, and it feels real now, the extension of her stay, with its vague, unsettled shape, its messy convergence of desires and impulses. The sounds from the televi-sion have settled into a groove, and they drift about her head, shapeless, for a few minutes, before it becomes clear that the voices on the dial are speaking in English, with a laugh track underneath. She listens to the dialogue of the American sitcom; it sounds at once strange and familiar. She squeezes her eyes even tighter and turns on her side, plugging her fingers into her ears, not wanting to hear the banter about sons and curfew, not wanting to be reminded of home.

CHAPTER 22

When Meiling shows up at the spa she is ten minutes late, and she hurries through the French doors, an apology on the tip of her tongue. But then she sees Rosalyn on the divan in the corner of the bright, airy waiting room, laughing and sipping a cup of tea, surrounded by staff, with someone bringing her a plate of strawberries, and someone else holding an armful of nail polish bottles, showing them off to her one by one.

"Rosalyn." The name is still strange in her mouth. Meiling smiles and walks over, but there is no place for her to sit. Rosalyn jumps up, spilling tea, and goes to hug Meiling while a young woman bends down to the white carpet and blots up the stain with a towel. "Welcome, Ms. Zhou," some of the staff members say hello, "nice to see you again. Thanks for calling ahead and letting us know about our special American guest! Just look at the hair on her!"

Alan is meeting them here, in an hour and a half. Meiling insisted that they would be fine at the spa on their own, knowing that he would be bored by massages and pedicures. She had raced through work this morning, telling Vice President Wu that she would be unavailable for the rest of the day. "Good," the older woman said with uncharacteristic warmth. "You've been working too hard, and we're in decent shape right now. You deserve to take a little time for yourself, Xiao Zhou. Why don't you think about taking a few days off too? You and Li Jing and Pang Pang could go away for the weekend. Just the three of you."

Now she has turned off the sound on her phone, she's taking off her clothes and jewelry, slipping under the towel on the massage table in the double room before the masseuse comes back in. Next to her Rosalyn slurps a glass of cucumber juice and sets down her purse, nervous laughter bubbling out of her throat. Meiling turns her head to the other side and closes her eyes, listening to the sound of Rosalyn stepping out of her skirt, unsnapping her bra. They lie there, waiting, and the silence in the room feels tense, as if this intimacy needs chatter to buoy it up, into the realm of friendship. Meiling is aware of Rosalyn's breath, her squirming on the other table, and when the door finally opens it feels like a reprieve. The masseuse's hands, slick with oil, press down on her shoulders, and she takes a deep breath, trying to relax.

Only it feels wrong, the masseuse's hands. Meiling twists her head and looks over her shoulder. The woman above her is a stranger, not her usual masseuse, the one who has attended her for as long as she has been coming to this spa. She turns to the other side and sees that her masseuse is working on Rosalyn instead. Xiao Wu throws her an apologetic smile, shrugs, mouthing, "The boss told me to work on the *lǎowài* today."

The same thing happens during their facials. Her usual aesthetician hovers over Rosalyn in the next seat, and some other girl, with thick, clumsy fingers, presses down hard on her face with a hot towel, making Meiling wince in pain. During their pedicures Rosalyn laughs when her feet are tickled and mimes broadly to indicate her pleasure. Despite the language barrier, Rosalyn's obvious delight in their work charms everyone. The usually cool and calculating owner of the spa comes to chat with a handful of broken English phrases, giggling with Rosalyn as if they were long lost friends. Meiling looks in the mirror on the opposite wall and is startled at the dark circles under her own eyes, her sallow, dull skin. Next to her, Rosalyn is the picture of health, with a farmer's glow, her hair spinning red and gold around her face.

It's a relief to sees Alan waiting outside the door of the spa, careful and composed in his shirt and tie. Meiling and Rosalyn both start talking as soon as he walks up to them, as if they've been holding all their words in, and then they both stop and gesture for the other one to go ahead.

"Thank you so much," Rosalyn says. "It was such a treat! I feel thoroughly relaxed, and that staff was *so* nice. Please, let me pay for half of that."

"I hope that was all right." Meiling waves off Rosalyn's wallet. "It's the least I can do after all that you've done for Li Jing."

On Huaihai Road people stare and whisper, pointing at Rosalyn, her hair smoldering in the sun, her white arms swinging wide. Meiling and Alan walk a half step behind, self-conscious, listening to the murmurs, to the random English phrases shouted from the crowd. They go to Fendi, to Printemps, to the exclusive designer boutiques that Meiling visits every season for new clothes. She is thankful for Alan's presence next to her, especially when the salesgirls all flock around Rosalyn, holding articles of clothing up against her body, shouting to the back for a bigger size.

Alan says, quietly, "*Lǎowàis* always get a lot of attention. I'm used to it by now, but it must seem kind of strange. I hope you don't let this bother you, Ms. Zhou. It's not her, it's what happens with every white person in Shanghai."

"It doesn't bother me." Meiling tries to be blithe, but then they both turn and watch Rosalyn laugh again when she comes out of the dressing room in a bright gold tank top and looks at herself in the mirror, salesgirls pawing at the shirt, surrounding her.

"Is it really always like this?" Meiling bends her head close to Alan's.

"Always."

"You'd think we'd all be used to them by now."

"Maybe in a few years it won't seem like a big deal, but for now, everybody sees them, and it's still like seeing dollar signs."

He'd spoken with a subtle sneer. It was, Meiling thinks, the first time Alan has ever offered an opinion to her, and it makes her look at him in a new light. She turns to him and opens her mouth, but Rosalyn has walked up with a shopping bag in her hand, laughing, grabbing Alan by the arm. The three of them head back out to the blistering sidewalks, Rosalyn leading the way.

In the empty luxury of the next high-end boutique, Rosalyn looks bored and out of place among the sober palette, the slightly sexless clothes. She makes a face and asks if they can go to Huating Market instead, and Meiling, startled, nods and tries to keep herself from wincing or rolling her eyes. The market is full of clothes with fake labels and cheap trinkets. Meiling has not been there in years and has no desire to go there now. But after all, she has set aside this rare afternoon off to accompany the American around the city. They hop into a taxi and then they are on their way.

In the crowded, open-air market clothes hang in clumps on the walls of booths, bright and logoed, the loudness of the fabrics hiding their lackluster quality, their crooked seams. Sellers and buyers shout and laugh, haggling, getting into fights and then making up over a lowered price. Everyone stares at Rosalyn, looking her up and down, and she walks through the alley with a self-satisfied smile, at ease with all the attention. People shove Meiling and Alan to the side, hollering Chinese at them but staring at Rosalyn. "Hey! Tell your American friend to buy some necklaces . . ." ". . . Tell her these are real Prada bags, straight from the factory . . ." ". . . Tell her I'll give her a deal if she gives me a kiss."

Meiling shrinks back and tries to navigate through to the next set of stalls, tries not to touch anything, as if the merchandise might stain her skin. Rosalyn dodges away to peer at a booth fringed with garish scarves. Meiling watches her smile sideways at the seller, haggle, lean forward so that the man gets a glimpse of her cleavage. Rosalyn laughs with delight when the seller agrees to her price, and comes back victorious with a purple scarf veined in gold. "What a steal," Alan translates, flatly, and Meiling turns away, hiding her distaste. How unnerving to see this woman, her husband's doctor, looking coy and flirtatious, beaming with pleasure, holding cheap rags in her arms.

Meiling tries to reconcile this new side of Rosalyn Neal with the image of the American doctor in her white coat. Rosalyn had always seemed extroverted, the way Americans were said to be, but she had seemed professional and concerned too, giving no hint of the vanity that she wears now, in the middle of the crowd. It is hard, Meiling thinks to herself, to know anything about a person from another country; their foreignness, perhaps, always obscures their personality. You couldn't know them like you could someone from China, someone whose habits and contexts you're familiar with, someone whose face you could read as easily as a novel, penetrating through the hidden layers, rooting out the subtext.

"I'm getting a lot better at bargaining!" Rosalyn's voice is smug and she nudges Meiling in the side, giddy, as if they are the best of friends. "You haven't bought anything yet. Let's find something for you. Maybe some new summer sandals? Or look." She grabs Meiling's arm and pulls her toward a stall. "Aren't these dresses beautiful?"

When Meiling flinches away it is an instinctive act, without malice, but she can see it register, can see by the other woman's expression that her own face has betrayed her disdain.

"I don't know if they're quite my style. They're very . . . colorful."

Rosalyn takes a sharp breath and steps back. "Whatever you say."

"Rosalyn—" It's strange, too, how you can tell so easily when someone has taken offense, despite the barrier of language, and Meiling reaches out toward the American but then draws her hand back, wanting to apologize, not knowing what to say.

Rosalyn, though, is already turning away, lifting her chin like a jilted lover, pulling the just-purchased scarf out of the plastic bag, winding the cheap, glittery velvet around her throat.

WHEN MEILING TOLD him they were going to have dinner with Rosalyn and Alan, the four of them, he wanted to laugh. He must have given himself away by a twitch of the face because Meiling lifted her eyes to his again. "Dr. Neal is our guest," she said, serious and stern. He nodded. That's what he does now. He nods yes or shakes his head no. He listens to her voice, full of facts but betraying no emotions. He combs through his brain for the spelling of words in English, trying to remember back to long-ago lessons in Virginia, and types the words into the electronic dictionary. "Need toothpaste" or "Son. Take to school." The dictionary spits the Chinese equivalent out at Meiling. Last week, he typed the words in and watched her listen to the translation: "Tomorrow. Visit cemetery." She had shaken her head. "No time," she said. "I have to go buy some things for Dr. Neal, to put her room in order and prepare for her arrival."

He doesn't like it, having Rosalyn in their apartment, but Meiling does not ask him what he wants. She does not ask him how he feels, what to do with his father's things, or whether he wants to spend the evening with Rosalyn and Alan. His life has been arranged for him. The only thing left to do is wade through it, solitary and mute.

On his way to the restaurant he walks behind four young men in shirts and ties, watches them laugh their way down the sidewalk, slapping each other on the arms. He lowers his head to stare at the ground but their voices—loud, edged with adrenaline and relief—still come through; they complain about their bosses and the crappy pay, they tease each other about their wives and girlfriends. He can understand every word out of their mouths, but their easy friendship, the way their voices are part of the city and all its revelries, has been closed off to him. What makes it even worse is that he can listen in. He's been removed from everyone else, but he still stands on the edges of their scenes, envying their effortless chatter, but always entirely alone.

Before, there had been two restaurants among their regular haunts: the restaurant at the Swan Hotel had been for everyday meals with the family; the Ginko Leaf, with its restrained décor and decadent food, had been for special occasions, to impress extended family or guests. His father had loved it here, loved the sharp formality of the service, the sense of occasion that accompanied every meal. When Li Jing walks in he is glad to see an unfamiliar face at the hostess station, but then the manager is rushing to greet him with a handshake, the man's hand squeezing him hard and then letting go.

"Mr. Li. Can I just say . . ." The man takes his glasses off and puts them back on. "I'm so glad to see you again—not even as a customer, but just because we miss you. We were so sorry to hear about Professor Li. If there's anything we can do—"

Li Jing had been a public man, before, at ease with bellhops and politicians, careless with his affection. After he came home from the hospital there were cards in the mail and containers of food on the table, telephone calls left by people he barely remembered, visits from college classmates and business associates. He told Meiling not to call anyone back. He sat in the living room and listened to the buzzer ring, not getting up, not letting anyone in. Language, he thinks, is what he used to spin those casual webs of friendship. Without it, he cannot bear to be in the same space as all those who had laughed at his jokes or been enraptured by his stories. He will not sit in silence and be the recipient of their plodding words of pity.

So he nods at the manager but keeps his eyes downcast. He sits down at an empty table and turns his face away from the room. A waiter comes by with tiny plates of pickled cabbage, with tea. Li Jing does not look up but taps two fingers on the table in silent thanks, remembering how his father, imperious and unapproachable to the rest of the world, always had a kind word for busboys and waiters.

The table is next to a private room, and he can hear voices inside talking about the tumbles of the stock exchange, can pick up the cadences of negotiations, bargains being struck. There are certain things about the world of finance that he does not miss: he does not miss its ruthlessness, its sense of false urgency. But there was a strange kind of camaraderie there too. In the end, he supposed, it was all about the numbers, it was all about the profit, but to get there, along the way, you had to depend on getting to know people, making them like and trust you, charming them into handing you cash or tips or ideas. He had liked the way it filled his life with strangers and acquaintances, the way every swell and dip of the market came attached to faces and conversations.

From the room he hears a young man's voice, familiar and brash, slightly slurred by drink. "Leaving SinoVenture was the best decision I ever made. Everyone knows Li Jing lost his mind in the explosion. I had to jump off that sinking ship. Your company is where I should be now—I promise that you won't be sorry."

When he hired Zhang Qing the young man was already brash. He had said, "You won't be sorry" then too, and Li Jing, wary but clear-eyed, had said, "We'll see." Now Li Jing peeks in through the door and sees the president and hiring manager of a competing firm stand up from the table, gather up their bags. Zhang Qing, sloppy but pleased, shakes the two men's hands and hurries to the door, holding it open for his new bosses.

Li Jing turns around and walks off quickly, heading into the narrow corridor that leads to the bathrooms. When the men don't follow him his heart slows and he clenches his fists before going back toward the dining room; at the mouth of the corridor, he peeks out, but stays in hiding. The three men are stopped by the door of the restaurant. Over their shoulders he can see Meiling and Rosalyn and Alan. He tries to get a clearer look at Meiling's face, but it is half obscured, unreadable. In the hushed restaurant their conversation carries clearly. He can hear Zhang Qing's smug "Hello, Mrs. Li," and at the sound bile and anger swell up into his throat.

"Xiao Zhang." Meiling's voice drifts sharp but slow over the room.

"How nice to see you again. I had planned on calling you, to see how you are. It's too bad those investors pulled out of starting a new company with you, but things in finance are always difficult, especially for those just starting out. You understand, don't you, why we had to let you go? It was just business—you just weren't a good fit."

Zhang Qing tenses and the two men next to him laugh nervously and introduce themselves. They bow at Meiling, dazzled by her beauty, but also by the sense of power she seems to wield, her cool but electric poise. She receives them like a queen, and Li Jing finds himself amazed at her transformation, the way she vanquished Zhang Qing, the precision of her cut, the smoothness of the delivery. He did not know that her streak of superiority—usually so well hidden—could be extended to the business world. He does not know what to think of it now.

"Is Li Jing joining you this evening?" Zhang Qing says, trying to land a punch.

At the sound of his name Rosalyn turns and stares at the strange men for the first time. Alan is more discreet, but Li Jing can sense the translator's discomfort, his awareness of the tension underneath every word.

Meiling's laugh is the one she uses to make everyone else feel like a fool. "I wish," she says, smiling sideways at the two men, ignoring Zhang Qing. "No, Li Jing's still recovering, he's practically on vacation, lucky him. After all these years of working so hard, he deserves one, don't you think? In any case, things are going very well without him. Have you seen our numbers from the last four weeks? Now if you gentlemen will excuse me, I have a new client"—she gestures toward Rosalyn—"to wine and woo."

The three men walk out the door and Li Jing stays in the hallway for a moment, sticking his hands in his pockets to keep from punching the walls. But then he swallows his anger and heads over to the table, sits down with his eyes locked on to the carpet, his heart thumping. When he hears Alan's voice, he looks up and the three of them are coming closer, Rosalyn reaching him first, giving his arm a squeeze.

When he turns to see Meiling's reaction she has her head bent toward Alan. He tries to catch her eye, but she will not look up or even acknowledge him to say hello.

"James," Rosalyn sighs, "am I glad to see you."

He pulls out the chair next to him, and when Rosalyn sits down without hesitation there is nothing to do but scoot the chair forward. Meiling sits down across from him and finally meets his eyes before looking away. "Mr. Li." Alan nods and glances at the two women, before giving Li Jing a look of discomfort. Alan, he has a feeling, notices everything.

The manager, still solicitous despite Li Jing's silence, comes over with only one menu, placing it into his hands with deference. Before, he had been the one who always ordered the meal for the entire table, but now he sets the menu down as soon as the manager walks away, turning to the one person who seems happy to see him.

"How was shopping? Spa?" he says.

"Fine. It was fine. The spa was very nice, and shopping was—shopping was fine."

Since Rosalyn walked in, her face has been oddly hesitant, but when she looks at him her smile is genuine and lovely, exposing a smear of lipstick on her teeth. Across the table Meiling is consulting Alan about the menu. When the waiter comes over she places the order with authority, without having asked Li Jing or Rosalyn what they want to eat. Shoving back the memory of her at the door, her voice saying, "Things are going very well without him," Li Jing tries to smile at his wife, lays his hands flat across the table, closer to her fingers. Without meeting his eyes she moves her arms off the table and puts them in her lap, her face blank, her unmoving, unseeing smile making his gesture obsolete.

Once before, he had reached out for her, and once before, she had pulled herself out of his reach. Last week, Pang Pang was standing in front of them with his earnest face, trying to recite a poem he'd learned in school, tripping over the words. Their eyes had met and she had smiled; her face looked like the face he remembered, without the annoyance and tension that seemed to have been etched in her skin after the accident. He reached out and brushed the top of her thigh with the back of his fingers. She recoiled from his touch and drew back as if she had been stung. He could see her squint, her face tightening as she turned to stare at the part of the wall that still held a mark from where he'd thrown the computer. He got up abruptly, walking away from the scene of his crime, unwanted, impotent all along.

So he has tried to keep his head down, keep his hands to himself, stay out of her way, and focus on Pang Pang. With Meiling at work until late in the evening, he has been the one picking Pang Pang up from school, and they've established a routine of walks in the park and video games in the living room, weekly visits to the cemetery, half-clandestine dinners at fast-food restaurants. He is quite certain that she would disapprove, if she knew, of Pang Pang eating at KFC, at McDonald's, but there is something comforting about these places; they look exactly how they had looked when he was a kid in Virginia. He had longed for them then, when eating a Happy Meal was an expensive treat. Now he can be anonymous in the garish spaces, pointing to pictures of cheeseburgers and chicken nuggets, just another dad indulging his son.

The restaurant starts to buzz from the conversations of the dinner crowd, but a long, blank silence is stretched over their table. Rosalyn bites her lips and starts to speak. "I'm excited about the concert. Aren't you?" she says to Meiling and Alan. "I never go to this kind of stuff back home in Oklahoma. What about you, Meiling?" The name is funny, twisted ajar on her tongue. "Do you guys often go to classical music concerts?"

When Alan's translation dies down, Li Jing watches Meiling looking off to the side, one eyebrow raised. "We have season tickets to the Shanghai orchestra, which plays at the Grand Theater. I've never heard of this . . . East Sea Regional Orchestra before."

He has known, always, about this side of Meiling, her beautiful élan that verges on cruelty or snobbishness at times. When they had first met, he had liked that about her, the way she could, with a glance or a few words, place herself out of reach, cutting someone off at the knees. Later, when she'd walk away from him or dismiss his jealousy with one tilt of her chin, he had been infuriated but still enchanted. Earlier, he had hated the way she talked to the businessmen, the way she dismissed the need for him in front of them, but he had been willing to acknowledge the necessity of it, willing to see it from her point of view. But now, watching her with Rosalyn Neal, he feels wounded on the American's behalf. He remembers, years ago, how his father used to call Meiling "the ice princess," and he wonders what his father would think of her now.

"I am happy to go to concert." He smiles at Rosalyn, leaning into her infinitesimally, for show, glad to see her face relax again. When she was on the verge of leaving he had been relieved, knowing that he would miss her, but knowing that she had a dangerous pull on him. Now that she is next to him he considers her once more: her pale, freckled face should not have been beautiful, but there is a certain warmth to it that he can't define, that makes it, always, pleasing to look at. He chats with her about the afternoon, asks her about the concert, feeling protective, reveling in their camaraderie. Out of the corner of his eye he tries to watch Meiling and gauge her reaction; he wants her to see that he can do this, that he can talk and laugh with ease and fluency, the way he used to. But she does not seem to be paying him any attention. She keeps looking down at her lap as if distracted or immune.

When the food comes everyone relaxes a little, lets themselves be absorbed into the rituals of the meal. "For our guest." Meiling picks up a drumstick with her chopsticks and deposits it onto Rosalyn's plate. Rosalyn smiles and tries to return the favor, but accidentally drops a piece of fish into the soup. Li Jing watches as the dark sauce that had clung to the fish spreads like an oil spill, as the fish sinks to the bottom, muddying up the clear vegetable broth. When Alan ladles the soup into everyone's bowls Meiling takes a small sip of hers and then discreetly pushes it to the side. She turns her head away to root through her purse for a handkerchief, and all Li Jing can see is the back of her head, the black shine of her hair covering up her thin, delicate skull.

SHE CAN SEE that the two of them talk easily, Rosalyn and Li Jing, and she wants to be glad for him, be glad that he can talk to someone, even if it's not her. But listening to them talk in the other language feels like being strangled, centimeter by centimeter, word by word. She tries to focus on Alan, but he too is paying more attention to the other conversation, unsure of whether to translate or respond.

It is the first time she has been at a restaurant with her husband in more than two months. It is the first time, she realizes, that she has really looked at him in weeks. She studies him while his head is turned to Rosalyn: he's wearing a light gray suit without a tie, the top button of his white shirt open, looking debonair, almost windblown. She always liked that quality, the sense of something slightly wild in him. He has gotten very tan during the summer, his face almost brown, with a hint of pink in the cheeks. Rosalyn says something, looks sad or pensive for a second, and he leans into her, with a determined expression on his face. Meiling's mind stutters and tries to remember; something about his look is so familiar. It makes her jerk back, hard, into her chair. She rattles the table, knocking a glass onto the floor.

"I'm fine," she says, although no one has asked. "I'm fine."

Something about that look of his making fear race up her spine.

Alan bends down to pick up the shards of the glass, and she knows he can see how hard her legs are shaking under the table. He touches the tip of her shoe for a moment, but then he gets back up with a calm face and a gathered napkin in his hands. He says, "It broke clean."

There is still the rest of dinner, and then dessert, and then a taxi ride over to the concert, Alan in the passenger seat, the three of them squeezed tight in the back. By the time the orchestra shuffles onto the stage to tune up, Meiling is so grateful for the distraction that she doesn't even grimace at the screeching coming out of the instruments, just stares up into the lights hanging on the ceiling of the high school auditorium, their brightness almost blinding. Rosalyn breaks from her conversation with Li Jing suddenly, pointing out a blond man with a cello sitting four seats in from the stage. "That's her friend," Alan explains, "the gentleman playing the cello. His name is Danny Barrett."

The music begins, loud and heroic; the instruments take a second to come into harmony, and then they march forth, plodding and methodical. The program, which features the blond man prominently on the cover, promises Dvořák's *New World* Symphony and Beethoven's Fifth. Meiling listens as a single clarinet slips out of tune, listens to a hiccup in the tempo, the brass section a touch slower than the strings. The orchestra handles the bombastic passages of music with puffed-up gusto, but falters during the quiet moments, playing without subtlety or grace. There's a whispered din over the room as the audience murmurs, restless. Two rows in front of them, a woman is knitting, obliviously, and the hiss of her needles can be heard between movements.

The music goes on, without intermission, for what seems like hours. Meiling leans back in her seat and tunes it out—she is exhausted from the day, from being deferential to the irritating Dr. Neal, from the encounter with Zhang Qing, from the forced intimacy of their dinner together. All of it had felt like a façade, stretched thin to cover her decimated life. She looks over to her left: Li Jing looks bored, Alan is stoic as always, and Rosalyn is entranced, leaning forward, her shirt gaping, her scarf messy and vivid around her neck. When the orchestra lurches toward the last notes of the Beethoven it speeds up, the conductor jabbing his baton wildly into the air; all the instruments manage to come to a stop at the same time, and polite applause breaks out across the auditorium. Meiling puts her palms together reluctantly. Already Rosalyn is getting up, jabbering, "Wasn't that great?"

The folding chairs on the stage make scraping noises as the orchestra players get up, talk and laugh, accepting congratulations and goodbyes. But there is a pall of embarrassment over the entire stage, too, the players not quite meeting each other's eyes. "Danny!" Rosalyn throws

herself at the blond man, and next to her, Meiling can feel Li Jing going very still, staring at the couple, who are now hugging, talking easily back and forth. He takes two steps forward and sticks his hand out
for the other man to shake. "Li Jing is congratulating Mr. Barrett,"
Alan tells her, without prompting. "He is saying that it was a very en-
joyable concert."

In a moment they're all standing in a circle, Rosalyn making the
introductions, Alan filling in the details for Meiling. The blond man introduces himself to her in clumsy Chinese; when she gives him a back-
handed compliment on the music he looks taken aback, recognizing
the challenge in her voice. But then he turns to Rosalyn, and the two
of them are off, talking in English, until Li Jing interrupts and joins in,
diverting Rosalyn's attention. Meiling stands next to them, with a stiff
smile; she is shut out of their conversation despite Alan's best efforts.

Danny suggests that they all go to a bar, and to Meiling's surprise, Li
Jing doesn't even hesitate before nodding yes. She starts to decline, but
then Rosalyn pleads for her to come, and she looks at Li Jing, the tense
way he's holding himself, how he's still staring at Rosalyn, as if he's angry
with her, as if he feels betrayed. "Will you come, too?" She turns to Alan
and he nods, gravely, making her smile and giving her courage. They
follow Danny down the street to an Irish pub full of white men watching soccer, howling like animals, and at the bar, everyone else orders
beer, so she does too, cupping it between her palms, taking a tiny sip.

"So you're Rosalyn's famous patient. I suppose I have you to thank
for getting her here to Shanghai. Isn't she great? Cheers to Rosalyn."
Squeezed into a booth, with his arm around Rosalyn, Danny raises his
glass, looking at Li Jing on the opposite side.

They all lift their glasses but Li Jing clinks his hard against Danny's
glass. "Cheers," he says. "Don't know—where I would be . . . without
her."

"It's lucky for the both of you that I'm sticking around for a while
then," Rosalyn says, preening. She looks from one man to the other
with a smirk on her lips.

They talk more, the three of them, about Rosalyn's stay in Shanghai, the men suggesting places for her to travel to and things for her to do. Alan translates the conversation for Meiling, tries to keep up with the fast exchanges, until Meiling shakes her head. "Stop," she says. "There's no need to translate everything."

You can sit at the same table, drink the same brand of beer, but be completely and utterly in two different universes, without any points of intersection. Li Jing looks over to Meiling sometimes, puzzled, looking like he wants to ask her something, but then he'll be pulled back into the other conversation, where Meiling can almost hear how smoothly the words unroll from his throat. They are arguing about something now, the two men, and their voices are raised, Rosalyn's laughter pealing out between them. Meiling feels as though there are things churning hard in her chest: hope, because he has that vibrant, belligerent tone in his voice again, and bitterness, because it is in another language, for the sake, perhaps, of another woman.

"Are you all right, Ms. Zhou?"

"Call me Meiling, Alan."

"Meiling, then. How are you feeling?"

"I'm fine, I'm just worn out. I don't think I've ever been this tired in my life."

"You need rest, you need to take care of yourself, too," Alan says.

"That's funny. That's what my father-in-law used to say too. But"—she sits up straight—"someone has to take care of things. It's fine. It's just for a little while."

On the other side of the table Danny still has his arm around Rosalyn. He strokes her bare upper arm with his fingers, hesitates, and then pulls her jaw toward him, kisses her on the lips. Meiling notices Rosalyn's surprise—she does not look especially pleased, but then she relaxes into Danny's embrace, she lets him kiss her for a moment longer before pulling herself away, pink-cheeked. Next to Meiling, Li Jing swallows and shuts his jaw tight, jutting it forward, with a familiar, stormy look on his face.

It strikes her like a fist, the recognition of his look, now, and earlier too, across the table at the restaurant. He looks exactly like how he used to look at her, infatuated and resolute, with a certain light in his eyes, his lips pressed together in determination. For so long he had looked at her like that, even after she was his, but she does not know when he stopped, she has not seen that look in his eyes for months, maybe even years. Seeing it now, from the sidelines, makes her feel like throwing up. She blanches, and when Alan lays a warm palm on her back she shoves at him until he moves out of the booth. Then she runs to the bathroom and gags into the toilet. Nothing comes out. She tries again, but it is just a dry heave; she will not even have the pleasure of purging her horror away. She stands up straight in the stall for a second, trying not to touch anything, trying to get her breathing under control, and sees that the walls and door are covered with unrecognizable graffiti, English phrases plastered ugly and dense. The black marks seem to close in on her, they swim closer to her eyes, there are so many letters of the alphabet gathered together, incoherent, so many imaginary insults like daggers coming toward her. Her legs start shaking again, her knees buckle, and she crumples down to the edge of the toilet, listening as the door to the bathroom opens and laughter and shouting come rushing in before fading away.

CHAPTER 23

For days after, Meiling tries to tell herself that she was mistaken, tries to shake off the memory of the looks on his face. It's only natural for Li Jing to form an attachment to Rosalyn, but it would never go further than that; he has never given her any cause for jealousy before. In a few more weeks, Rosalyn will go back to America, and perhaps by then, Li Jing will be able to speak Chinese again. The future looms before her, without focus, but she tries to place her faith in it, in the impossibility of anything besides his body by her side and his voice in her ear again. She will not allow herself to think anything else.

She still rolls out of bed early in the mornings, glancing over at him, watching his face, which looks hard, even in sleep. Before she goes to work she prepares breakfast for all of them, leaving the table set with wedges of melon, bowls of porridge, pieces of toast, empty mugs waiting for coffee or tea. When she is at the office she does not have time to think about anything else; she lets herself be plunged into that other world with its own signs and demarcations, its own strange logic and speed. On the rare nights when she is not working late she will come home and make dinner, eating in silence with Li Jing and Pang Pang, each minute a silent torture that she almost enjoys, because it is the only thing, really, that they still do as a family. She'll read to Pang Pang after. Then she'll fall asleep, only to be jerked awake by Rosalyn coming home late, in the middle of the night. Rosalyn, heedless, opens doors and lets them shut with a bang, her high-heeled steps heavy-footed in the hall. The one bathroom in the apartment has a door leading out to the hallway, and another door to the master bedroom. When Rosalyn flips on the light Meiling can see a thin bright line at the edge of the floor, hear water rushing out of the faucet or the sound of bristles scraping against teeth. Once, as she woke up, she became aware of Li Jing's still body next to her, his breathing shallower than it was during sleep. They lay there, not moving, and listened to the most intimate of sounds from the bathroom, the flush of the toilet, its thunderous whirlpool plunging Meiling into isolation and despair.

The phone at her desk rings, shrill and persistent. She has begun to hate the telephone. Her voice is flat and venomous when she says, "Hello."

"Meiling! Is that you? I've been trying to get ahold of you for weeks."

The thick, unhurried voice crawls out of the mouthpiece, familiar-sounding, tinged with amusement. "Now, tell me," the person says, "are the rumors true, have we really lost you to the dark underworld of . . . finance?"

"Lao Chen? Is that you?"

"Have you really forgotten me so quickly?"

The sound of her old boss's voice floods her chest with warmth. "Lao Chen, it's so good to hear from you. How are you? How's everything at the office? Did Ge Dong's wife have the baby yet? And the Japanese translation, is it already out?"

She swivels away from her desk and watches planes land and take off outside the window. She thinks of her old office, with the dilapidated trellis outside where tiny clusters of grapes grew in late summer, the big, airy room where they all sat, their wooden desks piled high with manuscripts, thousands of books lining the walls. "Tell me everything . . ."

She trails off, a tinge of melancholia in her voice. "I've missed so much these past few months."

"It's not the same without you, Meiling."

She had liked being the only woman in the small office, surrounded by men who wore their bookish masculinity like a badge of honor, who treated her as though she were a cross between a little sister and an object for seduction. After Pang Pang was born she cut back her hours; during the two days of the week when she went into the office, the men always clustered around her, asking for advice about girlfriends or daughters, teasing her about her expensive outfits, sniffing her perfume. It had given her so much pleasure, this part of her life that was hers and hers alone. She takes a breath now and looks back at her computer screen, with its restless columns of numbers and abbreviations.

"I've missed you guys," she says. "But everything here is just . . ."

"There's no need to explain."

Lao Chen had been a friend of Professor Li's, and at Meiling and Li Jing's wedding banquet, when she was newly graduated and toiling away at a real estate company, he offered her the job of his assistant as a favor to the professor. Back then, Lao Chen was already a well-known editor at a prestigious press. In the years since, he has become the publisher of the press, and Meiling a senior editor. Under Lao Chen, she learned to read and edit, massage egos and divvy out rejections. Since the accident, she has avoided his calls, avoided wondering whether he would disapprove or be angry at her sudden departure.

"I'm sorry we didn't get a chance to talk at the funeral," she says. "The truth is I hardly talk to anyone now—there's just too much to do. Thank you for the gifts that you sent to the house, and thank everyone else in the office too, for thinking of us. You've been friends with Professor Li for decades—it must have been hard on you too."

They pass memories of the professor back and forth, laughing a little at some of his antics over the years. Lao Chen asks after Pang Pang and Li Jing, and Meiling wants to know about manuscripts and acquisitions. She remembers what a pleasure it is, always, to talk to him; he fills her up with news and gossip about people they know in common, making her laugh with his description of an awkward encounter between two feuding writers. She is a little startled at herself when she comes up with a barb about one of the men in question, and Lao Chen bursts out laughing. "You always did have a sharp tongue, Meiling."

It has been so long since she has talked like this, at ease, and she feels a sharp sense of longing for her old life stabbing at her. Here, in the world of computers and skyscrapers, exchange rates and shares, she is an amateur, lucky but precarious, fumbling her way through. Before, in the world of poetry, she had belonged: how sure of herself she was then, how certain she had been making decisions syllable by syllable.

"As nice as it is to talk to you," Lao Chen says, "there's a reason that I called today. Tian Dan contacted me earlier this week. She's ready with her next collection, and she was annoyed to find that her favorite editor wasn't around."

"She wants to work with me again?" The words tumble out of Meiling and she laughs a young, carefree laugh of surprise.

"She said she wouldn't dream of working with anyone else. She said that she liked the way you ordered the sequence of poems in her last book, and said something else, about how you have a way with commas."

"Hardly," Meiling grumbles, rolling her eyes. "I told her to add commas in twelve different places, for clarity. She looked at me and told me to let my hair down and have more sex. She said that overpunctuation was a sign of sexual repression."

"You never told me that story!" Lao Chen is laughing on the other end of the phone. "She did add four of those commas, though, far more than she would have done with anyone else. Anyway, she's back, and she's looking for you. I know you're busy, but you can't pass this up! Everyone says she's going to win the national prize for poetry one of these days. It would be a coup for the house, not to mention great for your career."

There is a knock on the door and then her assistant sticks her head in. "Ms. Zhou." She points to her watch. "It's eleven o'clock."

At her ear Lao Chen keeps talking, saying something about sending a messenger over with the manuscript this afternoon.

"Ms. Zhou." The assistant again, louder this time. "Did you forget the eleven o'clock meeting? Everyone's already waiting for you in the conference room."

Meiling tears through her desk looking for the meeting agenda and the quarterly report. The time, she sees with a flinch, is already 11:08. "Lao Chen," she interrupts, and then says, in one burst so that he can't get a word in, "thank you. Thank her for thinking of me. But I just can't right now. I'm sorry—I'm so sorry."

He is still talking when she hangs up. She collapses back against her chair, shaking, but there is no time to think about anything now. There are staccatoed bursts of pain cluttering her stomach, voices in the back of her head screeching at her, but she grabs the papers and heads down the hall, trying to forget the voice on the phone.

Inside the conference room six perfectly composed faces look up, expectant. She sits down, forces herself to take a deep breath and smile in apology. "The first item on our agenda," she begins, reading her notes, on autopilot, "is to review the past six months and talk about broad strategies for the rest of the year." She glances at them, and around the room eyes stare back at her, impassive. "Well, shall we begin?" she says, dully. "Let's talk about our performance from January to June, and start strategizing for the next two quarters."

"Ms. Zhou." The chief financial officer is apologetic but firm. "I think something else needs to be addressed. I know we haven't talked about this much, and things are running very smoothly, but for future planning and company stability, we do need to know—Ms. Zhou, are we expecting Li Jing back sometime soon? Is he interested, or . . . capable of reassuming the post at this point? Or will you continue on as acting president of SinoVenture for the rest of the year? What about next year? Will you continue on at the company then?"

"No . . ." she starts, "of course not . . ." But then she has to close her mouth; she doesn't know what else to say. The rest of the year, and then *next year.* The months unravel before her eyes. Will he talk again, now, or next year? Is he even trying, in Chinese, or is he happy just to talk to Rosalyn Neal, laugh with her in English, his head close to hers? The present, which she has thought of as temporary, as *just for now* since the accident, has stretched on for months. She has sacrificed her work and her time and her energy for his recovery, but she cannot see an end in sight.

Vice President Wu cuts in, saving her. "I think we can all agree that despite some rocky moments, leadership has been stable, and the bottom line reflects that."

This is what makes it acceptable: the bottom line. As long as she can continue to turn a profit, she will be expected to stay on for next year, maybe even the year after that.

Vice President Wu is still talking. ". . . the question of the future in terms of positions and responsibilities, I imagine, is a longer discussion, more appropriate for a separate meeting. Let's not talk about that now."

The meeting moves on, to portfolios and advertising, salaries and bonuses. Meiling offers few responses and keeps looking down, at the table, *next year*, the words drumming in her head over and over until the syllables break down, losing all meaning. When the meeting is finally over, she heads back to her office and sits rigid in her chair, staring out the window, not seeing a thing. She does not want to think about the future, does not want to think about next year. *Next year*; just the possibility of it makes permanent the conditions of the present, as if the future could be planned based on his silence, her own presence at the helm of SinoVenture, and Rosalyn Neal in their home, with her easy laugh, the hours they spend together every day.

WHEN LI JING picks Pang Pang up in the afternoon the boy erupts with a stream of carefully practiced English. "Dad," he says, "my name is Li Gepang." He keeps talking, dispensing all the English he had been saving up from summer school classes in one unbroken paragraph. "I am eight years old. This is my father. Father, where will we go to eat dinner? Father, I would like pizza and hamburgers, please. How do you do today?"

"I am . . . well today!" Li Jing crouches down and looks up into Pang Pang's determined face, astonished, shaking his head slightly. "Your English is very good, Pang Pang. We eat pizza or hamburgers today. McDonald's, or Pizza Hut?"

Pang Pang darts his eyes to the ground and back up to Li Jing, panicked, not understanding the response. Li Jing grabs his son's hand and squeezes it as hard as he dares, trying to pour all his gratitude and relief into it. "Pizza?" He repeats in English, slowly this time. "Or hamburger?" He is afraid of his own face, knowing that it is being lit by grotesque desperation, and so he turns away, not letting Pang Pang see him bite down on his lip, hard enough to draw blood.

English, in Pang Pang's voice, sounds stilted, with a hint of a British accent from the language tapes his summer school uses. But the syllables are oddly beautiful too, quivering, taking on more coherence with every repetition until they begin to feel like a balm. "This is my father. This is my father. I am eight years old. How do you do today."

Dr. Liu had suggested that Meiling and Pang Pang learn English at the very beginning, but Li Jing had dismissed the idea then—it seemed like defeat, like accepting his aphasia as a permanent condition. He was the one with the wound in his brain, the misfiring neurons, a stuttering, useless tongue. He held out hope that all the words would come rushing back in, but months passed, and Chinese is no easier than it was when he woke up and ran his fingertips across the porous bandage on his head.

He stares up at leaves on the late-summer trees, so dense that they seem to stretch over the street like a solid canopy. Next to him Pang Pang is taller, his face still small but his arms and legs stretching out. "How do you do," Pang Pang keeps muttering to himself, "this is my father." The English phrases—on Pang Pang's tongue—seem to open up new fears, but possibilities too, and what if Meiling learned just a little bit of English, enough to get them through this . . . "Pang Pang," Li Jing blurts out, with an almost painful smile stretched across his face. "Let's go home."

The apartment door is unlocked, and Meiling's purse lies half open on the kitchen counter. He picks it up, feeling the grain of the leather beneath his fingertips, and hangs it in the front closet, in its rightful place. "Mei-ling." The syllables in Chinese are still off, awkward in his mouth and hard to grasp in the brain, but he says it again, turning it into English, turning *Meiling* into a different sound, softer, without the shifting inflections. It takes on different shading now, it sounds like music; he repeats it to himself, and listens to the shower running through the bathroom door.

The television clicks on, filling the apartment with the sounds of a cartoon. He stands in the hallway, closes his eyes—thinking that it could be six months ago or a year ago, the sounds of the shower, of the television, filling up this space. It is an ordinary moment, made precious, now, by the rarity of these ordinary moments. What he is missing is the sound of his father rustling newspapers in his room, clucking disapprovingly at the latest reports. Li Jing presses his palm against the wood of his father's door, and then twists the doorknob, walking in.

It smells different, though he cannot pinpoint how. All the furniture has stayed the same, all the books are still on the shelves, but there is a different blanket on the bed, and the framed photographs have disappeared. A glittering necklace hangs from the corner of a chair, and the calligraphy brushes on the desk are desiccated, gathering dust. His father would practice Chinese calligraphy in the morning for an hour every day, writing characters so beautiful that they looked like paintings. Over time he stacked one finished sheet on top of another, a palimpsest of days, but when Li Jing opens the bottom drawer of the desk the drawer slides out far too easily, without the weight of reams of paper, without years of mornings laid down in ink. His father's books and brushes are still here, but gone are his father's face, his father's handwriting. In the drawer there is a hairbrush, a package of American vitamins, and a makeup bag. A compact of eyeshadow has fallen open, and the bottom of the drawer is dusted in glittering bits of green and gold.

He walks over to the wardrobe in the corner and yanks the door open. Instead of somber Mao suits and sweaters in khaki and gray there are shiny dresses in purples and reds shoved onto the hangers, high heels haphazard across shelves. Faced with Rosalyn's things, with Rosalyn's presence, Li Jing can only reach out and touch a corner of a chiffon sleeve. Rosalyn. He has tried to avoid thinking of her, but after the turns of his life over the last few months she seems to have embedded herself into his life, into his home. Perhaps even into his heart.

What he feels for Rosalyn seems like an impossibility in Chinese. Chinese is a language without tenses; it sets emotions into permanence, unwilling to acknowledge changes over time. No, his affection for Rosalyn only exists in English, a language that sharply delineates the past, present, and future. He liked Rosalyn. He is falling for her. But there will be no future for the two of them. Dangling on the corner of a hanger is a gray T-shirt, about to fall off. He holds it up: it's enormous, with U OF O on the front, in big letters, two small holes near the collar. The shirt—whose it was originally, why she might wear it now—is incomprehensible to him, just as her life half a world away is unimaginable. He crumples the shirt in his hands. The worn cotton material is soft, almost warm to the touch.

The shower turns off with a squeak. The cartooned voices still stream out from the television. *"Meiling,"* he repeats the name—with its new course and inflections. He sees her face, at the restaurant and after the concert, guarded and blank, but now it occurs to him that she must be so exhausted, she might be as scared as he is. In her tightly seized face he imagines she is hiding all her fears, she is hiding all the grief he has brought to her, the unbearable burdens he has caused over these few months. He wants to apologize or make it easier, but he does not know how. He thinks that maybe if they can just get away from this apartment and all its memories for a little while, the three of them, then maybe her face will loosen up, maybe she will smile once more, maybe he can call her by her name—the same name but a different sound.

When Meiling walks into the room her hair is still wet from the shower, her cheeks are scrubbed pink, and she wears glasses instead of contacts, looking so young, looking like that girl with the yellow backpack. Li Jing starts to smile—they'll go away for the weekend, they'll go to Hangzhou, just the three of them, he'll try harder—but when he takes two steps toward her she opens her mouth wide as if she is about to scream. Her face has twisted itself into horror and disgust.

"Meiling." He says her name in the only way he can. She backs away, staring not at his face but at his chest, as if into his heart. He looks down and sees the gray T-shirt still bunched in his hands, his fingers fisting the material. When he lets go of it, the shirt flutters gracelessly down the front of his pants, falling into a heap at his feet.

Before he can say anything Meiling has run out into the hallway. *"Meiling,"* he calls out, *"No! It's not . . ."* but she doesn't even turn around. In the living room Pang Pang's head is alert, twisted toward them. Li Jing shoots him a look of anguish, and they both watch Meiling take a suitcase out of the front closet, watch the smooth silver buckles catch the sunlight, flaring bright.

"What are you doing?" English, English again. Speaking English in the apartment feels like firing a shot, but English is all he has. *"Meiling. Stop!"*

There is nothing to do but follow her as she goes from one end of the apartment to the other. He's right on her heels, so close that drops of water from her hair spray onto his skin. In their bedroom she begins throwing clothes and underwear into the open suitcase. *"What are you doing?"* She can't understand him, doesn't even want to understand him, but the English phrases tumble out and he flails in their midst, trying to grasp on to something, anything. *"Where are you going? Stop, please stop!"*

Pang Pang steps into the room and thrusts the electronic dictionary into Li Jing's hands. "Mom," he says, a hitch in his throat. "What's going on?"

"Go to your room, pack a bag for yourself." Meiling barely raises her head. "Clothes, and your toothbrush, and an extra pair of shoes, and a few books. Don't argue with me, Pang Pang. Do it now."

Pang Pang stands in the doorway. "Dad?"

"Go to your room—now!" Meiling calls out. Pang Pang hesitates for a moment before running out the door.

All along she has not stopped moving. She has been piling clothes into the suitcase without order or care. Now the suitcase is almost full. She tugs at the zipper and it makes a hissing sound, baring its teeth, closing the case.

"*Please,*" he says. The long syllable of English quivers in fright. His fingers feel too clumsy for the tiny keys of the electronic dictionary, but he forces himself to slow down, to type in the right combinations of letters. "Why?" The dictionary chirps out in Chinese. When Meiling does not respond he presses the keys again. "Why? Why? Why?"

"I have to get out of here." She is breathing hard, shaking her head. He wants to touch her, wants to put his arms around her, but he knows she would jump away if he came any closer. "What a fool I've been." Her back is turned to him and her voice is shaking. "I've been an idiot not to see what's going on between the two of you."

"No." The electronic dictionary makes the Chinese syllable sound crisp but bland, so he switches to English, useless English. At least in English he can pour his feelings into his voice. "*No, Meiling. Please don't go. I'm sorry. It's not what you think!*"

She shoves the suitcase off the bed and turns around. He tries to plead, cowering before her, putting his palms over his heart. "*Meiling, please,*" he begs, but her face doesn't change. It is hard, full of scorn, the skin so tight he's afraid it'll crack.

"I have to go." She has gotten ahold of herself and her voice is quieter now, almost indifferent. "I'm taking Pang Pang with me. I need time to think."

He cannot stand it anymore and lurches forward, tries to grab her arm, but she steps back fast. "Li Jing." There is a note of warning in her voice. "Don't touch me."

"Where?" The dictionary chirps. "Where? Why?"

"To my parents' house." She walks into Pang Pang's room and all Li Jing can do is follow her there. Pang Pang has taken a travel bag out from beneath the bed, but it sits on the floor, empty, while the boy stands pressed up against the wall, his hands tucked behind his back. Meiling is quick to the closet, grabbing T-shirts and socks. "We're going to your grandparents', Pang Pang," she says, "won't that be nice."

"Please don't." He hates the dictionary, hates the placid woman's voice coming out of the tinny speakers, hates the way it feels in his hands, plastic, toylike. But it is his only recourse. He switches over to English again. *"Not Pang Pang. Please. Not Pang Pang."*

She stalks into the bathroom and comes out with two toothbrushes. Then she slings Pang Pang's bag over her shoulders, she is already walking away. Half an hour ago he was walking down the street listening to Pang Pang's words in English, staring up at the leaves, thinking ahead to fall. Now it's as if a bomb has gone off—he knows it's his fault, he knows he has hurt her again, but he doesn't know how to fix it or explain.

"When? When?" he asks her through the dictionary, still at her heels. She won't turn to look at him and so he has to keep following her. "Back. When?"

"I don't know. I don't know." When she answers his questions she doesn't even break stride. Her voice is quick and harsh, spitting contempt. "Don't worry, you'll have Dr. Neal to keep you company. I don't expect that you'll miss us at all."

CHAPTER 24

On her way back to the apartment Rosalyn stops at a liquor store that caters to foreigners and buys two expensive bottles of gin: one to take to Clarissa's party that night, another as a gift for Meiling and James. She is not sure if the gift is appropriate, too much or not enough, but the intricacies of her relationship with James and his wife have become too byzantine to unravel, as if there were a set of governing rules, but no one is willing to translate them or shine a light. She stays in their home, eats their food, every Monday an envelope of cash with her name on it appears on the dining table. But it is impossible to tell whether she's supposed to be guest or hired help, whether their apartment is supposed to be hotel or home. She does not question it too much: the life that's been arranged for her here in Shanghai feels stolen, as if she's on the run, delaying extradition. She ignores the tension splintering through the apartment and wills herself oblivious, letting herself be carried along, knowing that she will leave it behind in time.

So the days ripped away easily. The heat made her exhausted and delirious. In sleep, she thrashed, waking up with her body coiled tight. But during the day the hours were smothered by little things, here and there, and she was saved from having to think about her life, about what she was really doing here still, after these empty months. She had not wanted to go back to the hospital, and so she did not have access to the MRI unit, the gantry, or the imaging software. She gave up on further developing her computational model, and decided to focus on the practicalities of his rehabilitation. They started, in the mornings, with exercises in English, which Li Jing dispatched with increasing ease. Then there were videotapes and voice recordings for speaking Chinese, and both of them tried to follow along, laughing and making light of their mistakes. She made him repeat all the iterations of each tongue-twisting phrase, but she could hear the imprecision of his syllables, could watch his face darken with frustration before he tried to shake it off. He would persuade her into finishing early and heading out into the city, and she always succumbed, letting him drag her out of the apartment, letting him show her another part of his Shanghai.

They went to temples and public squares. They went to the science museum and a toy store. He tried to show her where he lived as a teenager only to find the *longtang* entirely razed, the site of new construction. He took her to the university where his father had taught—outside his father's old office the newspaper obituary hung behind glass, the professor's face in black-and-white seeing everything. They walked through flower markets, spent afternoons in department stores, riding escalators, buying sunglasses and chopsticks. There was an easy camaraderie between them, but there was a caginess too. They were careful not to touch, careful not to talk about his marriage or her divorce. She asked him about his distant past and he talked about his childhood in America in a tone of discovery. He did not ask her questions about Ben or Danny or about the future, and she was grateful for it. On the streets, with English coursing between them, setting them apart from the crowds, the two of them existed in an entirely private universe.

In the afternoons, when James headed to the hospital for his sessions with Dr. Liu, Rosalyn took naps in her bedroom, prepared for nights out with her friends. Without noticing it she has memorized the schedule of comings and goings in the apartment. She tried always to leave before Li Jing brought Pang Pang back from school, before Meiling came home, and then she stayed away until late at night. She had Danny and Clarissa and Patrick in the evenings. Night after night they drank and danced and laughed, everything fizzing like a flute full of champagne.

When she returns to the apartment this time it's already late afternoon. She braces herself for an awkward meeting with Li Jing and Pang Pang, but all she hears is silence when she walks through the door. What she sees, though, is a mess: a pizza box on the floor, the closet door open, discarded bags of food littering the table. She puts the bottles of gin down and wonders if she should try to clean it up, but it is not her house, she does not know where anything goes, and so she walks back to her room, leaving it all untouched. It reminds her of returning to her parents' house as an adult: of how she'd leave the dishes unwashed in the sink or forget to make her bed in the morning, things she would never have done in her own home. The luxury of being removed from her everyday routines is unsustainable, but for now, she shrugs her shoulders and opens her wardrobe, looking for the night's outfit with jaded anticipation. Clarissa is having one of her monthly martini parties tonight, and it will be, she thinks, all the same people that she sees all the time, air kissing as if they actually like one another. Danny will be there too. She has been putting him off with one excuse after another since he kissed her at the bar, in front of James. She feels a vague sense of guilt for leading him on, but he has always known that this wasn't real, that she would leave. Seeing Danny now, even in a group of people, feels awkward in a way she does not want to examine. He was the one who knew her first, and now, his gaze, when it flickers over her, is full of questions and doubts.

She puts on a green satin dress she bought from Huating Market. The dress is cut like a traditional *qipao*, with gold embroidery that echoes the gold in her hair, but it ends, abruptly, in the middle of her thighs. Then there is eyeshadow and mascara and blush and lipstick, then her platform shoes, and a smile to herself in the bathroom mirror, trying to convince herself of the good time to come.

She wanders into the living room. Outside the balcony doors, the sunset shoots through smog, smothering the city in a radioactive glow. She flops down on the sofa and lets her knees knock together, not knowing why she is dreading the night ahead. One rounded corner of a video game control unit sticks out underneath the coffee table, and she picks it up, turns it over in her hand, pressing on the arrows and buttons.

Sometimes she catches Pang Pang looking at her, studying every detail as if she were a question he is trying to find the answer to. She has been trying hard not to think about the boy, about the three of them, James and his wife and his son. Now she wonders if they are out having dinner together in some dark and cozy restaurant, what they do when she is not here. The thought of them—as a family—should not be surprising, but she has tried her best to push it aside; she has acted as though his life, too, is as without constraint as hers has become in Shanghai. There are so many things that she tries not to think about now. Sometimes late at night she wonders if he feels anything besides gratitude and camaraderie when he is with her, she wonders what happens between him and his wife when the door closes, across the hall.

The thought of him with Meiling, laughing with her, touching her, cuts into Rosalyn like a thin, precise razor blade, the cut so fine that you have to press at the skin for blood to come welling up out of it. She tries to shake it off and walks toward the bathroom. There's no point in thinking of any of it, she tells herself, and tries to imagine ahead, to Clarissa's party, the clamor of it, all the people, Clarissa's beautiful apartment under dim lights and the haziness of gin.

A small sound comes out of the master bedroom, a cotton-mouthed sound without shape or clarity. Rosalyn jolts in surprise, and then the sound comes again, muffled.

"Hello?" she calls out, knocking on the door. "*Nihao?* Is anyone there?"

The curtains are closed, the lights turned off. When her eyes adjust to the dimness she sees James on the bed, his head in his hands, rocking back and forth. She sits down next to him, peering into his face. "James." She smooths her palm over his hair. "Are you okay?"

It darts into her heart, the pleasure of touching him. She can feel the spiky ends of his hair beneath her fingers, the heat of his body so close to her. "It's okay," she says. "Whatever it is, it'll be okay."

When he looks up his eyes are wild. He shakes his head, hard, and she puts her palm on his cheek, wanting him to be still.

"What's the matter, James?" She says it so tenderly that it comes out as a whisper, his name fading into a lisp. "What's wrong? Tell me. It'll be okay, I promise."

"She left." He tries to hold himself still but under her palm she can feel him trembling. "She came home, took Pang Pang, left. Said she needed . . . to think."

"Meiling left? Where did she go? When is she coming back?"

"Maybe she's never coming back . . . for me. Maybe . . . giving up on me."

"She's going to come back," Rosalyn blurts out, and then says, more quietly, "Don't be scared."

"What am I going to do?" He is blubbering now, his words shaky. "What if . . . she not come back. Why would she? What am I going to do?"

"It's going to be okay," Rosalyn says, hauling James to his feet and letting herself hug the full length of him, letting her body absorb his tremors. The room—their bedroom—is just as meticulous and cold as the living room. With James in her arms she shakes her head, angry on his behalf, wondering what kind of woman Meiling was that she could just leave him behind, could shut her heart against him and walk out the door with their son.

"What am I going to do?" He looks into her face. "Don't want . . . to stay here, by myself. And Pang Pang! Gone! What am I going to do?"

"It's okay, James. Just breathe." She holds his eyes for a few seconds and puts her palms on his cheeks, rubbing his skin as if she can erase his fears. In the dim light of the room, with the silence of the apartment stretching on, it feels like they are the only two people in the city. She stretches up and presses a kiss to his temple.

"Whatever happened with Meiling, whatever it is—she's not here right now, and things are going to be okay. I don't think you should stay here right now. In fact, I think we should both get out of here, go have some dinner. And then, if you want, you should come to a party with me," Rosalyn says, leading him by the hand. "Whatever it is—you can forget about it for now, you can deal with it tomorrow."

HE WANTS TO wipe away all his fear, his sadness, he wants to be as indifferent as Meiling was when she so easily left him behind. So at dinner he drinks a bottle of wine and smiles at Rosalyn from across the table, caressing her fingers. It is as if there's an unspoken agreement between them not to refer to the scene back at the apartment. They gossip about his other doctors or talk about American TV shows from the seventies instead. For stretches of minutes he can forget, he is almost happy, and he marvels at Rosalyn, at her laughter, the way she can so easily absolve him of everything. In the cab on the way to the party they sit pressed together in the center of the backseat. He likes the way she feels under his arm, likes the adoration he can see glowing out of her face.

He walks into the stranger's house with Rosalyn's hand in his. She smiles at him before letting go to hug the hostess, and her smile slips a bright note of courage to the base of his spine, putting him at ease.

"Clarissa," Rosalyn says. "This is James. James, our fair hostess Clarissa."

The woman opposite them is wearing a long, skintight red dress cut so low that he can see the black lace of her bra peeking out. She raises her eyebrows and does not even try to be discreet as she looks him up and down through her glasses, assessing him.

"Hello," she says, "so you're the one Rosalyn's been playing doctor with."

Next to him Rosalyn cringes, squeezing his hand hard. He has met women like Clarissa before, women with this particular kind of posturing, slightly embarrassing with their sexual bravado. "A pleasure, Clarissa." He is careful to enunciate every syllable clearly and steps forward to kiss her hand with a charming, giddy smile. "Yes, I am lucky, I am the reason that Rosalyn is with us. She . . . is a treasure, yes? Lucky me. Lucky all of us."

He can feel Rosalyn's astonishment at his glibness, but he simply smiles again at Clarissa and leads Rosalyn into the living room. Clarissa's house is an old Shanghai mansion painted blood-red and done up in gilt and kitsch. Along the edges of the room antique furniture gleams with elaborate, curving edges, and when he looks up he sees parasols in pinks and yellows and reds looming, covering up the ceiling in a kaleidoscopic pattern. *Lǎowàis* gather in clusters with drinks in their hands, shouting, laughing with each other. Out of the corner of his eyes he sees Danny Barrett coming and he tightens his hold on Rosalyn before turning with a look of surprise and exaggerated pleasure.

"Danny! So . . . nice to see you again."

"Hey, James." Danny is turned toward him, but he's looking at Rosalyn, trying to catch her eye. "I'm surprised to see you here. Recovering quite well, aren't you?"

"I am. And you? Practicing cello? Next time I see you . . . hope you play in professional orchestra."

Danny opens his mouth in shock and closes it again. Rosalyn glares back at Li Jing and goes to hug Danny, trying to hide her smile. Li Jing is already walking away. He goes to the bar and fixes two martinis, taking his time. When Rosalyn comes up to him, alone, he hands her a glass and lifts one eyebrow.

"How is . . . your boyfriend?"

"He's not my boyfriend," she shoots back, blushing.

"Does he know that?" Li Jing laughs, taking a gulp of his drink.

"Yes. Well, maybe." She rolls her eyes but he can tell she is not displeased. He nudges her with his shoulder and she leans into him, pushing him back. They laugh but then they both look away from each other, Rosalyn blushing harder, the stain on her cheek bleeding down to her neck.

All evening long, his mind keeps drifting back to Meiling's face, and he sees it again now, the way it was lit up with contempt, the way it dismissed his claim on her. He takes a gulp of his drink and tries to leave her behind too. He wants to forget the whole afternoon, forget the idiotic way his heart had surged before she shattered all his hopes. But his voice, in English, begging her, courses through his brain again and again. "Please," he hears himself saying, but she wouldn't listen. When they left, Pang Pang had turned around with a helpless, beseeching look, but Meiling just kept going, as if she couldn't hear him. She walked out the door without ever looking at him again.

Now it is Rosalyn's face that he sees. She is leaning in close, smiling and animated, her eyes feverish, her lips half open, waiting for him to say something. After this summer of losses she is the only one he has left, and he pulls her in, buries his face in her neck for a moment before letting go. "Are you okay?" she whispers softly. "I am fine," he says. "I am great." He wants to show Meiling that she matters as little to him as he does to her, and so he takes a step back from Rosalyn and shrugs into a practiced ease that feels good against the skin. "Let us enjoy the party," he says, putting his arm around Rosalyn's shoulder, pressing his fingers into her bare arm.

Clarissa's house looks like a set, with lacquered snuffboxes and velvet drapes, thick, intricate rugs on the hardwood floor. The lights are dim, and candles flicker around the room, giving everyone a look of determined glamour, all shadows and screens. They all stand around as if they're waiting for their close-ups, he thinks, the women tilting down their chins with alluring smiles, the men with their eyebrows permanently cocked, their faces feigning boredom and insouciance. Everywhere there's English, with its smooth vowels lollygagging, its accented permutations. There's a buzzing in his head from the wine and gin and the smoke and the voices, the loud, discordant music coming out of the speakers, the heavy, cloying scents from incense sticks in corners. Rosalyn is across the room now, her green dress bright in the middle of a small circle of people, Danny at her elbow, trying to insert himself into the conversation. Li Jing watches her for a second, watches her furrow her brows and then smooth out her forehead. She does not turn to look at him but there is a kind of alertness in her body, and he knows that she is as aware of him as he is of her.

He turns away and introduces himself to an older English couple. They are in China to sample and track down tea varieties for a British tea brand. He draws them into a conversation about leaves and picking times, about fermentation and brewing vessels. They are delighted by his attentions, by his expertise, and by his slow and mysterious command of English. Both halves of the couple have long and melancholy faces. For a moment the man's white hair, his face, and the determined timbre in his voice remind Li Jing so much of his father that he stutters. But then the blue eyes of the stranger come back into focus and he shakes off the thought, smiling again, all charm, light as air.

"Yes, the English do know teas. Second in this . . . in tea knowledge . . . perhaps, only to the Chinese."

Despite having been out of practice he finds it easy to return to that older, more gregarious version of himself; he has always been a natural at gathering a crowd during parties. Other people join their small circle, a journalist dispatched from Ohio, the teenage daughter of the ambassador from New Zealand. He chats with them, makes them laugh, but all along he is conscious of Rosalyn's location, he is reminded of her hold on him. She careens through different pockets of people on the other side of the room, chatting with acquaintances and friends, and he can pick out her laughter, sometimes, the sound of it jumping out of the din, singular, like a strand of glittering beads. She looks up with heavy eyelids and their eyes meet for a moment. He smiles, raising his glass, glad that he does not need her, but knowing that she is his lodestar.

"James." The ambassador's daughter tugs on his arm, drawing out his name in her nasal voice. "I need your help. Do you know of any tattoo parlors in Shanghai? I'm going to get a tattoo, either a bird or a daisy, right here." She points to her chest.

He looks down at the girl's large, pale breasts, rising out of her black corset. He exaggerates his expression so that his ogling is more than blatant, so that everyone is smiling and her young face twitches, wavering from bravado into uncertain amusement.

"Alma." He says her name slowly. He knows that his elliptical English has become an exotic and necessary part of his effect, and he plays it up, drawing out every syllable. "I will not tell you. Please, I beg you . . . don't be rash. Why would you want to"—he pauses and looks around—"spoil your own . . . perfection?"

Everyone bursts out laughing, Alma loudest of all, her black lipstick a gash on her face, her hands holding on to his arm even more tightly. Not far from him, Rosalyn glances over while she shakes hands with a man who has just walked in, and then she lifts the man's arm over her head, spinning underneath as if she is on the dance floor, smiling up with the certainty of drink.

Li Jing walks through a long, dark hallway to wait outside the bathroom. He closes his eyes for a moment, leans into the wall, trying to make the pulsing in his head subside but taking another gulp of his martini, wanting its oblivion. The bathroom door swings open, and a young Chinese man in a dress shirt and a skinny tie walks out, blinking, hovering at the door for a long moment. He looks down the hall into the living room, at the people passing through the doorway, the glow of candles and dimmed lights, and takes a step toward them, but then hesitates and draws back. Finally he notices Li Jing, and he starts to stammer but then his eyes focus in recognition.

"*Duì bu qǐ.*" The man speaks Chinese as if it is a relief. *Excuse me.* "Some party, isn't it? I only know one person here, and he's busy flirting with some woman so he's abandoned me. It's kind of awkward." He moves closer to Li Jing and whispers, "I think you and I are the only two Chinese guys here."

Li Jing is sympathetic, but there is nothing he can say. He nods and makes a sound of assent. The young man, who looks as though he's still in college, glances from side to side to make sure that there's no one nearby, and keeps going, pouring out sentence after nervous sentence.

"I mean, they've got the expensive alcohol, that's for sure. But there's no food, and everyone's just standing around. What's the point of that? I have to tell you, I was kind of excited to come tonight. A real foreigners' party, I thought. But this is kind of boring, isn't it?" He straightens his tie and smooths his hand over his hair. "I don't know who I'm even supposed to talk to. My friend—this German exchange student in my department—left me on my own, before he introduced me to anybody. Do you know anybody here?"

The problem isn't listening to Chinese. He can understand every tone, every word, even the things that the young man doesn't say, the things that are humming beneath his jumpiness, his rapid-fire jabber. The problem happens the moment the other person falls silent and looks at you, waiting, and then you just stand there, your mouth open and useless, shaking your head.

"I . . ." Li Jing stammers, wanting to apologize for so many things. "I am sorry."

The young man registers the English phrase as an insult. "Pardon me." He switches to English too, and then flushes dark. Li Jing watches as he walks down the hall and stands at the doorway to the living room, looking left and then right before disappearing into the crowd.

Inside the bathroom the walls are plastered with old Chinese news-papers, yellowed and blurry from age and water damage. The light-bulbs glow under dense red shades so that they look like lanterns, and when he looks into the cloudy mirror his face is murky; he can barely recognize himself. He takes a deep breath, trying to sober up or clear his head, but the room smells like perfume and cigarettes. He feels like he's being smothered.

He walks out, and instead of going back to the living room he heads away from all the people, toward the half-open door on the other end of the hallway. Clarissa's bedroom is cavernous. From the markings near the ceiling he can tell that walls have been torn down, and older, smaller units merged to make the single room. Now the space is dominated by an antique four-poster bed with the mattress raised high and pink canopy panels pooling onto the floor. Everywhere he looks the walls are covered in satin and candlelight. There are mirrors and birdcages, paintings of courtesans, and vases on pedestals. An old armoire stretches to the ceiling and one door is propped open, showing off a sumptuous riot of fabrics and colors, dresses tumbling out, gleaming darkly.

It looks, he thinks, like an opium den or a brothel. Like something from a television show, signifying sin and moral decay. He sits down on an armchair and rests his chin in his hand. Clarissa walks in, her face naked with exhaustion for a moment, but then she sees him and sways, catching herself with a practiced smile.

"James," she says, her voice low. "Well, well, well. I see you've found your way to my bedroom."

"Hello, Clarissa. The party is great."

"If it's so great, then what are you doing hiding out in here? Or did you come here looking for me?"

Even drunk, Clarissa advances on him smoothly, with a predatory languor. He considers her for a second, trying to think it through despite the buzz in his head. He has been propositioned by a number of women before. Being a wealthy man in Shanghai meant that he was the object of more than a few pursuits despite being married. He would never be so self-righteous as to say that he hadn't been tempted, at times. But his heart, with its hopeless, unwavering devotion to his wife, had not been touched, and the thought of having an affair always seemed pointless whenever he went home and basked in the pleasure of seeing her smile.

He does not want to think of her smile now, does not want to think of the empty apartment, of Pang Pang being gone too, of the way she just took off, leaving him behind. Clarissa is sitting on the bed and giving him an appraising look. He stays still, and in the quiet he can hear the din from the living room, the laughter and music and conversation making him feel more alone.

"Hey you guys!" Rosalyn pushes through the door and spills some of her drink on the floor. "What are you doing in here?"

Then, taking in the scene, she starts to laugh.

"Clarissa," she says, tender and admonishing. "Where's Steve? I didn't see him out there tonight. What are you doing? I think you've had one too many drinks."

"Steve and I broke up." Clarissa stands up again and sighs dramatically. "He's left me, the bastard, for this bitch who just got here from California. She's a cow, and about fifty years old, but supposedly she's a record producer, therefore good for his career. I hate Steve. Steve can go to hell. I need a distraction, I need someone else to play with."

"Oh darling!" Rosalyn says, and he watches the two women hug. Then they whisper to each other, tightly enclosed in something female, some instinctive cocoon built at will. Clarissa nods at something Rosalyn says and then her face is glowing again. She looks at him, pushing her glasses up the bridge of her nose. With a tilt of her eyebrows she says, "I was just looking after him for you."

"Well, thank you. I think that'll be all for now." Rosalyn catches his eye and smiles.

"Anytime." Clarissa saunters out of the room. "Bye kids. Be good."

Now who would advance on whom? Rosalyn's face is pink, he notices, and her eyes are bright, glazed over.

"So," she says, "you were the quite the hit out there."

He shrugs. "Fun party. Nice people."

She sits down on the bed, exactly where Clarissa had sat before, and leans back, propping herself up on her arms. "What were you going to do if I hadn't come in?"

He gets up out of the armchair but stands still, at a distance from her. "Going to . . . put her to bed," he says, pausing before finishing the sentence, "so she can sleep it off."

The blanket on the bed is bright red, with intricate yellow designs on it. Rosalyn runs her palm over the silk, and then rubs it, thoughtlessly, in her fingers. He keeps standing there, not wanting to take a step forward but not wanting to leave either. Finally, she reaches out with one hand, and he walks into her arms, leaning down for a kiss.

They had kissed once before. He had pecked her quickly when he thought she was leaving Shanghai. That kiss had felt inconsequential, like a goodbye. This kiss, now, her lips and her tongue and her skin soft beneath him, feels like something else. She reaches up and grabs the back of his neck, pulling him down so that he has to rest his weight on her. He can feel something seizing the bottom of his stomach, this ache, and he cannot tell if it's shame or longing or rage. She feels soft and expansive, almost liquid, and so warm to the touch he wants to burrow closer, to draw from her heat. When she begins to open the buttons at the neck of his shirt he freezes up for a moment, like an animal who has just picked up the scent of a predator in the wind, but then her hands are touching his face and he closes his eyes and gives himself over to her, letting himself forget, letting himself sink.

VII

FALSE MOONS

A flock of birds is singing outside the window of his grandparents' house. Pang Pang turns to them with fury, trying to shush them so they won't wake his mom up. She twitches and rolls over but stays asleep, and he slips her shoes off her feet, setting them down on the floor gently, so as not to make a sound. His mom had lain down in bed with all her clothes on after they got to the house, falling asleep right away. He stands guard over her now, watching her, counting her breaths.

At dinner, his mom is still asleep in the next room, so he eats quietly, whispers to his grandma and his grandpa about flying kites, about going down to the river tomorrow morning. He sets aside a bowl for his mom, putting a scoop of rice on the bottom and covering it up with a pile of cabbage and pieces of chicken. Then he drifts along at the table, and when his grandparents go to sleep at eight o'clock he sits in the dark house, thinking about the day, trying to sort out all the details, tracing over every moment. He hadn't wanted to leave his dad behind—his dad's face looked sad and scared. But then his mom's face on the airplane was so white and her hand gripped his so hard that he was afraid for her too. He watches the clouds fade from orange to black out the window. He doesn't know who to worry about more, or what to do.

In the morning his mom's smile is brighter. They eat breakfast together and she tells him he gets to decide what they'll do during the day. The river calls out, so do the trees where you can climb up into the branches, but he doesn't want to leave the house just yet, and so he tells her that he wants to play hide-and-seek. His grandparents are sitting on the porch, snapping the roots off bean sprouts. He recruits them to play, and tells his mom that she has to be the one to find them. When she's counting to a hundred he knows just where to go.

It's not a big house, but the rooms have little nooks and crannies and the ceilings are high. He can hear his mom starting out in the kitchen, and in no time at all she has found his grandma. She laughs in triumph. "Dad! Pang Pang! I'm coming to find you," she shouts.

It takes her a little longer to find his grandpa. While she's looking, she comes into the room he's hiding in, looks under the bed and into all the corners and behind all the furniture and even into the closet. But he's found a good hiding spot so she doesn't see him. She walks back out and soon he can hear his grandpa groaning from the other end of the house.

"You got me." His grandpa's voice is gentle even when he's been caught.

"Two down, one to go!" his mom says, loud, as she comes closer.

He squeezes his legs to his chest and makes himself very small. He has climbed onto the very highest shelf in the closet and sits behind the winter coats bundled and tied down with string. The door of the closet is slightly open, and if he presses his face to the shelf and looks through a crack in the wood, he can see parts of the room below and a small corner of the kitchen. His mom comes in again, calling out, "Pang Pang, where are you?" He keeps quiet. She rolls her neck and closes her eyes and collapses onto a white, spindly chair by the bookshelf.

"I'm taking a break," she says to the air. "But get ready, because when I get up again I'm going to come and find you!"

She takes a thin book down from the shelf and opens it, putting it close to her face. She flips through a few of the pages, and then slams the book shut. She looks sad, he thinks, like how he imagines a heroine in a fairy tale might look, before everything gets fixed. Then she is shouting again. "Break over. Here I come!"

From his perch he can see her rummaging through the cupboards in the kitchen, even opening the fridge. And then she disappears onto the porch. "I thought you guys had to stay in the house. I hope you haven't gone outside." He listens hard to her footsteps, and then the sound of a door being opened—the back door, he thinks. She's probably in the small, drafty room in the back of the house where his grandparents keep old cardboard boxes and hang sausages to dry from the rafters. Her voice is sharper now, and it carries a faint echo. "Pang Pang, come out! I give up. You win!"

The house has no attic, and the closet extends high up, all the way into the sloping ceilings. Where he's sitting it's almost completely dark, with little stripes of light coming in from below. The dark feels warm on his skin, like it's petting him, and he leans back against the bundle of parkas, settling in. A hinge on the rod below gives up a tiny squeak and he freezes, terrified of being found, but then he hears her and she's outside the house again, shouting, "Pang Pang! Where are you? Come out, please, just come out."

She runs fast through the house, and when she comes back into the room, her hair has come out of her ponytail and her face is tight and pointed. She lies down on the floor and looks under the bed, then she's in the closet, right below him, digging through the stacks of sweaters, grabbing jackets on hangers and shoving them aside.

He holds his breath and watches her. She's so close that he can reach out with his foot and touch the top of her head. Her hair is shiny and black, just beneath him, but then he can see a few strands of white hair glittering, right in the middle, where there is a flesh-colored, zigzagging part that exposes her scalp. She stands still for a moment and he starts to reach out his hand, open his mouth, but then she is walking away, fast, walking out of the room and down the hall.

His mom, he thinks, is slipping out of his grasp, just like his other grandpa slipped away, just like everything—their whole family seems to be slipping away. She's almost never home anymore, and when she is, she always seems so distracted, as if she's there, but not really there, as if she's thinking about something else.

"Pang Pang! Please come out!" She stands in the middle of the room, rubbing at her eyes and then swiping the back of her hand just beneath her nose. His grandpa and grandma are calling out his name too now, their mermaid voices low and insistent. "Pang Pang," they say. "Where are you? Come out, you're making us worry."

The walls are so close to him, the space is so dark, when he closes his eyes he can convince himself he's sitting in a tiny cell, that he's sitting inside a time machine. He wants things to be the way they were before, when his other grandpa was still alive and his dad laughed and told jokes and his mom picked him up at school and then they sat down on the couch, him with his homework and her with her poems. Now everything's different and there's a stranger living in his house—he's not sure whether she's an ally or a spy. Maybe if he just sits here, in this tiny space, for long enough, he can make time go backward. He screws his eyes up tight and tries to concentrate hard, thinking of the Swan Hotel, seeing the pieces of the rubble on the ground and then trying to build it back up, like a movie being played in reverse.

His mom is in the kitchen again, blowing her nose, and she's crying now. She says his name and her voice is so quiet he can barely hear her.

"Pang Pang," she says. "I'm scared. Where are you? Please be safe. Please."

He hadn't meant to make her even sadder than she was. "Mom," he cries out.

She turns around in a whirl and comes into the room, staring hard in every corner. "Where are you? Pang Pang, where are you?"

He grabs the rod below him and then flips himself down, landing on his hands and knees in a pile of quilts, crying out from the impact. She is already taking big, wobbly steps toward him, and then she is holding him tight and close as if she never wants to let him go.

THE DAYS SEEM longer in Sichuan. Two days without responsibilities means barefoot walks with Pang Pang by the river, rereading books of poetry she loved as a teenager, playing endless games of mahjong with her parents, sitting still outside, letting the sun burn her feet until they feel a pleasant, almost abrasive tingle. It feels like a vacation, Meiling thinks, or an escape.

It is the early afternoon now, and her parents have retired to their room for their naps. Pang Pang, too, fell asleep while they were sitting on the porch, and she lets him stay there, on one of the big wicker chairs, leaving the door open a crack so that she can still see his thin legs dangling below the seat of the chair.

She turns on her cell phone for the first time since she left Shanghai. There are voice mails from her assistant and from Vice President Wu about closing prices and meeting agendas, but nothing that cannot wait for a day or two. When she hangs up she keeps staring at the phone, wanting to dial home, but then she draws her hand back and puts the phone down. What could she say to him? "Are you in love with Rosalyn Neal?"

She thinks of the word for *love* in Chinese: *ai*. The sound of it rings false in the ear. Growing up, it was not a word that she heard in real life. Actors said "I love you" on television, their faces in close-ups, but even then, the words rolled off their tongues with an awkward gait. To Meiling, love had never been about saying the word *ai*. Instead, it had been about the way he dropped everything to take her to the hospital when her back hurt, the way he married her despite his father's disapproval. Love is about taking care of someone without being asked, about sacrificing yourself, about protecting the other person. Not long ago she would have said that pain was just another side of love, that it deepened love. Not long ago she would have said that words have nothing to do with love.

In a French movie she saw a few years ago, the heroine screeched, *"Je t'aime! Je t'aime!"* over and over again. The subtitles, written out, were almost embarrassing to read—no Chinese person would ever repeat that phrase in the same way. But the words on the sound track rang out like a song, with their own course and flow. Perhaps in French, perhaps in English, with an American woman, the concept of love is entirely different. Perhaps love, in a different language, rushes through and spills out more easily, the words carrying the feelings along.

When she left the apartment he was still calling out to her. Without understanding the words she could hear the desperation in his voice, and she kept hearing his voice in the elevator, in the car, in the airport lounge as their flight was about to board. Pang Pang's face was scrunched up in fear. "When are we coming back home?" he asked her, but she had no response for him. She wanted to turn back and rush into Li Jing's arms, but she had not been in his arms for months, and she kept seeing his face as he stared at Rosalyn Neal, she kept seeing his hands on Rosalyn Neal's shirt, holding it close to his heart.

She dials a number, almost hangs up, but stays on the line, listening to the ring.

"Hello," the voice on the other end comes on.

"Alan," she says. "It's Zhou Meiling." She doesn't know why she's called Alan, but he was the only person she could think of, the only person she wants to talk to.

"Meiling! Do you need something translated?"

"No, that's not why I called. Actually, I'm in Sichuan right now, with Pang Pang, at my parents' house."

"Is Li Jing with you?"

"No. He's not. He's back in Shanghai. With Dr. Neal."

She hadn't thought of it that way until now, hadn't thought about the fact that she has left Li Jing and Rosalyn alone in the apartment. The idea of it—of not just his face or the way he looks at her, but of them physically together, kissing, holding each other—is impossible to imagine. Yet once the image rushes into her head it will not let go. Would he really . . . ? She shakes her head, not even wanting to voice the question, not wanting to give it legitimacy. Alan's voice is in her ear, asking after her.

"I don't know Alan. I guess I'm fine."

He sounds like he's about to say something in response, but he pulls himself back, and they stay on the phone, letting silence stretch long between them.

"Alan?"

"Yes, Meiling?" His voice is clipped and careful.

"I called you because I didn't know who else I could talk to. I don't understand what's happening anymore. Maybe it's all in my head, maybe I'm the one who's blowing it out of proportion, but Alan, do you think—"

"Do I think . . . ?"

She fidgets with her hair, curling a small section of it around her fingers and then pulling at her scalp, hard. "Do you think there's something going on between Li Jing and Dr. Neal?"

His breath catches but she doesn't know if it's out of surprise or secondhand guilt. His voice, when it comes through, is slightly garbled. "I don't know, Meiling."

"That night, when we all went to dinner, I thought there might be something between the two of them, but . . . did you see anything then? Or am I just being paranoid?"

Alan takes a deep breath. "They do spend a lot of time together, Mr. Li and Dr. Neal. But it's only natural for a doctor and her patient to become close, isn't it?"

"Never mind, Alan. Forget I asked. I should go. I know I'm just being crazy."

"Wait, Meiling." Alan's words hurry out. "You're not being paranoid. I thought I saw something too, that night. And I know Dr. Neal well enough to know that she seems to care for Mr. Li. I just didn't know if it was my place to say anything."

She listens to him with the phone pressed tight against her ear and her eyes closed. His voice, always so transparent before, as transparent as glass, seems to have thickened, the syllables now distorted.

"Meiling?" After another silence he calls out, checking to see if she's still on the line. "I don't know any more than you do. I just thought I saw something between them. But Dr. Neal is only here for another few weeks. She'll be gone, out of your lives soon enough. I'm sure they haven't . . ."

Meiling stands up abruptly, takes a step forward, and walks straight into the table, the sharp edge of the wood slamming into the soft part of her stomach. The pain makes her give a small grunt and she sits back down again. Alan is still talking, and there is something about his voice, even now, that makes the words sound like they're being translated from a foreign language, from some entirely other world.

"I don't know Mr. Li very well at all," Alan says, "but I don't think he would—"

"He wouldn't. Or at least, he wouldn't have before. But he's like a stranger now. I don't know what he would or wouldn't do anymore."

"He's still the same person."

"Is he? I used to be so sure of him. I was so smug that when Professor Li thought there was something going on between Li Jing and Dr. Neal, I practically laughed in his face. But he was right. I was the one who was being a fool. I wish he were still here now. He'd know what to do."

"Meiling," Alan says. If she didn't know better, know how unruffled he is by everything, she would say that he sounds like he's in pain. "Whatever happens between you and Mr. Li, it's going to be all right. Dr. Neal is leaving soon. And you've done so much for Mr. Li—he must see that, even if things are hard for him now. I've watched you, you've been taking so much responsibility, you've done everything that you could. You've been the perfect—"

She interrupts him. "Don't say that, Alan. I'm not perfect. Trust me, I'm far from it."

"Meiling, I've seen how much you've sacrificed . . ."

"No, stop. Really! I can't listen to you talk about how much I've sacrificed and what a perfect wife I've been. Everyone wants to think that I'm so docile or perfect, that I have the perfect life. If you only knew . . ."

Alan makes a noise in his throat that could have been agreement or disbelief. She keeps talking, the words pouring out on their own. She has this feeling that if she just keeps talking, filling up space and time with her voice, things will begin to make sense, that possibilities too awful to think about will begin to recede.

"It's true—I had a really nice life. Looking around me, at other people—I knew that I was lucky. I married a man who adored me, and we met when we were both just students. But then he became very successful, and we became very rich, through no effort of mine. We have a wonderful son, even though I wasn't sure that was going to happen, I have a minor but respectable career, and my father-in-law, I suppose, was a person of some importance. Everything came so easily to me. Maybe it was all too easy."

"You were lucky, but you were also good, and brave. You deserved all those things—" Alan's voice sounds like it's being dragged out of him.

But she isn't listening. She's already starting again. "I lived a charmed life. Other people seemed to think that it was perfect. Maybe it was perfect, or at least had the appearance of it. But I was ungrateful. That's what no one knew about me. I felt like my life had all these limitations—I never really got to be on my own, I've never had my heart broken, my entire adult life was about my husband, and my father-in-law, and my child. And sometimes I thought: I wouldn't mind if all this fell apart so that I could find out what I'm really made of. So maybe the explosion was all my fault. Maybe I was the one who made it happen."

Alan starts to protest, but she will not let him get a word in. "You have no idea, Alan," she says. "I'm not the perfect wife. I'm not a good person. We're both talking around the possibility of Li Jing having an affair with Dr. Neal as if the idea of it is inconceivable. And I admit it, the idea of it is awful to me—not just because he would be having an affair, but because he would be having an affair with her, of all people. But why wouldn't he? People have affairs all the time. I almost did."

Alan makes a slight choking sound on the other end of the telephone.

"I've never told anybody. Sometimes I don't even like to remember it. But a few years ago, I met someone through work, and he was so . . . different from Li Jing. He was so irresponsible, and never had any money, and I couldn't imagine him being a husband or a father—that would have been a joke! But we had certain things in common, he and I—we liked the same poems, we saw the world in the same way, somehow. I found myself drawn to him, maybe because he was so different from Li Jing, and maybe because I wanted to test myself. I wanted to let myself fall for him, and see what would happen."

"And you . . . ?"

"I didn't do it. I couldn't sleep with him. But it wasn't, I think, because I was so committed to my marriage, or out of some sense of morality," she says, enunciating every syllable crisply. "No, it was probably because I was really only in love with the idea of him, with the difference of him. I wasn't actually in love with the person. And I'm glad, in the end, that I didn't cross that line. But the truth is, I crossed a lot of lines. I lied to Li Jing for weeks. I took so much pleasure in the man's company and in how reckless I felt. I was awful, and if Li Jing had ever found out, I'm not sure he could have ever forgiven me. Whatever is happening between him and Dr. Neal, he's so much more honest about it. Not me. I never let on a thing."

She has never told anyone all this. She has kept it wound up tight inside herself like a ball of yarn. Now she wants to unravel the whole thing, make a mess of it, not give a damn. She laughs, and the sound of it is bitter and awful.

"Li Jing always put me on a pedestal, and I liked it there, I thought I belonged there. I was so sure of him, though. I never thought about the possibility of him wanting to be with anyone else. That's just not how our relationship worked."

"Meiling . . ." Alan starts, but then falls silent.

"Have I shocked you? I'm sorry then—I probably shouldn't have told you. But you see, you shouldn't put me on a pedestal either. I'm not an innocent, or the injured party. I had a charmed life, I was thoughtless and deceitful, and maybe all this is fate's way of paying me back."

"I don't think . . ."

"I asked Rosalyn Neal to stay on, I invited her to move into our home. I was so arrogant—despite what the professor had said, and now they're together, in the apartment, and I'm the one who made that happen too—I left them there. I wouldn't listen to him, I wouldn't give him that satisfaction before I left, and I took Pang Pang with me because I was angry, because I wanted to punish him for looking at her that way. But he was only looking at her. He wasn't as good at deception as I was. What an idiot I've been." The words are hard to get out, so she grits her teeth. "I have only myself to blame. I need to get back to Shanghai before anything else happens."

"You can't blame yourself."

"It's his birthday tomorrow. I had forgotten—isn't that awful?—until Pang Pang reminded me last night. We'll go home in the morning. I hope it's not too late . . ." She trails off.

"And what if it is too late? What if he's with her?" Alan's voice takes on a savage quality.

Something sharp and revolting wrenches through her stomach. "No, he won't be. You were right before—he is the same person. It's my fault, all of this. I shouldn't have come here, and now I have to go home."

She gets up and goes out onto the porch, watches Pang Pang sleep with one hand thrown over his face to block out the sun. "Alan," she says, sincere, "thank you, for everything, not just for the translation, but for being my friend."

"Of course, Ms. Zhou. I wish you a good afternoon and a safe flight," he says without inflection, pausing, and then, "Goodbye, Meiling."

"Goodbye."

She hangs up the phone and sits down in the chair next to Pang Pang. Out here, it's so quiet that you can hear the soft hiss of the cornstalks in the wind, the barking of dogs. Despite what she said to Alan, despite the certainty she feigned, she can feel her legs start to tremble, and she has to bite down on her lower lip, hard, so that the sobs pulsing in her throat get swallowed up. Pang Pang shifts in the chair but stays asleep. He drops his arm and turns away from her, exposing his face to the light.

CHAPTER 26

"My birthday today." Li Jing says the words casually, barely looking over at Rosalyn.

"Today?" She is walking into the living room and makes an exaggerated stop, windmilling her arms, staring at him.

"Thirty-three. Middle age."

"Nonsense!" she says. "Why didn't you say anything to me? If I'd known I would have gotten you a present. I'm a big believer in birthday celebrations, you know. They do only come around once a year."

Late morning sun pours into the apartment, over the lines of the furniture, bleaching the bright wood of the tables, making the vases in the glass cabinet dazzle. He sinks back onto the couch and shakes his head, letting himself indulge in self-pity for a moment: his thirty-third birthday, but no one besides Rosalyn is here. He hadn't realized it until he woke up this morning, but he was hoping that Meiling would have remembered, that she and Pang Pang would have slipped into the apartment in the middle of the night. He wanted to wake up and find her lying next to him, smiling, giving him a kiss, wishing him a happy birthday. But there wasn't even a card or a telephone call.

"Well, what are we going to do to celebrate today?"

"Nothing," he tells Rosalyn. "Forget it."

"Oh no you don't. You're going to have a great birthday." She will not let him sour her enthusiasm. She looks at him now, all determination and cunning. "Give me ten minutes to get dressed, and then we're going out."

Her hair is still wet from the shower, the dark red strands matted against her scalp, and pieces of them crawl across her cheeks, connecting her freckles, making her look like a creature come out of the sea. She's wearing a bright blue tank top and it's been mottled by streaks of water, parts of the fabric bleeding dark, clinging tight. She gets up, and then bends down again. Her face is close to his, and he can see the hesitation in her eyes before she leans forward to kiss him, before she wraps her arms around his shoulders and presses him to her body.

"Birthdays should always start with a kiss and a hug," she says, backing away.

He has not touched Rosalyn since Thursday, since Clarissa's party, and she must have known that he was avoiding her, because she stayed out all weekend, coming back to the apartment only late at night, tiptoeing through the halls. Now she is offering him this kindness, as if he has done no wrong, dissolving the knot of guilt in his stomach. He looks up at her and she is smiling a warm, uncomplicated smile.

"Thank you," he says.

He wants to say something more than that, to explain himself, to say that despite the impossibility of the situation, the insanity of it, that he—what, that he wishes things could be different? Different—but how?

All weekend he felt as though his skin had been flayed open; he walked through the city without seeing a thing until he could no longer feel his feet. It was a city that shuttered itself against him now, all its voices chiming in, but its heart impenetrable. He was isolated in its every crooked *lóngtáng*, the curve of its every highway, but he walked on for hours, until he found himself in front of Fudan University, all the way on the other side of town. Rows of bicycles were slotted into racks next to the main gate. The students walking by the tree-lined paths looked so young, their faces animated and the echoes of their laughter like smoke rings in the air. He tried to find Meiling's old dorm, but the campus had become unrecognizable. Pathways had been rerouted; new, sprawling buildings cut him off. He wandered as if in a maze, until finally, he realized that the dormitory had been razed to make room for a soccer field covered in artificial turf.

Rosalyn comes back out into the living room in a blue-and-white polka-dotted dress. She does a little turn in front of him, and her skirt flares out in a circle, showing off her legs. He lets her usher him out of the apartment, lets her touch his face and help him forget. When she laughs in excitement he laughs too. She is so carefree and he lets the infectiousness of it seep into him, drop by drop.

"Come on, birthday boy." She grabs his hand and pulls him into the sun. "Let's go buy you a cake for breakfast."

"WHAT DO YOU usually do on your birthdays?" Rosalyn says.

"Go to work. Have dinner, maybe with friends, maybe the four of us." He shrugs and opens his palms. "Not a big deal, birthdays."

"Nonsense." She charges ahead. "I don't know who you think you're fooling, but everybody wants to be fussed over on their birthdays. Okay, let's see, where should we go, what should we do? Definitely something fun, and unusual. What do you want to do that you never get to do?" She looks back and narrows her eyes. "What would be a complete and total waste of time? Good for nothing but entertainment and pleasure?"

They go to Starbucks for breakfast—it is the only sit-down place vaguely resembling a pastry shop that Rosalyn knows how to get to from the apartment. Even with the exchange rate, the prices for frappucinos and coffee are outrageous. But it is familiar, and she substitutes a cranberry muffin for a birthday cake, singing to him, making everyone else—well-dressed young couples and expats dawdling over English-language newspapers—turn to look at them, joining in, clapping at the end of the song. He laughs and she is struck, from across the table, by how very happy he looks, how young he is. He has this very strange quality of being completely absorbed in a particular mood, his face committed to a feeling so that no other expression, not the one from a moment before, and not the one that would come a moment after, seems possible in the moment of his happiness, or of his anger, or of his charm. It is easy to forget the look he wore in the morning, the look of defeat, how much he missed them, his longing etched between his brows. When he laughs it seems as though he has been laughing for-ever. This does not seem like a man who had ever been sad or afraid.

She drags him to the movies in the late morning, luxuriating in the dark, air-conditioned theater at eleven a.m. They have chosen a roman-tic comedy from America, assuming that the sound track would be in English, but once the movie begins to play they discover that the actors have been dubbed. They stare at each other and begin to laugh. Chi-nese voices come out of the mouths of the blond leading man and his Latina costar; their lips move and move on the screen, never matching up to the sounds coming out of the speakers.

"Shall I translate?" James is laughing so hard that some of the other people in the theater glare back at them. "I am . . . not Alan, but I can understand movie. I can explain it to you. Oh, she says, 'Go to hell!' but now, she trips, falls—right into his arms!"

Terrible romantic comedies with predictable plot elements need no translation, and she is happy just to lean into his shoulder, feel warm puffs of air above her face as he laughs at the pratfalls on the screen. Halfway into the movie he puts his arm around her shoulder, pulling her farther into him. She pushes the armrest between their seats up, out of the way, and then her body is flush against his, they are hip to hip, side by side. The screen flickers with montages under sunny skies and peo-ple in ball gowns and tuxedos, but she is no longer paying attention, she is staring at the tail of his untucked shirt, she is trying to classify the texture of his skin. She looks across the row, at other faces in the dark, the glow of skin under the movie screen lights, and then puts a hand on his thigh, feeling his muscle jump and flinch before settling back down, tighter now, humming with tension.

In the three days since Clarissa's party he has been avoiding her, leaving the apartment early in the day, or staying in his bedroom with the door shut, the sound of his pacing filtering out, irregular but relentless. She did not know what he was thinking but she forgave him his absence. Forgiving him meant that she could forgive herself too. It meant that perhaps they could forget anything happened between the two of them. She did not feel guilt, for what happened between them was so singular and strange, so without the possibility of a future, that it seemed like it could do no damage as long as Meiling did not find out. But still she was sorry, even though a part of her hated Meiling for the way she left James behind. She was sorry for the other woman, and sorry for herself too: for all the ways in which she and James could only talk to each other they could not talk about this thing between them, this eclipse that could only happen in passing, that could not hold on or sustain itself.

Today feels like a day stolen out of a long chain of days. When they get out of the movie theater the sun is straight above them, the light gritty, sharpening the edges of buildings, the windows glaring down with a cool menace.

"What now?" he says, grabbing ahold of her wrist, not paying attention to stares from passersby.

"Oh, so you're leaving it up to me? It's your birthday, but if you want me to take charge I will. You better get ready—we're about to have some fun. Let's see, we've gone to the movies. What else should we do?"

They go into stores for hats and water guns. They run through a park shrieking, dodging past crowds, shooting sprays of water at each other on man-made hills and across obstacle courses. Instead of going to a fancy restaurant for lunch she takes him to the food court at the top level of the No. 1 Department Store. They grab red plastic trays and walk around the circumference of the giant room, stacking up plate after plate of deep-fried snacks, poking at them with their fingers, stuffing them into each other's mouths.

She gesticulates wildly to the cashier at a store to no avail. But then she sings "Happy Birthday" and then points at a lighter, making a flicking motion with her fingers. "Aha!" The cashier is triumphant and digs out a packet of birthday candles from beneath his counter. Rosalyn is smug when she looks at Li Jing, grinning hard, saying, "You just wait!" There is the cake she had bought at the food court, smushed into a Styrofoam box, and later, another one at a dessert shop on Huaihai Road, and a sundae at an ice cream store. She makes James eat each piece, watching him groan and roll his eyes but watching him laugh like a kid too. Each time she lights a candle and sings "Happy Birthday," being as goofy as she can, relishing his giggles, the way his arm swings easy and loose around her waist, the way he presses a kiss to her face.

ALL THE LIGHTS are off, the curtains wide open. Meiling drops their bags on the floor and walks down the hall flipping light switches, calling out, but no one answers back. No one is home.

"Dad!" Pang Pang insisted on carrying the birthday cake all the way from the taxi. The box is so big he can barely see over it. He stumbles in now, calling out, "Where are you! We're home. Happy birthday!"

It's nine o'clock at night. Their flight was delayed and then delayed again. She called at noon, leaving a message saying that they'd be in Shanghai by the evening, but when she looks at the answering machine she sees the blinking red light; when she presses PLAY she hears her own voice and then Pang Pang's too, wishing Li Jing a happy birthday, telling him they are on their way.

She sways for a second, the air too thin, but then Pang Pang is by her side, still holding the cake, looking up at her face. "Where's Dad?" he says, in a careful voice. "It's his birthday. Where is he? Why isn't he home?"

"He probably just went out for a walk. I'm sure he'll be home soon. And then we'll be ready, with cake and sparklers and birthday wishes. Now go wash your hands and put on a clean shirt, any one that you want. I'll set everything out, and then he's going to be so surprised. He's going to be so happy to see us."

When she hears the faucet start in the bathroom she lets out a breath she didn't realize she'd been holding. From the minute she stepped into the apartment she had felt a hollowness inside her, and it expands now, making her jumpy, rattling her bones. She washes her hands in the kitchen sink and starts to clean, gathering up the half-empty glasses cluttered everywhere, wiping away the rings of water that have gathered on wood. The clock on the wall ticks too slowly, slower than the beat of her heart, and when she has done all the dishes she looks at the clock again: it's now almost nine-thirty, but there are no steps in the hall.

Pang Pang comes out of his room brushing sleep out of his eyes, setting out plates and spoons. She helps him untie the intricate bows on the cake box, and then they are lifting the cake out together, setting it down on the table. Pang Pang studies it again, looking from every side to make sure the frosting is symmetrical and unmarred, that the words in the middle of the cake—*Happy birthday, Dad!*—are still intact. The red lines of text on the butter-yellow frosting are squiggly and messy; Pang Pang had insisted on writing it himself: he did it slowly, holding his elbow in the air at the bakery until it started to shake. He considers the words now, and puts a bouquet of sparklers right in the middle. "Is it okay that we only have ten sparklers instead of thirty-three?" he says, and she nods yes, blinking away tears.

At ten she turns on the television, wanting both of them to be distracted, wanting the rush of images and sounds to carry them away. Pang Pang sits next to her on the couch but keeps staring at the front door, not moving his eyes. The television screen flares bright, filling the room with gargled voices, but it makes Meiling feel even more unsettled, so she turns the sound off and looks away. Soon, she is looking at the door too, focusing on the singular pane of wood, willing it to open, willing him to come home.

Pang Pang bends down and picks something off the carpet, holding it up to the light. She can see a long, insidious strand of hair, the color of rust, looping and curling itself around Pang Pang's small fingers. She pulls him into her side and cradles him, prying open his hand to let the strand of hair fall to the floor, feeling him shake in her arms. When he finally falls asleep, later, she carries him tenderly to his bed, stands there looking at his face, and then walks, barefoot, back to the living room. She turns the lights off and strikes up a match, lighting the sparklers on the cake, letting them hiss away. Then she pulls the sparklers out, leaving a cluster of holes in the icing. She holds them like a wedding bouquet, both hands clutched tight around their spines, and walks to the balcony. Points of orange light dart under her chin, shooting off and trailing into the air, puncturing the dark. Stepping onto the cement of the balcony she stretches her arms out in front of her and the tiny, fizzing constellation in her hands looks brighter, the sparks jumping, swallowed up by the dark.

The sparklers burn down to her fingertips and she lets go of them, watching the flares of light falling through space, watching them as they get extinguished. Below her the city is lit up in traffic signals and headlights, the angled roads and curving highways glowing white and ferocious. They could be anywhere in the city, she thinks, at a bar, on a dance floor, in the back of a taxi, entwined in a hotel room. The calm she has been struggling to hold on to since yesterday threatens to snap, and all the rage and resentment and fear come flooding in. She walks back inside, closes the sliding door and then pulls the drapes shut, blocking out the world, sitting down to stare at the door again.

IT'S TWO IN the morning, no longer his birthday, and Li Jing leans on Rosalyn's arm as he tries to put the key in the lock. She starts giggling at his tipsiness, his lack of coordination, pawing at him, biting down on his earlobe. When he finally gets through the door they are both laughing, in each other's arms, and then he sees Meiling, lying asleep on the couch, a birthday cake behind her on the table. All at once his hand is shaking. He drops his keys and they fall soundlessly into the carpet. Next to him Rosalyn lets go and takes a step back but he does not even glance at her. He walks over to Meiling and stands there, looking down at her carefully made-up face, at the gray, puffy circles peeking out below her eyes, at the way she has pressed her palms to her stomach, one hand on top of the other.

She twitches and blinks once, waking up smoothly. When she sees him she begins to smile. "Li Jing," she says, with this look of relief on her face. He is terrified to move, terrified to say anything back to her, wanting this moment to stretch out, wanting—

Behind him Rosalyn shifts her weight from one foot to the other. He watches Meiling's eyes go from his face to a spot over his shoulder, and then her eyes narrow and her face seizes up.

"Where have you been?" She pushes herself off the couch, backing away from him.

He opens his mouth but nothing comes out except a gagging sound. He tries to say her name, "Meeei . . . ," but she is already scrambling back, her arms up in front of her body, showing him her open palms. He takes two steps forward, tries to touch her hand, but she flinches and shakes him off.

"Don't touch me! We came back . . . we've been waiting for you, and all this time, you were with her."

"*I . . . was . . .*" English starts to erupt, but he tamps it down, shaking his head.

"I was worried that something had happened to you. Pang Pang sat up waiting, asking where you were. And all this time you've been with her. How could you?"

He wants to say: *I only left because I didn't think you were coming back*. He wants to explain how afraid he was, how humiliating it had been to beg her to stay and see her walk out despite his pleas. He wants to grab her hand and calm her down, take away the tension that he can see in her forehead, the set of her shoulders. Her pale, seething face stares at him, daring him to speak, and he wishes, more than anything, that he could talk to her, that he could try to explain.

"Mom?" Pang Pang stumbles out of his bedroom, blinking hard. "Dad! You're home. Where have you been? We got you a birthday cake, look! Happy birthday!" He tries to run up to Li Jing but Meiling catches him around the waist. He is still calling out in Chinese, "Happy birthday! Happy birthday!"

Li Jing reaches out for his son, but Meiling pushes Pang Pang to stand behind her, blocking him. "Dad," Pang Pang says again, and then looks over at Rosalyn, who stands in the kitchen, her eyes wild, not knowing where to look. Meiling crouches down and Li Jing watches her eyelids flutter and her mouth try to hold still. "Pang Pang," she says quietly, "go to your room. I'm talking to your dad now."

"Dad? Where were you? We've been waiting all night."

Meiling pulls Pang Pang to her and they both stare at Li Jing, Pang Pang confused and shaking, Meiling's face freezing up. He is not sure he has ever seen her face so stiff, so much like a mask of contempt. "Pang Pang," she says again. "Go to your room."

Pang Pang looks at her, and then swings his eyes up to Li Jing. At a small, jerky nod from him the boy takes a step back, out of his mother's arms. He stares at them all again, Meiling and Li Jing and Rosalyn, and then he turns around and runs as fast as his legs will carry him, the thumping of his feet on the carpet followed by the sound of his door slammed shut. Meiling takes two steps after him but then stops and rests her hand against the wall. She keeps her back to Li Jing, to Rosalyn, as if gathering something within herself. When she turns around her hands are holding her elbows against her body. Her mouth is so pursed that her cheekbones jut out of the skin like two violent slashes, the hollows underneath them tight and quivering. She looks, he thinks, beautiful and terrifying, like a statue. He wants to walk up and touch her face, but he stays still, waiting for her to attack.

"Your father," she says, "warned me that this would happen. He would be ashamed of you. I'm glad he is not here to see this."

Instead of the shriek he was expecting, her voice is quiet. But she has struck with the hardest blow imaginable. He thinks of his father through the smoke, lying on the floor of the Swan Hotel, not moving. He thinks of that morning, his father in bed, his bloodless face.

"She's your doctor. She lives in our house. It's too much." Meiling shakes her head and her hair swings forth but then falls down into its usual, perfect symmetry. "This is pathetic. You're pathetic. Your father and I arranged for Dr. Neal to come here and help you get better. We had no idea that we were actually finding you a new girlfriend."

Rosalyn, who has pressed herself against the counter, leans forward now, trying to get a word in. "Meiling, I'm so sorry. We didn't mean to . . ." She trails off. Her English, stuttering and soft, drifts into the air like poison.

Meiling ignores Rosalyn, not even giving the other woman a glance. "What? Did you need someone to make you feel . . . strong? Like a man? Fine, but how dare you do it in our house, in front of our child, with a woman who sleeps in your father's bed." She draws herself up so that she stands as tall as she can, with her shoulders back and her chin lifted high. She looks at him with more scorn than he knew her capable of, and even now he marvels at her control, at the precision of her cut, at the impeccable cool that she wears like a crown.

"So what have you been doing to feel like a man, really? You sit around and watch television, you play your video games. You throw things at the wall and scare your child. You lose all control, you take no responsibility for your actions. You go out with your American doctor, you go to bed with your American doctor. That last part would be impressive, if she wasn't so easy, and you weren't such a fool."

The words come at him like nails being hammered, pounding in to his head. He tries to keep standing straight, but his knees buckle and he almost falls over before Rosalyn catches him and pulls him back up. He wrenches himself out of her arms but it's too late. Meiling is laughing now, the sound of it contemptuous and sharp. Listening to her laughter, he feels lower than low, like a cockroach, like he is nothing.

"That's just great," she says. "Dr. Rosalyn to the rescue. You can't do anything without her, can you? It must be nice, to have people around who are so accommodating. After all, you have me to clean and cook and run the company and take care of your child, and you have her for conversation and a little fun on the side. Not a bad deal, the way I see it. You must be proud of yourself. Despite not lifting a finger to do anything it's all turned out quite well for you."

He wants to scream, but he has no voice, no words with which to combat her. He has to stand there and take it, let himself absorb each syllable like a bullet. Inside his throat there is only English, useless English, and he grunts roughly before clamping his mouth shut. He touches the scar on his skull, traces the thin, jagged line of it beneath his hair. Though the scar is hidden now, it would always be there, a marker of the brain damage that will always be a part of him. He bangs his forehead against the wall, wanting it to break open again, wanting to drown out the sound of her voice.

"I'm sick of this, Li Jing. I can't stand it. I know you don't give a damn, I know you don't care about anything. But to do this to me now, to do this to your son . . ." Her voice is fading, sounding softer, more splintered. When he looks up her eyes are closed and she is shrinking into herself. Despite everything he has this urge to reach out, to make it better, but then she opens her eyes. She shakes her head and smiles a terrible smile.

"What have you done?"

He squeezes his eyes shut, wanting to squeeze it all away, but inside him there is only a thorny, choking blackness, a bottomless echo. Since the accident he has destroyed everything he's touched: his father, his marriage, his family. Meiling is only confirming everything he already knows about himself, and there is nothing that can let any of it out, no release valve that can save him or expel the ugliness inside.

Meiling comes closer, her eyes boring in. "Stop it!" Rosalyn says, taking a step forward. He tries to get away from the both of them, turning into the hallway, opening the door to the bathroom. "Don't walk away. We're not done." Meiling catches up to him, wrenching his arm back, shouting in his ear.

She is louder now, so loud that he knows Pang Pang, even with the door closed, can hear her every word. It takes all his strength not to grab her and shake her to make her stop. He holds on to the bathroom sink with both hands, squeezing the porcelain as hard as he can, trying to make his arms stay still.

"What have you done?" she says. Her mouth is so close to his ear that he can feel her breath. "What have you done to me? To us? You've ruined everything."

His right hand lets go of the sink and hurls itself at the wall next to the mirror. He can feel the solidity of the plaster, its resistance against his knuckles, and then his hand punches through the wall, his arm vibrates all the way up to his shoulder. Meiling backs away, looking horrified and afraid.

"You . . . what are you doing? Every time this happens you hit something, or break something, and . . ." She takes another step back and flattens herself against the wall. "I can't be here right now. I can't do this anymore."

"James . . ." Rosalyn is in the hallway, helpless. "James, what can I do?"

Meiling pushes past her, and turns around to stare at Pang Pang's door for a moment. When she takes a step forward, Li Jing cries out and rushes to the door, blocking it with his body. "I can't be here right now," she says, looking away, wildly. She stands still for one moment, fixes her eyes on him and then on the door of Pang Pang's room. He almost calls out, looking at her standing there, her eyes glassy, filling with tears. But then she shakes it off. When she speaks she's pleading and quiet. "I can't be here right now. Tonight—I just can't. Pang Pang—stay with him. I can't—I can't."

What she doesn't say, but what he knows is true, is that she can't be with him anymore. Then she is walking down the hall, grabbing her purse off the kitchen counter, walking out the door, leaving him behind again.

CHAPTER 27

When Rosalyn wakes up there is still the hole in the wall next to the vanity in the bathroom, still a birthday cake on the dining room table. She starts to reach for it—for the stiff, lurid roses made of icing, little bits of crumbs at the bottom edge of the cake—but then she draws back as if the cake were evidence at the scene of a crime, meant to be left intact, left alone.

So it wasn't a dream, in another language, or a half-remembered scene from a film. She sits down at the table, and after a minute, she moves over to the next seat, into the shade. It's another day of that brutal, scraping sunshine coming in through the balcony doors. She is sick of sunshine. She is sick of this immaculate apartment. She is sick, she thinks, of herself, of what she has become.

She lays her head down on the table: the surface of it is smooth, with faint traces of lemon and vinegar. She realizes, with a start, that Meiling must have wiped it clean last night before they had come home, wiped away the layer of dust and crumbs that had gathered on it over the weekend. Rosalyn stands up and walks back to her room, throwing open the armoire to look at her suitcase, on its side, with the luggage tags from her flight here still attached. She thinks of Meiling's face, last night—she had recognized that almost unbearable look of pain, and she hates herself for being part of the cause.

Rosalyn hears the door to Pang Pang's room opening. She stands frozen for a moment, and then steps into the hallway. When she looks up, James's face is empty and guiltless, as if it, too, had been wiped clean during the night.

"Good morning, Rosalyn. I hope you slept well."

Pang Pang walks out of his room and past her dragging a travel bag behind him, not saying hello.

She steps closer to James. "What's going on?" she whispers. "Where is Meiling? Did she come back last night? Did you talk to her?"

He ignores her questions and walks into the master bedroom. Rosalyn steps over the threshold, but stays near the door. When he pulls a duffel bag out from behind a chest of drawers Rosalyn clutches at the hem of her T-shirt and leans back, asking, "Are you going somewhere?"

"Yes," he says, moving around the room, throwing clothes onto the bed. "If she can leave we can leave too. Go pack. *We* are going on a trip."

Then James smiles a strange and easy smile. His entire face looks so bland and careless that something inside her sounds a warning bell.

"I want us to go—away," he says. "I want to show you a beautiful place."

She looks at him, wanting to guard herself against his charm, but something about the mixture of his vulnerability and his assurance draws her in. "I don't know, James. Do you really think this is the right time for us to go away?"

"Just for the weekend. Just for a break," he says. "Please, Rosalyn? Just leave this behind, just for the weekend."

She wants to mention Meiling again, but the name will not roll off her tongue. His face, so close to hers, is glowing, his black eyes compelling her to say yes. She shivers and leans forward, pressing her cheek against his. She cannot refuse him anything, it seems. "Where do you want to go?"

"It's a surprise."

"Well, you should give me a hint or two. Otherwise I won't know what to pack."

An hour later Rosalyn is standing in front of the apartment complex, holding Pang Pang's hand, waiting for the car. Pang Pang squirms in her grasp, his wet, hot palm trying to break free, but she keeps her hold on him, gripping him tight and then smiling down. "It's okay," she says, talking just for the sake of talking. "Hold on, your dad is coming." When James pulls up, Pang Pang hurls himself away from Rosalyn. She watches him throw himself into the passenger seat, slamming the car door shut.

"Sorry." James picks up her suitcase and sets it down in the trunk.

"It's perfectly understandable. He's probably pretty upset right now. James, are you sure this is a good idea . . . ?"

He closes the trunk and then opens the back door for her, bending at the waist but not answering her question. "We will have a good time. Now, we drive for two hours. Then we will be there. Find a comfortable seat."

On the highway out of town the sun blazes down, trapping heat in the car. Rosalyn keeps asking for the air conditioner to be turned up. "Too cold," James says, but he turns it up another notch anyway, grinning at her in the rearview mirror.

"Well, I'm hot," she shoots back, and then when she sees the lift of his eyebrows and a slight nod she blushes, ducking her head. She is perched in the middle of the backseat, leaning forward so that she can talk to him over the loud hum of tires on cement. She glances at Pang Pang out of the corner of her eye, studying him, looking for similarities and differences between father and son.

Pang Pang doesn't move, except for occasional twists of his head to follow something out the window. Despite how much he looks like a smaller, softer version of James, with the same face, Rosalyn decides that he has obviously inherited something of the fortitude of his mother, her steeliness and resolve. There is something astonishing, she acknowledges with a pang, about seeing discrete components of personality and looks passed directly from parents to children, recognizing the thread of genetics, the strength of its bind. She leans forward and turns to smile at Pang Pang, humming a little song underneath her breath. He turns his head and stares out the window, not meeting her eyes or giving an inch.

Rosalyn calls Alan from a rest stop, wrinkling her nose and holding her breath outside the ladies' room. "I'm with James . . . with Li Jing, and with Pang Pang. Everything's fine. I'm sure Meiling knows, I'm sure he told her, but tell her, just in case. I can't explain right now, Alan, but they're fine. James and Pang Pang are both fine."

She hangs up the phone and thinks, for a moment, of how it might look to someone who hadn't heard the cruelty in Meiling's voice or seen the sadness on James's face last night, who hadn't held his bloody knuckles under the faucet, cleaned them and wrapped them up in bandages. But then she hears cars honking from the parking lot, all these horns, held long and short, making her heart leap, and she walks back into the parking lot, shading her eyes, looking for the blue sedan, the man and the boy inside.

On the long, belting road past the tollbooth, there are not as many cars, and they speed up, past fields of green, past occasional three-story houses with tiled roofs, dotting the landscape like chapels. Rosalyn puts her head next to the window, opening it a crack. The wind pours in, with a whooshing sound, with the familiar smell of mud and rain and green things growing in the sun. She strains her neck to look at Pang Pang again, and he is low in the seat, hunched over, playing a handheld video game, not taking his eyes off the screen. In front of him the landscape moves past the windshield with its greens and blues, its flatness, its vast stretched-out wings. It reminds her of home. She wishes, with a moment of annoyance at the child, that she was sitting next to James instead, staring at the lines of his jaw, the shape of his sunglasses, letting the world outside move over her.

She has barely traveled outside of Shanghai since she arrived, but now she is glad to have left it behind. There is a freedom to staring at row after row of soybeans and corn and everything else being grown, out there, the repetition of it so familiar across kilometers and miles, across languages and oceans, across the vastness of geography. When she closes her eyes and focuses on the momentum of tires across asphalt, the sensation of soaring takes over. Her nerves flare steady, a cool surge of speed rushes into her body, and she feels herself blowing past all of it, finally on her way.

The road signs hang overhead, each word repeated in Chinese, pinyin, and English. Rosalyn reads the names of cities, the exits not taken, and when they finally pull off the highway the sign says HANGZHOU: WEST LAKE. She remembers now that Danny had wanted to take her there, but she had put it off again and again, not wanting be alone with him on an overnight trip. Danny, who had been her first friend in Shanghai, will probably never want anything to do with her again. After Clarissa's party he would not return her calls, and when Rosalyn finally talked to Clarissa, the other woman had been abrupt in her dismissal. "We all really care about Danny," Clarissa said before hanging up, taking responsibility for their entire social circle. "Goodbye, Rosalyn. Have a nice life." All her friendships in Shanghai had dissolved in one night, but the losses, like everything else here, don't seem to register at all.

They pull into a parking lot, and before the engine is shut off, Pang Pang is leaping out of the car, racing to the doors of a sprawling, dark-wooded building that peeks out from between trees. Rosalyn starts to race after the boy, but behind her, James is lifting out their luggage at leisure, calling her name.

"It's okay. Let him go." He shuts the trunk with a bang. His sunglasses have stayed on his face for the entire trip and they do not come off now. "Pang Pang knows where to go. We came here, we used to come here . . . all the time."

Some of the clerks at the West Willow Inn seem to recognize James, but they are too well trained to raise an eyebrow at his choice of languages or companions. Soon, a bellhop is leading them past a canopied walkway, and they are surrounded by tall, leafy stalks of bamboo, green everywhere. She has not realized how much she missed the color green until the car trip, with its endless fields, and now this hotel that has sprung up like something out of a fairy tale where everything is fresh, plants and trees and grass all around them. In front of her Pang Pang is saying something to his dad, and James nods and stoops down to pick him up, holding him so that Pang Pang is looking back, straight at her, not blinking at all.

Their suite is an offshoot of the main building, with a private entrance, and a hammock swaying in the breeze, between two huge, ground-sweeping willow trees. Rosalyn stands back and takes in the scene while James walks into the room and sets Pang Pang down. "This is beautiful," she says as she follows them in, sweeping her eyes over the austere luxury of the place. Neither father nor son responds to her. They are already communicating in a kind of mimed shorthand: Pang Pang's thin voice lilting into indecipherable snippets of Chinese, James's grunts and gestures and short snatches of English answering back, making itself understood.

The bellhop, directed by James, has deposited her things in one of the bedrooms, and now Pang Pang is taking his father by the hand, pulling him into the other bedroom. She walks into the room that has been designated for her and her alone: the room is all polished wood and clean lines and soft fabrics, and it looks, she thinks, oddly like James's apartment, the same kind of restraint, the same cool whisper of money coming out of every surface. On the other side of the living room James clicks the door shut and then walks toward her, leans against her doorframe.

"This is some place," she says.

"I thought you would like it."

"How's Pang Pang?"

"Fine. Tired. But fine. He naps now. He is tired from . . . the last few days."

She nods as if he has explained everything, but there are so many other questions she wants to ask. Why did he bring her here, and how long will they stay? How does he feel about her? And what will happen between him and Meiling? Yesterday, they had roamed through Shanghai laughing, celebrating his birthday, determined to not think about the past or the future. Last night, it felt like everything had been dragged out into the open, all their faces exposed, everything old shattered between them. She wonders if there is any hope for new configurations of feelings. She wonders what will happen once they return to Shanghai. But in the car, they had been quiet, almost dreamy, and now in the hotel room too. Asking too many questions would invite a kind of scrutiny—by whom, she isn't sure—that she knows she is not prepared to deal with. So she lets the questions fall away from her and walks up to him, puts her arms around his waist. "Thanks for bringing me here," she says, not meaning *here* as in the hotel room, but *here* as in away from all the rest of it, away from the questions and their answers.

CHAPTER 28

During dinner on their first night in Hangzhou, Li Jing watches as Rosalyn stares at Pang Pang, catches his eye and then places an extravagantly carved radish on top of her head. Pang Pang's face flickers for a moment. He doesn't laugh, but gives her a curious look. From then on, he watches her out of the corner of his eye, chewing thoughtfully, looking down but sneaking glances, as if he doesn't want to be caught looking at her. She simply smiles back, cheery and winsome, her chopsticks all wrong in her fingers, the occasional shrimp or string bean falling just as it's about to reach her lips.

Later she plucks a piece of lotus root from beneath the lacquered duck and fondles it in her hands, sticking her fingers through the holes in the cream-fleshed disk. With Pang Pang watching she holds it up to her face and tries to hang it on the skinny tip of her nose. The lotus hangs on for a second, adhering to skin either by sauce or by sheer will, but then it comes flying down, falling into her plate, splashing Rosalyn's pink T-shirt with dots of oil. She laughs that laugh of hers, the one that seems to hold multiple frequencies and timbres all at once, wrapping them up and then letting them loose. Li Jing would like to fall into that laugh, so that it's everywhere, all around him, touching his skin. He sees Pang Pang watching her laugh too, holding his small head to the side, considering her, and wonders if her laughter makes his son feel the same way he does, as if it would provide a haven, a hiding place, somewhere safe and warm.

The rest of dinner is near-silent, with occasional phrases of English floating up. It is as if he and Rosalyn are both biting their tongues, keeping quiet, not wanting to exclude Pang Pang, not wanting to give him a reason to flinch. There's a slow thaw on the boy's face now, and he looks up more, with curiosity and wonder; sometimes he mutters, "How do you do" or "Father and I eat" in English. When they leave the restaurant Li Jing gestures to Pang Pang, moving his fingers to ask if he wants to take a walk, and Pang Pang nods with a shy smile, letting himself fall into step next to Rosalyn, trying not to look at her face.

In summer the days stretch long and thin. At dusk, the faded pink at the edge of the sky makes everyone glow. The sidewalks are less crowded here. Headlights and street lights seem to emit less wattage. They wander into a park, and a pathway, lined with trees, unfolds with only a few other people strolling by. A squirrel darts in front of them, freezes, and then scrambles away. Pang Pang gives a squeal of delight, chasing after it, but the squirrel has leaped onto a tree trunk and climbs it fast now, scrabbling the bark with its paws, heading for a branch, and then a twig, climbing into the sky.

When they catch up to Pang Pang his lower lip is jutting out, his shoulders slumped over. "Where did the squirrel go?" He whinnies like a small horse. "Come back, Mr. Squirrel. Come back!" Li Jing crouches down and take the boy's hand. "Pang Pang loves animals," he says in English. "In Shanghai, there are no animals outside the zoo."

Behind him Rosalyn makes a clicking sound with her tongue, as if acknowledging what he said. But then she makes that sound again, and then again. Pang Pang and Li Jing both turn back to stare, but she just holds a finger up to her lips and keeps making the sound, scattering it in an irregular rhythm, walking slow-footed but careless, as if she were a girl on a country road, whistling a tune out of the side of her mouth. On the side of the path a small, shaking squirrel darts out from behind a rock, but stays there, quivering, staring at Rosalyn. She gestures for Pang Pang to follow her, and keeps walking, keeps making the click-clacking sound with her tongue.

Soon she is a pied piper of squirrels, with four tiny creatures following them, staying a respectful distance back on the path, but still scampering forward when they are left too far behind. Other squirrels peek out from behind bushes or climb over to the tops of branches, letting themselves be seen, making visible their secret animal world. Next to Li Jing, Pang Pang is shaking in excitement, his eyes huge and black in his face. He whips his head around to stare at all the squirrels, and then turns back to Rosalyn in wonder. She keeps clicking but makes a gesture for Pang Pang to come closer. When he does, she grabs him by the hand and opens her mouth big, showing him how she curls her tongue and touches the tip of it to the roof of her mouth. He mimics her. His first clicks are loud and wet. The squirrels on the path behind them stop in their tracks and hold their front paws under their chins, as if considering the noise. Pang Pang looks up at Rosalyn, panicked, and she pats his hand, clicks her tongue, taking a few steps forward, letting the squirrels listen, and settle, and come to them again.

Soon they are both making that small, clicking sound with their tongues, trailed by a pack of squirrels under the darkening sky. Li Jing watches them share a smile. He watches Rosalyn point out a small, black squirrel on a tree stump on the side of the path. Pang Pang's face is smooth and radiant like the moon. He laughs freely now, startling the animals, letting go of the nervousness that has kept his small body scrunched up and afraid. The two of them are facing each other and giggling, wordless but together, and even though he has stopped walking it feels to Li Jing as though something is shifting beneath his feet, bedrocks that he thought secure moving into new configurations. He is thinking *what ifs*, he is thinking of the future not as a single path unfolding but as open waters, awaiting navigation, full of possibilities.

IN THE MORNING they drive past yellow-walled temples and streets lined with silk merchants, follow winding paths that take them higher and higher up the mountain. Rosalyn shouts and gasps at the sights, wanting to stop everywhere. Li Jing glances over at Pang Pang and they exchange knowing looks in the front seat, wiggling their eyebrows, squirming in the heat that blazes through the windshield. How strange it is to be here in this familiar place with his son, someone new in the backseat. She is chattering now—"We'll definitely have to go back to that silk market later . . ."—and the sound of her English zooms around the car, making everything seem new. It feels like they are in a movie about their life, suddenly, doing all the same things they do but with a different language on the sound track, a new female lead.

Pang Pang has slipped out of his seat belt and now he climbs onto his seat to look back at her. She makes a face, putting her palms together to bow to him, and he starts giggling, the sound of it unrestrained, bright, and a little wobbly. Something has been altered, Li Jing thinks, threads rewoven in the air so that there are precarious connections among all three of them now. The threads shimmer and glow, stretching taut. He looks at Pang Pang, and then at Rosalyn. It is as if he has stepped into a dream, an alternate reality of familial life. The heat glazing over one reality and shifting to another, the heat gathering into a palpable contentment of the heart, the heat making him think, *Why not?*

His mind is edged with a kind of madness or magic, making everything look like a mirage. This is not the path he has chosen, but it is some other path that might have been his. They get out near the top of the mountain and climb up a set of endless steps, Pang Pang bounding ahead and then darting back, shouting in Chinese, "Hurry up!," shouting "Come on!" The leaves throw their shadows over them, shaking, making a soft, murmuring sound, like the faintest of applause. Up another set of steps Li Jing remembers that day at the Swan Hotel, the sketches his father was judging, for a memorial here in Hangzhou. He wonders what the memorial was for. He wonders which parts of the past need to be remembered, which parts need to be left behind. He imagines a life in which his father had never moved back to Shanghai, imagines meeting Rosalyn Neal at a university in America, or a gas station, or a hospital. He turns to look at the round, freckled shoulder of the woman next to him, wanting to reach out and touch her pale, smooth skin.

"It's beautiful here." She is gasping to catch her breath but the sentence still slips out, low and husky.

"Yes," he says. He looks at the beads of sweat clinging to her temples, the jut of her collarbones, the damp shimmer where her tank top scoops down to expose her skin. "Beautiful."

"Oh James." She turns and pleasure pours out of her face. "Thank you so much for bringing me here."

Every time she calls him *James* her voice startles him with its easy intimacy. The syllable goes on and then trails away in a hiss, like a sting. The name seems to call out for someone else. When he thinks of *James* it sounds like the name belongs to another person, someone he knew a long time ago. But for her he would be *James*, for her and this other life that he might have had.

IN THE TEAHOUSE near the top of the mountain, Rosalyn sips from a steaming mug, letting the bitterness of the tea wash down her throat, letting it clean her insides. The day has gotten muggy. Her entire body is slick with sweat, even in the shade. But she keeps drinking, the heat of the tea burning her mouth, and when she gets to the bottom of the cup, when tender shoots of leaves brush against her tongue, she slurps them in, chewing the soggy wet flakes, sucking the astringent taste out of every last leaf.

Pang Pang finishes drinking his soda and shoots off like a puck, a slur of a sentence reaching Rosalyn and James after his body is already out of grasp. They watch him run out of the pavilion and disappear around the corner, a blur of white. Rosalyn starts to get up, but James's fingers circle her wrist, pulling her back down. Her skin is slippery and hot. It is the first time he has touched her all day. She feels it not as a jolt but as relief. The trembling that she had not been aware of quiets down, and her body settles in, calmed by his touch.

"This tea is wonderful," she says. "I should buy a bag of this tea."

He smiles and stays silent for a moment, as if he were amusing himself with a private joke. "The tea is nice," he says, "but what you're tasting is really the water. The water here is special. It's drawn up from a well deep in the ground. In fact, that's where Pang Pang's gone now. He went to see them pull it up, out of the well."

He keeps his hand on her wrist. She swallows the tea leaves she had kept flat against her tongue and looks into his eyes, which seem even more black in the sunlight, not giving away anything. The world closes in on the two of them so that she can only feel his fingers cuffing her wrist, squeezing it gently, and see the dazzling gold of his face, the black of his eyes. She leans in, closer to him. The air is so thick with humidity that she can barely breathe. Her body feels as though it's melting away. The sunscreen she had slathered on in the morning smells like coconut and sand. Her eyes flutter shut, but even through her eyelids she can see the brightness of the sun, his head a shadow close to her. He brushes his lips against hers, pulling back, and she keeps her neck arched, her eyes closed, waiting for contact again.

His lips do not come back to hers. She pulls away and opens her eyes. The light blinds her for a moment, and then she sees him watching her, something unreadable in his face. She smiles, as if to say, *I understand*, or *Kiss me later*. When she squints she sees his mouth twisted down in a grimace, but then her eyes adjust and she realizes that what she had seen was just a trick of light. He had been half smiling the entire time and now he has both of her hands in his, under the stone table, without her noticing how it happened. He brushes his thumb against the inside of her wrist, and the assurance of the gesture seems to her the most intimate thing, closer than even his kiss. She blinks but his face is still there, in front of her. She wonders what his face might look like in ten years, in twenty, if seeing it every day would ever rob it of its power over her.

The day is spent on mountaintops and in souvenir shops, with easy murmurs, full of gestures and repetitions. They have not brought the electronic dictionary but they do not seem to need it—the three of them understand each other easily, without too many words. Pang Pang is chatty, slipping between Chinese and a few phrases of English, asking this or that so that James can nod or shake his head to make things clear. James acts things out so that Pang Pang will understand, making a game of it, making them all laugh. By the time they finish dinner the most wonderful nausea is rising out of Rosalyn's stomach. She has barely eaten anything; the nausea clutches at her chest, filling it up. She takes Pang Pang's small hand in hers and walks out of the restaurant into the soft, creamy night. The leaves are so thick above her head that she can't see past them to the moon or the stars but the lights in the parking lot blaze dazzlingly white.

Pang Pang says something quickly and then gestures at her.

"Let's go to the lake," James says, a softness in his voice that she has not heard before.

When they get into the car Pang Pang lets her have the front seat. He contemplates her face, clicks his tongue a few times in her squirrel call, and then says something else to his father, nodding his head with authority.

James laughs and turns to Rosalyn. "Pang Pang says we have to go on a boat, because you have not been here before. We used to . . ." His voice cracks and his face falters for a moment before he blinks it away. "Pang Pang loves boats, loves going on the lake in a boat. He wants you to go too. We both want . . . you to see it, feel this."

Then they are drifting across the dark mirror of the West Lake on slow planks of wood. Small waves rock the boat, gently, and she feels her joints loosen, feels her body sway back and forth to match the tide, the unsteadiness beneath her matching how she had felt on the inside all day long. "This is lovely," she says to no one in particular, and no one responds to her now. James and Pang Pang sit on the bench across from her, their faces barely lit from the small gaslight that hovers by Pang Pang's foot. The gondolier stands behind them with his sweep, moving the boat across water, looking like a shadow, the looseness of his clothes giving his body a vague, smoky outline. Rosalyn closes her eyes and opens them again, as if she is afraid it would all disappear, but no, James and Pang Pang are still there, the boat, the lake, the moon.

On the shore buildings are lit up as bright as torches, yellow windowpanes from restaurants and hotels falling into the lake so that the edge of the water is patterned with light. But the shore is getting farther and farther; all the shores are fading away from them. The boat drifts into the dark heart of the lake, the sound of water slapping against wood like the sound of a heart beating. She braces her arms on the bench and throws her head back. The gray-blue of the sky and a bright moon are all that she can see. The moon hangs so heavy and full that she feels as though it were pressing down on her. The world keeps moving underneath her body, swaying back and forth, and she thinks that if the world keeps swaying long enough her bones might disintegrate and melt into her flesh. Could she stay here forever, with this boy and this man and the gondolier standing tall, anchoring all of them, taking them away from the shore and into unknown waters? She follows the light of the moon to a series of tiny pagodas rising out of the water all around them. The moon pours into the pagodas through the openings and then it is reflected, doubled, landing on the surface of the lake here, and there. So many moons scattered like pale petals on the glossy, black surface of the lake. She breathes out a gasp of pleasure and when she looks at James he is smiling at her as if her face were giving off its own fevered light, as if her face, too, were a reflection of the moon.

When the boat clanks against the shore James holds out his hand. She takes it and steps onto the land, feeling rattled and off-kilter, as if the unsteadiness of the water is where she belongs, more than the solidity of the earth. The three of them walk along the edge of the lake, under willow trees, past teahouses with people laughing and playing cards. They stay silent, still wanting the air of calm from the lake, but the lights and the voices trickle in. Rosalyn feels as though she were waking up from a dream.

A woman's voice blares the same four syllables over and over, her sales pitch like a siren in the night. Little kids run on the path, unleashed, chattering, chewing open-mouthed and giddy. Rosalyn wants to stay still, keep this feeling of contentment inside her. She is so full of the feeling that at any moment it might spill over, and so she walks carefully, silently, looking at the cracks in the pavement, holding on to herself, wanting to keep the feeling intact.

Pang Pang says something and the sentence scratches against her ear. Next to her James nods and digs bills out of his pocket, handing it to the boy, gesturing for him to go ahead. Pang Pang dashes to a stand selling lotus roots, disappearing into the blur of small bodies at the end of the line. Rosalyn drifts closer to James, feeling the heat of him, feeling as though there is a concavity under his shoulder for her to stand in, feeling as though if he touches her she might never let him go.

James turns toward the lake, walking past a cluster of shrubs and trees as if he were about to walk into the water. She follows him, and in a few steps they have hidden themselves away from the shore and its revelry. They can hear the laughter and conversation behind them, but they are facing the dark lake again, watching the shapes of boats pass slowly across the water, watching so many moons lying open everywhere.

"James." She whispers his name and he puts his fingers up to her mouth, shushing her. The tips of his fingers are cold, and she opens her lips, wanting to say something else, she doesn't know what. She licks his skin instead and then pulls herself away. "James, I . . ."

All the sounds still come in through the ear, the selling and the laughing, the conversation and the clinks of glass. When his mouth seals down on hers the world does not quiet as she had wanted, but goes on clamoring, the sounds louder, more tumultuous, the sounds buzzing in her head. His tongue in her mouth is insistent, as if rooting out causes or betrayals. His hands splay across her back and press into her like shackles, his fingers hard on her skin. She wriggles in his grasp and then her arms circle around his shoulders. When she brushes the back of his neck she can feel little sharp tufts of hair, and she runs her hands farther up, holding his head in her palms like a globe. A familiar oblivion sweeps over her, a kind of sinking into the black lake until she is submerged. Now she hears things as if she were underwater, and she keeps running her palms over his cheeks, past his ear, to touch the skin on the back of his neck, pressing herself into him more.

When he lets go of her mouth and she opens her eyes the world flutters for a moment. She tilts her head back, the leaves above her look almost white in the moonlight, shuddering in the trees, and past them there is the faded ink of the sky, the stars obliterated by the brightness of the moon.

She would have liked to stay here forever and she turns to him now, her palms clutching at his shoulders, wanting to tell him. "I—"

He pushes her away so fast that she stumbles backward. For a second she thinks she might fall into the water, but then her feet find their balance, and she is looking up at his strangled face, a moan tearing out of his throat.

Pang Pang stands in front of them, with three lotus roots gathered in his arms like a bouquet of flowers. He looks at them, his eyebrows pressing down into a black line, and then his mouth is open as if he is about to scream. Nothing comes out, not even a breath. James takes a step forward, bending down. "Pang Pang!" The boy stands still for a moment, staring at Rosalyn and then shifting his eyes to his father's face. Turning his back on them he shoots off around the corner, past the shrubs, the patter of his feet on cement already getting quieter, fading away from their stunned, useless bodies.

CHAPTER 29

All he has are his legs racing across the footpath, his voice with its repetition of a name. The night air rushes into his throat, heavy and thick, choking him. "Pang Pang!" he tries to scream, but his voice comes out as a rasp. He darts across headlights and honking horns to the other side of the street, into a black parking lot with cars like silent, sleeping creatures. No shapes moving. Turning in a circle he sees the neon signs of fast-food restaurants. Tall hills of grass and pale flowers under the moon. A hotel squatting on top of the slope like a fortress, tense and foreboding. Lampposts casting their spotlights onto empty circles of tar.

He runs back to the footpath edging the lake. How far could a boy's legs carry him in a matter of seconds or minutes? Every small body yields hope, but when he sees two pigtails hanging down the back or an anonymous face the hope is extinguished like a candle flame snuffed out between fingertips. There are so many pale T-shirts catching the light, moving across dark, but none of them is Pang Pang's. He tears through the crowd, bending down, searching, still wordless. He runs past a couple necking on a dark bench, and then turns back, passing them once more, his groan parting them for a second before their lips come together again.

There are so many people, the path dotted with them. They stroll loose-limbed and lazy. Their contented bodies lean against trees and sprawl across the grass. Their voices blend together until everything sounds like carelessness, like laughter. Their shadows waffle on the ground, blue and blurry. He stops in the middle of a crowd and clenches his fists, all their faces before him. The only face he wants to see cannot be found. He jumps up as high as he can, swiveling his head around to try to see better, but there are only more people, more faces, eyes and noses and glasses and mouths, none of them the right ones. The black night is pulling its shade over everything and all around him things look murky, the dark swirls of water, the shadowed bodies moving to and fro, the thick trunks of trees and hedges of shrubs hiding things, hiding bodies, everything veiled, people and their faces and little boys with their quick limbs. How easily they become lost. How easily they might stay lost.

He begins running again. The air pushes back and he hurls himself forward, breaking through its resistance, dodging around old people inching forward with canes, past clusters of kids blocking the way. The shore is endless, the footpath keeps unwinding in front of him, and he follows its curves. He zooms in on small figures in white T-shirts. He grabs a boy from behind and turning him around sees a pair of startled eyes behind glasses. The boy is the right size, wears the right-colored T-shirt, but he has the wrong face, and Li Jing lets go of his shirt as if throwing him away. The woman next to the boy starts shrieking but already Li Jing is running again, leaving them behind. "Pang Pang!" His voice is louder now, and he no longer gives a damn about pronunciations and tones. "Pang Pang! Li Gepang!"

Panic rises up until his vision is dotted with bright glares and he can no longer see straight. He pulls up next to a man selling pirated DVDs on the ground and takes a deep breath, trying to slow his heart down and clear his head so that he can come up with a plan. The lake is still on his left, stretching its bare, black face up at him. The moon is still illuminating the footpath, throwing its milky light onto cement. He decides to head back to where he last saw Pang Pang, saw his small, pale face set in shock, saw his thin, bare legs carry him away. He would go back and start there again, head down the other direction, explore every shrub and crowd gathered on the shore, find his son before—before it's too late.

"Pang Pang," he yells, trying to keep his voice steady. He sees a pack of people under the open pavilion of a teahouse, and he runs to them, searching every table, all the people laughing, playing cards and mahjong. They gape at him with curious looks. "Hey, who are you looking for?" he hears someone say. "Pang Pang," he screams the name again and pulls himself farther into the heart of the crowd. Now someone is tapping him on the arm, and he jumps around, almost grabbing her by the shoulders before retracting his hands.

"*Shénme shìqín?*" The woman's white hair is pulled back tight into a bun and her face is carved with deep wrinkles. She looks at him, sympathetic. *What is it?* "*Nǐ zài zǎo rén ma?*" *Are you looking for someone?*

He opens his mouth to say something, say anything, but all that comes out is a gurgle of the tongue. "Pang Pang," he says, feebly, and she searches his face with her hooded eyes. He is gasping, desperate for language, staring at her, willing her to understand.

"*Shénme shìqín?*" she asks again, slower this time. *What's the matter?*

He can see a gold tooth in the back of her mouth, almost by the throat, and its glint reminds him of seeing his mother's gold earrings late at night, when she bent down and kissed his forehead, putting him to sleep. Her skin never became marred by wrinkles, he thinks now; she never got a chance to be a grandmother. He had forgotten about the glint of gold in the dark and the memory pierces through him. All the things he has forgotten. All the things he is not ready to leave behind.

The old woman is still staring at him, and her face looks weathered and kind, as if nothing could surprise her. Sounds crowd up in his throat, but he can only open and close his mouth. He shakes his head, not wanting to jangle the air with all the English words on the tip of his tongue. "Pang Pang." He says the name again and lets his head fall to his chest.

"*Aīya!*" the woman exclaims. "*Zhēnde bùhuì shōu de ma?*" *Why can't you talk?* He knows that she is just trying to understand, but the frustration, so plain on her face, still makes him feel utterly useless, as if he is letting someone else down now, as if Pang Pang is running farther away with every second of his silence.

Everyone else at the teahouse stares, curious, slightly snickering. Li Jing looks at them as if pleading, and then he is cutting his hand back and forth around his chest, trying to indicate Pang Pang's height, trying to make it all clear to the woman in front of him. He opens his mouth and tries to blurt out a syllable—"*Ta . . .*" *He . . .*—and it feels like a marble trying to jump across the threshold of his throat. He tries again. "*Wo de . . .*" *My . . .* Then the two syllables for *son* dart away. He closes his eyes, feeling as though he were clawing in a pool of murky water, sounds and ideas slipping through his fingers.

Trying to find the two syllables for *son* is like running into a wall, so he tries to go around. He looks down at his feet and thinks about the word *child*. The meaning of the first syllable comes to him in a flash: "small." He searches for the Chinese, opening his mouth as if the sound might leap out, independent of his brain.

Small. A single syllable. He tries it again. "*Xiao.*"

And then he repeats the sound over and over, grasping for the right tone, trying to figure out what's supposed to come next. "*Xiǎo . . . xiǎo.*" *Small.* A small person. A small offspring.

He's got it now and he swings his head up, desperate, looking at the woman, trying to string the sounds together. "*Xiǎo hai xiǎo hái. Wǒ de . . . xiǎo hái.*"

But she has forgotten the question, already looking away. The volume of the crowd has swallowed the sound of his voice and she is standing there with her hands on her waist, murmuring to a middle-aged woman next to her, saying, "What a pity. He must be a deaf-mute."

"No, I'm not . . . I can speak," he starts to say in English. English is so much easier, the sounds now come out of his throat without hesitation, but English is useless. He watches the woman turn away with another shake of her head, and then he throws his arms up and runs back toward the lake, hearing the roar of curiosity behind him dying down like a wave receding from shore.

The boats on the surface of the lake drift by with infinite leisure, methodical, men at the rears, helming them with slow plunges of their sweeps. Lovers whisper under trees and crouch by the water, their shapes dark, blurry, lurking at the edge of his vision. Endless streams of headlights and taillights blinking yellow, blinking red, unravel across the road that rings the lake. On the other side, there are restaurants and hotels, places packed with people and noises where a small boy might get disoriented, get lost, get kidnapped, disappear without anyone's notice.

He wants to shout, wants to ask every person on the path whether they've seen a small boy in a white T-shirt, running away. But the words, the questions, the phrases demanding help stay lodged in his brain, refusing to come out of his throat. If he could just talk to someone, if he could only say something, anything, then maybe he'd have a chance, maybe he'd have a direction to follow. But he is so alone, with the wrong language in his brain, nothing that will make them understand, and he has to find Pang Pang with only his legs and his eyes and the repetition of a name on his tongue. No one else will help him now. He spins in circles and stares around him. Despite the bright windowpanes in the distance and the streetlights that dot the footpath, the world is still dark, every shape hiding in different densities of gray. Panic keeps flapping its frantic wings inside him, threatening to break out of his chest, but he smacks his palms against his forehead to calm down, pressing on his skull to rid himself of the thing that wants to explode and leave him shattered and useless. He needs to focus and think. He needs to keep himself together and keep running. Pang Pang is still out there, somewhere, alone in the dark, and it is just a matter of time before he finds him, it is just a matter of time before they can go home.

The lake plays hide-and-seek through the trees. Sometimes it shines through without interruption, its endless lapping water flaring bright with moonlight, dotted by boats and small islands. Other times there are plaits of leaves that hang thick like curtains, tree trunks interrupting the scene like borders on photo negatives, shrubs so tall they block the view, foliage that could hide a small boy under its arms, could hide a man and a woman kissing under the moon.

"Pang Pang! Pang Pang!"

In the distance, he can hear Rosalyn's voice calling out, getting closer. Her voice, with its honeyed accent, its low, husky sound, drifts through the night with languor.

"Pang Pang! Where are you?"

Without thinking he runs away from her voice. He crosses the path and darts into a crowd of people watching two men playing Chinese chess, dodging his head, keeping his face away from the light.

"Pang Pang! Where are you? Come out come out wherever you are."

That rich, low voice with its long vowels of English and its unhurried drawl makes it sound as though she were playing a game. It sounds too much like her laughter, like something without urgency or fear. And so he waits until the voice fades away, until she has left him behind, before heading out onto the footpath again, looking left and then looking right, not knowing where to go.

The woman selling lotus roots is still there. She's calling out the same thing over and over again. "Lotus roots! Lotus roots! Three for five yuan! Lotus roots!" There's a line of little kids gathered in front of her. Li Jing watches them hop from one foot to another, watches them stuff change into the pockets of their shorts and start gnawing on the roots, their faces flush with happiness. This is where Pang Pang would have been coming from, before, and then he walked toward the lake, turning slightly into the shrubs. Li Jing stands on the exact spot where Pang Pang had stood in shock, where he saw his father's lips on Rosalyn's, his father's hand on her back. The tree trunks there are pale, mottled where the bark has peeled off. Leaves hang off the branches, sickly, like clumps of fur. He stands facing the lake and looks out past the empty shoreline to a small, dark island that rises out of the water like a turtle shell. From where Pang Pang was standing their bodies would have blocked the island from view, their torsos pressed together would have obliterated the topography of the lake.

A small body pushing through air, running away. One minute Pang Pang was there, and the next minute he was not. What would a boy do? Where would he go? The stifled blades of grass beneath Li Jing's feet do not give up any clues.

Li Jing looks at his watch. Each tick of the second hand seems to him a small bomb detonating. An hour and a half. Anything could have happened in an hour and a half. He breaks into a run again, scanning every face on shore, looking behind lampposts and tree trunks. The surface of the lake shimmers smooth and violet; all the boats are docked now, now that it is almost the end of the night. On the shore people begin to disperse, walking toward parking lots and hotels, leaving behind heaps of seed casings, cigarette butts, empty beer bottles, and paper cups. Only groups of young men with their shirts unbuttoned stay behind playing cards, their loud voices rattling clear without the muffling din of crowds. Li Jing listens to their every syllable and tries to gather the words, tries to remember all their sounds, wanting the Chinese to sink in, wanting the words back so that he can ask for help.

"*Wǒ de . . . xiǎo hái . . .*" He practices forming the words in his throat. How does he say *my child is missing*? He opens his mouth again. "*Wǒde xiǎohái.*" Starting over, blank, *my child . . .* what next?

"James!" Rosalyn runs toward him. She drags her feet and winces with every step. "Any luck? We're going to find him, I swear we will."

She stops in front of him and reaches out to his face, but he takes a step back, not looking at her.

"I don't know," he says. "I don't know where he is." Having to articulate it makes everything harder. The sound of his own voice speaking English, with its terse finality, makes him start to shake. That ball of panic rises up again, clawing at him so that his body feels like it's about to brim over, so that his skin is trying to keep something uncontainable within it, and failing. He grips the trunk of a young birch, as skinny as a wrist, and holds on, pushing his fingers against its bark, wanting to snap it in two.

Rosalyn steps closer with her hands held up in front of her body. "It's going to be okay," she says. "We'll find him."

Over her shoulder, on the far shore, there are small points of light going on and off like fireflies. He looks out onto the water, and now there is only a singular moon with its dense, white face, casting a circle of diffuse light past its edges, onto the quiet, murmuring waves.

"James." She presses herself against him and breathes hot and moist onto his neck. "It's going to be okay. Everything is going to be okay." She winds her arms around his body and he feels as though he is sinking into her flesh again. The skin of her shoulder against his face is cool and soft, calming him down. Her hushed vowels try to soothe the pounding in his head.

"It's going to be okay."

He pulls his head back and looks at her face. It is a face that exposes her heart to him, a face that only sees him. Her lips are quivering, and he can see past them into the darkness of her throat. He wants to kiss her, wants to pass his fear into her like a puddle of mercury, a poison slipped into her mouth. He squeezes her instead, clutches at her torso, wrapping his arms tight around her rib cage, trying to crush her with every ounce of strength he has. He can tell by the way her muscles tense up, the way she is trembling, that he is squeezing too hard, squeezing the breath out of her. She twists in his grasp, letting go of him and bracing her arms on his wrists, trying to push him away. But he keeps squeezing, wanting to knead his fingers into the meat of her, wanting to wring out her flesh, wanting to feel the dark pit of her heart beating against his bare hands.

"James," she gasps and then crumples in his grip. "It's okay." Her voice is edged with pain now, but she is still trying to reassure him, still repeating herself. "You're going to be okay. Everything is going to be just fine."

A small boy's body crashing through the night, reckless and afraid, but *he* is going to be okay, everything is going to be *just fine*. He pulls back and stares at her. Anger, hot and lucid, threatens to spike out of him, attacking her, and he has to look away. He loosens his arms and feels her body expand against his, feels her dragging long, shuddering inhales of air into her lungs. She has kicked off her thin, plastic flip-flops and he can see that her feet are marred with cuts and gashes the color of raw meat from running around the lake, but still she reaches out for him, her murky pupils full of worry, searching his face.

All the other times when she had looked at him, when she had put a soft palm on the thin, hollow shell of his skin, when she had said, *It's going to be okay* with her eyes trained on his face, not seeing anyone else—who was it that she saw? Who was this singular person carved out of the context of his life—without family, without history, without language—that stood before her, shaking, hysterical, needing the calm of her touch?

He stands still with her body against his, closing his eyes, listening to the exertions of water toward shore. The sound of the lake trickles a calm into his body so that anger and panic lose their edges for a second, retracting their claws, smothered by the implacable tides. Since the explosion everything seems to have been happening to someone else. Calamities unfolded in a reel, one after the other: first himself, then his father, and now his son. He remembers Meiling waking up after Pang Pang was born, how weak she looked then, her eyes still glazed over with pain. He had been terrified that something would happen to her, that she had been put at risk for the sake of carrying a child for him. It was

only after she smiled and asked for her son that he looked at Pang Pang
for the first time. Until then, a child had only been an abstraction, but
then there was that tiny face, the smallest fingers imaginable. Now, in
front of him, is Rosalyn's face, offering up sympathy, escape, maybe
even love. But who is she looking at? Who is this person standing in
front of her, and what does she see with those eyes of hers, the ones that
have already forgotten Pang Pang, that are focused on him, and only
on him?

"James," she says.

At the sound of the name he grabs her upper arms and throws her
off, taking one step toward the water and then shrinking back. Behind
him he can hear the soft, flapping sound of her skirt blowing in the
breeze, and when he finally turns around, the dark shape of her is at the
edge of his vision, she looks at him with an uncertain face. He closes
his eyes again, so afraid. What is he doing here, looking at her, when
there is a small boy with bone-china limbs running around a lake?
"Pang Pang," he calls out, but his voice is thin and useless. Anything
can happen in an hour and a half.

He starts running again. Her steps follow him, the slap of her feet
on cement making her cry out in pain. He stops but doesn't turn
around.

"Don't follow me," he says. "Just don't."

"James!" Her voice is a lament. "I'm just trying to help."

"That's not my name." He jerks his head and flicks his wrist as if batting something away from his face. "Don't call me that. Just go."

Without waiting for her reaction he begins running again, pumping
his fists, taking giant steps as if he's jumping over hurdles. "Pang Pang,"
he screams, and the night swallows the sounds but then he is screaming
again, repeating the name. The tree trunks, with their scaly, cracked
barks, look like they've been broken into pieces and stitched back together, trying to weather the times. The lake shines its dark face up, as
deceptive as a mirror, not betraying a thing. He runs away from Rosalyn, leaving her behind, crashing into a world where his son is alone

and lost. "Pang Pang," the two syllables over and over, the only sound that he can hear, the only thing that still makes sense in his head.

BY THE TIME Li Jing pulls the car into the parking lot of the West Lake Willow Inn, the sky has lightened to a pale gray, and rain clouds are dripping opaque onto the edge of dawn. All night he ran and drove around the perimeter of the lake, stopping and starting again, prowling past the façades of cafés and gift shops, exploring hollowed-out temples with their huge statues of sitting Buddhas behind which a small body might have lain down for a nap. The lake changed color hour by hour, going from black to deep purple, fading to the color of smoke, and then tinted orange at sunrise, until finally all hues deserted the water and it swam dull and gray, separated from the gray skies by the dark, listless rim of shore.

He turns off the car and sits with his hands on the steering wheel for a minute, turning phrases over and over in his mouth, chewing them like gum.

First, *"Wǒde xiǎohái . . . diàole."* My child . . . lost.

Then, *"Jǐngchájú?"* Police station?

The phrase he dreaded most of all was *"Mèilíng, Pāng Pāng . . . diào le."* Meiling, Pang Pang . . . lost. He repeats it over and over again, trying to get used to the pain. Would she scream or yell? Or would she just seize her face up again, lift her chin, and say, "I knew you were useless. You don't deserve Pang Pang. You never did." He is the one who has taken their son away from Meiling and brought him here, to Hangzhou, to see him kissing Rosalyn Neal under the moon. He can make no sense of anything, but he knows that Meiling has been right all along, that he is pathetic, that all of this is his fault.

He gets out of the car and tries to practice the phrases in Chinese again, the words skeletal and bumbling, the sentences barely coherent, shapeless on his tongue. Every syllable is imprecise and slurred. *Meiling, Pang Pang . . . lost. Police station? My child . . . lost.* First, he'll go back to his room and call Meiling on the telephone, try to explain to her how this is all his fault, try to tell her that he will not sleep until he finds their son. Then, he'll find someone to help him call the police station and nearby hospitals, and after that, he'll go to every restaurant beside the lake again, every souvenir shop, every hotel lobby, calling out Pang Pang's name.

When he walks around the main building he sees that the curtains are open and the lights are on in the suite. His heart expands and contracts painfully in his chest, and he runs toward the door, past the rustling bamboos with their pale joints that circle the stalks like wedding rings. Rosalyn is sitting in the living room, her skirt bunched around her knees, her eyes open and her face slackened by defeat. When she looks up at him he shakes his head, wanting to tell her . . . to tell her that it doesn't matter anymore, what was between them; that he is the one who has messed all of this up, and that he's sorry, terribly sorry, that she should just go back to Shanghai and then go back to America and forget about him. But then she is looking at him with a strange expression and her mouth is open. She is saying something but the rush of blood in his head makes it impossible to hear. She gestures toward the open door of the bedroom on one side of the suite, and he follows her hand to see a small, dark shape on the blue sea of the bedspread. The shape tosses its head and turns over so that it lies on its back now, and he can see the small chest rise and fall, can see that tiny, tender face, the black eyebrows pressing into the half moons of Pang Pang's eyelids, the small mouth murmuring something in sleep.

Sometimes she misses the view from their old apartment on the thirty-fourth floor. She misses standing on the balcony and seeing so much of the city, looking across at the haphazard skyscrapers, letting her eyes rest on the tiny patch of bright green grass behind the girls' high school a few blocks over. She lives her life on the ground now, trudging between her office and their new apartment on the second floor of a six-floor walkup. The apartment is not so far from the one they had before, only a ten-minute walk away, but it looks out onto a wall of concrete, barbed wire looping at the top.

The city keeps shifting, only now there is no way for her to see the skyline change at dusk, no way to count the steel girders going up day by day, watch buildings being torn down and new buildings going up in their places. But who can really keep up with the city, the way it changes constantly? She had asked him to meet her at the Shanghai Family Diner on Huashan Road, but the restaurant has shuttered its doors sometime in the weeks or months since she last visited. The windows are covered in newspaper, already yellow at the edges.

"Meiling!" Alan calls out from across the street, held on the other side of the intersection by the red light. The wind whips by and strands of his hair fall onto his forehead. She watches him smooth them back and give her a small, self-conscious wave. The light changes and he trots across the street. When he is about a meter in front of her, he pulls up, hesitating for a second, before extending his hand.

"Ms. Zhou. Meiling," he says. "It's nice to see you again. It's been a long time."

"Hello, Alan. Or would you rather I call you Shao Anli? It's nice to see you too."

"Alan is fine," he says. "How are you? You look . . . you're looking well."

She ignores his remark and gestures to the restaurant. "I'm afraid that we're going to have to go somewhere else."

He considers this for a moment, and then tells her that there's another restaurant, not far, that they could go to. She falls in step next to him, and they walk quietly, passing children on their way home from school. The last time she had talked to Alan had been on the phone, from Sichuan, almost exactly three months ago. Since then, in the middle of everything else, she has thought of him, from time to time, thought of the mildness of his voice, thought of the way his glasses reflect the light so that it is impossible to see the expression in his eyes.

When they round a corner the sun is shooting straight down the street from the opposite side, making it a canyon of light. Meiling stops in the middle of the sidewalk, squinting at the shadows of passersby, fast-moving bicyclists, telephone poles, the road sparse with cars. She pulls the collar of her jacket tight against her throat and hitches the strap of her bag, heavy with manuscripts, higher onto her shoulder. Fall is creeping into winter, and the light, yellow and cool, makes everyone look scarred, overexposed.

Alan has walked on ahead but comes back to where she is standing still. "What is it?" he says.

She shakes her head and crosses the street. Between two tall buildings there is a gap where an oversized truck idles near neatly stacked sheets of concrete and glass. When she gets closer she sees a giant hole in the ground beyond the truck. The hole is rectangular and deep, with clean edges, embedded with concrete beams. Men in hardhats take measurements inside, shouting out commands.

She has not walked down this street since it happened, always taking the long way around, but there is nothing left of the Swan Hotel here, no debris or broken windows, no linens from housekeeping, no broken plates from the kitchen. Instead, a billboard next to the truck says SUNSHINE REAL ESTATE and displays photographs of bright living rooms, children playing at the edge of floor-to-ceiling windows, the city a backdrop. LUXURY CONDOS FOR THE NEW MILLENNIUM, the billboard says. PERFECT FOR YOU AND YOUR FAMILY.

"Meiling? Is this . . . Is this where it happened?"

"I'm sorry." She turns away. "I seem to have acquired a terrible habit of looking at real estate prices everywhere. We bought a new apartment in September, and sold our old one. I looked at so many listings my eyes went blurry, and now that it's all settled, I find that I can't stop looking."

"I didn't realize you had moved."

"The old apartment was too big. A change of address seemed best . . . for all of us."

Alan stays quiet for a moment, and then he says, "Of course." Something in his voice makes Meiling look at his face. His eyes are cast down, unreadable behind the lens of his glasses. His nose is thin and exacting, but his mouth is small and kind. He looks up at her, and she can see the quickest trace of disappointment before he shakes it off. "It make sense," he says. "This way—you can leave things behind and start over, the three of you."

She reaches out to touch his arm, but he has already walked ahead of her, into the blinding light. When they get to the next block it is a relief to be out of the sun's abrasive reach and she walks faster so that she is right next to him, so that she can say, softly, "I don't think it's possible to start over, I don't know if I want to. But we had to sell the old apartment. It was too expensive, and we hadn't paid all of it off."

Alan doesn't say, "I'm so sorry," the way her friends did. He doesn't say, "Maybe things will get better," or "You don't know what the future will bring." He simply nods and considers her without pity or worry. "It sounds like you've taken the time to plan for the future," he says. "I'm sure you did the right thing."

The truth is that the new apartment—a misnomer, really, since the building was constructed in the late seventies and has not held up particularly well—is utilitarian but charmless, with bars mounted outside the windows. But it's adequate, even spacious, with a living room and two bedrooms and a small study that she sleeps in every night. She had the walls buffed and painted, shelved her books and hung her pictures, and the rooms became tolerable; in the evening, they were almost pleasant. But seeing all her things in a new context, months later, still seems wrong. She doesn't think she'll ever get used to it. She doesn't know if it'll ever feel like home.

"I simply did," she tells Alan, "what had to be done."

He takes her to a small café with squares of sunshine on the checkered floor. The room is empty but warm, and a waitress is slumped over a table near the kitchen, napping during the mid-afternoon lull. "I hope this is all right," he says. They sit themselves down at a table by the window. "It's fine." She smiles. "I had meetings with authors all morning long and I skipped lunch, so this is perfect. I'm free for the rest of the day, Alan. I'm glad we're getting a chance to talk, just the two of us."

The waitress walks over to take their order with her ponytail astray, her voice dreamy, as if the world were moving at a slower speed. When Alan asks questions about the specials Meiling studies him from behind the menu. He is not particularly handsome, Alan. He has an indecisive, nebbishy quality to his face, and his cheeks are dotted with pockmarks. But he is careful and solicitous, suggesting dishes but turning to her for approval before placing the order. When the waitress leaves, Meiling catches him staring across the table at her the way one might stare at two young people kissing in a dark corner of the park: discreetly, but with a veiled look of longing.

"So you've gone back to your job in publishing," he says. "Are you pleased?"

"I am. I'm working full time, which I haven't done in years, but I'm quite enjoying it. There's more travel now—sometimes I have to take trips out of town to conferences or universities. And the money—well, it is poetry, after all. But it's nice to be doing something for me. All of this . . ." She gestures carelessly as if the rest of her life can be flicked away. "It's more bearable that way."

She does not tell Alan that the excuse of work allows her to be away from Li Jing as much as possible. She does not tell him that on trains or in hotel rooms late at night she sorts through the thin, precarious options for her life, trying to bargain herself into some imaginable future, not knowing how to go on. When she looks up again he is pressing his napkin to a spot on the table, absorbing the ring of water the waitress had spilled around her glass. She smiles at him and leans in. They both begin to speak at the same time.

"And Mr. Li . . . ?"

"How are you? How's your work . . ." she starts, but flinches. They gesture back and forth for the other one to talk. Finally, she wins out. "Go ahead," she says.

"I received an e-mail from Dr. Neal a week ago," he says. It is the first time either of them has mentioned Rosalyn, and Meiling can feel something stiffen, her lower back, with a vague echo of pain. Out the window the late afternoon sun is still sweeping through the street, and now there is a hard wind blowing, whipping women's hair about their heads, picking dead leaves up off the pavement. It is strange to talk to Alan now, without someone's English next to her ear, without a need for translation, without looking at someone else's face while Alan's voice goes on and on.

"She's back in America, for good. She asked after you, and Pang Pang, and Mr. Li. She wanted to know about how all of you were, but I replied that I didn't know. I don't think Dr. Neal and I will go on corresponding," Alan says, his voice careful with meaning. "But I do hope Mr. Li is well. Is he . . . is he still working with Dr. Liu?"

Alan tries to be discreet, tries not to come right out and ask the questions that seem to dog her now, in her role as Li Jing's keeper. *Is he back to normal now?* people asked. *Can he talk again? In Chinese? It's such a shame, a man like that. Will he be a burden to you for the rest of your life?*

"He's still working with Dr. Liu. The Chinese . . . it came back, a little. It's a lot better than it was when you knew him. But still, it takes him a long time to say anything. He's never going to be 'normal,' not the way he was before."

The answers to the unasked questions are almost rote now. She can recite them without betraying any distress or sadness. "His English is always going to be the much stronger language for him. He's fluent in English. He'll never be fluent in Chinese. But he seems to have finally accepted his condition. Dr. Liu has been teaching him ways to compensate, and between that, and the dictionary, he's doing a little more now: he can go to the grocery store by himself, he went to a parent-teacher conference when I was out of town. Still, he has to hunt around for every word and rehearse every sentence until he feels comfortable with it. When something unexpected comes up, he starts to panic."

"I assume, then, that he couldn't go back to work?"

"No. Even if he wanted to it would have been very difficult. He was torn about it, I think, but ultimately he didn't want to—all the things he couldn't do anymore just made him feel too awful. I think that maybe he's been doing something on the computer, some kind of trading over the Internet—who knows. I considered continuing on at Sino-Venture too, but in the end, I thought it would be best to sell the company. It was too much, on top of everything else."

She does not tell Alan about the difficulty of finding a buyer for the company who would keep it intact. She does not tell him that Zhang Qing is the chief strategist for the investment group that took over SinoVenture, or that half of the employees, including Vice President Wu, have been laid off. The question of the company had been a terrible one—she knew that she did not want to continue, and every time she brought up the question of its future to Li Jing, his face sharpened into a kind of grotesque focus. He wanted it desperately—his old job, his old self—but then he'd sigh and start to brim with anxiety, he'd twitch and turn upset and she was afraid he might throw something or punch a wall or . . . she didn't even know what else she was afraid of. So she began to omit details about the situation. Over time, she stopped talking about it entirely. And he? He never brought it up either.

She handled the sale of the company on her own, sold the old apartment and purchased the new one on her own. Money, which had been entirely his domain before, became her responsibility, while he went to the supermarket, picked Pang Pang up from school, and cooked dinner, leaving the leftovers covered in plastic on the dining room table, waiting for her to come home.

"I'm sorry to hear that things have continued to be difficult. Mr. Li, does he have . . . help?"

"If you mean a translator or a caretaker, then no, he doesn't. I'm not sure Li Jing would want someone hovering over him all the time. At least the therapy with Dr. Liu seems to be having some small results, though it's very expensive."

"It's manageable, though, with the money from the apartment, and the company?"

"It's manageable," she says, "but we have to be very careful with it. My salary is negligible, so that money is going to have to last a long time."

She tries to smile, but when she meets Alan's eyes her lips begin to quiver and she has to look away. There is no one she can talk to about any of this—not her friends, who no longer understand, not Professor Li, who would have understood, but who is gone, and not Li Jing.

Not Li Jing, who keeps staring at her in wretched regret, but whom she cannot talk to, whom she is not sure she can ever look at again without pain shooting up her spine, making her reel each and every time. She takes a large gulp of tea and swallows, looking at Alan, at the way his lips are pursed, almost disappearing into his face. Alan, she thinks, might understand. Alan, she thinks, with his glasses, and his kind mouth, and the way his face lights up at the sight of her, might offer escape.

"What about you?" Her voice sounds unnaturally bright. "How have you been in the last few months?"

"The same," he says. "I have my regular clients. And I have some new clients. I am exactly as I was. The people change, but most of what they talk about stays the same."

She looks at him with her head tilted and leans forward. "I always wondered—why did you decide to be an interpreter? Your English is so fluent. There must be a lot of other options open to you."

Alan shrugs. "It never made me rich, but I've never wanted for much. The job is easy and flexible. It was never supposed to be a life-long career."

"And do you still like it?"

"I'm not sure. But sometimes you get used to doing something, and it's too much of a bother to change it."

"I can understand that." Her face lurches into a grimace. "But translating, it must be hard too, sometimes—all the things you have to help people say, all the things you hear."

He meets her eyes eagerly. "Exactly. You do see too much, because people forget about you. They forget that you're there, and the things they do when they're in a foreign country, when they think no one is watching—"

"Like they don't care what kind of damage they do." When Meiling interrupts the words come like marbles dropped on the floor, plinking one after another. "Because they'll just leave at the end of it. They have the option of leaving. The rest of us don't."

At her outburst Alan reaches out and covers her hand with his palm. She jerks her hand back. "They slept together." Her voice is thin and low. When Alan says, "Meiling," plaintive, half reaching out once more, she leans back into her chair and piles her hands into her lap. "I had guessed it, but he was the one who told me, after they came back from Hangzhou. I don't know if it made him feel better to confess. But it made me feel even worse—the confirmation of what I already suspected."

It was Li Jing's betrayal, but it is her humiliation to bear. For months she has been keeping the knowledge inside herself, not letting it out, so that all its damages would be inflicted on the underside of her skin, so that none of the scars he'd wrought would be visible to the world. Now she has blurted it out and she looks up, daring Alan to say something. Alan does not register shock or try to make excuses for Li Jing, and for this, she is grateful. She sits back and lets the noise from the restaurant filter in. The tables are beginning to fill with groups of high school students laughing and playing cards, their heads close together, their voices so carefree.

"Did you know about them?"

"No," he says. After a minute, he tells her, "I must admit that I am not surprised."

"That's funny. I was." She snorts, inelegant for once. "I had suspected it, even taunted him with it, but I still found myself surprised when he finally told me. He must have practiced that particular speech for days."

They sit in silence and pick at their meal, taking small, careful bites, pushing food around on their plates. The cloth napkin on her lap has a fleck of green on it, and she shakes it out and puts it on the table, smoothing her palm over her lap. Knowing that she was meeting Alan, she had put on one of her favorite dresses in the morning, but now the pale gray crepe feels absurdly formal beneath her fingers. She puts her hand back on the table but he does not reach out for her this time. Her hand lies limp, half open, before she clenches it into a fist and pulls it to her side again.

Finally he says, "What is it that's going to happen now?"

Talking, to Alan, with only their words between them, in only a single language, is much harder than she imagined when she had struck this bargain with herself. Already, she has said too much, and now she returns to her script, knowing that he will pick up every subtext. "Alan, I'm wondering if you have the time . . . for private lessons. That is, I'd like to learn English, and I'd like you to teach me."

The waitress clears the table and sets down a platter of oranges. Alan, not meeting her eyes, picks up a wedge and chews off the flesh methodically. The oranges smell tart and sharp, they glow ferocious in the light. "Meiling," he says, and hesitates before asking, "why are you doing this?"

She answers a different question, speeding up her voice, hiding its tremor. "He's never going to be able to speak Chinese, not really. Not the way he did before. And the doctor says he doesn't have the ability to even relearn it. That part of his brain is gone. But he speaks English well, and Pang Pang is learning English in school, and they're starting to talk to each other more easily now. So if I learn to speak English"—beneath the table, her fingers are knotted tight together—"then that'll be something, won't it?"

"You'll keep trying," Alan presses her, "even after everything that's happened?"

"Don't you understand? I can't leave him." On this she is firm, and she looks straight into his eyes. "Not like this, not right now. We're married, no matter what he's done, no matter how bad things get, I can't be the one to leave. I can't leave him like this. But . . ." She swallows and then says the words too quickly, wanting them to get out, otherwise— "But we don't have to live the same life together. We're not . . ."

She trails off and looks away. Outside, the wind has died down, and the sunlight almost looks balmy from behind glass. She is afraid to look up at Alan, afraid that he will not see anything, or that he will see straight through her. When he stays silent she keeps looking out the window. The shadows of people on the ground are so long they look like they're on stilts.

"Does Mr. Li get a say in the matter? What does he think of all this?"

"What does it matter what he thinks? He's the one who—"

Alan flinches but then schools his features, expressionless. She squeezes her eyes, angry at her own lack of control. Alan always manages to see every gesture, hear every intonation in every word. She had wanted to smile blithely and hint at the subtext, but Alan is refusing to make it easy or play by her rules.

"It doesn't have to be this way, Meiling," he says. "Some things can't be changed back to the way they used to be. Sometimes you have to move forward, try to go on."

"Don't you think I know that?" She raises her voice but then looks around the restaurant and begins again, in a harsh whisper. "I know that things can't go back to the way they used to be. But what else am I supposed to do? I know—I know this isn't good enough, that I'm not doing enough, not for Pang Pang, and not for Li Jing. But what else can I do? Leaving him isn't an option. I have to try to make it bearable for him. But where does that leave me? I need to make it bearable for me too."

She pushes her plate away and looks up. He stares up too, and the ceiling light glares off his glasses. Laughter drifts over from the next table, loud and crass. The waitress comes by and lays down the bill, but neither of them reaches for it, and it flutters and cartwheels off the table and down to the floor.

"I know what you're thinking," she says. "You're thinking that I should either forgive him everything, or let him go. Well, I don't know how to forgive him, I don't even know if I want to forgive him— maybe that's a terrible thing to say, but it's my right to say it, isn't it? As for letting him go, do you really think I could? Is that what you would do, if you were in my shoes?"

He doesn't respond, doesn't look at her. She watches his Adam's apple bob up and down.

"I'm sorry," Meiling says, "I'm just so tired. I've thought and thought about this so much. But it feels like there's no real way out."

"Meiling . . ." The pity in his voice makes her name sound like a slur. "You can't martyr your life away."

"I don't want to," she says. "That's why I'm here."

She has laid all her cards on the table, and now she sits up straight and tries once more. "I'd like for you to teach me English, Alan. Just once or twice a week. I can't pay you much. But I can pay you, a little. And I wouldn't need lots of your time. Alan, I—"

His voice is gentle. Too gentle. "There are classes you can take," he says.

When she doesn't answer he is even quieter. "Classes might be the best thing, for someone like you. But if you're interested in private instruction, I can recommend several other people . . ."

"Of course." She picks the napkin up off the table and folds it once, and then twice, folding it until it is a tiny square, something she can clutch tight in her hand.

"Meiling—" he says.

"If you could give me a list of names and classes—"

"It's just not . . ." He takes off his glasses and cleans them with the hem of his shirt. His face is taut, and his eyes—now that she can finally see them—look fogged over, like there's a layer of grease swimming on top of his pupils. She tilts her chin and looks at him, determined to be brave.

"You're not thinking straight." He shakes his head. "It's just . . . it's just not a good idea. I don't know what it's like, I don't know what you should do, but you can't go on like this. You—"

"Stop," she says, and then begins again as if he hadn't been talking at all. "English classes. Why didn't I think of that? I can take them in the evenings. If there are any particular ones you'd like to recommend, I'm all ears."

"Meiling. I didn't mean—" he starts, but seeing the expression on her face he closes his mouth. When the waitress comes, they both bend down and make a grab for the bill. Beneath the table their eyes meet. Alan freezes for a second, staring. Meiling reaches out and plucks the bill from his side before rising smoothly.

"No," she says, with a tight smile. "Please, Alan, it's on me."

WHEN THEY SAY goodbye Alan shakes her hand for too long, opening and closing his mouth in silence. She wants to tell him that she understands, but before she can begin the light is changing at the intersection. She turns and walks away, past all the stopped cars. When she looks back from the other side of the intersection he is still waving. She doesn't wave back. She walks down the street at a punishing pace, until she knows she is out of his sight. The sun is closing in on the edge of the horizon now, and she lets her eyes be dulled by its rays, she tucks her hands into her pockets. Soon it will be winter. Soon it will be next year. On her right is the entrance to the park, and without thinking she walks past the gate and then she is inside, on a tree-lined path, leaving the street behind.

Workmen walk past her in their lime-green uniforms, picking up garbage, sweeping away leaves. She keeps walking down the wide, straight path until it stops, and then wanders into trails winding through the man-made hills, walks around the small, dim lake, listening to its quiet hum. Above her the branches are almost bare, sprawling away from tree trunks the way arteries shoot out from the heart. The park is so small that soon she is back on the main path. She stands at the edge of it and stares at the entrance of the park, toward the blur of bicycle wheels, toward the car honks and the streetlights flickering on and the world waiting outside.

She sees them walk in, their bodies smudged at first, and then their outlines sharpening, getting closer. Li Jing is holding bags of groceries in one hand and grabbing onto Pang Pang with the other, and he moves slowly, stiffly, he is hunched over, jerking himself forward with every step. She takes a step back into the shadows, out of their sight lines, and watches Pang Pang look up, his small face smiling, animated, but his voice too far away for her to hear. They laugh together, the two of them, and for a moment Li Jing's shoulders loosen and he glides ahead with his old swagger, but then with Pang Pang on one side and heavy bags in his other hand he is pulled back into the gait of an old man, he is awkward and lumbering once again. It is almost painful to look at him, to remember the ease of the man she fell in love with and to see him now, trudging on.

When they are close enough she can hear their voices stumbling over each other. They are speaking in English, the foreign words spinning toward her and then spinning away. She takes another step back, pressing herself against a tree trunk, and as they walk past her, walk farther into the park, their voices fade and she stares at their backs, at their bodies disappearing behind the cluttered hills. The sun, hanging low above the horizon, has gathered clouds around it like layers of tulle, and as it blazes with its last light, its last palm of warmth, she steps into the path once more. She is not sure what she is doing here, in this park. She knows that they come here every weekday afternoon, after Li Jing picks Pang Pang up from school. Since Hangzhou he has painstakingly written out a schedule for himself every day, using the computer to translate it into Chinese. He leaves the printouts for her every morning, and on each one is a different apology, the words always simple, like "I'm sorry," or "I regret so much" or "Thank you for everything," but always underlined, by hand, as if the translation is in no way adequate for his sentiments. Over the past three months she has let the schedules pile up at her desk until the pile began to look like an unbound notebook, growing higher and higher. She does not like looking at the pages but she needs them nearby. She does not acknowledge the words of his regret—to acknowledge them would give him an opening that she is not willing to grant.

But now she has wandered into this park and into their routine, into a space that she can only remember from a time that seems so long ago, from another life. She told Alan that she does not want to forgive

Li Jing, but as she stares into the vivid orange of the horizon, she realizes that she does not know how to forgive him, she does not know what she might say if he stood silent in front of her, how they could leave the past behind and begin once more.

She looks up, wildly, at the rock behind which they disappeared, and then starts to walk out of the park, speeding up, letting her high heels crash down hard with every step. When she breathes in the air is clean and crisp, with the faint smell of burning leaves. She keeps walking, but then she looks down to the ground. On the path, patterns and shapes darken the cement, stretching forward like an ordered set of shallow etchings.

There are words written in water on the ground beneath her feet. The strokes are tangled up in each other, gathering together into characters and lines and stanzas. The calligraphy is masterful, like something you might see across a scroll, in a museum. Meiling leaps back as if she has accidentally stepped on a priceless work of art.

When Li Jing and Pang Pang come around the pond and back onto the path, come toward her, she can hear their voices speaking English, and then they stop, and she knows that they have seen her. She forces herself to stand still: she does not know how to begin, but she will stand still. When they finally walk up, she is still looking down, and she can see the tips of their feet in front of her, next to the wet characters of Chinese. Both of them with their feet pressed together carefully, formally, as if they are about to salute.

"Meiling."

Will she ever get used to the sound of her name in the same voice she has listened to for so long, but with blurred edges, different caresses of breath? Before she can react Pang Pang grabs ahold of her hand and squeezes it tight, as if he will not ever let go of her. "Mom." He is so bright with hope that she has to press her lips together to keep from flinching. "Mom, what are you doing here?"

She holds herself still when Li Jing comes to stand on the other side of her, not touching her. She does not draw away from his warmth when she can feel the heat of him close by, can feel his breath trembling, disturbing the air. She lets Pang Pang tug her hand forward but they walk around the calligraphy, not marring it with their steps. The gray slabs of the pavement are burning in the setting light. The words, written in water, begin to fade in the last rays of the sun.

"Meiling." He says her name again, and the slip of sound crawls into her, abstract, as if it were an invented word. She looks up, and beneath the skin of his face every muscle seems to be contorting in pain. His eyes are pleading, his mouth is opening and closing, and she can see him groping, trying to string a sentence together, looking so afraid, wanting to blurt something out but not wanting to mess it up.

"I," he says in Chinese. "You . . ." His breath flares out of his nose in short, panicked bursts. The veins in his neck are pulsing hard, and his cheeks are filling with blood, turning red. His jaw twists and turns, futile and silent. His lips hover open, and just behind them she can see the tip of his tongue, the dark recess of his mouth.

"Meiling." One more time. Pang Pang is digging his fingers into her palm and when she turns to him he wears the same determination on his face. It is too hard to keep looking at the both of them, so she looks down at the ground. The calligraphy on the path stretches on, like a scroll unraveling itself. Closer to the entrance of the park the words become darker, every stroke denser, until every corner of every line is intact, untouched by the thin heat of the sun.

Beside her Li Jing is still struggling to talk. "Thank you . . ." He can barely get the syllables of Chinese out of his mouth and then he grips his head with his hands. "I . . ." he says, swallows, and tries again. "I . . ."

She cannot look at him, can no longer stand still, and takes two steps forward, trying to leave him behind.

On the path ahead of her, there is a crowd gathered around a young woman crouching on the ground, one long braid down her back. She moves her arms over the pavement, as if she is trying to embrace the earth. The people next to her lean in, watching the curve of her elbow, marveling at her skill. There is a calligraphy brush in her hand, and next to her, a plastic soda bottle with the top cut off is filled with water. With long, smooth motions, the girl dips the brush into the water, and then moves the brush reverently over the ground, painting intricate lines and curves. The strokes converge and characters appear. Each word glistens under the fading light, wet with promise and deceit.

"Meiling." His breath on her ear. He opens his mouth but nothing comes out. She turns to look at him, and he tries again, fails. "I . . ." She shakes her head and reaches out, almost touching his lips with her fingers before drawing back.

She turns away but Pang Pang is at the other side of her, slipping his hot hand into her palm. Li Jing touches her shoulder, grabs the strap of her bag and slides it down her arm, adding its weight to the groceries in his other hand. On the ground before them the girl moves closer to the park gates on flattened knees, blazing words on the path. The sun pours over the pavement, illuminating the lines crisscrossing on the ground, even as its faint heat begins to lift the words from view. The crowd moves with the girl but Meiling stays rooted in the same spot. She looks down, and beneath all three of them the lines are fading, the words evaporating into the half dark of the evening air.

"Let's go home," Pang Pang says. The sun has slipped over the edge of the horizon, and trees, people, man-made hills all shiver in the shadows. He tugs her hand forward and she drags her feet after him. Li Jing, on the other side of her, touches her elbow and she stares down to where his fingers are exerting the lightest of pressures on her arm. But she holds still, she does not flinch or draw away. Then she lets Pang Pang walk them past the girl on the ground, past the wet streaks of language, and out into the night.

ACKNOWLEDGMENTS

For their support, insight, and friendship, I will always be grateful to: Mikael Awake, Jason Boog, Benjamin Holt, Elizabeth Keenan, Madeline McDonnell, Max Novick, Dr. Usha Reddy, Brian Selfon, and Randi Silberman.

I could not have experienced Shanghai as fully as I did without the friendship of I-Shin Chow, Violet Feng Du, Liu Mengjie, and Lisa Movius. I am also deeply thankful to my family in Shanghai, and to the city itself.

I am indebted to my agent, Elaine Koster, for her astute guidance, patience, and grace. My editors, Hope Dellon and Helen Garnon-Williams, made this a better book with their intelligence, incisiveness, and care. Thanks also to the excellent teams at St. Martin's Press and Bloomsbury.

Hedgebrook, Dr. Neil Hochstadt and the late Adrienne Reiner Hochstadt, the Espy Foundation, the Anderson Center, the Jerome Foundation, Jentel, and Ragdale all provided invaluable time and resources, without which this book could not have been completed. POV and my colleagues there also provided me with time and encouragement. I am very grateful to have received their support.

THE LOST AND FORGOTTEN LANGUAGES OF SHANGHAI

by Ruiyan Xu

About the Author

- A Conversation with Ruiyan Xu

Behind the Novel

- "Language Lost and Found"
  An Original Essay by the Author

Keep on Reading

- Recommended Reading
- Reading Group Questions

For more reading group suggestions,
visit www.readinggroupgold.com.

 ST. MARTIN'S GRIFFIN

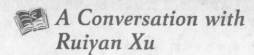

A Conversation with Ruiyan Xu

In *The Lost and Forgotten Languages of Shanghai*, all three protagonists at times feel estranged and isolated from their surroundings. Why do outsiders fascinate you?

We can start with the obvious—I moved to the United States when I was ten, and I was the outsider. I didn't understand the language, I didn't know the culture, and in my elementary school class, I was totally lost. I still feel lost sometimes—albeit to a lesser extent. Because I didn't grow up here, there are references I miss, a kind of understood shared history or feeling that Americans have who grew up here together, watching the same television shows, seeing the same events through the same perspective. And so I find myself, sometimes, feeling as though I'm watching things from a distance when I am supposedly participating in them. We can call that "Ruiyan as Outsider, Part One."

"Ruiyan as Outsider, Part Two" started when I was eighteen, visited China, and became an outsider again. I spoke English, read English, wrote English every day for eight years. And so speaking to everyone in Chinese—family members, passersby, shopkeepers—became incredibly awkward.

Simultaneously, in Shanghai, culturally, even physically, everything had changed so much—it didn't feel like a homecoming. Or, at least, it didn't feel like only a homecoming. And I had changed too, of course. So even if China had somehow frozen in time, I wouldn't have been able to just step back in.

Obviously I'm not the first person to experience or try to write about this feeling. Immigrant fiction, for example, often deals with the sense that you'll never feel entirely at home in either culture. Non-immigrant writers know and deal with this, too. Writers can almost be defined as professional out-

> "Writers can almost be defined as professional outsiders.... You often have to step outside of a situation to observe it."

siders. It's just part of the job. You often have to step outside of a situation to observe it—to choose the right details—to reshape a mess of events into a narrative.

What did you research for your novel, and what did you make up?

The story takes place in the summer of 1999. I lived in Shanghai during that summer, and I probably couldn't have set the novel in Shanghai during any other period. When I came back and began writing the book, my memories determined, or at least informed, how I depicted the city in my book. I drew on specific images and scenes that I could recall. But just as important was the feeling the city had while I lived there—a mixture of old and new and glittering and impoverished. So even when I made things up, I stuck to the ambience I experienced firsthand. Generally, though, the book's interior spaces were imagined, though perhaps informed by specific memories. Outside spaces tended to come from what I could more specifically recall.

My book follows a character who loses the ability to speak. His condition is called aphasia. I first read about aphasia during college, and I immediately felt some personal connection to the disease—a sense of recognition. Moving to the United States as a child, fighting through a new language, and then later losing my original language…aphasia seemed like an exaggerated, accelerated version of what I had experienced myself. So even before I started writing my novel, I had studied it through my coursework in cognitive science and neuroscience.

Probably no two writers will agree on how to research for fiction. My method is to read as much as possible on the topics or themes relevant to the story

I'm writing—to read widely, but also to read haphazardly. Eventually I decide I'm ready to write. But it's hard to write with a medical text next to you and the Internet open on your laptop. So I take all of the books and articles and whatever else I've read and put it away. And then I just write. My assumption is that the prep work will inform my writing, that all the information I picked up will come out almost unconsciously.

At certain points during the revision process, I had to go back and fill in details—and I needed to do supplemental research. I'd check on things I thought I had made up—little details of the book—and sometimes they turned out to be true. Who knows; maybe I read about things similar to those details during my initial research, put them into the novel without remembering where I'd gotten them from, and now was relearning them all over again. Or maybe I just guessed right. Anyway, in terms of the medical research, I sent my manuscript to a doctor friend to make sure I didn't get too much wrong, and was quite relieved when she gave me her approval.

Which writers helped inspire this novel? Who influences your writing, and how?

I was just graduating from college when I started this book. I was reading Marguerite Duras, Michael Ondaatje, and Susan Minot, and all of them had at least some influence on my style. The style of those writers, at that formative age, definitely penetrated. I responded to the saturation (for lack of a better word) of their prose, I think, and wanted to create that feeling in my own work. But my style has changed too, over the years. Prose style, for me, was and remains a moving target, one I think about a lot, and something I often question myself about. I

"[Writing]... allows you to see the world differently, as if writing was actively sharpening your vision."

will always be in love with words and sentences, but these days I find that my writing feels a little looser, my sentences aren't quite so careful. It's definitely been interesting.

It's hard to say that other writers are *direct* influences on this book. There are, of course, writers I love (W. G. Sebald, Marilynne Robinson, Alice Munro), but they are all geniuses. Geniuses are impossible to crib.

At one point, when I was struggling with the structure of the novel, trying to figure out its shape and pacing, I was drawn back to some of my favorite nineteenth- and early twentieth-century writers: George Eliot, Henry James, Edith Wharton. They wrote about flawed men and women, about the links between marriage and money, about bad choices and lack of foresight. And so much happens in all those books! So those novels made me think about my characters in a different way—about how they, despite their best efforts, were trapped by their languages and cultures and circumstances, by the society around them. Maybe the choices they made were the only choices they could make.

Apart from books, did other works of art play a role in the creation of *The Lost and Forgotten Languages of Shanghai*?

That's a difficult question to answer. I don't know if any works of art directly played a role. I did listen to a lot of Arvo Pärt during the writing, but it wasn't so much an inspiration as it was an accompaniment.

The messier answer, and probably the more important one, is that just about everything that passed through my life during the years I was writing my book could have played some role in how I wrote it.

It's one of the advantages of writing a novel. You spend so much time with it that you start to see the world through the prism of the book. Everything is potential material. You notice new things, notice old things in a different light, notice everything more intensely through whatever you're working on. Something you overhear, a work of art you see, some random gesture or the shape of a room—anything can fit into a character's life or plug into some dramatic moment. This is one of my favorite things about writing—the way it allows you to see the world differently, as if writing was actively sharpening your vision.

It's even more fun when this happens by accident. You've stepped away from the book and you're going through everyday life, and the novel is hidden away but still shaping itself in the back of your mind, and then all of sudden you see or hear something that just drops into place and completes a scene.

To capture some of these things, I take notes, especially if I'm in the middle of working on something. Maybe the notes make it into the book, but more often than not I don't look at them again. I think taking notes just trains me to observe, to take in details and be able to evoke them when they're needed. You grow extra sensors when you're writing—does that sound silly? The world becomes more alive to you. Some of what you see is terrible, and sometimes things are so strange or beautiful that you can't quite believe it. And all of it makes me more engaged with being alive, and I hope it makes me a better writer. It definitely makes me a better person.

"[Shanghai] is, and always will be, my city."

Excerpted from "Among Strangers: An Interview with Ruiyan Xu" by Brian Selfon, *Fiction Writers Review*, © 2010

 *An Original Essay by the Author*

"Language Lost and Found"
by Ruiyan Xu

When I was ten years old, I moved from Shanghai, China, to the United States. I didn't speak any English then, and I remember being so frightened, for I was in an entirely new place, a place where I didn't speak the language. The day before fifth grade started, I remember pleading with my mother to let me stay home; I was scared to not understand, and not be understood.

Eight years later, when I returned to China for my first visit back, English had become the only language I was fluent in. After not using Chinese for so long, I could no longer read or write it, and even my spoken Chinese had deteriorated to the point where talking to my family in Shanghai was slightly difficult and awkward. At eighteen, I was afraid of saying the wrong thing or not being understood all over again. It made me frustrated and sad, for I felt as though I had abandoned—through my own neglect—my first language. And I began to realize that I had slowly lost access to my childhood, my memories, my relationships with family members, and my cultural history through my estrangement from my native tongue. I didn't remember the names of my childhood friends—because their names were in Chinese. My conversations with my grandparents and cousins were shallow—it seemed impossible to get to the heart of the matter without the right words. I couldn't read the books that I'd loved as a kid at all. Taxi drivers and shopkeepers assumed that I had been born and reared abroad. That keen sense of loss I felt then—the idea that when you lose a language you also lose so many other things—has stayed with me ever since.

When I came across the concept of aphasia in a cognitive science class in college, I immediately felt a sense of connection to the disease. After all, isn't aphasia—suddenly losing the ability to produce or understand a language—a rapidly accelerated version of what I had experienced? The idea of writing about a fictional character with aphasia took root in my head, and when I returned to Shanghai at the age of twenty-one, this time for a three-month stay, that idea grew roots and expanded, taking on more details. Thus began *The Lost and Forgotten Languages of Shanghai*.

In telling the story of Li Jing—a Chinese man whose first language is English, and who sustains a brain injury that results in bilingual aphasia—I am quite literally exploring what happens when someone loses a language. Li Jing is isolated from almost everyone around him. His loss of language causes him to lose many things: control of his company, close relationships with his family members, and his own previously unquestioned ease in the world. But it is in his relationship with his wife, Meiling, where his aphasia causes the most damage. Because they can't speak to each other, and because of their own unwillingness to try to find new ways to connect, Li Jing and Meiling are no longer able to communicate. Their relationship begins to break down; they resent each other but do not understand each other; and Li Jing begins to turn to Rosalyn Neal, his American doctor.

The stories of Li Jing, Meiling, and Rosalyn unfold against the backdrop of contemporary Shanghai. Shanghai, for me, is almost another character in the novel. In writing about the place I grew up in, and the place I returned to as an adult for brief periods of time, I got to experience the beauty and mystery

of Shanghai all over again. The city is undoubtedly dazzling and glamorous and cosmopolitan. It is also isolating, full of customs and traditions, with certain indecipherable codes of conduct that are difficult for outsiders to penetrate. It is, and always will be, my city. And I hope that some of the facets of this remarkable and vibrant city come through in *The Lost and Forgotten Languages of Shanghai*.

For most of the book, Li Jing's aphasia seems as though it is damaging the lives of the three protagonists beyond repair. The loss of language, in whatever form it may take, is hard to recover from—it shatters not just our ability to speak, but our relationships and our senses of selves too. Still, with each loss there are things we might learn, about how to reach each other in new ways, about how to reform our connections with loved ones. For even when it feels impossible to communicate—with family members, with friends, with colleagues, and strangers—isn't it still important, isn't it still up to us, to keep trying?

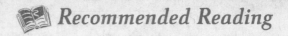 *Recommended Reading*

In the Eye of the Sun
Ahdaf Soueif

This depiction of a young woman's journey
from Egypt to England, her intellectual and physical
awakening, and her straddling of different cultures
and languages, gave me a sense of recognition
when I read the book. I love that it portrays a
woman's interiority so well.

In the Skin of a Lion
Michael Ondaatje

I read this book in college, and it was a revelation.
I didn't know you could write novels like this—
for it's a novel that shifts quickly but precisely among
different landscapes and characters and times.
Ondaatje is one of my favorite authors for his rich
prose, his vivid descriptions of space, and his
sympathy for those on the margins of history.

The Song of Everlasting Sorrow
Wang Anyi

One of the most important contemporary
Chinese writers gives us this expansive and
fascinating tale of a woman caught by
history in twentieth-century Shanghai.

Native Speaker
Chang-rae Lee

A sensitive and sharp examination of
an Asian American man in New York City.

The House of Mirth
Edith Wharton

Lily Bart, the irresistible but flawed heroine of
this novel, is one of my favorite characters in all
of literature. She reminds us that women are
not often in control of their own fates, and that
people are often trapped by their circumstances.

Selected Stories
Alice Munro

Each of these short stories is a gem, encompassing
more life and blood than most novels. Every time
I read Alice Munro, I am awestruck by her clarity
of vision, and her wisdom.

The Man with a Shattered World:
The History of a Brain Wound
A. R. Luria

A real-life account of a man with a severe
head injury. Absolutely fascinating, and gives
an unparalleled glimpse into the struggles
of the brain-damaged patient.

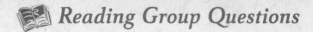 *Reading Group Questions*

1. How do you think your life would change if you suddenly lost the ability to speak your primary language? Would you still be able to hold your current job? How would your relationships with your loved ones change?

2. Rosalyn comes to Shanghai partly as a result of her divorce. She says that in Shanghai, she has "found a whole new solitude." What else does Rosalyn find in Shanghai?

3. What do you imagine Rosalyn to be like in her normal life, in the United States? Do people behave differently when they travel? Have you ever taken the opportunity to behave differently when you were away from familiar surroundings?

4. Meiling thinks: "Love is about taking care of someone without being asked, about sacrificing yourself...words have nothing to do with love. [But] perhaps in English, with an American woman, the concept of love is entirely different. Perhaps love, in a different language, rushes through and spills out more easily, the words carrying the feelings along." How might Meiling's concept of love differ from Rosalyn's? Do you think the concept of love is different in different languages and different cultures? Have you ever had an experience where love meant different things for you and someone you were close to?

5. Professor Li passes away in the middle of the novel. Would the lives of Li Jing, Meiling, and Rosalyn have been different if Professor Li stayed alive? Why might his presence have made a difference in their lives?

6. After Li Jing's accident, Meiling tries to keep his company afloat, but does not spend a lot of time with Li Jing himself. Discuss the relationship between Meiling and Li Jing after the accident. Why do you think they grow apart? What could each of them have done to change this?

7. Meiling invites Rosalyn to come to a spa with her. Over the course of the afternoon, each woman judges the other harshly. Are Meiling and Rosalyn's differences the result of different cultures, different languages, or different personalities? Why can't they get through to each other despite the presence of Alan the translator?

8. At the end of the book, Meiling and Li Jing seem to reach a tentative reconciliation. Do you think they would have stayed together if they didn't have a child together? What do you think their relationship will be like going forward?

*Keep on
Reading*